GRAVE DEVOTION

TROUBLED SPIRITS

J.R. ERICKSON

DEDICATION

For Carrie. Here's to another forty years.

AUTHOR'S NOTE

Grave Devotion is inspired by a true story. To avoid spoilers, that story is briefly retold at the end of this book.

PROLOGUE

She blinked, eyes gritty, eyelids impossible to hold open by sheer will. They slipped closed and seconds passed in darkness.

Open, she silently commanded them. *Open*. And finally, they did.

Trees whizzed by on the darkened road outside her passenger window. She'd passed out, forehead resting against the glass. A line of spit dribbled from her lower lip down her chin.

She shifted and her head rolled—impossibly heavy—off the window. It flopped back to the passenger seat. Her head was even heavier than her eyelids, her arms heaviest of all. Merely twitching her fingers took every shred of her strength.

Beside her, the man drove, eyes forward. Headlights illuminated the dark road. Bushy trees huddled behind the ditches. If there was a moon, she couldn't see it. Everything beyond the headlights faded to black.

She focused on her foot, realized one of her flats had fallen off. She wriggled her toes and when she moved her foot it lurched an inch, but that too took great effort. An empty plastic bottle crunched as her foot struck it. She remembered the bottle of water the man had given her, how the cap had felt oddly loose—no resistance when she'd unscrewed it for a drink.

He didn't look at her, concentrating on the road ahead, hands locked on the steering wheel. Though he didn't look at her, she sensed he was aware of her, aware that she'd begun to move a tiny amount, aware that whatever he'd put in her water was losing potency.

They seemed to be going fast. The engine and the tires on the road filled the car with a steady rumble.

She had no idea how long she'd been unconscious, how far he'd driven her, but in the minutes since she'd woken, they hadn't passed a single car from the other direction. No streetlights interrupted the endless forest.

He leaned forward, his body tense. She sensed his growing anticipation.

If they reached their destination, it would not be good for her. Years before, she'd taken a self-defense class. The instructor had pounded one message into the women relentlessly. *Fight! Do not be taken to a second location. Chances of survival decrease significantly if the perp gets his victim to an alternate location.*

She fumbled her fingers in her lap, felt the reassuring metal clasp of her seatbelt in the buckle. Her eyes drifted to him. No chest strap crossed the red fabric of his Izod shirt. Lower, she studied his seatbelt buckle. It wasn't connected.

She had one chance, but didn't know if she could command her hands to do what had to be done.

He let out a sound, a sigh of pleasure. She feared they were close now. He inched forward in his seat.

She shot out her hand and grabbed the wheel, yanked it sideways. He didn't have time to react and he lost control.

Her stomach dropped as the car went airborne, jumped the embankment and smashed headlong into a tree.

1

———

Five Years Later

"Wait. Isn't that your mom?" Stevie asked. She leaned forward and pointed through the windshield.

Kale cringed and rolled down his window. "Mom, what are you doing?"

"Kale!" His mom peered into the car. "And Stevie! What a pleasant surprise." She held up a painted sign. "I'm marking this squirrel. Look at this." She gestured in disgust at the flattened black squirrel on the dirt road. "There must be four speed limit signs on this road, at least. Twenty-five miles per hour. How do you kill one of God's creations at twenty-five miles per hour? Truly, it's chilling."

Kale frowned at the sign, which stated in all capital letters, 'WHAT IF THIS WAS YOUR CHILD? SLOW DOWN!' A red arrow pointed down at the carcass of the squirrel. "Good grief, Mom. Isn't that a little extreme?"

"Extreme? What's extreme are the ruffians who think Chapel Road is a racetrack. Do you know I found two beer cans on the road yesterday? Two." She struggled to hold up her fingers while continuing to wiggle the signpost into the ground.

Kale bit his cheek and didn't look at Stevie, who he imagined was fighting laughter. Their friend Zach had fishtailed on the road two days

3

previous and beer cans in the back of his dad's pickup had gone airborne. Stevie had yelled at him to pick them up, but he'd only slammed on the gas and rocketed down the road when a light had come on at Mrs. Drabble's house. The widow occupied the only other house on that stretch of Chapel Road.

Mrs. Drabble was a cranky old woman with three aging chihuahuas who barked furiously if anyone got near her when she was outside. Kale and his siblings had often been forced by their parents to take food and gifts to Mrs. Drabble, and in person she was every inch the cantankerous old lady she'd always seemed from afar. She'd once smacked Kale's sister Zinnia on the top of her head with a wooden spoon when Zinnia had accidentally stepped on one of the mostly blind chihuahuas.

"That's terrible, Mrs. Goodwin," Stevie said, leaning across Kale toward the driver's window. "I mean, Lucy." Stevie blushed.

"Thank you, dear. For protecting our planet, and also for doing your best not to call me the name of my mother-in-law. She may be deceased, but her name still makes my toenails curl." Lucy shifted her attention to Kale's windshield. "Kale, you have paper under your windshield here. This is exactly how litter happens, young man." She wiggled an envelope free.

"What is it?" he asked as his mother handed him the envelope. He pulled out four free passes to the Muskegon County Fair and Carnival.

"Awesome," Stevie said. "Somebody must have been putting those on cars at Taco Tom's."

"You guys ate lunch at Taco Tom's?" Lucy frowned.

Kale gently elbowed Stevie back to her own seat. "All right, Mom. We'll see you back at the house."

Lucy gave the sign one final thwack and then looked back up at them, beaming. "Oh, good. Thorn needs help with his math homework and your dad's gone to the auction to look at a rake-hitch. You two could help, right?"

"Where's Aster? She's the math whiz."

"Oh, off at the movies with her girlfriends. Hopefully it's not one of those R-rated ones that she and Thorn like to watch, full of blood and guts."

"We'd be happy to help," Stevie said.

Lucy grinned and clapped her hands. "Perfect. I'm just going to finish up my walk and then I'll be back. I have a ham in the crockpot and a table covered in vegetables from the garden. We're going to be eating zucchini until we turn green."

"Great," Kale mumbled, easing off the brake and inching his car forward.

"These are for tonight," Stevie said, reading the tickets.

"Text Ben and Zach. We were going to go anyway, might as well go tonight."

Stevie pulled out her phone and typed messages to their other two friends.

Kale turned off the dirt road onto the cracked pavement driveway that led back to the sprawling Victorian mansion. The former funeral home had seen better days. Years before, the Goodwins had painted the gray exterior white, but time had taken its toll and the white paint had curled and fallen away, leaving patches of gray exposed.

"We should seed your front lawn," Stevie said. "It's looking scorched."

"Yeah." Kale brushed a hand through his dark curls. "This summer has been so hot, it's fried. My mom has all the hoses out back for the garden, so this part of the yard is pretty neglected."

As they climbed from Kale's car, Kale spotted his twelve-year-old sister Sage. She squatted next to her bike, red-faced as if frustrated.

"What's wrong, Sage?" Kale asked his little sister.

"The bike chain came off again and I can't get it back on."

"Here." He knelt beside her and threaded the chain back into the chain ring.

She smiled and hugged him. "Thanks, Kale."

"You're welcome. Watch out for the third root."

"That one's my favorite," she said, climbing on her bike and pedaling off down the driveway.

"The third root?" Stevie asked.

"Yeah, the trail she rides has some big tree roots, which are fun, but the third one's a little tricky. I smoked it one year and flew right over the handlebars. Remember when I came to school that time with the sprained wrist?"

"Oh, dang, yeah. She's up for that? Biking in the woods?"

"Sage is indestructible."

"Yeah, she's pretty hardcore," Stevie agreed.

They watched Sage pedal furiously away, veering toward a little wooden ramp she'd built earlier in the summer. She hit the ramp, caught air, and landed with a thud before turning onto the grass path that led to the wooded trail.

"She's still feeling good?" Stevie asked. "I mean, she looks good, totally healthy."

"Yeah. In remission for three years now."

"That's awesome. Those were some rough years when she was sick."

Kale watched Sage until she disappeared into the woods, marveling that she was the same girl who'd been bedridden, so thin and pale she'd practically disappeared into the white sheets of the hospital bed.

"Yeah," he said. "They were."

~

It took nearly an hour to wade through Thorn's backlog of late homework assignments.

"Thorn, seriously, why do you have so many late assignments for summer classes?"

Thorn shrugged and tossed his wavy blond hair. "Homework is busywork. Even Dad says so. The school just wants to distract us from the actual problems of the world. They're doing the government's dirty work, getting us brainwashed young so we can be more cogs in their capitalist machine."

Kale sighed and leaned his head back.

Stevie waved him away. "Go take a shower or whatever primping you have to do before the fair. I'll finish helping with the homework. Thorn"—she pointed a finger at Thorn—"sit your butt down so we can get through this."

Thorn, who'd been gazing longingly at his dirt bike propped outside, rolled his eyes and sat down. "Fine, but we're just playing into their hands."

~

Kale and Stevie met Zach and Ben at the entrance to the Muskegon fair.

"Looks like rain," Ben said, holding up a hand as if drops might start suddenly splattering his palm.

"Nah. My dad said it's moving south and should pass us by," Stevie disagreed as they lined up at the ticket booth.

"Yes!" Zach pumped his fist. "The Zipper. I frickin' love that ride."

Kale nodded, watching the swift-moving clouds, some heavy and dark. He thought Ben might be right about the rain.

"How many?" the woman at the ticket booth inquired.

"Did you guys buy extra tickets?" Kale asked. "Looks like these free passes are good for rides until six o'clock."

"Just get the wristband," Stevie said. "It's a way better deal."

Kale eyed the prices and reluctantly pulled twenty dollars from his wallet. He didn't mind paying for the rides, but hated to shell out twenty bucks and get rained out in half an hour.

"Where first?" Ben asked.

"The Zipper," Zach announced at the same moment Stevie said, "The Pirate Ship."

"Rock, paper, scissors," Stevie said.

She and Zach each held out a hand.

"Rock, paper, scissors, break," they said in unison. Stevie held her hand flat, palm down. Zach's hand was curled in a fist. Stevie waved her palm over Zach's fist.

"Paper wins," Stevie said. She pulled off her backward ball cap and secured her blonde hair in a short ponytail.

As they passed by the Zipper, Zach gestured at the carny working it. "Look, Hulk Hogan joined the carnival."

The carny did vaguely resemble the once-pro wrestler. He was enormous with a bushy white-blond mustache.

"Mamma mia," Zach said. "Look at *her*."

He nodded toward the girl working the Pirate Ship. She was stunning, and out of place amongst the carnies at the fair.

As they filed up the ramp to the ride, Zach swaggered past the girl, tipping his ball cap. She barely acknowledged him, surprising considering most girls immediately reacted to Zach. He'd always been the handsome one in their group, naturally well built with square shoulders and shaggy blond hair.

Kale filed through the line behind his friends. As he passed the girl, their eyes met. He slowed, stumbled over his too-big feet and walked into Stevie's back. The seconds stretched, as if time were taffy, and in those seconds a powerful force gripped Kale and directed his attention toward the girl as if saying, 'Look, look at her—she is important.' And she was and he didn't know why, but he felt instantly as if he knew her or wanted—no, needed—to know her, and she looked back at him with the same intensity.

"Walk much?" Stevie laughed.

Kale blushed and ripped his gaze from the girl's, following Stevie into the second row on the Pirate Ship.

The girl had turned her attention back to the line of people, and Kale studied her. Black glossy hair framed her face in one of those cuts where her hair was longer in the front and brushed her chin. A line of silver earrings adorned one of her pale ears. She was angular, with sharp cheekbones and eyes a startling green.

The ride began. The steady whoosh filled Kale's ears as the enormous ship swung forward on its pendulum, then back, picking up speed. Kale couldn't take his eyes off her and when his stomach dropped, he didn't know if it was the ride or the green-eyed girl.

2

___

When the ride ended, they walked single file down the ramp that spit them through a gate on the opposite side of the ship, where Kale could no longer see the girl.

"Now the Ferris wheel," Zach announced.

Stevie groaned. "The Ferris wheel? What are you, eighty?"

Zach produced a flask. "No." He gave her an annoyed look. "I'm trying to get us all a little tipsy."

"I'm tipsy enough with the rides," Ben said, his color slightly green.

"Are you going to ralph?" Stevie asked. "Because if you are, I'm not riding in one of those carts with you."

"I'm fine," Ben grumbled.

They approached the Ferris wheel and boarded a cart with two benches on either side. Their knees touched when all four sat down.

The guy working the ride pulled the lever that sent their cart airborne, where it abruptly stopped so more passengers could fill the cart behind them.

Zach handed the flask to Kale.

Kale took a swig and grimaced. "What the hell is this? Wine?"

Zach shrugged. "It has alcohol in it, doesn't it? That's all I could snag when I stopped by my parents' house tonight."

Kale handed the flask to Stevie.

"You know this is a terrible idea, right?" she asked Zach as they

9

reached the highest point on the wheel. She took a drink and shuddered as if she'd just swallowed a spoonful of medicine.

Zach grinned. "Like my mother always says, I've made terrible ideas a calling card."

"I'm pretty sure I've never heard your mother say that," Ben said, waving the flask away when Stevie offered it to him. Ben was never one for drinking anything besides water and an occasional root beer.

Kale gazed over the side, searching for the girl operating the Pirate Ship. He couldn't make her out.

They drank the flask in turns, passing it amongst the three of them. As the liquor took effect, Kale surveyed the scene below. More people had arrived. They stood in lines at food concessions and games. Children carried enormous bags of cotton candy. Across the midway, the Haunted Funhouse belted out a creepy circus song.

When the ride ended, Kale followed his three friends. The wine sloshed in his stomach and his head swam.

"Come on," Stevie said, linking her arm through his and dragging him toward a ride that sped in circles, where rock music vibrated from the speakers. "We're doing the Himalaya."

"I hate the Himalaya," Ben mumbled, eyeing the ride queasily.

"Man up," Zach told him, jumping in line behind a throng of teen girls who giggled and smiled at him.

As the ride started, Kale caught sight of the green-eyed girl again. She'd left the Pirate Ship and stood near one of the work trailers, a soda cup clutched in one hand. A new song belted from the speakers —'Crazy' by Aerosmith. The ride picked up speed and soon Kale was whipping in circles, strobe lights piercing his eyes, dizziness rushing through his head and gut. He caught glimpses of her each time the cart circled back.

He saw her laughing, head tossed back, throat exposed. Her eyes caught his, a flash of eye contact before he was thrust around the corner, up the incline only to face a belly-dropping descent on the other side. Each time he circled around, he caught a glimpse of her. He watched her undoing her studded belt on the next round. She held the belt in her hands and snapped it at the man she was talking to, the carny Zach had called Hulk Hogan thanks to his bulging muscles. A total blockhead, practically the opposite of Kale with his delicate features and wiry body, strong, but always too thin for his liking.

The ride ended and Ben insisted on the Haunted Funhouse, which they fumbled through almost drunkenly, thanks more to their most recent ride than their few sips of wine. From the Funhouse, they ran to the Zipper. Ben bowed out. As Kale handed his ticket to the burly carny, he again caught sight of the green-eyed girl at the Pirate Ship. Their eyes met. The Hulk Hogan carny barked at him to get in the metal cage and Kale broke the stare, catching a dark look from the Hulk look-alike.

After they rode the Zipper, Zach pointed at the High Striker game. Bunches of purple elephants hung as prizes from a pole next to the game. "I want to do that," he said. "Show off these guns." He flexed.

"Water guns," Stevie said.

They walked to the game and Zach gave the carny five bucks and picked up the large mallet. He swung it above his head and brought it down hard. The puck shot halfway up the tower.

"So sad. Better let a woman show you how it's done," Stevie said, taking the mallet. She whacked the base, and the puck inched above Zach's high score.

"Ben? Kale? Come on. Can't show me up," Stevie teased.

"All right. Fine." Kale reluctantly coughed up five dollars and took the mallet. He swung down and hit the base. The puck surpassed both Zach and Stevie's placements, but only by an inch. "Boom," Kale said. "Didn't even know my own strength. Did I win one of these?" Kale gestured at an elephant.

"Sorry, man," the scraggly guy working the game told him. "You gotta get all the way to the top."

A woman wearing a rumpled blue dress and black flip-flops walked to an electrical pole near the game. She plastered a flier against it and stapled it into place.

The carny rolled his eyes. "Here we go again."

"What's she posting?" Stevie asked.

"A missing person's flier. Her sister disappeared from a fair quite a few years back. I've seen her at other midways. She makes the rounds every summer. Sometimes she's drunk, weaving all over, waving those fliers in our face like we killed her sister."

"Is her sister dead?" Stevie asked.

Kale watched the woman, who batted her hair from her face and headed for another electrical pole.

"Gotta be dead," the carny said. "It's been six years. Ain't nobody that good at hide 'n' seek."

"Ben? Want to give it a try?" Kale asked, holding out the mallet and trying not to stare at the woman.

"Nah. I'm saving my money for fries and a caramel apple."

"Guess your stomach's feeling better," Stevie said.

"It is now that I had five minutes of not spinning in circles," Ben quipped.

"Bumper cars first," Zach insisted. "Then food."

"Fine." Ben sighed.

"Hey," a voice called as they made their way toward the bumper cars. Kale turned and saw her, the green-eyed girl, stepping between two games. He felt it again—that magnetism, that spark. She held out the purple elephant he'd been trying to win at the High Striker game. "You forgot this."

He took it. Their fingers brushed, and a jolt coursed up his arm, lighting an explosion of nerves in his stomach. "Umm... I actually didn't win that."

She smiled, tilted her head, and then lifted a finger to her lips. "It can be our secret. Here. Give it to your girlfriend."

Kale frowned and glanced to where Stevie, Ben, and Zach stood in line for the bumper cars. "Oh, no, Stevie? She's not my girlfriend. Just my friend. Friends forever, actually, since we were babies." He kept talking, unnecessary words rolling out, but he couldn't seem to stop.

"Then give it to your friend." She turned away and then glanced back over her shoulder. "See ya around." She walked away, disappearing behind one of the games.

He gaped at her, the stuffed elephant clutched in his sweaty hand. After a moment, he willed his legs to move and hurried over to Stevie.

Her eyes widened as he handed her the elephant. "No way! Did you just go back and win this? I swore that game was rigged."

"No... I... someone gave it to me. The girl running the Pirate Ship ride earlier."

"The carny?" Stevie asked. "Ooh la la."

"Damn," Zach said, leaning over Stevie's shoulder. "That girl was hot. I wish she'd give *me* a stuffed elephant."

Stevie elbowed him back. "Get on the ride, ya jackass. You're holding us up."

Ben had already chosen a shiny blue car and had his hands planted at ten and two.

"Here comes the rain." Ben held out his palm as they walked to the concessions.

The first drops splattered the top of Kale's head.

Despite the rain, they rode until dark, when they were thoroughly soaked and worn out. Kale glanced behind him a final time, reluctant to leave, hoping to catch one final glimpse of the girl with the green eyes. As he scanned the mostly deserted midway, puddles lit by the colorful carnival lights, he sighed, disappointed.

They were halfway across the parking lot when he turned back and spotted her emerging from the exit.

"Hold on," he told his friends. He jogged over to her.

She smiled at him as if amused. "Yeah?" she asked.

"Hi again. I wondered, do you want to… I mean…" His mind went blank. Not a single word rose to his lips.

She waited, smile growing wider.

"Do you… will you be here tomorrow? Meet." The jumble of words made no sense, and yet she nodded.

"Yeah, I'll be here tomorrow. Meet me at the entrance at four. Here's my number." She pulled a marker from her apron and grabbed his arm. She popped the top off with her teeth and held the tiny cap between them as she scribbled a series of numbers on his forearm in red marker. Without giving him a chance to say more, she turned and walked away.

Kale watched her, his mouth dry, his whole body charged. He walked back to his friends, who stood clustered between his car and Zach's truck.

"What was that about?" Stevie asked.

Kale grinned. "I think I've got a date."

3

"Ugh, what's all the noise? Jeez," Kale grumbled, trudging into the kitchen where bright light streamed through the windows, rendering him momentarily blind. His siblings and parents sat around the kitchen table.

"Summer Scrabble. Duh," Kale's sister, Calla said, filling a glass of orange juice.

"Good morning, Kale," his father called. "Nice of you to join us."

"Must have been a late night." Zinnia snickered.

Kale's mother got up and hurried over, standing on tiptoe to kiss his cheek. "Good morning, my handsome boy. Here, let's get you some pancakes." She heaped three pancakes on a plate, added a pat of butter and doused them in the maple syrup they'd made the year before.

"Thorn," Aster snapped. "'Sdub' is not a word."

"Sure, it is. I sdubbed my toe. See? It's a word."

"'Stub,' not 'sdub,'" Zinnia corrected.

"Says who? Come on. It's a word if I use it. I literally sdubbed my toe this morning."

"Nice try," their dad said.

Sage stood and walked to their mother. "I think I'm going to go back to bed, Mom."

"You are?" Lucy frowned and put a hand to Sage's forehead. "Not feeling well?"

"Just really tired."

"Okay." Lucy kissed her daughter on the cheek. "Why don't you go lie in the big room on the couch? Grover can keep you company."

Sage shook her head. "It's too loud. I'm going upstairs."

"Okay, honey. I'll check on you in a bit."

Kale took his plate, but his mom followed him, adding two sausages and a scoop of chopped bananas. He sat at the table, yawning as his siblings and parents argued over the Scrabble board.

"Mom and I stayed up until ten and still missed you. What time did you get in?" his dad asked.

"Around eleven," Kale said, scooping a bite of pancakes into his mouth and thinking of the girl he'd met. His skin prickled where she'd written her phone number, and he kept his sleeve pulled down so his family wouldn't see it.

"Do they have the Gravitron this year?" Thorn asked, arranging a word on the board. "I love that ride."

"The puke-a-thon, more like," Aster disagreed, wrinkling her nose at Thorn's word. "Thorn! 'Wamper' is not a word."

"Huh?" He leaned in, nodding. "I had a wamper of a goose egg the other day. It's totally a word."

Calla laughed and pushed Thorn's letters off the board. "You're the worst Scrabble player ever."

"Now, now," Lucy said, clearing a few of the breakfast plates. "He's very creative. That's a good thing."

"Not when you're playing Scrabble it's not," Aster disagreed. "It's chaos."

"There's creativity in chaos," Thorn countered.

K ale had managed to shower without wiping away the girl's number, but when his mom called up the stairs, letting him know Stevie was there to pick him up, he quickly added it to his cell phone, then scrubbed it off his arm to avoid the razzing he'd get from his friend.

His mother caught him at the bottom of the stairs and attempted to fluff his already unwieldy curls before thrusting a sack lunch into his hands. "I made you a hummus and avocado sandwich and put some of your dad's toasted coconut energy balls in there. And I added some extra for Stevie, too."

"Okay, thanks, Mom." He bit back the reminder that he was twenty and that he and Stevie usually stopped for fast food. He'd told her as much a hundred times before, and his mother still insisted on making him a bagged lunch as if he were eight instead of twenty years old.

He trotted to the truck, which was hooked to a trailer of lawn equipment, including two push-mowers, a grass seed-spreader and a pile of tools ranging from weed-whackers to garden shovels.

"Hey, what's up?" Stevie asked as he jumped into the passenger seat.

"Just another day in paradise," he muttered, dropping his lunch in the backseat.

"Oh, come on! Look at that house? You live in an old funeral home, for Pete's sake. That's so cool. If you were in a band, that alone would practically guarantee you a number one hit."

"Unfortunately for me, the musical talent was bestowed on Zinnia."

"Every talent was bestowed on Zinnia, no offense, but that's not my point. So what if you're still living at home with your gigantic, loud family? I'd pay money to live in your house."

"Want to rent my room?"

"Ha, as if. My parents already think my renting the apartment above my aunt's garage is too far away. I can only imagine if I told them I was moving across town."

"They can come too. Why not? The more the merrier, as my mom says. We already have eight in there. Why not make it eleven?"

"I guess this means you're still feeling sick of life at the Goodwin Casa of Chaos."

"Not just that. It's everything. What am I doing? I'm almost twenty-one. I live at home and I'm taking general studies courses at the college. I have no money, no career plans, no hope of ever moving out at this rate."

"Come on. It's not that bad."

"Easy for you to say. You've known you'd take over the family business since you were ten."

Stevie laughed. "Hardly. I'm pretty sure my dad envisioned Jacob taking over the business until Jacob admitted he wanted to be a lawyer and headed off to law school. That threw a wrench in Dad's gears."

"Even so, you always wanted to run the store and stay in that business. You must have said it a hundred times."

"There's stuff you want to do. Look at the leatherwork you've done." She pulled out her wallet, engraved with her initials. "My dad said you should go into business for yourself. Make belts, wallets, watch bands. We'll carry your stuff at the store, put a little display by the counter."

"Sounds like a lucrative venture."

"Since when are you looking for the big money?"

"I'm not, but it might be nice to get a car someday that doesn't have a dead battery every time the temperature drops below thirty degrees."

"So you're saying lawn care is not the life for you?"

"It's fine for now, for the summer, but obviously we're not going to be doing this business in the winter."

"Zach talked to his dad about getting a plow on his truck and plowing this winter. Maybe investing some of the money from the business this summer into getting another plow truck. We could do that, me, you, Zach and Ben. Lawn care in the summer, snow removal in the winter."

"Isn't your dad asking you to take on more hours at the store?"

"Sure. I can do both."

"Plus school?"

"What else have I got to do? I like working. At the store, I'm with my family. Doing lawns, I'm with you guys. It's the best of both worlds."

Kale sighed. "Yeah."

He couldn't tell Stevie that it didn't satisfy him the same way it did her. He loved his friends, but for the previous year, he'd felt stifled. Trapped in the big house on Chapel Road, suffocated by his family. He'd never seen the world. The few times he'd left Michigan, he'd been crammed in his parents' van, stuffed between two of his sisters as they road-tripped to some family gathering in a nearby state—Ohio or Wisconsin. Technically, he had seen California since he'd been born there, but his parents had trekked back to Michigan when he was three. He had no memory of life out west.

"Zach said Paul Mickles is having a house party tonight. Might be fun."

"I can't. I'm, umm"—Kale rolled down his window—"meeting the girl from the fair."

"That's tonight? She moves quick."

"She said to meet her at the entrance."

Stevie whistled. "You've got a hot date, huh?"

"I don't know what it is."

~

After work Kale put on his going-out shirt—a black v-neck with gray stripes. He stood in front of the mirror. It looked like he was trying too hard. He pulled it off and dropped it on the bed. He tried on three more shirts, finally settling on a plain black t-shirt.

As he started down the stairs, he passed Zinnia walking up.

She eyed him. "What are you, Goth now?"

"Huh? Why? What?"

"Black shirt, black shorts, black hair. Put on some mascara and you could be Marilyn Manson's curly-haired brother."

"Whatever," he mumbled, but he bypassed the first floor and went to the basement to the laundry room. Three stacks of clothes sat on the dryer. He sifted through and found a gray Radiohead t-shirt.

Kale heard a voice drift down the hall. He walked out and peered into the craft room. Sage sat on the floor staring at the corner. A single rocking chair sat there, empty.

"I'm not afraid," she said, as if someone sat opposite her.

"Sage?"

She turned and smiled. "Hey, Kale. What's up?"

"Who are you talking to?"

She gestured at the corner of the room as if that explained it and then stood, wincing a bit and touching her forehead. "Want to bike some trails?"

"I would, but I'm heading out to meet someone. Raincheck?"

"No rain for days," she said, "but sure, we still have time."

~

When he arrived at the fair, Kale felt jittery. Excited, but afraid the girl wouldn't be there. She'd have blown him off. She was too pretty for him, too cool—the kind of girl Zach got no problem, but who rarely gave Kale a second look.

As he walked to the midway entrance, he fiddled with the leather cuff on his watch. No one lingered near the ticket booth, and his face fell.

He took out his phone and punched the number he'd programmed under the name 'Fair Girl.' It rang and rang with no answer and no voicemail.

She'd stood him up. Or, worse, maybe she'd forgotten about him altogether. What an idiot he'd been to think she was remotely interested.

He put his hands in his pockets and scanned the midway, searching for something to do that wouldn't leave him feeling awkward and alone. He saw the darts game. Above it hung rows of colorful stuffed monkeys. Sage loved monkeys. During her sick days, she'd consumed every book and video she could find about Jane Goodall and insisted when she grew up, she wanted to move to Africa and study chimpanzees.

He walked to the game.

"Five bucks. No losers. Everybody gets a prize," the man, short and acne-scarred, told him.

"How many balloons do I have to break to get one of those?" Kale pointed at the monkeys.

"Gotta bust ten. Five bucks gets you five darts."

Kale opened his wallet, eyed the meager contents. He could spare ten dollars for Sage.

"Here." Kale handed over the cash.

The carny stuffed the money in his apron and set ten darts on the ledge.

Kale lifted one, aimed at a yellow balloon, and was rewarded with the satisfying pop as it exploded. He hit three more and grinned, almost forgot that the beautiful carny had stood him up. He bit his lip, lifted his fifth dart, and focused on a red balloon.

"Trying to win me a prize?" a voice asked.

He released the dart too soon, and it wedged between two balloons. Kale turned to see the green-eyed girl standing just behind him, smiling.

4

———

"Sorry I'm late. I had to help restock prizes in skee-ball," she explained, tucking a strand of black hair behind one ear.

"That's okay. Umm… hi." He smiled.

"Hi to you. Can I try?" She stepped to the darts and winked at the carny. "Fluffy, how's the evening going?"

"Good, until you stepped up."

She hit balloons with the five remaining darts. She gestured at the monkeys. "Which one do you want?" she asked Kale.

"Uh-uh. No way. He missed one," the guy said.

She looked at him. "Don't be a pain. He missed one because I distracted him."

"It's okay," Kale said.

"Which one?" she asked again.

Kale tried to ignore the look of fury that flashed across the carny's face. "Umm… the blue one, I guess."

"Perfect." She climbed onto the ledge, reached up and pulled a blue monkey down, handed it to Kale. "Thanks for being a sport," she told the guy she'd called Fluffy.

"Pleasure's all mine," he muttered, reaching beneath a table to grab another stuffed monkey.

Kale and the girl walked away from the game. "I think you pissed him off," Kale said, glancing back.

The man watched them, his mouth in a thin line.

"Fluffy lives in a perpetual state of being pissed off. It's important that I give him an excuse now and then to have the permanent scowl he carries around."

Kale laughed. "Well, thanks. My little sister will love this."

"Good. Let's walk and talk. I only have twenty minutes."

"Sure, yeah. I didn't think to ask if you're working tonight."

"I'm working almost every night. This is a four-day push, and then I'll have a couple days off."

"Sounds exhausting," he said, a little knot forming in his stomach at her mention of moving on to another town.

"It is, but we have some time to recuperate before we start all over again. I'm Annie, by the way. Annie Carson."

"Oh, yeah." Color rose into his neck. "I didn't even ask your name. I'm Kale Goodwin."

She glanced at him sidelong. "Kale? As in the green leafy stuff?"

He blushed deeper and pulled at the collar of his shirt. "My mom has a thing for plants."

"Well, it could be worse. You weren't named after a homicidal nurse."

"Annie?" he asked.

"Ever heard of *Misery*? The book by Stephen King?"

Kale frowned and nodded. He'd heard of it, but never read the book or watched the movie. He had no intention of admitting it to her, but he'd never been able to stomach gore and horror, whether written or on the screen. "Your mom named you after a character in a horror book?" he asked.

Annie looked toward the rides as if distracted. "Something like that. Want to go ride the carousel?"

He grinned, assumed she was joking. In the distance, the carousel revolved slowly, kids clutching the brightly painted ponies. Nostalgic carnival music drifted on the breeze. Carried too were scents of deep-fried dough and salty French fries. Kale's stomach grumbled. He'd forgotten to eat at home and now his mouth watered.

"Come on," she said, sliding her hand into his, a gesture that sent an electric shock to the center of his brain.

For a moment he felt light-headed, dizzy as she dragged him toward the carousel, and then her fingers in his registered and a kind of euphoria stole over him.

She glanced back, and Kale's whole body buzzed from the eye

contact, the closeness of her. He wanted to stop, twirl her around, and kiss her.

They reached the carousel, and she pulled him past the fence and jumped on as it moved. Kale didn't think, simply followed her, nearly tripped on the platform and had a fleeting image of himself getting dragged beneath the carousel, wrapped around some impossible-to-stop gyrating wheel that would pulverize him before the carny could halt the ride. He righted himself and stumbled behind her as Annie wove through the grinning maniacal horses.

"Here she is," Annie announced, swinging a leg over the back of an emerald-green dragon with painted flames rippling from its dark lips.

She tilted her face back and held her arms out to either side as if she were flying. The flashbulbs sparked behind her and the music, old-timey, almost haunting, made the scene feel dreamlike.

"Get on," she told Kale.

He almost climbed on behind her—a ridiculous notion. There wasn't room on the dragon. He'd have slid right off the slippery plastic. After another moment of studying the horses dumbly, he selected a black stallion on her opposite side. Its bridle was red; its legs curled as if in a sprint.

Kale mounted the horse and clutched the golden pole that rose out of the stallion's nape. He turned and watched Annie, who lay back on the dragon, her dark hair fanning over the colorful rump.

Beyond her, Kale spotted the carny manning the ride. It was Hulk from the evening before. He glared at Kale with unconcealed hostility.

When the ride ended, Annie grabbed Kale's hand and pulled him off the platform.

"Break time is over for me," she said. "I have to work the Lucky Duck for a couple hours. Care to join me?"

"Yeah. Definitely." He cringed at the eagerness in his voice.

The guy working the game handed Annie his apron, but said nothing as he stepped from the game.

Yellow rubber ducks floated by on a constantly moving river of water.

"I'll get bitched at if I let you back here, but you can sit on a stool. This game never fills up."

Kale sat at one of the little swivel stools in front of the ducks. "How did you get into this?" Kale asked. "Working at the fair, I mean."

Annie tilted her head, a smile on her lips. "The lure of the midway, the call. Maybe I had it my whole life and then one night… it just broke through all the other noise. I knew this was where I was meant to be, so I packed my bag and I joined up. Took me a minute to convince my first boss I could hold my own against the guys. I think he was mostly worried about my sleeping in the bunkhouse, but I've never had any problems."

"You stay in a bunkhouse with all the other carnies?" Kale thought of the guy with the blond mustache and his guts wriggled. He wanted to pick her up and carry her away from the carnival, ensure the guy never laid a hand on her.

"Sure. They're not as rowdy as they seem, not all of them anyway. It's like having a pack of really crazy older brothers. None of 'em would dare mess with me because the rest of them would kick his ass. I also have a tent. That's where I'm sleeping this week. I alternate between the tent and the bunkhouse."

"It's been so hot at night. How do you sleep?"

She smirked. "I get a feeling we're accustomed to very different styles of living. Where do you live? An apartment? A dorm room somewhere?"

"At home actually, with my parents." He wished he could have said an apartment or a dorm room. Anything would have sounded cooler than with his parents.

"Hmm… how old are you?" She reached beneath the ledge and pulled out a plastic bag of lollipops. "Want one?"

He shook his head. "I'm twenty, almost twenty-one."

"Why are you still living at home at twenty?"

"Money, mostly. I'm paying for college, trying to save up for a new car. I have a business with my friends, Zach, Stevie and Ben. They were here with me last night. We do lawn care."

"Don't you want to move out? Be on your own?"

"Yeah, I do. I've wanted it more lately—started getting that wanderlust bug, I guess—but… even though I've worked over the years, I've always had school and needed to help with things at home, so I just haven't been in a position financially to do it. And, well… I have a lot of freedom. It's not like I have a curfew or anything."

"A curfew," Annie mused. "It's been a long time since I had one of those."

"I haven't had one since I turned eighteen. My siblings all still do."

"How many siblings do you have?"

"Five. I make six."

"You have five siblings?" She gawked at him, eyes wide, lollipop filling out her right cheek.

"Yeah. Crazy, right?"

Annie pulled the lollipop from her mouth and tossed it in the trash. "I can't even imagine it. Do you guys… like each other?"

Kale laughed. "'Love' is the word I'd go with. 'Like' depends on the day. I'm mostly kidding. We do get along. We fought more when we were younger. Sage and Calla still get into it pretty good. They're the youngest."

"Sage and Calla? As in…?"

"Plants, yes. I might as well just come out with it. I'm first, Kale. Then Zinnia, Thorn, Aster, Calla and Sage. Thorn and Aster. Four girls, two boys in our pack."

"Holy shit. Your mom must be exhausted."

"She is one of the most energetic people I've ever met. I'm serious. My dad calls her Hummingbird."

Annie shook her head slowly, as if struggling to make sense of it all. "And you all still live together?"

Kale imagined the house on Chapel Road—the former funeral home—and cringed. The story of his family only got stranger as the details emerged. He didn't have to disclose that part just yet. "Yeah. We have a really big house."

"You'd have to. Is your family rich?"

He grinned and shook his head. "Not even remotely. My parents inherited the house from my dad's father, Grampa Goodwin. He died when I was six, so we've lived there most of my life. Fortunately for my parents, it was paid off, otherwise we could never have afforded to live there."

"What does your dad do for a living?"

"He does a bunch of stuff, primarily buys and sells farm equipment. He'll get it at auctions, fix what's broken and sell it."

"Does your mom work?"

"In the cafeteria at my sisters' school during the school year. In the summer she and the girls sell flowers and vegetables in some farmers' markets."

"Seems like it'd be hard to afford a family of six kids with those jobs."

"My parents were, and still kind of are, hippies. We grow a lot of our food. We have chickens for eggs. There's a farm that we do an exchange with—we give them veggies, they give us meat. I was born on an organic farm in California. That was kind of their big dream to have something like that, but then my grandfather got sick and my parents moved home to help care for him. He left them the big house and by then they had Zinnia and I, and my mom was pregnant with the twins. It just made sense to stay put in the Chapel Road house. How about your parents? Are they still together?"

"No. I never knew my dad and barely remember my mom. I grew up in foster care, went in when I was seven."

"I'm sorry. That must have been hard."

She leaned toward him and lifted his arm, studying the blue and black yarn bracelet that encircled his wrist near his watch. His skin tingled where she touched it. "Beats sharing a bathroom with five siblings."

"Does it?"

She shrugged. "I like your bracelet. It's cute."

"My sister, Calla, made it for me."

"It's sweet that you wear it."

By ten o'clock the fair had thinned out and the carnival workers started shutting down the rides.

"Quittin' time," Annie said. "I need to change. These clothes are nasty. Want to come back to my tent?"

"Yeah, sure." Kale's palms had begun to sweat. Talking with Annie as she worked at the duck game had been easy. Now there were no distractions. He felt the intensity of her as they moved away from the rides.

"This is the back yard," she explained as they walked between two trailers.

A dozen or more tents occupied a field of patchy yellowed grass. The flaps on most of the tents hung open. Near a large blue tent, two men sat on canvas chairs near a grill. A radio played an oldies station. 'Black Magic Woman' by Santana drifted in the air.

"This one's mine," Annie said, unzipping a small red tent. "Welcome to my quarters."

He ducked his head to follow her inside.

A purple sleeping bag lay on the floor. In one corner sat an open duffel bag, clothes spilling out. A small plastic table held a battery-powered lamp, a box of graham crackers and two newspapers. Beneath it stood a shower toiletry basket with shampoos, body wash, and a pair of tattered red flip-flops.

"Cozy," he said.

"Have a seat." Annie patted the sleeping bag. She grabbed a paper bag and peered inside, drew out a bottle of Jack Daniels. She unscrewed the top and took a drink. She offered him the bottle. "Wait." She flirted with her eyes and pulled the bottle back. "You're not twenty-one. I could get in trouble for this."

He grinned, took the bottle and put his lips to the glass, tasted the whiskey, imagined he could taste her mouth as well. The whiskey burned, but he tried not to make a face.

"Lucky for you, I like trouble." She reached up and wrapped her hands behind his head, pulled his face to hers. She kissed him, their noses crushed together. Her eyelashes tickled his face. She tasted of root beer-flavored lollipop.

When she pulled away, Kale sucked in a breath, light-headed. "Wow," he murmured.

"For you too, huh?"

"Most definitely."

She kissed him again, longer this time, climbed into his lap and gently pressed him back until he was flat on her sleeping bag. He reached up and ran his fingers through her glossy hair, cupped the back of her head. She shifted her hips back and forth and he grew hard beneath her. He wanted to tear off her shirt, strip her naked. He'd never wanted a woman as much as he wanted Annie.

They kissed until their lips were raw, until the voices and music outside the tent had faded. It was nearly midnight when he looked at his phone and felt the first pinpricks of guilt that he hadn't called home. His parents would worry.

"I better go," he said. "I don't want to, but I should."

"Mmm…" she murmured. "I'll walk you to your car."

"You don't have to do that. You're all cozy in here."

She traced her finger from his forehead down his nose to his lips. "I want to, then I can kiss you one more time."

They strolled, holding hands as if it were the most natural thing in the world, across the field of tents and campers and into the parking lot.

The lot was mostly deserted. A crumpled piece of paper whispered across the concrete and caught on a cinderblock parking barrier.

Kale stopped at his driver's side door. Annie stood on tiptoe to kiss him.

"I do wish you could stay," she said.

"Me too." He hugged her, inhaling the citrus scent of her hair. She squeezed him back, sighing into him. Kale wanted to walk back to the tent with her, crawl inside, and wrap his body around hers.

"Okay. Goodbye, Kale."

"Bye, Annie." He opened his door but didn't slide in. He watched her turn and start across the parking lot. "Annie?"

She looked back.

"Can I come back tomorrow?"

She smiled. "You better."

She disappeared beneath the arch that opened into the midway. Kale laughed out loud, struck by the feelings that had gripped him and most of all, perhaps, shocked that of all the guys in the world, Annie was interested in him.

Something crunched beneath his foot as he moved to climb into his car. He peered down to see the paper that had blown into the concrete parking block. He picked it up and unraveled the crinkled sheet.

The face of a pretty young woman with bleach-blonde hair stared out. 'Missing' was posted in large black letters across the top of the page. The bottom half of the paper, which had likely contained the girl's name and details, had been torn away. Crumpling the paper, he walked to a trashcan and tossed it in.

As Kale pulled from the parking lot, his lights swept the dark rides in the midway. For an instant, he thought he saw a figure, someone standing near the back of the funhouse. He tilted his rearview, but could see only the dark silhouettes of the carnival rides.

5

Kale woke with memories of the night before unspooling in his mind. He grinned and practically jumped out of bed, skipped downstairs. He thought of Annie as he stood at the counter, absently spooning cereal into his mouth.

"Why are you grinning like the Cheshire cat?" Calla asked, startling Kale from his daydreams.

He frowned. "I'm not. I just slept well." Not entirely true. He'd woken several times after intense dreams about Annie where they were passionately kissing on some high-above-the-earth ride and then he'd suddenly be plummeting toward the ground. "Where is everybody?"

"Sage is riding her bike. Mom is in the garden. Thorn and Aster went down the street to walk Mrs. Drabble's dogs. Zinnia is in her room."

"Where's Dad?"

"Meeting somebody to sell a hay baler."

"All right, let Mom know I went to meet Stevie to do some lawns."

~

"Hey, Kale," Stevie called. "You already put grass seed there. About three times, I think. What's up with you today? Too many rounds on the Tilt-A-Whirl last night?"

Kale stopped throwing the seed and moved to a bare spot in the customer's yard. "How was the party last night?" he asked.

"Lame. All people from high school, which is to be expected." She shrugged. "I would really love to spend one evening hanging out with guys who talk about something other than winning the state championship in soccer our senior year."

Kale laughed. "Yeah."

"I was thinking about catching a movie tonight. There's a new one with the Rock playing at the theatre."

"Damn. I totally want to see that, but I can't. I'm going back to the fair."

"Three nights in a row?"

He nodded, but avoided her gaze.

"Come on, spill your guts. What's up with you and the carny?"

"Don't call her that."

Stevie released an exasperated sigh. "Fine then, you and the Pirate Ship girl."

"Annie," he said.

"Annie," Stevie repeated.

"I don't know. I just…" He clasped both hands behind his neck and squeezed, looking up, seeing Annie with a wave of dark hair covering one eye, her smile as it spread and changed her whole face, made her somehow more beautiful than she already was. "I'm really drawn to her."

"Way to state the obvious. Are you gonna date her?"

"I'd like to, but…"

"But she lives with a travelling carnival."

"I guess. I haven't talked to her about any of that. I'm meeting her again tonight."

"And what's the appeal? Other than the physical. That's hard to miss."

Kale didn't have a satisfactory response. His feelings for Annie originated from the same mysterious place as so many of his impulses. Why did he love the sensation of soft leather beneath his fingertips? Why did he feel deeply nostalgic whenever he heard any song by Bon Iver? "Stevie, I don't have answers to all these questions. Why are you grilling me? I didn't pester you when you started dating Jordan Miller."

"That's because everyone knows the Millers. His dad is your dentist. This girl is an outsider."

Kale snorted. "An outsider? What decade are you living in?"

"I don't mean it like that. You don't know anything about her. I'm… a little worried."

He scowled at her. "Why?"

"Because that girl has a ferociousness about her. She might chew you up and spit you out."

He shook his head. "No way. There's something between us. I've never felt anything like it."

"All right, fine. I'll drop it. But keep your wits about you. Okay? I have a bad feeling about her."

"Yeah, yeah. Come on, I want to get this done so I can get home and take a shower."

"Don't you have classes this afternoon?"

"I'm gonna bail. I don't think my life will go downhill if I miss a few communications and math classes."

Kale found Annie waiting for him at the entrance to the midway. She stood with another carnival worker Kale had seen briefly the night before. He was a burly, bearded man with a laugh that carried across the parking lot.

"There he is," Annie said, waving. "Kale, this is Dan the Dragon, also known as Dan with the good cigars. May I?"

"Here you go, sugar," the man told Annie, handing her his lit cigar. She put it to her lips and took a pull. Dan reached out and shook Kale's hand. "Good to meet you, kid."

"Likewise."

Annie handed Dan his cigar back. "I'll see ya at showtime," she said. "Come on." She grabbed Kale's hand. "I've got an hour. I want to take you for a ride."

"I thought the rides didn't start until three?"

She laughed. "Not that kind of ride." She drew Kale through the parking lot to a shiny silver and white motorcycle. "It's Duke's. He'll never miss it."

Kale stared at the motorcycle, palms instantly sweating. He'd never ridden on one. The closest thing had been driving Stevie's dirt bike once. He'd made it about fifteen feet before crashing into her mom's lilac bush. "No helmets?" he asked.

Annie slapped the leather seat behind her. "Come on."

The logical Kale brain said 'hell no,' but his body stepped forward, swung a leg over the bike and settled behind Annie. He wrapped his arms around her waist and squeezed. She smelled like the cigar she'd taken a puff of and shampoo, the kind men used—sandalwood or cedar.

She started the bike, and they sped away from the midway, spitting up gravel as she turned onto the main road. He held her tight, squeezing his thighs and feeling her backside pressed against him. He wanted to slip his hands beneath her shirt, kiss her neck, but the fear of their speed held him riveted as they hurtled down the road.

They flew through town and onto the highway. She drove fast, zipping by the cars and semis going north. Fear and adrenaline pulsed through his veins in equal measure. At an exit with only a number, no city sign, she veered to the right, and the bike tilted with the curve.

Kale closed his eyes for a moment, quelling the rising panic that they might suddenly tip sideways and both go skidding across the pavement. They didn't. She slowed at the stop sign, quickly glanced each way, then sped on down the road, turning into an empty parking lot that faced a sandy embankment.

He climbed off, released a huge shuddering breath, and stared at her.

She hopped off the bike, surveying him. "How was that?" she asked.

He grinned. "That was awesome! Terrifying, but awesome. Holy cow." He ran and did an awkward little jump, as if shooting a basketball toward a hoop. When he turned back to her, she was laughing.

"Really though," he said, rubbing both hands against his wind-burnt cheeks. "I've never felt so... alive."

She walked to where he stood and took his hand, leading him toward the bluff. "Stick with me and you'll feel alive every day," she said.

He walked with her, their palms touching, fingers intertwined. Her hand was warm and soft and he couldn't imagine ever having to let go.

They crested the bluff and Lake Michigan stretched toward an invisible horizon. Waves frothed against the shore. Above them, the sun shined down from a smattering of smoky clouds.

Kale had seen Lake Michigan hundreds, maybe thousands, of times, but now it took his breath away. A bubble of unidentifiable grief ballooned in his chest. He squeezed her hand tighter, felt the ridges of her knuckles beneath his fingers. She turned to face him and when he looked at her, really looked at her, the grief transmuted to near-despair. The thought of losing this, the feeling he held now literally in the palm of his hand, paralyzed him.

"What is it?" she asked. "You looked sad."

He forced a smile. "I'm happy-sad. Does that make sense?"

"Yeah." She stepped closer, released his hand, and slipped her arms around his waist. She rested her head on his chest. "I can hear your heart," she murmured.

He stroked the top of her head, kissed the parting in her hair.

"Come on," she said, pulled her shirt over her head and ran across the beach. She stripped out of her shorts and ran into the surf wearing black underwear and a faded gray sports bra.

He hesitated, then yanked his shirt off and tossed it on the sand. He awkwardly pulled down his shorts, wishing he'd opted for boxers instead of whitey-tighties.

As he followed her into the lake, a surge of water rushed up to his chest. He gasped. "Holy crap, it's cold."

She laughed and went under, popped up and waded back to him. She wrapped her arms around his back, both of their skin clammy and slick with goosebumps. Her mouth was hot when she pressed it on his.

She pulled away and dove under, stood and jumped as a wave crashed into her. She surfed it back. He joined her, diving under some waves and jumping over others.

She swam out and Kale tried to keep pace with her, but he kept losing her in the swells. Annie continued swimming, head down, arms lashing the waves.

"Annie," he yelled, treading water.

She kept going and then finally, just as the worry took hold, she turned and started back. When she reached him, her breath was rapid.

They dragged themselves, spent, to the beach and lay panting.

Kale rolled onto his side and kissed her, feeling her body trembling against him. "You went so far. I was starting to get scared."

She gazed at him, eyes searching his. "Sometimes I want to swim forever. Swim and swim until my body gives out and I can drift down."

"Don't do that. You'd break my heart."

She tucked one of his curls behind his ears. "I might break it anyway, Kale. Not on purpose, but... I usually hurt the people I love."

"You're worth it."

"Am I?"

"Without a doubt."

"Maybe we'll be the modern-day Romeo and Juliet," Annie murmured. She traced a finger over his collarbone. "I'm so into you, I want to write bad poetry."

Kale laughed. "We are what bad poetry is made of."

She laid her head on his chest. "And good poetry too."

6

———————

At the carnival, Annie led Kale to the back yard. She stopped at a camper and slipped the motorcycle keys into a knapsack sitting on a small outdoor table.

"He never even knew it was gone." She winked at Kale. "I'm working the Pirate Ship. Free rides all night for you," she told him, her eyes twinkling.

"I'd be riding by myself?"

"Well, I can't run the ride *and* be on it."

Kale rode twice and then loitered around the metal gate, watching Annie work. She smiled at the little kids, making sad faces when they didn't reach the minimum height limit before whispering some secret in their ear that made them giggle. The men who boarded the ride looked at her with probing, carnal eyes and Kale felt a stab of jealousy each time a man's gaze drifted over her body.

"Kale?" she called after a ride ended and the group who'd been on the ship began to depart. "Would you run and get me a Coke?"

"Sure, yeah."

She blew him a kiss and then turned her smile back to the line of people waiting to board the Pirate Ship.

Kale wove through the steadily growing crowd and stood in line at a food truck. "I'll take a Coke and a water, please," he told the girl in the window.

As he started away, drinks in hand, he slowed at the mention of

Annie's name. A young woman wearing a gold scarf tied around her neck stood talking to a carny working a Whac-A-Mole game, a photo in her hand. Kale craned his neck to get a look at the picture, which vaguely resembled Annie with much longer pink- and purple-streaked hair and a whole lotta makeup.

"Are you sure it's her?" the woman asked, urgency in her voice.

"No. I ain't sure. Go ask her. She works the Pirate Ship."

The woman broke away from Kale, seemingly headed for the Pirate Ship, but apparently didn't realize she'd started off in the wrong direction.

The carny caught eyes with Kale and, though the man said nothing, his expression told Kale to warn Annie.

Kale ran back to Annie, arriving as passengers boarded the Pirate Ship. "There's someone looking for you. They had a photo and seemed kind of upset. A woman, twenties probably, with reddish hair and lots of…" Kale waved at his face, couldn't think of the word.

"Freckles?"

Kale nodded.

Annie paled. "I need to get someone to cover me. Hold on." She broke away from the crowd already lining up at the Pirate Ship and ran to the Gravitron. The guy returned with her, looking annoyed. Annie performed the switch two more times, ultimately working her way down to the Haunted Funhouse. "Will you do me a favor?" she asked.

"Yeah, definitely. Anything you need."

"Put my apron on and let people through. You don't have to do anything on this one. I'm just going to tuck myself into this little alcove here. It's super easy."

"Who is it who's looking for you? Someone you know?"

"Maybe. I'm not sure, but… it's a long story and I promise I'll explain later. Just not right now."

The lights in the Haunted Funhouse stuttered and popped. A steady stream of fairgoers flowed through the amusement, screaming as they wove their way down mirrored halls and peeked in the darkened rooms where severed heads and other horror scenes awaited them.

Kale's butt ached from sitting in the plastic chair, so he'd switched to leaning against the side of the funhouse, where he and Annie could talk while she remained hidden.

She asked him a million questions, wondering about his family, his interests, his plans for the future. He tried to ask those same questions of her, but Annie was evasive, often shifting the focus back on him, insisting that her life before the carnival was sad and not worth sharing.

"Favorite band?" she asked.

"Hmm… Empire of the Sun, Cold War Kids. I've been really into the Shins the last couple of years. How about you? What music do you like?"

"Techno mostly. It's fast and there are no lyrics."

"Why don't you like music with lyrics?"

She shrugged. "Songwriters want you to feel sad. I listen to music to dance, not cry."

A family of four walked past clutching bags of cotton candy and cheap stuffed plushie toys they'd won at the games. Behind them was the girl who'd been searching for Annie.

"That's her," Kale murmured.

Annie shrank further into the shadows. "Follow her. See if she leaves. She's walking toward the exit."

"Okay." He untied the apron and handed it to Annie.

He hurried down the funhouse steps, staying a good distance behind the woman. He studied her. She couldn't have been much older than him, but she dressed like someone who worked in an office, with slacks, black pumps and a shimmery blouse that matched her gold scarf —hardly an outfit for the county fair.

At the exit, she turned and walked beneath the arch. She glanced back at the midway, her face drawn, her eyes sad, and then she strode across the parking lot and climbed into a silver Volkswagen Jetta.

Kale hurried back to the Haunted Funhouse. Annie stood near the funhouse entrance.

"Did she leave?"

"Yep. Did you recognize her?"

Annie pursed her lips and shook her head. "I don't think so. No."

Behind them, the leering face that served as the Funhouse entrance released a sinister laugh.

"Go ahead. Take a gander through the Haunted Funhouse." Annie gestured at the yawning mouth.

Kale shook his head. "I'm not into getting creeped out. Plus, I already did it."

"Oh, come on. It's cheesy, not scary. Show me how brave you are."

He chuckled and pushed his hands through his hair. "All right, but if I scream like a girl, you'll have to come in and rescue me."

She kissed him. "I would be delighted to."

Kale stepped into the first set of mirrored mazes. His reflection appeared on every surface. He held out his hands and touched the smooth glass, feeling his way for an opening. He found one and moved along each corner, revealing another set of mirrors and another.

As he neared the end of the mirrors, he froze. Someone else must have come in behind him. The man looked oddly like him with glossy brown curls, but his skin had a jaundiced hue, and when Kale studied him, he started. The whites of the man's eyes appeared bloodshot and a black muck seeped toward his irises.

Kale spun, expecting to find the sick-looking man standing there waiting for Kale to move, but he wasn't there. Only Kale's reflection met him. He turned back, but the man no longer appeared in any of the mirrors. He must have been ahead of Kale and walked further into the funhouse. But how had he slipped in without Kale seeing him outside? Maybe when Kale and Annie had kissed?

Kale reached the end of the mirror maze, but found he didn't want to go any further. His stomach plunged at the prospect of what lay on the second floor, the disturbing scenes he'd been reminded of as people emerged throughout the evening.

Did you see the woman in the blood-filled bathtub? Soo creepy. That severed head was seriously gross!

He hated the thought of slinking back out though, telling Annie he was too spooked to go on. He gritted his teeth and moved forward, arms outstretched as he passed through the hall of prison bars filled with dangling metal chains.

A darkened stairway led to the second floor of the funhouse. It was pitch-black and Kale could navigate only by feel.

He reached out and his hands closed on something soft. Someone's hair. As he pulled back, the hair came with him, hair and something wet, like oozing flesh. He heard the plop as it fell from his hands onto the ground.

A trick of the Haunted Funhouse, he thought, but knew it couldn't be true. Such a prank would have the impossible-to-see stairs thick with slimy fake blood. Customers would be breaking ankles and wrists every time they set foot inside. It was a liability nightmare. No. There was something else at work, something connected to the man with the glossy black curls and the sunken red eyes.

Kale turned and ran face first into the wall at the bottom of the stairs. Pain exploded in his head and he bent down and cupped his nose, sinking to his knees as fireworks played behind his eyes.

On the stairs behind him, something moved. A wet, slouchy dragging sound and then a thump, thump.

It was coming after him.

7

He scrambled to his feet and burst through the dark curtain that led back into the chains. In the mirror maze, he caught his reflection—eyes wild, a red mark on his nose where he'd struck the wall—and suddenly the mirrors filled with another image and he screamed. The girl coming through the opposite way screamed as well and flung up her arms as if he was about to attack. Two of her friends shrieked and bumped into her.

"It's okay," Kale blurted. "Sorry. I'm... going back this way. I have to go out this way." He inched around them, pressing himself against the glass, and plunged through the opening back onto the entrance platform. His breath was ragged as he slumped against the wall.

Annie, who was chatting with two young men waiting at the top of the stairs to go inside, turned to look at him. All three of them did.

"Hey," she said. "I wondered where you went."

"That was terrifying!" Kale shouted. "Do not go in there if you have a heart condition."

He marveled at his own words, the outrageous tone. His heart thundered behind his ribs and he thought he might throw up, but still he tried to play the part and disguise his fear. He'd never had the stomach for creepy experiences and he was embarrassed at the level his mind had just played tricks on him in the Haunted Funhouse.

Annie grinned, then tried to muffle it as she let the two men pass.

"Enter if you dare," she told them. She turned to Kale. "Well, who knew you were such a showman? You trying to get hired or what?"

He chuckled, but it was more of a wheeze as his breath continued to come in gusts.

The girls he'd passed appeared on the upper platform, giggling as they took turns exiting the funhouse on the red swivel slide that offered the only means of escape.

"There he is," one girl said, pointing at Kale. "He works here, see. It was all part of the show."

"You totally freaked us out," one girl called to Kale. She gave him a thumbs-up as the trio walked away.

None of them had come scrambling back through the entrance. They weren't slick with blood, fake or otherwise. Neither was he, for that matter.

It had all been in his head.

~

At ten, the rides went dark, the music died and Annie and Kale made their way to the backyard, trailing the other carnies headed the same way.

Annie stretched and bent over, shaking her head and ruffling her hair. When she stood up, her dark hair was tousled.

"You look so beautiful," Kale said.

She kissed him, and he buried his hands in her hair. "Mmm… I need a shower. I smell like sweat."

"I like it." He kissed her neck, her collarbone.

"Walk me to the tent. I need to get my shower stuff. Then we can have some fun."

Kale accompanied Annie back to her tent, where she grabbed her toiletries, a towel, and a change of clothes.

He waited for her outside the shower trailer and watched the other carnival workers celebrating the end of another long day. Some stood clustered near tents, smoking cigarettes or cracking beers. He noticed the Hulk Hogan lookalike standing with two other rough-looking carnival workers. They were all drinking from red plastic cups.

"Hey there, handsome," a woman with bright red hair, roots gray, said as she walked up to Kale. "I hear you're Annie's sweetheart."

Kale smiled and held out his hand. "Yeah. I think so, anyway. I'm Kale."

"Kale, I'm Margaret. Wife of Dan the Dragon." She gestured at the man he'd met earlier that day. Kale waved, and the man gave him a nod. "We're cooking some burgers and dogs on the grill. You grab Annie and come join us, okay?"

"Sure. I'll talk to her about it when she gets cleaned up."

"You do that." Margaret winked at him and sidled along, stopping at a camper, likely to offer the same invitation to the man who sat in a canvas chair drinking a bottle of Mountain Dew.

Annie emerged several minutes later, hair wet on her shoulders, face scrubbed clean. She wore cut-off jean shorts and a loose button-down black sleeveless blouse. The buttons were slightly off, leaving one side of the shirt longer, which Kale loved for no reason he could pinpoint.

Annie stood on tiptoe and kissed him.

"You smell so good," he told her.

"Good enough to eat?" she asked, raising an eyebrow.

"Definitely."

She smiled and took his hand. "Let's go to the tent."

"One of the other ladies here, Margaret, invited us over. They're grilling."

Annie glanced at the group and made a face. "Are you hungry?"

"Not really, no." He should have been hungry, hadn't eaten for hours, but with Annie food was little more than an afterthought.

"Good. Then I'm not sharing you with anyone."

At the tent, she knelt, unzipped it and crawled inside. Kale followed. Annie closed the tent flap and then turned back to him, her eyes filled with emotion, something he couldn't quite name.

"What?" he asked.

"I'm telling myself this is real… that you're real." She leaned toward him, brushed her fingers over his forearm. His skin prickled.

"I know exactly what you mean."

"You do? You feel it too? This"—she fluttered her hand between them—"magnetism."

He nodded. "I've never felt anything like it."

"Me either. It's all-consuming. I barely slept last night. I couldn't stop thinking about you."

"Me too." He remembered his fitful dreams, moments where he'd awoken in his bed, sure she was lying beside him just out of arm's reach.

"You're not a virgin, are you?" she murmured.

He started, choked a little on his laugh. "What? No. Why?" He wasn't, though he'd only slept with one person, Noelle—a girl in his political science class at college. They'd dated for six months the year before and all he knew of sex he'd learned from her. It wasn't much.

"Just curious."

"Do I seem like a virgin?" he asked.

She climbed onto his lap and straddled him. She tilted her head, dark hair falling across one eye. "You seem like a nice guy, one of the good ones."

She kissed him and his body buzzed. Her hands drifted down, and she caressed the hardness pressing against his jeans. He swallowed.

"I want you," she whispered, her lips tickling his ear.

She unbuttoned her shirt. She wore no bra and her nipples were dark and pointed. Kale touched a cluster of round white scars on the left side of her rib cage. The flesh was raised beneath his fingertips. "What are these?"

She wove her fingers through Kale's. "They're burns."

"Burns? From what?"

"From cigarettes, and I don't want to talk about those now, okay? I just want to be right here with you."

Kale's eyes lingered another moment on the burns, and he imagined what she'd told him about growing up as a foster kid. "I'm so sorry, Annie."

"Shh…" She pressed her mouth on his.

When she wriggled out of her shorts, Kale took off his own shirt and flung it aside. They laughed as she fumbled with the zipper on his shorts, which got stuck halfway down and refused to release.

"Are you sure?" he whispered when she climbed on top of him.

"Shhh," she said again, quieting him by putting her mouth on his.

Kale gasped when she took him in her hand and slipped him inside of her.

~

K ale left Annie's tent just after midnight. They held hands as they walked to his car. It was as if they'd always been together, would always be together.

She wrapped her arms around his waist. "Will you come early tomorrow? I want to take you somewhere."

"Of course, yeah. How early?" He ignored the fact that he had class again the following day and was supposed to mow several lawns.

"Eight in the morning. That should give us time."

"Eight? You're not going to get much sleep."

"I don't need sleep when I'm with you."

He grinned and kissed her. "Me neither."

8

"Wait. Kale Joseph Goodwin, turn around," his mother commanded.

Kale turned.

He'd woken up just after six and showered and dressed quickly to ensure he'd make it to the midway by eight. He'd slipped into the kitchen for a cup of coffee, but spotted his mother near the stove and tried to retreat before she saw him.

His mother stood watching him pointedly, hands on her hips. She wore the same grass-stained white paint overalls she'd worn gardening for most of his life. "Are you headed to class?"

"Yep," he lied.

"And then doing lawns today?"

"Umm… no lawns today. I'm meeting a friend."

"The girl at the fair?"

He sighed and nodded. "Yes, Annie. Now I've gotta go. I don't want to be late for class."

"Then don't be, but here." She grabbed a banana from the table and tossed it to him. He caught it. "We're having family dinner tonight. Bring her by."

He groaned. "Mom, no. It's too soon."

"It's never too soon to introduce someone you care about to the people who care about you most of all."

"Well, I can't anyway, because she can't leave the fair. She has like an hour's break if she's lucky. I usually hang out with her at one of the rides or games."

"That's fine. The fair ends soon, doesn't it? Bring her after it's over."

"I'll think about it." He turned.

"One more thing," she called.

"What?"

"I need you to drop Calla at Penny's house. They're making fairy houses."

"I don't have time—"

"Kale." Her voice was serious. "I'm happy you've found someone. I am, but you still have responsibilities here. Understand? I need you to do this for me. I have six plants out of the pots as we speak and I need to get them in the ground ASAP."

"Fine. Okay, but she better be ready right now."

"Thank you," his mom said. "And bring Annie home tomorrow. I want to meet her."

Calla, as it turned out, was not ready, and it took Kale fifteen minutes of threatening to leave before she finally abandoned her project —stapling carpet to a cat tree she and Thorn had made. He drove fast and Calla complained he was tailgating, but he dropped her off with time to drive to the fair.

He parked in the carnival lot and texted Stevie.

Kale: Something came up and I can't do the Shepherd or Neff lawns today.

Stevie: Damn, really? What's going on?

Kale stared at the words, guilt making his stomach twist as he typed a lie.

Kale: My dad needs help.

Stevie: Okay. Want to meet later? Zach was thinking about a bonfire at his and Ben's place.

Kale: Probably not tonight. I'll call you tomorrow.

As he hit send, he spotted Annie walking across the lot.

She climbed into the passenger seat, leaned over and planted a wet one on his mouth.

"Hello to you too," Kale told her.

"Let's go," Annie said. "This is a bit of a drive, so pedal to the metal."

"Turn right at the next road," Annie told him, pointing. "You're not taking me to the woods for a ritual sacrifice, are you?" he joked as they turned down yet another deserted road thick with forests on either side.

"Not today, I'm not," she teased.

He glanced at the road sign and read it aloud. "Boneset Road."

"Yep, kind of a creepy name, huh?"

"It seems like it, but boneset is actually a plant," Kale explained. "Native Americans used it to treat colds and influenza."

"Well, aren't you the history professor."

He chuckled. "Hardly. I can thank my mother for my wealth of plant knowledge. Boneset is actually an aster."

"Like your sister?"

"Like her name, anyway."

They passed a large tree on the side of the road. The trunk was warped and scarred, the bark blackened. "Whoa, look at that tree," Kale said.

"Yeah, nasty-looking. I think somebody died there."

"Really?" He shuddered, noticing a faded bouquet of plastic flowers near the base of the tree.

"Yeah, a car accident."

"That's sad."

"See that trail right there?" Annie pointed.

Kale leaned forward and squinted through the windshield.

"There, turn left now." She nudged the wheel.

Kale turned the car onto a weedy path that barely looked big enough for an ATV, let alone a car. "We might get stuck," he said as the car bumped over a divot and nearly bottomed out.

"We won't. It opens up just ahead."

After the car scraped through a mass of prickly bushes and branches, the two-track grew wider and more defined. They were still driving in thick forest without any clue to what lay beyond, but at least he was no longer concerned they might get wedged between two trees.

"What is this place?" Kale asked.

"My uncle's camper. I've been coming here for years."

Kale glanced at her sideways. "Like… a biological uncle?"

She shook her head. "The brother of one of my foster dads. Really nice guy. He'd bring us foster kids out here and let us run wild."

"And he doesn't mind that you still come here? Use his place?"

"He moved out of the country years ago. Costa Rica or something. Livin' the good life as an expat. He left this place behind and I sort of claimed it. I've never seen anyone else out here."

"Hmm," Kale mumbled, not entirely comfortable with the arrangement. What if the former uncle showed up and found them?

"Don't worry," Annie said, putting her hand on Kale's thigh and sliding it to his knee and then back up, higher. When she started massaging his inner thigh, he momentarily forgot himself and closed his eyes.

"Kale, you're about to run us into a stream."

His eyes popped open and he realized they'd left the claustrophobic trail and emerged into an opening. A stream ran along one side of the property. At the back sat a long camper streaked in grime and rust.

"It's way better on the inside," Annie assured him.

"Really?" he asked, skeptical.

"Yes. Really. Park this thing. I'll show you."

Kale parked near the camper and turned off the engine. He followed Annie from the car and up to the camper. She stepped onto the cinder blocks that served as makeshift stairs. She pulled the door handle all the way up and then wiggled it. After a moment, something clicked and the door opened with a screech.

Kale grimaced. "Sounds like somebody just stepped on a cat's tail."

Annie grabbed his hand and pulled him in behind her.

The camper was musty with brown carpet. At one end stood a bench upholstered in faded checkered fabric. Dark brown cabinets and countertop comprised the kitchen. The front of the stove was orange. A little table with paisley benches sat opposite the small kitchen. A bundle of coconut air fresheners hung above the little metal sink.

"Home, sweet home," she told him and then grinned. "I'm kidding. This isn't home, although maybe it's the closest thing I've got."

"It has character," Kale said, picking up a plastic rat from the counter. "Friend of yours?"

"Friend, enemy, depends on the day."

Kale lifted the rat to face level. It had sharp little blood-soaked teeth poking from its long face. "Creepy," he said, setting it down.

"Let me give you a tour of the bedroom," Annie said.

Kale stepped into the narrow hall as she opened a door at the back of the camper.

"'Come into my parlor,' said the spider to the fly," she whispered, walking backward and holding onto both of Kale's hands as she guided him into a cramped little bedroom. She fell backward onto the bed and pulled him with her. Their foreheads bumped, and they laughed.

Annie kissed his ear, then bit it lightly. "Take off your pants, Mr. Goodwin," she murmured.

~

They'd fallen asleep, and Kale woke alone in the stuffy little room. They hadn't cleaned up after and he was sticky as he sat up.

"Annie?" he called.

She didn't respond. He stood and groped between the bed and wall until he found his underwear. They'd slipped under the bed. He crouched to grab them and saw a plastic binder. He wiggled it free and flipped it open to see newspaper articles sandwiched between the plastic dividers.

'Man Killed in Fiery Crash,' announced the headline on the first article. Kale frowned at the black and white picture of a car wrapped around a large tree. Tarps covered portions of the car and much of the vehicle was burned black. Kale eased the binder closed, not wanting to pry into Annie's private things.

He slipped on his underwear and carried his jeans into the main room of the camper. No Annie. He struggled into his jeans and opened the door, searched for her on the weedy property, but again didn't see her.

Thirsty, he trudged from the trailer to his car. He opened the driver's door and grabbed the Thermos of water he'd brought, gulped three large swallows. When he lowered the Thermos, he heard a sound that seemed to be coming from the stream.

He walked over and spotted Annie. She sat on a boulder, her shoulders hunched forward. She ripped furiously at something she clutched in her hands. Kale squinted and realized it was paper, several crumpled sheets. She tore them in strips and dropped them into the stream.

Kale stepped back, sure she'd be upset he was watching her. His foot landed on a branch that snapped.

Annie's head whipped around and for a moment she was unrecognizable. Her dark hair hung limp in her face. Her eyes appeared vicious and black, as if the pupils had expanded and crowded out all the color.

"I'm sorry. I didn't mean to—" Kale started.

She blinked and stood. "Hey, sleepyhead." With the words her face transformed. She smiled and hopped from the boulder back to the bank. "Have a good nap?"

"Yeah." Kale's gaze shifted to the stream, but it had swallowed the paper.

Annie looped her arm through his and steered him away, not acknowledging the strange moment. "There's something else I want you to see."

They walked hand in hand down a nearly invisible path in the woods. Before them the trees opened and revealed a small lake. Perched on the edge was an old wooden structure.

"What is it?" he asked.

"A boathouse." She started toward it.

"Are you sure it's safe to go inside? It doesn't exactly look structurally sound."

"It's fine. Do you think I'd ever put you in danger?"

Before he could answer, she ran up the rickety wooden steps and pulled the metal handle on a decayed wooden sliding door. The hinges screeched as the door opened.

Kale followed her into the dark space that stank of lake and mildew. The front of the boathouse was open to the lake and the water lapped against wooden decking, where once upon a time a boat had likely been moored. On the side of the room stood a narrow staircase.

Soft boards sank as he shuffled toward the wooden stairs, which shook as Annie skipped up them. He had even less faith in the stairs than the boathouse itself, but bit his tongue.

The upstairs of the boathouse was a large room, the boards more durable, the ceiling sloping upward to a peak in the center. A crisscross of beams ran overhead.

A mattress lay on the floor in the room's corner, surrounded by half-melted candles. A crumple of blankets sat in the center of the bed. No other furniture occupied the space, but he saw newspapers stacked along one wall.

"Have you stayed here before? Slept here?"

She grinned and nodded. "It's unbelievable. The sounds of the frogs and crickets and birds at night. It's so loud and yet peaceful. I want you to stay here with me."

He swallowed and glanced again at the bed. "Tonight?"

She stepped toward him and ran her hands up his arms. Goose-bumps rose along his biceps. He kissed her and would have agreed to anything in that moment.

"Not tonight," she murmured. "We'll come back in a couple of days when the carnival has moved and I have some time off. We can bring some supplies. Clean bedding, flashlights, food, and water. What do you say?" She kissed his neck.

"Mmm-hmmm... yes."

"Look at this," she said, leading him to a set of swinging double doors that reminded him of something in an old western saloon. She pushed them open to reveal a wooden platform jutting out from the side of the boathouse over the lake.

"Is this safe?" he asked, stepping gingerly on the soft wood planks.

"Sure." She wiggled her hips.

The deck shifted slightly, and Kale clutched the exterior wall of the boathouse. "That was not reassuring."

"It's fine. Come over here." She stopped with her toes right at the edge of the platform. "I used to jump off of this as a kid. Cannonball right into the water."

Kale shuffled toward her, wary of the drop to the dark lake below. He stopped just behind her and leaned forward.

Annie looked at him and laughed. "Are you afraid of heights? You handled the Pirate Ship pretty well."

"I'm not afraid of heights if I trust what I'm standing on," he said.

Annie took his hand. "Don't worry. I'll catch you."

He laughed. "I'm afraid if this thing collapses, we'll both go."

"As it should be. Romeo and Juliet, remember?"

Kale pointed. "See those white flowers at the edge of the lake?"

Annie shielded her eyes from the sun. "Yeah."

"Those are boneset."

"Huh... neat. I never knew that." She released his hand and walked back toward the doors. "I'm going to grab my sunglasses. It's bright out here."

Kale inched to the edge of the platform and peered into the lake. Weeds and cattails grew along the shore. The surface was thick with algae and water lilies.

Kale stared down at the murky water. Something drifted just beneath the surface. He squinted and then sank to his knees, hands gripping the boards as he tried to get a closer look.

His heart thumped faster as he studied what appeared to be a pale human face.

He recoiled. "Annie!"

"What?" She stepped back through the swinging doors, sunglasses clutched in her hand.

He glanced back at her, his stomach sinking. "You better come look at this."

She walked to the edge of the platform and crouched beside him. "What do you see?" she asked.

Kale turned back to the lake. He searched the dark surface for the pale face he'd seen only seconds before, but could no longer find it. "I saw..." He frowned and scanned the lake.

"What? A water snake? They're in there—some big ones, too."

"No... I don't know. That was weird."

When they left the boathouse, Kale wanted to get closer to the lake, but the shoreline was thick with weeds and soft at the water's edge. He shuddered and followed Annie back to the forest toward his car.

9

———————

"We could stop and grab lunch," Kale suggested on their drive back to the carnival.

"Better not. Mo's doing his big closing night speech. He'll be pissed if I miss it. I am hungry, though. Any chance you want to run and get some sandwiches? I'm so sick of fair food."

"Sure, definitely. I know a great deli. What kind do you like?"

"Whatever. Turkey, ham. No tuna."

"No tuna. Got it."

He stopped near the entrance to the fair. Annie leaned across the seat and kissed him. "I'm working the Pirate Ship again tonight. Meet you there?"

"No place I'd rather be."

~

Sandwiches took longer than he expected. A boys' summer baseball league had descended on the restaurant and Kale spent forty minutes waiting for two turkey and cheese subs.

When he arrived back at the midway, the fair was in full swing. The rides played their jovial, albeit mechanical, songs.

He found Annie at the Pirate Ship and they ate their sandwiches quickly. Fairgoers had started to trickle in, but none had yet lined up for the ride.

Kale thought of his mom insisting he bring Annie home for dinner. He wondered if Annie would think it was too soon. His family was a lot for any girl to handle.

"Why have you gone quiet all of a sudden?" she asked, pulling one of his dark curls so it sprang up.

"My mom wanted… I mean, I wondered if you wanted to come to my house for dinner tomorrow night. I could pick you up and bring you back."

"Your mom wanted?" she asked, cocking an eyebrow.

"She suggested it, but I'd love for you to come."

"And meet this giant family you've told me about? Sounds terrifying."

He grinned. "It is, and if you're not up for it—"

"No, I'll go. Why not? We'll be tearing down tonight and tomorrow morning and then pulling up stakes to head to Grand Rapids. You'll have to drive me to the next jump after dinner if you want me to come over, because this is my ride." She gestured at the midway.

"I'd love to," he said.

"Twenty-minute break," she said. "I've got to pee, but then let's go for a ride on the Ferris wheel."

"Want me to grab you a snack or anything?"

"How about a Coke?"

"I'm on it. Meet you back here or—?"

"At the Ferris wheel."

Kale walked to a food truck and ordered a Coke for Annie and a lemonade for himself. He sipped from his straw and cringed. It was sickly sweet. His mother made homemade lemonade, sometimes putting so little sugar in it his entire face puckered when he took a sip. The fair lemonade tasted like liquid candy.

He found Annie waiting for him at the Ferris wheel.

"Come on," she said, bypassing the line and leading him onto the platform. "Vinnie, this is Kale. Kale, Vinnie," Annie told the carny manning the ride as they stepped into the four-seater capsule.

Annie sat and Kale started to sit opposite her, but she patted the bench beside her. "Sit close to me," she said.

"It won't..." He tilted his hand from side to side. "Throw the weight off?"

Both Annie and Vinnie laughed.

"It's not a teeter-totter, man," Vinnie told him. "If it were, every fat guy gettin' on here with his kids would get dumped out and go splat on the pavement."

"Thanks for that image, Vinnie," Annie said, wrinkling her nose. "But he's right. The cars stay balanced regardless of the distribution of weight."

Kale felt a blush rising into his face. He settled beside Annie, their thighs pressed together and the car chugged forward and stopped as another pair of passengers departed and a foursome climbed on.

"That's Jasmine and Marco." Annie pointed at a couple several cars below them. "They've been working carnivals for over twenty years, had a carny wedding and everything."

"What's a carny wedding?" Kale asked.

"It's something special and rather mysterious. I've worked at a couple outfits now and they have different versions, but basically the show boss—Mo, in our case—stands with the couple at the Ferris wheel or the carousel. The couple says their vows, the show boss asks for the 'I dos,' and then they take a ride, one loop either on the wheel or the carousel, and voilà—married."

"Not a bad way to do it," Kale said.

Annie snuggled against him. "It's the way I'd want to."

The ride ended and Annie and Kale held hands as they walked back to the Pirate Ship.

"Ten minutes until the real work begins," Annie said as the carnival wound down.

"I hate that it's almost over," Kale murmured.

"Even the best things end," she told him. "You can hang around tonight and help us tear down."

"Absolutely. Yes. And I'll come help tomorrow and bring you back with me for dinner."

"Are you sure your parents approve of you dating a carny girl?"

"They're going to love you."

Annie laughed. "You're just saying that because you want them to. They might hate my guts."

"They won't."

Annie sighed. "Maybe it doesn't matter. Once this outfit moves along to the next town, you and I will probably fade away."

Kale stared at her, stunned. "What? No. Why would that happen?"

She shrugged. "Because it's what usually happens when carnies have flings with locals at the fair. You get your fill of the girl from the other side of the tracks, then you toss her aside."

"This isn't a fling, Annie. I'll come see you in Grand Rapids too. I'll be there every night if I can." She'd been in his life for mere days and yet... meeting Annie had been like the moment in *The Wizard of Oz* when suddenly the whole world was filled with color. He'd never felt so alive.

"What are we gonna do when it's a five-hour drive?"

"We'll figure something out."

"Okay." She kissed him. "If you say so."

At ten, the mood of the midway shifted. The music from the rides died and enormous speakers blasted rock music. The carnies and an additional crew who worked dismantling and building the carnival descended on the midway.

It took hours, but those hours felt like minutes as Kale and Annie joked and kissed and caught each other's eyes as they pulled down and loaded the dismantled rides. Once, as Kale was carrying a steel beam, the Hulk Hogan carny veered toward him and nearly checked his shoulder. Kale dodged the hit, but stumbled and nearly dropped the beam.

He thought, *Asshole,* but didn't say it out loud for fear the carny would take it as an invitation to get into a proper fight. Kale would have loved to deck the guy, but doubted he'd get more than one good hit in before Cliff's fists pummeled him into a bloody mess. It wasn't worth it.

It was nearly two a.m. when Kale kissed Annie goodbye and promised he'd return the next day.

The parking lot, which had been quiet the previous nights, was downright eerie as he walked alone, his tennis shoes slapping the concrete. He unlocked his car and climbed inside. A gift lay on his passenger seat, wrapped in satiny red paper. His name had been written on the front in black marker. Kale picked it up and gently tore away the paper, revealing a Shins CD.

Annie must have gotten it for him. He grinned and turned the key in the ignition.

Nothing happened.

"No…" he murmured. "Not tonight. Come on."

He tried again, but the car didn't so much as sputter. He'd have to get a jump.

Kale left the car and started back across the parking lot. From somewhere behind him, he heard a sound, as if someone had called his name, but it had floated to him more like a whispering wind than an actual spoken word. He turned and squinted into the darkness that edged the lot, but saw no one. He turned back to the midway.

"Kale…" The sound came again. Now it appeared to be arising from somewhere in front of him. As he searched for the source of the sound, his eyes landed on the Haunted Funhouse. From the back, the funhouse was only a distorted shape against the spotlights set up for the night-time dismantling of the rides.

Again, he saw the face of the man in the mirrors and remembered the thick plop as a clump of what Kale was sure had been hair and flesh landed on the stairs.

"You imagined it," he said out loud. "It wasn't real and now you're freaking yourself out. It wasn't real, it wasn't real." He repeated the words under his breath as he slipped back under the arch and headed for the rides, searching for Annie amongst the crew.

"Hey, Vinnie, have you seen Annie?" Kale asked the guy who'd let them on the Ferris wheel earlier in the evening.

"I think she headed for the back yard," Vinnie said.

Kale hurried to Annie's tent, which he found unzipped. She was kneeling inside, her hands in her backpack.

"Annie?"

She jumped and turned. "You scared me. I thought you left." She quickly zipped her backpack and climbed from the tent.

"Did you get me the Shins CD?"

She smiled. "Maybe. Do you like it?"

"I love it, and lucky for you, my car is so old it still has a CD player… and unfortunately a dead battery."

"Oh, no. The battery's dead?"

"Yeah. Do you think someone could give me a jump?"

"Or you could stay the night," she suggested, eyes twinkling.

"I wish. Soon though, okay?"

"Promise?"

"Yeah. Absolutely."

"Hey, Dan." Annie trotted over to Dan the Dragon, who'd stepped from his camper with a bottle of water in his hand. "Can you jump Kale's car? It's dead."

"Sure can. I was getting ready to pull the truck in here to load it up."

The three of them walked back to the parking lot. Dan slid behind the wheel of a green dually pickup. He drove and parked nose to nose with Kale's car.

"I've got jumper cables," Kale offered, pulling them from his trunk. He handed them to Dan and slid in his car and leaned down and popped the hood.

On a whim, he turned the key in the ignition. The car started. "What the…?"

Annie, who stood outside his open driver's door, looked surprised.

Dan stepped around the car and gazed down at him. "What's that about?" he asked.

"I don't know," Kale said. "It was totally dead when I was out here like five minutes ago. This makes no sense."

"Don't have time to be messing around," Dan mumbled. He handed the jumper cables to Annie, climbed in his truck and pulled away.

"I'm sorry," Kale said, color rising up his neck. "I swear it didn't start."

"Don't worry about it," she told him, carrying the cables to his trunk and closing the lid. She bent and picked up a crumpled piece of paper from the ground. She handed it to him. "I think this fell out of your car."

Kale smoothed it out and frowned. It was the same ripped 'Missing' flier he'd seen the night before. "Weird."

"What?" she asked, peering at the paper.

"I threw this away last night. I found it on the ground."

Annie narrowed her eyes at the image. She grabbed the paper, ripped it into pieces, and balled it up. "I'll throw it away for good." She kissed him again. "I'll see you tomorrow."

"I'll be here."

10

The following morning, Kale found his mother in the kitchen canning tomatoes with Zinnia and Aster.

"Annie's coming to dinner tonight," he announced.

"Who's Annie?" Calla asked.

"Kale's new girlfriend," Zinnia said.

"Kale's new friend," Lucy corrected. "And we're so excited to meet her. Are you doing lawns today?"

"Umm… no. I'm going to help Annie at the fair. They're getting everything pulled down for their next stop."

"Which is where?"

"Grand Rapids." Kale cut a piece of baked oatmeal from a pan on the counter. He took a bite and mumbled. "Mmm… this is really good. Did you make this, Zinnia?"

"Actually, it was Aster. You can thank her when you go outside to feed the chickens. She's collecting eggs," Lucy said.

"Okay, but it has to be quick. I'm meeting Annie and—"

"Kale. You can spare twenty minutes to help around here. Please feed the chickens and help Sage with the chain on her bike. It fell off again."

"She needs a new bike," Kale grumbled.

"And when you have an extra hundred dollars to buy her one, she'd love it," Lucy quipped.

Zinnia shot him a look that said to tread carefully, their mother was stressed. Normally Kale would have asked his mother what was wrong, offered to help, but he wanted to get moving so he could meet Annie.

I t was late afternoon when the last of the trucks pulled out of the carnival and headed for Grand Rapids. Annie settled into the passenger seat of Kale's car. She fiddled with the straps on her backpack.

"Nervous about dinner with my family?" he asked.

"I didn't think I would be, but yeah. I kind of am."

He squeezed her knee. "Don't be. They're cool, really. Weird, but cool. It'll be great."

This is your house?" Annie gaped at the enormous Victorian house when Kale pulled down the long driveway.

"Yep. This is our Casa of Chaos."

"Casa of Chaos?"

He laughed. "Aster coined that term, and we've all embraced it."

Annie's eyes were still wide and fixed on the house. "Aster is which sister?"

"Thorn's twin. They're both fifteen, but she was born forty seconds earlier, so she's technically number three in the pecking order."

"Jesus. You said it was big, but this place is huge."

"Well…" Kale bit his cheek and wished he'd just told her when he'd spilled the beans about his enormous family. "It used to be a funeral home."

"You're kidding, right?"

"No. If you're feeling morbid, I can give you a tour of the old embalming room."

Annie leaned back in her seat, nodded slowly. "Huh. Crazy."

"Do you want me to turn around and drive you back?"

She laughed. "No. I kind of dig it. It's cool."

He smiled, his shoulders relaxing. Though he'd been joking when he asked the question, some part of him had feared she'd say yes. "Then I guess you'll fit right in."

She slid her hand up his thigh and squeezed. "Of course I will. We were made for each other."

As he climbed from the car and hurried around to open her door, he felt giddy, as if the whole world had grown buoyant and golden. He wanted to kiss her, but already sensed eyes watching them from the windows. Likely his sisters, giggling and peering around the curtains, but probably his mother too, making no pretense about studying the girl he'd brought home.

They climbed the steps, and Kale pushed in the front door.

The house opened into a large foyer with a wide wooden staircase leading to the second floor. Stacks of laundry lay piled on the first six steps, one step belonging to each child. Faded rugs ran the length of the hall and the original wallpaper, dark green and speckled with white flowers, still covered the walls. Though his parents had done little in the way of renovating the house, they'd made it their own. The walls were decorated with framed family photos and watercolor paintings done by Kale's father, who'd had a lifelong love of painting plants, birds and animals.

Double glass doors, always open, led to the right into the Goodwins' family room, which had once been the formal viewing or funeral room. Kale still remembered the first time he'd set foot in the room for his own grandfather's funeral sixteen years before. That had been the last funeral in the home. Rows of wooden white chairs had faced the gleaming casket. His father had carried him up to the front to peer down at the deceased man with his powdered face and age-spotted head. He'd been so white and thin against the gray satin surrounding him. Within a year of that funeral, Kale had moved into the house with his parents and sister, Zinnia.

Kale took Annie's hand and drew her into the room, where Calla and Sage quickly ducked from the big window and ran back to the coffee table, where they'd been playing a game of Clue before abandoning it to spy on him.

He narrowed his eyes at his sisters, but grinned. "Sage, Calla. This is my friend Annie."

Annie gave them a little wave. "Nice to meet you," she said.

"Likewise," Calla told her.

"I like your earrings," Sage said, touching her own bare earlobes.

Kale glanced at Annie's earrings. He'd noticed them, but only vaguely. A silver moon with a suspended star hung from each of her ears.

"Thank you," she said. "Someone told me they're lucky."

Kale put an arm around Annie's waist and directed her back out of the room. "Where are Mom and Dad?"

"Both in the kitchen," Calla answered. "Mom's making squash and zucchini burrito bowls and Dad's decided to tackle some new tahini cookies."

"Tahini?" Annie whispered as they left the room.

"My parents make… eclectic food." Kale sighed. "My dad, especially, has made it his life's mission to turn virtually everything into dessert. In his defense, his creations are usually edible. Except for the beet and mushroom brownies. Ugh. Those were gross."

Annie wrinkled her nose. "Sounds like something you'd feed to a farm animal."

Kale grinned. "That's kind of their motto. Eating the way animals do. At least it started that way, but… I'm not sure even animals would willingly consume some of his crazy concoctions."

As Kale started down the hall, Annie tugged his arm. "Show me your room."

He heard his parents talking in the kitchen, knew they'd expect him to take Annie there first and introduce her, but he nodded. "Okay. Quick though. I don't want to subject you to the sound of my mom screaming that dinner's ready."

He led Annie up the stairs to the hallway that forked in three directions. Straight ahead lay his parents' master bedroom. Three additional bedrooms occupied the hallway to the left and another three to the right. His was to the right. He wracked his brain to think if he'd left anything embarrassing out, and worried he might not have put away his stack of *Star Trek* comics.

"The littlest one, Sage, looks like you," Annie said.

"Yeah, we both got my mom's black hair and blue eyes. 'The bookends are supposed to match,' my mother likes to say. The rest of the kids are blonde with brown eyes. They take after my dad."

They passed Zinnia in her bedroom. She was sitting at her desk, fingers clacking on the keys of her hand-me-down desktop, headphones on. She didn't turn.

"That's Zinnia," he said. "Next oldest after me."

"Is she doing schoolwork in the summer?"

"Writing a novel. At least she says it's a novel, but she won't let anyone read it."

"How old is she?"

"Eighteen."

"And she's writing a book?"

"Yep. She's pretty intense. Graduated valedictorian."

"Is she going to college?"

"Yeah. She has a scholarship to U of M, so she's heading there in the fall. It's been a tearful summer between her and my mom. I'm not sure she's going to enjoy being so far away."

Kale pushed the door open to his bedroom. It was a large, square room with a loft bed he'd built himself on the opposite wall. Beneath the bed was his desk, which was scattered with pieces of leather, tools and several wallets and cuffs. His walls were painted a pale blue, save one, which was covered in a mural of their now-deceased dog, Ernie, a German shepherd who'd been with the family until Kale was sixteen.

Annie stared at the image. "Is that your dog?" she asked.

"Ernie. My sidekick until a few years ago. We had to put him down. He was twelve and couldn't walk anymore."

"Did you paint this?" Annie touched Ernie's snout.

"My dad did. He paints as a hobby. Each of us has a mural in our rooms, though I'm the only one with Ernie."

Annie walked toward his bed and then hunched down to peer at his desk. She picked up a piece of leather and gave him a questioning look.

"Leathercrafting. It's kind of my thing, a side gig, I guess. I engrave wallets and belts."

"This is really beautiful." She held an unfinished leather cuff he'd been making for Calla, whose birthday was in the fall. She held it to her nose and closed her eyes. "It smells like you."

"I'll make you one," he told her.

She stepped toward him and slid her hands up his arms. She kissed his chin and then his lips. "Promise?"

Behind them, someone cleared their throat loudly.

Kale quickly stepped away from Annie and turned to find Aster and Thorn in the doorway, not bothering to hide their grins.

"Dinner's ready," Aster said.

"Great." Kale fanned his t-shirt out. "Aster, Thorn—this is Annie."

"Hi, Annie," Aster said.

"Hi," Thorn added.

"You're the twins," Annie said. "Great to meet you."

Thorn stared another moment at Annie until Aster grabbed his arm and dragged him away.

"See you downstairs," Kale told them, turning back to Annie. "I guess we better follow them or it will be my mom in that doorway."

In the hallway they encountered Sage, who tilted her head when she looked at Annie.

"You have a drifter," Sage told Annie, looking just past her.

Annie sent a puzzled look at Kale. "I do?"

"Mmm-hmmm. A girl. She's pretty, kind of looks like you." Sage squinted. "But with a birthmark right here." Sage pointed at her right cheekbone.

Annie stiffened.

"Oh, wait… and something else…" Sage touched her throat, then paled. "Never mind. See you at dinner." She turned and walked down the stairs.

11

Annie frowned at Kale. "Did your sister say I have a drifter? What did she mean?"

"Sage had cancer a few years ago, and... ever since, she sees people." Kale brushed a hand back through his hair. "Dead people. She calls them drifters. When she first started talking about them, my mom had a psychotherapist friend come over and check her out, but Sage didn't seem to have any mental problems. They thought maybe it was hallucinations from the chemo or radiation, and then they were worried the cancer was back and a tumor was causing the visions."

"Did they find anything?"

"No. And weirder is she would tell people about... like their dead loved ones. I know that sounds crazy, but it's true. I've seen her do it. The psychotherapist started crying and asking her all kinds of questions. Sage saw the woman's husband, who had died tragically in a hunting accident like five years before. It's pretty nuts, but... Sage says when you nearly die, you cross into the afterlife or whatever, and if you come back, you sort of leave a doorway open behind you. You can see other people who crossed over."

Annie frowned. "That's really creepy."

"Yeah. It weirded me out at first too, but I've gotten used to it." He wanted to ask Annie if she had any idea who Sage might have seen, but the topic clearly bothered her.

Annie trailed behind Kale as they walked into the kitchen.

"Mom, Dad—this is Annie." Kale stepped aside.

Annie smiled and held out her hand to Kale's mom.

Lucy studied Annie. "My goodness, Annie. You have very beautiful eyes. They remind me of someone. You're not from around here though, right?"

"No, further north."

Lucy pulled her into a hug. "Well, it's lovely to meet you. I'm Lucy. This is Frank, Kale's dad."

Frank joined the hug and Kale grinned at Annie, who smiled tightly.

"Okay, let her breathe," Kale said, breaking Annie from the hug and leading her by the hand to the table where most of the other kids sat.

Zinnia breezed in, grabbed the bowl of rolls from the counter, and added it to the table.

"Zinnia. Have you met Kale's new friend, Annie?" Lucy asked.

Zinnia smiled at her. "Hi, Annie. How much is my brother paying you to go out with him?"

Thorn guffawed, and Lucy gave him and then Zinnia an unamused look.

"Very funny," Kale said, rolling his eyes. "Pick whatever chair you want, Annie."

"Where are you sitting?" she asked in a low voice.

"Next to you."

Annie pulled out a chair and sat down, fidgeting with her fingers in her lap.

Zinnia's eyes lingered on Annie. "Have we met before?" Zinnia asked. "You look so familiar."

Annie shook her head. "I doubt it. I'd have remembered your name. It's very unique."

"That it is," Zinnia agreed.

"Annie, would you like water, tea, or carrot juice?" Lucy asked.

"Carrot juice?" Annie wrinkled her nose.

"Freshly made by Thorn and Aster this morning. It's delicious."

"Water. Thank you."

Kale helped Zinnia and his parents carry the rest of the food to the table and sat down.

"Tell us about you, Annie," Lucy said, tossing Thorn a clunky sprouted dinner roll. It missed his hands and struck his plate with a loud thunk.

"Watch out for those," Frank told Annie with a wink. "They feel a bit like a hockey puck to the head."

"Taste like it too," Thorn grumbled, biting into the roll.

Lucy shot him a look, then refocused on Annie.

"What would you like to know?" Annie asked, taking a tentative bite from her squash bowl and chewing slowly.

"Where are you from?" Lucy asked.

"Up north."

"Up north like the Upper Peninsula, or…?"

"No, not that far. Just… well, I moved around a lot, but mostly in the northern middle of the state. North of Grayling."

"Hartwick Pines is over that way. Lovely old-growth pine forest," Frank said, smiling. "A very special place."

"I've never been," Annie said.

"And your parents? Are they still in that area?"

Kale grabbed Annie's hand beneath the table and squeezed. "Annie grew up in foster care," he said.

"Oh, my." Lucy put a hand on her chest. "And here I am, poking and prodding when perhaps you'd rather not get into all that."

Annie's eyes lingered on Lucy, a curious expression on her face. Kale wondered if she was thinking about her own absentee mother.

"What was that like?" Sage asked. "Does that mean you lived with lots of families?"

Kale shot her a 'stop asking questions' look, but it sailed right over her head.

Annie smiled tightly. "A few. It wasn't great." She directed her attention back to Lucy. "I do prefer not to talk about it, if that's okay."

"Of course it is. I apologize for putting you on the spot."

"Does that mean you don't know your parents at all?" Sage asked, grunting after what Kale assumed was Calla kicking her beneath the table.

"My mother left when I was seven and I never met my dad," Annie told her.

"Well, I have some news," Zinnia announced, drawing the attention away from Annie.

"Which is?" Aster asked.

"I've decided to give up sugar."

Lucy frowned. "Well, dear, we don't even keep white sugar in the house. It's hardly a problem."

"Not just white sugar," Zinnia said. "All sugar except for fruit. No honey or agave or maple syrup. I'm giving it up. Do you know how many chronic diseases sugar is linked to? It's truly disturbing."

"The tahini cookies have honey in them," Frank said, face falling.

"It's okay, Dad," Zinnia assured him. "I've been eating your desserts for years. This way there's more for the other kids."

Aster and Thorn exchanged a tortured look, as if they realized they'd each have to eat an extra cookie now that Zinnia, easily the biggest sweets eater in the family, was bowing out.

"More for us then." Frank leaned toward Annie, smiling. "You'll love these cookies. One of a kind."

"You survived," Kale said when they climbed into his car after each forcing down a tahini cookie.

"They're nice," Annie replied.

"Yeah. I like 'em too. Thank you." He turned to face her. "I mean it. I'm sure it wasn't easy and I'm really grateful you were willing."

"I told you," she said. "We were meant to find each other. Meeting the family is part of the deal. Lucky for you, you'll be spared a similar fate."

He squeezed her hand. "I have a big enough family for both of us."

They spoke little as he drove Annie to Grand Rapids, where she rejoined the carnival. When Kale left her at her tent after kissing her so long his lips felt bruised, he walked back to his car, mildly terrified. What if he never saw her again?

His fears were absurd. She was crazy about him. They were crazy about each other, and yet something in his guts twisted with each step he took away from her.

At home, he avoided his parents' questions about Annie by holing up in his room.

"Hey, bozo. I just called your name like three times. Have you gone deaf?" Zinnia stood in his doorway.

Kale blinked at her. "You did? I was daydreaming, I guess, trying to figure out…" He held up a piece of chocolate-colored leather.

"What to make?" she asked, stepping into the room and walking to his table. "I'm a fan of this feather stencil, but it depends on what it's for."

"It's for Annie," he said.

Zinnia studied him, a half-smile on her lips. "That's what's going on, then. You're lovesick. Can't think, can't eat, can't hear people when they're yelling your name from three feet away."

Kale shot her an exasperated look.

"What?" she said, holding up her hands. "Am I wrong?"

Kale dropped the leather back on the table and sighed. "I don't know… No. You're not wrong."

She smiled. "I sure don't envy you, brother."

"And why is that?"

"Let me quote Ernest Hemingway: 'If two people love each other, there can be no happy end to it.' Or perhaps you'd prefer Oscar Wilde's take on the matter: 'When one is in love, one always begins by deceiving one's self, and one always ends by deceiving others. That is what the world calls a romance.'"

"Well, those are cynical perspectives."

"Have you ever known a happy ending?"

"Sure—Mom and Dad."

Zinnia shrugged. "They're the outliers." She gestured at his leather. "Go with Annie's initials and some Pablo Neruda. Maybe, 'In one kiss, you'll know all I haven't said.' Or, 'The moon lives under your skin…'"

"Oh, wow. Yeah. Those are good. Do you have a book by Neruda that I could flip through?"

"Yep. One sec." She left and returned a moment later, holding a hardcover book with a photo of the poet on the front. "And here, I sketched this of Annie."

She handed Kale a small unlined piece of paper. On it, she'd pencil-drawn Annie, dark hair cutting a line across her forehead, one sparkling eye fixed on something off to the side.

"This is amazing. You drew this today?"

"Yep, found myself wanting to draw her after she left. She's very pretty."

"Yeah." Kale sighed. "She is." He pulled out his wallet and tucked the picture inside. "What did you want? When you were trying to get my attention."

"Oh. Mom's on a rampage because you were supposed to take all the jarred food to the basement and rotate it in this week. You also haven't carried your laundry up from the stairs, taken out the trash, swept out the shed. Not to mention Stevie has texted me three times, wondering why you've been MIA at the lawn business the last couple of days. Mom doesn't know about that."

"Shoot. I'll finish this and then do chores."

"You sure you wanna do that?"

"What?" he asked, flipping through the book.

"Bring it to life, burn those feelings into leather. There's no going back once you've done that."

"Just tell Mom I'll be down soon."

"All right, but don't say I didn't warn you. And text Stevie back."

"Yeah. I will, later." He dreaded texting Stevie. All three of his friends were liable to be pissed he'd skipped out on lawns without messaging. Stevie wouldn't hold back in telling him exactly how she felt about it.

Kale skimmed the pages, reading the poems, feeling as if Pablo Neruda had captured exactly his feelings for Annie.

He settled on a single line that sent a shiver down his spine when he read it. *Neither night nor sleep could separate us.*

Using his branding tool, Kale burned the words into the soft leather. On the underside he contemplated what to add, then finally put 'KG loves AC.' He secured the ends with a small bronze infinity symbol and tucked the bracelet into a little white box.

As he stared at the little box, he experienced again the pang of fear that he'd never see her again. The carnival had moved. What if she'd made the fling comment because that was what he was to her?

He shook the thoughts away and stood.

As he carried a box of stewed tomatoes to the basement, his phone rang. He didn't recognize the number.

"Hello?"

"Kale, it's Annie."

"Annie. Oh, wow. It's so good to hear from you."

"You just dropped me off two hours ago."

He laughed. "I am smooth, aren't I? Clearly, I'm not well-versed in the art of playing hard to get."

"One of the many things I love about you."

"Where are you calling from? This isn't the number you gave me."

"I'm using Dan's phone. The other number was Margaret's. I don't have a cell, so I borrow theirs."

"Really? You don't have a phone?"

"Nope. Listen, we're going to be mostly set up by midday tomorrow, then we have the rest of the day off. I thought we could go to the boathouse and spend the night."

"Yes, most definitely. I'll pick you up."

12

The following day, Kale rushed through his chores, then started packing food to take to the boathouse.

"What's that?" Sage asked, peering into the picnic basket Kale had set on the table.

"Food."

"Well, duh. What's it for?"

"Annie and I are going on a picnic."

"Hmm… you really like her, huh?"

Kale added a bag of dried plantain chips to the basket. "Yeah. I do."

"She has a lot of drifters."

Kale frowned and rearranged the snacks. "As in…?"

"Yeah, spirits. And I don't think they like her."

He paused. Sage watched him with a somber expression.

"Why not?"

"Beats me. I could just feel it. They follow her, but they don't like her."

Kale opened the refrigerator and sighed. This was not a conversation he wanted to have right now. He grabbed two bottles of water and nestled them in the basket.

His mother walked in, carrying an armful of purple lettuce from the garden. "Can you put a colander in the sink for me, Kale? I need to get these washed."

"Sure." He grabbed the metal colander from the cupboard and plopped it in the cast-iron sink, flipping on the faucet.

His mother eyed the picnic basket, then dropped the lettuce into the sink. "Sage, honey, I pulled some cucumbers out there. Would you run and grab them?"

"Sure, Mom." Sage disappeared through the backdoor.

"Packing a picnic?" his mom asked, wiping her wet hands on her apron.

"Yeah. I'm meeting Annie."

"Did you eat breakfast?"

"No, I'm good. I had some coffee."

"Coffee isn't breakfast, Kale. Your brain can't function on coffee. Here." She tossed him a banana.

"All right. I'll eat it on the drive, and Mom…" He paused, knocking his banana on the rim of the picnic basket. "I'm not coming home tonight. I'm going to stay with Annie."

Lucy pursed her lips. "Is that a good idea? Where would you even stay? Not in her room, I hope. Does she even have a room?"

"I'm almost twenty-one. I can stay over with a girl."

"I'm not comfortable with this, Kale."

"That's okay, Mom. You're not staying over. I am." He wanted to turn and walk away, but his mother held him pinned with her gaze.

She closed her eyes and blew out a breath. "Okay. Fine. What can I do, after all? Forbid it? Be careful and… call me and Dad tonight to check in."

On his way to the fairgrounds, Kale stopped at a store and bought Annie a pre-paid cell phone. He slipped it into a gift bag in the trunk.

Annie stood waiting for him at the entrance to the midway.

"Ready?" he asked as she slid into the passenger seat.

"Am I ever. God, they were rowdy last night, drinking and fighting until after three in the morning."

"Really? Doesn't your boss get after them?"

"He did a couple times, but he sleeps in a camper with an air conditioner going and he snores so loud I can hear it in the showers. It's fine. I'm just looking forward to a night away. Specifically, a night away with you." She leaned across the seat and kissed him, sliding her hand up his leg.

Outside the car, somebody whistled.

Kale looked up to see Vinnie and another carny making kissing faces at them.

"All right, let's get out of here," Annie said, flipping the two men her middle finger.

Kale parked near the camper and turned off the engine. Annie had dozed off in the passenger seat. He put his hand on her arm and rubbed his thumb over her elbow. "Annie, we're here."

Her eyelids fluttered and she turned to look at him. "I was having the best dream."

"What was it?"

She wrinkled her forehead. "I don't remember exactly, but I was with you."

Kale kissed her, then went around to the back of the car. He hoisted the picnic basket from the trunk, and grabbed the duffel bag he'd stuffed with bedding, two flashlights, and matches over his shoulder. "Hey, Annie. Could you grab this one?"

She came around to the trunk, her own backpack slung over her shoulder. He nodded toward the red gift bag.

She flicked her eyes at him and smiled. "Is this for me?"

"Yeah. It's not much, just... well, open it."

Annie pulled the bag out and reached inside. She drew out the box that held the little flip phone first. "A phone?"

"Yep. It's just a pre-paid cheap one, but I didn't want you to have to borrow phones every time you wanted to call. I already loaded it with minutes."

She stared at the phone, her expression slightly troubled, but then she smiled and kissed him. "Thank you."

"You're welcome. There's one more thing in there."

She dug into the bottom of the bag and found the little white cardboard box. She opened it and removed the layer of tissue he'd tucked inside. Beneath the tissue lay the leather bracelet.

Annie lifted it out and turned it in her hands. She read the words silently. "I love it. It's so beautiful."

"Do you want to wear it?"

"Of course, yes. I'll never take it off."

"Except when you shower and swim. Leather doesn't hold up great in water." He unclasped the infinity symbol and secured the bracelet on her thin wrist.

She held it up. "It fits perfect."

"I hoped it would."

She threw her arms around him and squeezed. "Thank you." She kissed him. "I love you, Kale. I love you so much."

The words hung in the air, perhaps surprising them both.

"I love you too." He laughed, picking her up and carrying her to the camper.

In the early evening, after they'd set their stuff up in the boathouse, they lay on their backs on the upper deck and looked at the sky.

"That cloud looks like a skeleton," she said, pointing to a string of puffy clouds, one with a distinct pattern that reminded Kale of a ribcage.

"It does. And that one looks like a squirrel."

"And that one"—Annie moved Kale's hand so he pointed east —"looks like a penis with wings."

He laughed. "It's a bird, it's a plane. No—it's a penis!"

Even on the little porch, the air was thick with the humming of bugs and the dense humidity of summer. A mosquito buzzed near his temple and he slapped the side of his head, causing his ear to ring. "I should have brought bug spray," he said.

"I think there's some in the camper. I'll go look in a few minutes."

He picked up her hand and kissed it. "What's next, Annie? After the carnival. What do you want to do?"

"There is no next. There's only this."

"But don't you eventually want to do something different? Long-term carnival life doesn't exactly seem ideal."

"Why not? You get to travel. You have a built-in family of misfits. You're never bored."

"There isn't anything else you want down the road? A career? A family?"

Annie leaned forward, letting her hair fall in her face. "Not really, no."

He didn't say that he eventually wanted all those things, that he wanted them with her.

"What do you want, Kale?"

"For starters, I'd like my own place, an apartment. Down the road, I'd like to start a business doing leatherworking."

"Yeah?" She rolled to her side and gazed at him. "I think that'd be amazing. There are vendors at the fair who sell handmade stuff. You could talk to Mo about doing a booth."

"You think he'd be open to that?"

"Sure. You'd have to split the profits or pay for a booth or whatever. Maybe I could help you. I used to make homemade jewelry as a kid, beaded bracelets and wire earrings."

"I'd love that," he said. "Who knows, maybe we could really turn it into something. Set up a shop online, even open a store someday."

"Yeah," she said wistfully. "That'd be really amazing."

"Is there anyone from your childhood still in your life, Annie? Friends or…"

Annie shook her head. "I moved so often in foster care I never had many friends. I stopped holding onto people. It was safer to cut them loose."

"I'm sorry you went through that. It seems so lonely."

She leaned into him. "It's not anymore."

They built a fire and ate their picnic sitting on a blanket Annie had spread on the ground. Afterward they made love in the open, the trees and stars looking down. The smoke kept the mosquitoes away.

Annie snuggled into him, arm across his stomach. She played with the line of hair that trailed down from his belly button.

"Even this hair is curly," she said, twirling her fingers through the fine dark hairs.

"Yep, curly everywhere."

"I like it." She sat up and draped her hair across his chest. "My hair's always been so flat. I wish it was curly."

"Sage's hair is curly and it drives my mom nuts. It's hard to brush.

Mine's not so bad since I keep it shorter, but Sage has a horse mane, my mom calls it."

"It's so pretty," Annie said. "All that dark curly hair and those big blue eyes. She's beautiful."

"Yeah. Don't tell her that." He chuckled. "She's more into looking tough than pretty."

"Now *that* I understand." Annie stood and slipped into her panties and t-shirt.

"Where are you going?" Kale asked, sitting up and putting on his shorts.

"To pee and put this food in the camper so we don't attract the local wildlife. I'll look for bug spray too."

"Are there bears around here?"

"I've never seen one. I'm more worried about raccoons. Those little monsters will tear this place apart for a bag of plantain chips."

He laughed and helped her load the food back in the picnic basket. She headed off toward the camper and he stood and sat on an over-turned stump.

He watched the flames rise and fall. A gust of wind shifted the smoke and Kale blocked his stinging eyes.

As the smoke cleared, he spotted a figure emerging from the edge of the forest. He jumped up, eyes blurred, as the figure ran toward him.

His eyes widened. It was a young woman, her face twisted in terror. Her mouth was open in a silent scream, her hair wet and plastered against her shoulders. Something was wrong with her face and Kale gasped when he realized she was missing an eye. A black hole gaped in the right side of her face. She didn't slow or veer from the looming fire. Kale shrieked and waved his arms as she plunged forward into the flames.

Kale stumbled back, expecting her to charge into him, hair and clothes burning, twisting and writhing. She didn't. She wasn't there. Kale stared through the fire at the woods beyond. There was no sign of the girl.

Kale stood dazed, heart thundering. He took a few steps toward beyond the fire, searched as if she might have somehow changed course. She wasn't there.

"Hey." A voice spoke and Kale whirled around.

Annie walked toward him. "Look what I found." She waved a bottle of tequila.

He blinked at the bottle, then turned back to the forest.

"What's with the face?" she asked. "Don't like tequila?"

Kale rubbed his eyes and then gestured for the bottle. Annie handed it to him. He twisted off the cap and took a swig. It burned down his throat and into his nose.

She grinned. "I guess you do like tequila."

"Let's put out this fire and head up to the boathouse," he suggested, trying to steady his voice.

"I was just thinking that," she said, wrapped an arm around his waist and kissed him.

In the boathouse, they dropped little white candles in mason jars and propped them around the room. Kale unpacked the bedding he'd brought while Annie stripped the old stuff off the bed. The candles flickered as he and Annie took opposite ends of the blankets and whooshed them over the mattress.

"This one's pretty cute," Annie said as she fanned out a cream-colored blanket adorned with black paw prints on the bed.

"Aster made it," he explained. "She sewed them for all of us last Christmas."

Annie flopped back on the bed, grinning. "Bring that bottle over and let's give this blanket something to talk about."

K ale woke to the smell of death. It permeated the room, which was thick and hot. Disoriented, he fumbled for his lamp, but his hand smacked a bare wall. He wasn't in his bedroom and slowly he remembered. He was with Annie on the second floor of the boathouse.

He'd fallen asleep on the side of the bed that pressed against the wall. Nearly gagging from the stench, he scooted down and climbed off the mattress, staggering for the door that led to the swimming platform. He pushed through the swinging wood doors, careful not to veer toward the edges that dropped to the lake below.

Outside he gulped air, so much cooler than the stagnant air inside the boathouse. He sank to his butt and reclined until he lay flat on his back on the wood platform. Above him, the stars shone from the black cloak of a moonless sky. Somewhere in the expansive woods a pack of coyotes yipped.

Kale's eyelids were heavy. They slipped closed, and he drifted down.

"No..." he murmured, shaking his head. He sat up and then stood.

He slipped back through the boathouse doors, surprised to discover the rancid smell had evaporated. It had been so strong only moments before, but he could find no trace of it.

Kale returned to the bed and slid his foot along the floor until it bumped something hard—the flashlight. He knelt, grabbed it, and flipped the light on. Annie slept on her side, dark hair fanning across her pillow. She hadn't woken.

Kale made his way to the stairs. He suspected an animal had gotten into the boathouse on the first floor, though he wondered if the odor had arisen from the water that lapped the mostly rotted dock on the level below. He walked down the rickety stairs, quiet not to wake Annie.

On the ground floor, Kale scanned the space. The door that led from the woods into the boathouse was closed. Nothing could have entered that way. He stepped to the yawning hole at the front of the boathouse that faced the weedy lake. His beam of light did not extend beyond the stagnant patch of water that drifted inside the structure.

He shone his light into the water at his feet.

A school of silvery minnows darted beneath the dock. Weeds rustled further in the lake, followed by a loud splash. Kale again trained the beam of light on the yawning hole. Nothing.

He shifted the light down as something massive swam from the lake into the boathouse.

"What the..." Kale muttered, leaning forward as he tried to make sense of it.

The death smell returned, gusting toward Kale on the crest of the wave that unfurled as the figure moved beneath the water.

Kale stepped back, body tensed as the thing in the water stopped.

Hands, pale and slimy, the flesh curling away from yellowed knuckles, reached from the lake and gripped the dock edge. A head rose between the rotted hands. Wet brown curls clung in clumps to the pale scalp.

Kale's mouth fell open and his breath rushed out.

The face was bloated and misshapen. Sightless yellowing eyes glared from puckered eye sockets.

13

———————

Fingers touched the back of Kale's neck. He screamed and spun around.

Annie stood behind him, sleepy-eyed and frowning. "Kale? Jesus. what are you doing? Why did you scream?"

He swung back toward the water, raising the flashlight, but the thing that had been climbing out of the lake was not there. No rotted hands clutched the wooden edge. No corpse face peered into the beam of light. He shook his head, gestured with the flashlight at the thing that should have been there.

"What? What is it?" Annie peered past him, confused.

He grabbed her hand and pulled her toward the boathouse door, shoving it open. It screeched on rusted hinges. Kale dragged Annie from the boathouse, leaving her at the forest edge. He ran back and slammed the door shut and secured the rusted iron bar between the door handles.

"Let's go sleep in the camper, okay?" he told her.

"Whoa," she said, planting her palms on his chest. "Calm down. Why are you so upset?"

The light shook in his hand, the beam skittering across the grassy floor. "I don't know. I had a nightmare, I guess. I can't sleep in there." He glanced back at the boathouse, now only a dark silhouette behind them. He shined the flashlight on the exterior, suddenly terrified he'd see the bar sliding away, falling to the grass, a dark shape emerging from within.

"A nightmare?" she asked, following his gaze with her own much more skeptical one.

"It seemed real. Too real. Let's just go to the camper."

"Okay," she sighed, the word giving way to a yawn. "But you need to tell me about this nightmare."

Kale urged her toward the trail that led to the camper. "Tomorrow. I don't want to talk about it tonight."

He glanced at the boathouse a final time as they walked into the woods, but the structure had largely vanished into the inky shapes of the surrounding trees.

When Kale woke, the sunlight filling the room all but erased the previous night's terror. It had obviously been a hallucination. Perhaps in his fugue state, he'd slipped into dreaming while he stood on the first floor of the boathouse.

Annie stirred beside him.

"Wake up, beautiful," he told her, kissing her temple.

"Mmm…" She snuggled closer to him. "Let's just stay in bed."

"For how long?" he asked, rubbing her back.

"Forever." She peered at him through the hair that fell over her face. "Can't we? We'll just plant a garden out there. I can mend our clothes while you hunt for squirrels."

"What will we do in the winter?" He traced a finger down her spine, smiling as she shivered.

She rolled over and pulled him on top of her. "In the winter we'll hibernate like bears. We'll let the snow pack us in and we'll keep each other warm right here in this bed."

He kissed her. "Or maybe we should go to Canada. Hmm? Find a little cabin in the middle of nowhere. Or Mexico. We could live in a hut on the beach, catch fish for dinner, swim naked in the ocean every night."

"Let's do both." She pressed her hands against the center of his chest. "You know what this feels like, this crazy love? It feels like annihilation, like what I was before you is gone. We're this now, you and me, us."

Kale's breath caught in his chest. He felt it too, felt things he hadn't imagined existed before her. "I love you, Annie. I'm insane for you."

"Good. Sane is boring."

~

"I hate that our little getaway has already come to an end," Annie said as they packed their stuff to leave.

"Me too," he told her, leaning over and kissing her. "I thought after I dropped you off, I'd run home, get cleaned up and come to the midway in Grand Rapids."

"Really?" She perked up. "I'd love that."

"Then it's decided."

As they started from the camper, Annie's bag caught on the doorhandle. It slipped from her shoulder and spilled onto the floor.

Kale knelt and helped her gather the contents: sunscreen, chapstick, a small bottle of hand lotion. He held up a hunting knife covered by a plastic sheath. "This looks scary," he said, handing her the knife.

"You remember where I work, right?" she asked, tucking the knife into her bag. She stood and stepped from the camper.

Kale started to follow, then spotted an I.D. card that had skittered under the table. He reached and grabbed it.

It wasn't Annie who looked back at him, but another young woman who slightly resembled her. He read the name 'Norma Fenn' with an address in Leslie, Michigan.

"What is this?" Kale asked, holding up the I.D. as he stepped from the camper.

She snatched it from his hand and stuffed it back into her bag, mouth in a line.

"Annie?"

She sighed. "I knew I'd have to tell you sooner or later. I was just hoping for later."

"Okay..."

"I have a stalker... or had a stalker. I guess I don't know if he's still after me or not. It's part of the reason I started working for Brisby Amusements, to get away from him, to hide. The I.D. is my friend Norma's. She gave it to me, so I had an extra if I ever needed it to get a job or whatever. We look alike enough that it works."

"But you go by Annie."

"I stopped using Norma when I started working for the carnival. I move so much, I figured he'd have lost track of me by now."

"Did you get a restraining order or..."

"Yeah, but it made no difference. Guys like Byron don't exactly adhere to pieces of paper if it's standing in the way of what they think is theirs. His whole family is involved in law enforcement. He knew better than anyone how useless a restraining order was."

Kale rubbed his face. "The woman at the fair that day looking for you, was she connected to him somehow?"

"Maybe. I hope not, but if she was... then he's learned where I'm at."

"How did you know him? How did he get fixated on you?"

"I dated him. We went out for about a year and he just was obsessed. He was so jealous, always searching through my stuff, following me. I finally ended the relationship, but he wouldn't let go. He'd show up at my house, call my friends, hack into my email. I got the restraining order, and that's when he attacked me. He waited until late one night when I was outside alone. He threw a bag over my head and shoved me into his trunk. He took me out to the woods and... did stuff, terrible stuff."

Tears welled in Annie's eyes and Kale wished he hadn't pushed her for more information.

"It's okay," he said, putting an arm around her and squeezing her against him. He kissed the top of her head. "You don't have to tell me anything else."

14

When Kale arrived home after dropping Annie at the midway, his mother met him at the door. She held an envelope in her hand.

"This letter says you've missed four classes." His mother didn't look at him. She stared instead at the letter in her hands as if expecting him to say they'd made a mistake, a simple clerical error. Someone else was cutting class.

"I'm… I'm not sure if I want to go anymore, Mom. I was never sure. I talked about working, maybe traveling."

"And then you committed to school. It was your choice, Kale. We encouraged you to consider other options, take some time."

"I know. So why do you seem bothered by this?"

"Because dropping out in the middle of the semester is avoiding your responsibilities, not to mention the waste of money. By all means, take a break, but finish the summer semester first."

Kale sighed.

"This is because of Annie. Right? You're running off to be with Annie."

"I'd hardly call it running off. Mom, I'm twenty. I'm an adult."

"I'm worried about you making all these dramatic changes for a girl you just met."

"I feel like I've known her my whole life, all my lives."

Lucy smiled, but with effort, as if the smile weren't built on joy but despair. "I understand that feeling, honey. I do. But… sometimes our feelings are so powerful that we ignore logic."

"You've been telling me my whole life to follow my heart. I'm finally doing that and now you're saying to stop."

"I'm not saying to stop. I'm saying to slow down, to zoom out and look at the big picture. Annie's not going anywhere. You can finish the semester and still date her."

Kale sighed and glanced at his watch.

She put her hands on her hips. "Have somewhere more important to be?"

"No… it's just I wanted to jump in the shower and…" He didn't want to admit that his only interest was in seeing Annie. "And then I'm going to the fair."

"You just spent the night with her."

"I know."

Lucy set the envelope down on a hall table and wove her fingers together, pressing her hands to her lips.

"Mom." Calla stood at the top of the stairs.

"Yes, honey?"

"Sage feels sick. She's asking for you."

Lucy gazed a last time at Kale, wearing a mixed expression of disappointment and sadness—the sort that arises as something slips away slowly, like losing a balloon and watching it drift higher and higher until it was gone.

Guilt gnawed at Kale's insides as he watched his mother trod up the stairs, not her usual springy self, but heavy, slow.

S howered and changed, Kale hurried from his room and down the stairs, hoping to avoid his mother and any more lengthy discussions about his unfavorable life choices.

He started toward the kitchen to grab a snack and paused, hearing his parents' voices.

"I'm worried about him. He seems…" his mother said.

"In love?" Kale's dad interrupted.

"You think I'm overreacting?"

"I think you're being the protective mama bear we all know and love. But do I think Kale getting swept into a summer romance is a tragedy? No. I think it's good for him. Remember the summer we met? My God, I get red in the face just thinking about it."

Lucy laughed. "Now I'm blushing," she said.

Kale peered around the corner and saw his dad spin his mom in a twirl and then kiss her.

"Get a room," Thorn said, ambling into the kitchen and opening the refrigerator.

"We happen to have seven rooms in this very house," their dad said. "Maybe we should take yours."

"Very funny," Thorn answered, rooting around in the fridge.

"What do you need, honey? Want me to make you a sandwich?"

"Mom, I'm fifteen. I can make my own sandwich."

"Goodness," she said. "You're a bit snappy this afternoon. Is something wrong?"

Thorn sighed and faced his parents, crossing his arms. "Leland just passed his driver's exam and his parents bought him a truck for his birthday. It's a hunk a' junk, but it drives. I don't even have a learner's permit yet."

"I told you, when you're sixteen, you and Aster can start driver's training."

"But all my friends will be driving at sixteen. I'm the only one—"

"Thorn, please." Lucy's voice grew shrill. "You know how I feel about this. Driving is a huge responsibility. Cars can be very dangerous."

"Mom, just because you got in an accident—"

"Thorn, stop!" Frank's voice silenced him.

"Fine. Whatever," Thorn snapped.

Kale turned and headed for the front door. He eased out and climbed into his car, knowing he should have told his parents he was leaving, but not wanting to walk into the hornets' nest brewing in the kitchen.

A car blocked him as he was about to back out of the driveway. He craned around and spotted Stevie stepping from her mom's blue Volkswagen.

"Shit," he murmured, not bothering to turn off the car. He rolled down his window.

"Wow. Really? Not even going to get out of the car?"

"I'm just leaving. I'm running late."

"For what, exactly? Sure as hell not class or work."

He sighed and bit his cheek, wanting to tell her to buzz off, leave him alone. Why did everyone feel entitled to lecture him about his life? But it was Stevie, his friend for longer than he even had memories. He turned off the engine and stepped from the car.

"What's up?" he asked, shoving his hands in his pockets.

"That's what I want to know. What's up? I've called and texted you like ten times and you haven't called me back."

"I've just been… really busy."

"Do you remember in eighth grade when Zach started going out with that girl from south Muskegon?"

"Tiffany," Kale answered. "Yeah. I remember."

"And remember what a douchecanoe he was being? Like blowing us off every weekend so he could make out with that chick who treated him like total crap whenever her friends were around?"

"I said I remember."

"And remember how we swore we'd never be like that, never throw each other under the bus for a piece of ass?"

"Annie's not a piece of ass."

Stevie glared at Kale. "You met her like a week ago. We've been friends for twenty years. We've been friends since before we could wipe our own butts. Doesn't that at least warrant a return phone call?"

"I'm sorry. You're right. I've kind of been a jerk."

"No. You haven't kind of been a jerk. You are *currently being* a jerk. You're talking to me, but you're not even here. I might as well be telling this to that tree over there."

"I'm sorry. I am. What if we hang out tomorrow? Can we do that? I promise I won't bail."

"Fine. Me and Zach and Ben are going fishing at Mud Lake. We've gotta go early so we can do lawns in the afternoon. It'd be nice if you'd show up for those, too."

"I will. I promise. I'll meet you at the dock."

"Seven a.m.," Stevie said.

"Got it. Seven a.m."

~

The scolding he'd gotten from his mother and Stevie plagued Kale the entire drive to the fair, but he quickly forgot when he found Annie.

She broke away from the Pirate Ship and ran and jumped into his arms, kissing his face and neck. He laughed and swung her around.

"Oh, shoot, we better stop." She giggled, dragging Kale back to the ride. "Mo's over there talking to Vinnie and he'll bitch at me if he sees us canoodling on the midway. I kid you not, that's what he told me during the meeting today. 'Annie, no canoodling.'" She laughed.

Kale grinned, grateful he wasn't the only one taking heat for their relationship, but more grateful still that Annie seemed unfazed by it.

The evening passed in a blur of talking, stealing kisses and plotting the epic adventures they'd go on in the future.

"I've always wanted to visit the catacombs in Paris. I mean, I never thought I'd actually go, being broke and all, but that's probably the big dream."

Kale made a face. "The catacombs? Underground tunnels built out of dead people? Umm… no. I'll go to Paris with you, but you're not getting me into those tunnels."

"Oh, come on. They're dead. They can't hurt anyone."

"That's literally the opening line for a horror story."

Annie laughed and looped her arm through his. "Don't worry, I'd protect you from the big, scary dead people."

"Listen, we don't want to be stuck in a black tunnel beneath the earth if the zombie apocalypse begins."

"I'd take my chances with the dead over the living any day. Why don't you stay tonight?" she asked when they reached her tent.

"I want to." He kissed her. "But I promised Stevie I'd go fishing with them early. They're pissed I've been blowing them off and I think I better get home before midnight tonight. I've been gone so much and it's bothering my mom."

"Everybody's worried I'm stealing you away, huh?"

"Nah. They're just not used to me having a life."

She wrapped her arms around his waist and kissed him. "I'll miss you."

"I'll miss you too."

15

———

Kale woke to the ringing of his cell phone. He opened his eyes and blinked into the dark room, fumbling his hand along his nightstand.

Annie's name was on the screen. The time was four a.m.

"Hello," he said, voice thick.

"Kale?" Her voice sounded small, scared.

He sat up. "Are you okay?"

"No… I'm… I'm having a really hard time. Can you come get me?"

"Yes, absolutely. Where are you?"

"I'm, umm… I don't know. Hold on."

"You don't know?"

"Well… I went into downtown Grand Rapids with some of the guys last night and… I had a couple drinks. I think someone slipped me something. I just woke up."

"Holy shit, Annie. You think someone drugged you? I'm getting dressed right now."

"Someone was following me after I left the bar. I was all dizzy and I kept hearing their footsteps. I finally hid behind a dumpster and I must… have like passed out. My face is throbbing like somebody slapped me and my knees are all bruised."

"Where are you?"

"I can see a motel across the street and there's a street sign, Miller Road. The motel is called the All Night Inn."

"Okay, I'm coming now. Where did you wake up?"

"In some car. I vaguely remember pulling on doors until I found one unlocked." She began to cry.

Propping the phone between his ear and shoulder, Kale struggled into shorts. He grabbed his t-shirt and hurried out of the room and down the stairs.

"I don't know whose car this is. I'm all alone."

As Kale opened the front door, he heard his name.

"Kale?" Sage's voice.

"Hold on, Annie." He peered into the sitting room. "I've gotta run, Sage."

She sat on the couch, a blanket snug around her waist. Grover slept in a ball of rumpled gray fur in her lap. "Be careful, okay? Just now when you opened the door, something slipped out in front of you, a dark shadow."

"Okay, sure. I'll be careful. Try to get some sleep." He ran to his car and climbed in. "Are you still there?" he asked Annie.

"Yeah," she whispered.

"Okay... okay," he murmured, mind whirring. "Listen, maybe you should hang up the phone and call 911. If someone drugged you—"

"No!"

Kale squeezed the wheel, rage bubbling in his stomach at the thought of someone hurting her. "I know that's a scary idea, but hear me out, okay? If someone drugged you... they might have... have..." The words 'raped you' was on the tip of his tongue. He couldn't spit it out.

"They didn't," she said.

"How do you know?"

There was silence on the other end and he realized what a stupid question he'd asked. Of course she'd know. It was her body. How could she not know? Then again, maybe she didn't want *him* to know. "I still think—"

"I'm not calling the police, Kale, and I don't want you to say it again. I'm not. I won't. Not ever under any circumstances."

He didn't understand her reaction, but knew better than to push her in that moment. "All right. I'm coming, but I'm forty-five minutes away. Go into the motel lobby and wait for me there."

"Will you stay on the phone with me?" she asked.

"Of course, yes."

They didn't talk much, but sometimes Annie would mumble into the phone.

"I'm a lost cause, Kale," she whispered.

"Hey, don't say that. Never say that."

"I'm broken and you can't fix me."

"Annie, please. You're scaring me. I'm on my way and I need you to be strong right now. Okay? Can you do that?"

"Mmm-hmm."

Kale sped down the dark, mostly empty streets. The usually forty-five-plus-minute drive took him less than thirty. When he finally pulled in front of the motel, he forgot to put the car in park and it started to roll as he stepped out.

"Shit, crap," he muttered, clutching the door and jumping back in. He slammed his foot on the brake with the car only inches from hitting the bumper of a white sedan.

He put the car in park, turned off the engine and took the keys to ensure he didn't accidentally lock them inside. "I'm here," he said into the phone, striding toward the motel. He pushed through the double doors.

The lobby was dingy and lit by a dim blue light. No one stood behind the desk.

His pulse quickened when he scanned the space, which included a scattering of chairs, and found them all empty.

"Annie?" he said into the phone.

She hadn't spoken in a while. He'd suspected on the drive she'd fallen asleep, but now…

"Annie?" he called out, his voice reverberating in the lobby.

A rail-thin man with a scraggly goatee stepped from the room behind the front desk. He eyed Kale suspiciously.

"I'm looking for a woman with dark hair. She was in here—"

"The vending area," the man interrupted, pointing down the hall.

"Thanks." Kale hurried down the corridor.

A red 'EXIT' sign flickered at the opposite end, casting an eerie crimson glow on the misshapen walls. He spotted her through the dirty glass door. A single spindly table and chair sat between two large vending machines—one filled with soda, the other with candy and snacks. Annie lay face down on the table, her forehead propped on her stacked hands. Her legs were bare and looked stick-thin. She appeared smaller, meeker in the yellow-green fluorescent light.

Kale opened the door and went to her, squatting. He wrapped his arms around her, lifted her head, and pulled it into his chest.

She blinked at him, her eyelids heavy and red-rimmed. "You're here," she murmured.

"I'm here. Come on. Let's go."

He helped her stand, but her legs wobbled. He picked her up, cradled her. She wrapped her arms around his neck, rested her head on his chest. As they passed the front desk, the thin man watched, but said nothing.

At his car, Kale sat Annie down and opened her door. She slid into the passenger seat and pulled her knees to her chest. When he climbed into the driver's side, her teeth chattered.

"I'm so cold," she whispered.

"You are?" he asked, surprised. It was warm out, but he could see her lips had a blueish tinge.

"Can we just get a room in there?" She nodded toward the motel. "So I can take a bath."

He looked beyond her, back at the motel with its grubby floor and overflowing garbage cans. He wanted to take her to his house, where she could sink into the big claw-footed tub on the second floor and climb into his bed. Where they could wake up hours from now and eat whatever his mother had whipped up for breakfast, stuffed French toast or scrambled eggs. But he knew that choice would also come with his family's questions and noise, their curious gazes.

"Not this one," he said. "I'll find some place decent."

'D ecent' turned out to be a Holiday Inn near the highway. Kale handed over cash and hoped the woman at the front desk didn't demand I.D. He wasn't yet twenty-one and some hotels refused to rent to guests under the age.

The desk attendant did ask for his license, but barely glanced at it. She gave him a key card for Room 206 and reminded him that breakfast started in an hour and checkout was ten a.m. He'd shelled out ninety bucks for a hotel room they could stay in for five hours.

Kale returned to the parking lot and gently shook Annie awake.

"We can go in," he said. "Come on, let's get you to the room."

Kale helped Annie from the car. She leaned heavily on him as they walked to the side entrance and up the carpeted stairs. As they moved down the hushed corridor on the second floor, Annie stopped him.

She looked up at him, eyes swimming. "Thank you. Thank you for rescuing me. I've never had anyone to call in moments like this. Never. You saved me."

He smiled and pushed a piece of hair out of her face. "That's giving me a lot of credit, but you're welcome. There's nowhere I'd rather be than right here with you."

In the room, Annie stripped off her clothes and climbed in the bath. Kale sat on the edge of the bed. The adrenaline of the last hour had worn off. Tiredness pulled at the corners of his eyes. He lay back on the bed, legs dangling off the side, and let his eyes slip closed. The burble of water into the tub lulled him to sleep.

He woke to Annie unbuttoning his shorts. She pulled them off. She stood naked, her hair damp on her shoulders.

"You should sleep," he told her, but his body had already begun to respond to her touch.

"We will," she whispered, climbing on top of him. "But first I want to thank you."

16

A shrill ringing ripped Kale from sleep. He fumbled for his cell phone, disoriented. It took him a moment to realize he wasn't home in bed, but in a hotel room with Annie. She lay curled against him, her legs entwined with one of his. He looked at his phone on the opposite end of the bureau, reached his fingers, but couldn't grasp it without waking Annie and moving her aside.

He ignored it, hoped the sound didn't wake her, and drifted back to sleep.

When he woke for the second time, daylight spilled through the partially open curtains. Annie's side of the bed lay empty. Kale sat up, blinked at the alarm clock. It read '10:12 a.m.'

"Shoot," he muttered.

Checkout was ten a.m. He picked up the black phone on the bedside table and dialed the front desk.

"How can I help you?" a cheerful woman asked.

"Hi, sorry. I'm in Room 206. Can I request a late checkout, please? Eleven a.m."

"Yes, we can do that. Enjoy your morning."

He sat the phone down and stood, stretching his arms overhead. The bathroom door stood open. No Annie in there either.

He moved to grab his cell phone, but it no longer sat on the nightstand. He checked the floor, but it hadn't fallen.

"Huh," he said, reaching back to a bleary memory of waking up to the ringing of the phone. He hadn't moved it, had he?

Kale shrugged on his shorts. He grabbed his t-shirt off a chair. His cell rested on the floral cushion beneath his shirt. He stared at it, then at the nightstand.

"Weird," he said, lifting it up and cringing at the barrage of missed calls and texts.

Stevie, Zach and Ben had all tried to reach him that morning. He opened the line of texts from Stevie, scrolling back to the first she'd sent at seven a.m.

Stevie: We're at the dock. Boat's in the water.

Stevie: Hello? Are you coming? We're going to miss the good fish.

Zach: Dude, we even picked up those nasty jelly donuts you like and you're going to bail?

Ben: You better wake up because Stevie has steam coming out of her ears.

Stevie: I just called Zinnia and she said your bed is empty. Where are you?

Stevie: Okay, we're waiting five more minutes and if you're not here, we're going without you.

Zach: You suck, bro.

Interspersed in the messages were two texts from Zinnia to call her ASAP. He also had five missed calls from Stevie, one from Zach, and three from his mom.

"Hey!"

Kale jumped at the sound of Annie's voice. She stood in the hotel doorway holding up a Dunkin' Donuts bag and a cardboard carrier with two cups of coffee.

"Breakfast?"

Kale frowned at his phone, guilt heavy in the pit of his stomach. He'd forgotten he'd agreed to the morning fishing trip. Now Stevie would really be pissed.

"Yeah, sure," he said, returning the phone to the chair. He wanted to put off dealing with the barrage of anger a bit longer.

Annie took the bag and coffees to the little table. She handed him a coffee. "I put cream in yours," she said. She pulled out two donuts. One was a glazed twist and the other was jelly-stuffed with white frosting.

He stared at the jelly donut and glanced at his phone.

"A lot of their donuts were cleaned out," Annie explained, following his gaze. "You choose."

"Jelly all the way," he said, picking it up and taking a gooey bite. It lacked its usual uplifting effect. The donut tasted too sweet, the texture of the jelly slimy on his tongue.

～

"I've got to call Stevie," he said after he'd parked in the carnival parking lot.

"Okay. I'll go get changed." Annie reached for her door handle.

Kale put his hand on her arm. "No. I think you should wait for me. The guy who drugged you last night might be someone you work with. I think I should go with you."

"Are you sure? I don't want to be the reason your friends are mad at you."

"I'm sure. Hold on."

Kale called Stevie. She didn't answer, and his shoulders relaxed. "Hey, Stevie. It's me. I'm really sorry about this morning. Something serious came up and I couldn't be there. Call me when you can. Please don't be pissed."

As he hung up, his phone rang. He expected to see Stevie's name on the screen, but it was Zinnia's.

"Hey," he said.

"You need to come home," Zinnia blurted.

"Why? What's going on?"

"I don't want to talk about it on the phone. Just get here as soon as you can."

"Zinnia, just tell me."

"No. Come home, Kale." Her voice was harsh, but he could hear tears bubbling behind her words.

Kale stepped from the car. "I have to go home, Annie. I'm not sure what's going on, but that was Zinnia and she didn't sound okay."

"Go, of course. Don't worry about me. Call me later." Annie held up her new phone.

"I will. As soon as I can. I'm sorry to leave you like this."

"Don't be. I can hold my own, Kale, last night excluded. I hope everything's okay."

Kale frowned and nodded. "Me too. Hey." He braced his hands on her shoulders. "Be careful, okay? I'm worried about you with those guys."

She bunched his t-shirt in her hands and pulled him closer, kissed him. "Don't worry about me. Take care of things at home. I'll be here."

17

———

When he arrived home, the house sat eerily quiet.

"Mom?" he called as he pushed through the front door.

No response.

He found his parents in the back garden. They sat together on a wooden bench his father had carved from a black walnut tree that had been felled by a storm years before. All the Goodwin kids had engraved their initials on the bench with a pocket knife.

His parents sat close together, their faces blotched and red. His mother was hunched forward, her garden mat bunched in her white fists.

"What is it? What's wrong?" Kale asked.

She swiped at her tears at Kale's arrival. His dad, too, did a quick rub beneath his eyes and sat up straighter. He patted the seat beside them and, though they barely fit, Kale squeezed onto the wooden bench. He didn't ask the question again, knew the answer was coming, and wasn't sure he wanted to hear it.

"It's…" his mother started, but her words caught in her throat.

"Sage," his dad finished. "The cancer is back."

Kale squeezed the bench and stared hard at the pile of weeds his mother had pulled from the garden.

Sage, the baby of the family—the pixie or gremlin, depending on what she was up to. The cancer had appeared the first time when she was six and the three years that had followed were a blur of hospital visits and midnight prayers. His parents had tried it all—special diets, natural remedies, energy healers, chemo, trial drugs, and in the end, something had worked, but now…

"When did you find out? I thought everything was fine."

"She hasn't been feeling well. We went in last week for a check-up, figured she had a touch of summer flu. We got the call this morning."

"How bad is it?" He didn't need to ask the question. His parents' faces held the answer.

"We don't know for sure," his dad added quickly. "Mom, Sage, and Zinnia are going to Ann Arbor tomorrow for more tests."

"You're not going?" Kale asked.

"I have to meet a farmer who's buying a skid steer. It's a big deal and we can't afford to lose it."

"Where is Sage? Where are all the kids?"

"In the movie room doing a Tim Burton marathon."

"Good. That's nice for Sage."

Sage had a Tim Burton obsession. The mural their father had painted in Sage's room several years before depicted Jack Skellington perched on the edge of a curling hill in front of a massive yellow full moon.

"I'm going to go see her," Kale said.

He left his parents in the garden and slipped into the house. Downstairs, he eased open the door into the movie room. Light spilled into the space. His siblings lay sprawled across the two large sectionals. Sage lay curled on her side on the long end of one couch, her head in Zinnia's lap. They all looked at him as he slipped into the room.

Kale squeezed onto the end of the couch next to Sage. "How ya doing?" he asked.

She smiled and teetered her hand from side to side. "Been better."

On the screen, *The Corpse Bride* played.

"Mom said you guys are heading to Ann Arbor to meet with the doctor tomorrow."

Zinnia made a sound, and Kale glanced her way. Tears streamed down her cheeks. He leaned over and squeezed her shoulder. She nodded, but kept her eyes locked on the screen as if she couldn't look at him.

"How's Annie?" Sage asked.

"She's fine. Probably running the Pirate Ship at the Grand Rapids fair right about now."

"Maybe I could go sometime. I didn't make it to the fair this year."

"I should have taken you," Kale said, stomach sinking. In years past, they'd always done a family night at the fair, all the Goodwin kids plus some of their friends. This year, it hadn't even crossed his mind.

He settled in between his sisters and watched the rest of *The Corpse Bride*. As the credits rolled, his parents crept in and the Goodwin kids scooted together to make room. They watched *Edward Scissorhands* and *Beetlejuice*.

It was nearly eight p.m. when Lucy insisted they break the movie marathon and eat dinner. She and Frank pulled out sandwich fixings and a fruit salad Calla and Aster had made.

"Can we eat in the garden?" Sage asked.

"That sounds like a fine idea," Frank told her, kissing the top of her head.

They sat in the garden, plates balanced on their knees. Kale perched on an upturned stump. He laughed as Thorn and Aster reminisced about the time Sage had kept stealing the neighbor's dog. She felt bad he was tied up outside, and she would untie him, walk him home, and hide him in her bedroom. Her parents finally realized what she was doing one afternoon when they found her and the mud-covered Border collie asleep in her bed.

The stories went on and on. They all had stories of Sage's various antics over the years.

It was almost ten when Sage said she was sleepy. Lucy and Zinnia accompanied her into the house. Aster and Thorn tackled the dishes while Calla too went to bed. Kale sat alone with his dad for a few more minutes in the garden, smelling the gardenias and jasmine.

"Are you worried, Dad?"

Frank Goodwin sighed and traced his finger over his children's names on the bench. "There's a quote, I can't remember by who now, but it says something like the greatest gifts we can give our children are roots and wings. I feel confident we've given all six of you those things. Sage, for all her earthly leanings, has always had very big, very bright wings. If she flies early, as some of God's angels do, then we will go on. We will go on as the seedling goes on after the forest burns. Surviving is something we Goodwins know how to do. And as the son of a mortician, I should be uniquely qualified to survive such a terrible sacrifice. But it would be a lie if I said I was ready to face the death of one of my children."

Kale grew still as he listened to his father. He'd never heard the man allude to the possibility of Sage's death. Their dad usually steeled himself against such conclusions, refused to entertain any glass-half-empty beliefs, but now…

"I think I'll go to bed," his dad said, standing. "Good night, son."

Kale watched his father, shoulders sagging, walk to the house and disappear inside. Lights blazed in two of the upstairs windows—Sage's and Calla's. Kale looked at his own bedroom window, a dark square in the pale façade of the house.

He suddenly, desperately missed Annie, wanted nothing more than to bury his face in her hair and cry.

He called her phone, pacing around the garden as it rang without an answer.

"I could be there by eleven," he murmured. She'd still be awake. The whole midway buzzed for a couple hours after the fair shut down for the night.

Kale hurried into the house. He found Aster and Thorn in the kitchen, their faces drawn. Aster sat on the counter, her legs dangling over the side. Thorn leaned against the wall. They stopped talking when Kale walked in.

"You guys okay?" Kale asked.

"Peachy," Aster grumbled. "Of course we're not okay. Sage has cancer again."

"Yeah." He shoved his hands in his pockets, knew he should do the big brother thing and offer words of wisdom, at least a listening ear, but he felt hollow. He wanted only to be with Annie. "I'm going to run over to the fair and see Annie. If Mom or Dad asks, will you let them know?"

Thorn and Aster exchanged a significant look, but he didn't push for an explanation. If he did, he'd get roped into an argument. He could sense one brewing.

"I'll see you guys tomorrow," he said.

He parked in the largely deserted parking lot at the Grand Rapids fairgrounds. Warmth emanated from the cracked concrete as he hurried toward the midway. He didn't bother with the entrance, but followed the side to the wall of work trailers that backed the carnival rides.

Scents of hot dogs and burgers filled the air. A group of carnival workers, including Margaret, her husband, Dan, Fluffy and a few others, sat in lawn chairs while a carny Kale hadn't met manned the grill.

He beelined for Annie's tent. "Annie?" he called, tapping on the nylon.

No response.

"She isn't in there," a man standing near a tent several feet away called out.

"Do you know where she is?"

"Nawp. Saw her head off thataway 'bout a half hour ago." He pointed toward the heart of the midway.

Kale walked through the deserted carnival grounds. The hulking rides loomed silent and watchful, their lights and sounds extinguished. Popcorn and discarded cups littered the cement and edges of parched grass.

Nerves jumbled in Kale's legs and hands. He'd tried two more times to raise Annie on her cell phone with no luck. He suspected if he'd peeked in her tent, he'd have seen her phone lying discarded inside.

A scream erupted across the midway, Annie's scream. It came from the Haunted Funhouse. Kale broke into a run.

18

____

"Annie?" he shouted as his feet banged on the steel steps into the funhouse. He took them two at a time and plunged into the yawning, fang-filled mouth of the leering monster who granted access to the interior.

He immediately ran into one of the mirrored walls and smacked his face. Groping, he pushed forward, hands sliding over the mirrored surfaces.

"Annie?" he yelled again.

She didn't respond.

He stumbled out of the mirrors and into a long dark hallway hung with thick chains. Deeper into the haunted funhouse, he could no longer see much of anything. The chains knocked against his face and hands as he thrashed forward. The darkness was stifling. It would be so easy to get turned around, lose his sense of direction, become totally lost.

"Forward, this is forward," Kale whispered to himself, attempting to calm the tremors of panic inching up. He remembered his phone and snatched it from his pocket, fingers trembling as he turned it on and found the flashlight icon. He illuminated the space in front of him, releasing a relieved breath as the darkness at least partially dissipated. "Annie! Where are you?"

Silence and then her voice, tiny and scared, from the floor above him. "Kale?"

He moved faster, finally reached the end of the steel bars that led into the narrow stairway to the second floor. As he stepped into the stairway, he remembered the thing he'd encountered the last time he'd been in the funhouse, the flesh and hair that had pulled away from its head. Terror gripped him, but he steeled himself against it and hurried up the stairs.

"Annie?" he called out again.

"I'm here," she said, louder this time. "Up here."

He reached the top of the stairs, which sent him through the circular opening that revolved when the ride was running. On the opposite side, he plunged into another maze of tight halls, plastic balls up to his ankles. He kicked them away as he walked.

The hall branched in either direction, leading into rooms with severed heads, bodies in bloody bathtubs, which he didn't shine his light into. He remembered the one that had chilled him most of all when he'd walked through it with Stevie—a woman sitting at a vanity gazing in the mirror, some mechanical contraption causing her to swipe a razor blade back and forth across her bloody throat.

As he moved down the hall, someone suddenly rushed from a dark room.

He gasped and held up his light, catching Annie's terrified face in the beam. She recoiled, blocking the light with her hand and falling backward as if not sure who stood on the other side. She turned to flee.

"Annie, it's me," he said, stepping forward.

"Oh, Kale," she sobbed, throwing herself against him, nearly knocking him over. "Oh, my God. I was so scared."

He held her close. "What happened? Why are you in here?" Her body trembled against his.

"Let's get out of here first, okay?"

He kept his arm tight around her waist as they maneuvered through the last of the hall that spit them onto the balcony overlooking the midway. The night air was a welcome sensation after the claustrophobic funhouse.

"The slide's the only way down," she said, hurrying toward the plastic spiral slide.

"You go first," he told her.

She shook her head. "No, together. I don't want to be down there alone, not even for a second."

"This is going to be a tight squeeze," he said, sitting on the slide, Annie wedged between his legs.

They slid down slowly, Kale pushing with his hands to keep them going while Annie held his phone. When they climbed off, Annie's gaze darted around the empty midway as if searching for someone.

"What happened? What is it?"

"Let's start back," she said, tugging him back toward the area where the other carnies were. "I went for a walk," she started. "And… I heard footsteps behind me. I turned a couple times and didn't see anyone, but I was afraid to double back to my tent because I kept hearing them and thinking someone was following me. Finally, I waited and then looked back really quickly. I saw a man in a dark hood and dark pants. I panicked and ran into the funhouse. I heard him come in behind me, so I went upstairs and hid. Then I heard you call my name."

Kale turned and looked back at the funhouse, chilled by her story. "Who do you think it was?"

"It was Byron. It had to be. Somehow, he's found me."

"Annie, this is serious. If this guy found you, chased you into that funhouse tonight, he probably intended to hurt you. I think you need to call the police."

"Kale—"

"I know," he interrupted her. "I know you don't want to and you think he's got them all wrapped around his finger, but if you do nothing and he does hurt you, how will you prove it was him? You need a record of what's going on."

"I'll think about it. Okay? But… I don't want to talk about doing that right now. Let's just go to my tent."

Kale eyed the carnies scattered around the back yard. He searched for Hulk Hogan amongst the faces, but didn't see him.

Margaret waved, and Kale gave her a nod before following Annie into the tent.

Annie climbed into his lap and he draped his arms around her, resting his chin on the top of her head.

"What happened at home?" Annie asked. "Why did your sister call?"

The news that had been delivered hours before seemed light years in the past, but now it rushed back with startling sharpness.

"It's Sage," he murmured. "The cancer came back."

"Oh, no." Annie twisted around and looked at him. "I'm so sorry, Kale. Poor Sage."

"Yeah. It's really hard news. Last time the cancer nearly got her. She's been in remission, finally getting to a be a kid again, and now it's back. It's not fair."

"No," Annie sighed, curling deeper into Kale. "Life is definitely not fair."

They lay together, not speaking, and after a while Annie drifted to sleep. Kale thought of his room at the Chapel Road house, the somber breakfast in the morning. He wiggled his phone from his pocket and texted Zinnia.

Kale: I'm staying with Annie at the midway tonight. Please let Mom and Dad know.

Annie was already up when Kale emerged from the tent the following morning. She appeared in shorts and a t-shirt, her hair wet.

"Hey, sleepyhead," she told him, kissing him before kneeling to slide her shower stuff into the tent.

"Good morning," he murmured. "I can't believe I slept this late."

"It's not even nine," she said.

"I know, but still. How'd you sleep?"

"Good, thank you. If I'd been here alone last night, I probably would have opted for the bunkhouse. It stinks of man fart, but at least it feels safe."

"Does it feel safe?" Kale frowned and looked at the bunk trailer where two carnies stood outside smoking cigarettes. One was shirtless, his shorts hanging so low his hip bones poked from his pale skin. He had a tattoo of a three-headed dog that stretched from his neck to his navel. "Are you sure it's not someone in the carnival following you? That Hulk Hogan lookalike, maybe?"

"Hulk Hogan lookalike?" She smirked. "That's hilarious. Cliff does sort of look like Hulk Hogan. But it doesn't make sense that Cliff would be following me. I'm ten feet away from him in a tent. If he wanted to do something, it wouldn't be hard."

"That's not very reassuring."

"I'm just saying I don't think it's Cliff."

"Have you thought any more about calling the police?"

"And saying what exactly? Someone drugged me at a bar? I saw a person walking in a hoodie at the midway after dark? How can I prove any of it? And worse, if I bring up Byron, they're liable to reach out to him and then, if he doesn't already, he'll know exactly where I'm at."

"I'm worried about you, worried you're not safe here."

Annie pulled her leather bracelet from her pocket and offered her wrist to Kale so he could secure it. "Then stay with me."

Kale sighed. "I want to, but—"

"Join the carnival. It's only for a couple more months. It's a great experience. It's like taking a year off to backpack Europe, just a little less refined." She laughed, but Kale could see she meant every word.

He studied her eyes, so intent on his—pleading, hopeful. There was a certain pull toward the carny life, an electricity not so unlike the magnetism between him and Annie. It felt like freedom.

The image that cut through his reverie was Sage. Sage, who was likely beginning cancer treatment all over again. The thought of those awful months of treatments and doctor's appointments, fundraisers, waking to the sounds of Sage vomiting at night, or, worse, crying…

"Are you worried about leaving Sage?" Annie asked.

He nodded. "I helped a lot when Sage was sick last time. Took the kids to practices and events, helped with bills because my dad had to take time off."

"Well, school doesn't start again until the fall, right? Your siblings are on summer break. Your sister, Zinnia, is home. Maybe this is the perfect time. You deserve to do something for you, Kale. It's not wrong to do that."

She was right. It wasn't fair that the burden of caring for the other siblings fell on him. What would a couple months hurt, choosing himself for a change? And then he'd commit to helping more when school started up again. Maybe he and Annie could even fix up one of the outbuildings, make a little apartment, live at the Chapel Road house together.

"Do you think they'd hire me?" he asked.

She grinned. "Are you kidding me? You'd be the star of the show. Mo would do backflips to get someone like you on the crew. We can go talk to him right now if you want."

"Okay, yeah. Why not, right?" Kale laughed, but it rang hollow beneath his ribs. It wasn't that he didn't want to—he did. He wanted to so badly he could taste it, but the thought of telling his parents made him feel sick.

"Come on." She dragged him toward a camper near the back of the field. It was one of the nicer ones, with a large awning that protected a little patio table and chairs.

A man stood outside the camper, trimming his fingernails. He looked up as Annie and Kale approached.

"Heard you went AWOL a couple nights ago," he said to Annie. "Some of your family was worried you might not make it back."

"I'm okay, just… had a little too much to drink, I guess."

Kale wanted to tell the man the truth, alert him to the fact that someone in Annie's so-called family had likely drugged her, done God only knew what and abandoned her in an alley, but he bit his tongue.

"Mo, this is Kale. Kale, Mo. We were wondering if Kale could get a job," Annie said.

Mo eyed Kale up and down, then spit a clump of tar-like chew on the ground. He inserted another wad behind his bottom lip and returned to his fingernails. "We could use another guy. Lost Billy at the start of the month."

"Kale's brilliant," Annie told him, holding tight to Kale's arm.

Kale looked at her, surprised. No one had ever called him brilliant—such compliments were usually reserved for his sister, Zinnia. He was the oldest and the first son, but had always lacked his sister's direction and smarts.

"I'll need a few minutes alone with him. Go on, git." Mo waved Annie away.

She kissed Kale on the cheek, then narrowed her eyes at Mo. "Be nice, Mo."

He grunted but said nothing. After she'd gone, Mo gestured at Kale to follow him. "You gotta meet the big boss. He's the one who decides, and just your luck he's here today."

"Like in the Mafia?" Kale asked, smiling.

Mo cocked an eyebrow. "Round here, Tony Brisby is definitely the Don."

"And what if he doesn't like me?"

"Then you'll be buying a ticket to see your girlfriend like everyone else, but I wouldn't worry much. You seen this crew. He ain't all that picky."

The big boss was a short, soft-looking man with a rim of silver hair that ran ear to ear while the top of his head was bald. He sat in a reclining lawn chair wearing Bermuda shorts, a Hawaiian shirt, and pristine white tennis shoes. A jumble of paperwork rested on a plastic table beside him.

"Mo. How's it coming? Everything on schedule?" he asked.

"Yep, right on time. I've got a guy here looking for a job."

Kale stepped forward and extended his hand. "Hi. I'm Kale Goodwin."

"You got a decent handshake, Kale Goodwin. I'm Tony Brisby. You got a record?"

Kale straightened up, surprised. "No."

"Okay. You got any problems with drugs?"

"No."

"Booze?"

"No."

"Girls? You out chasing girls all the time?"

"No."

"You runnin' from something?"

Kale thought of the big house on Chapel Road, his boisterous, crowded family, Sage. "No."

"You look like a college boy. You in college?"

"Technically, yeah, but… I'm taking the semester off."

"Are ya now?" Tony picked up a plastic bottle of lemonade and unscrewed the cap, considering Kale through shrewd blue eyes. He didn't take a drink. "How do your parents feel about you doing this?"

Warmth rose into Kale's face. "I haven't told them, but I'm twenty, so…"

"So you're a man and you can do what you want, huh?" Tony took a sip of his lemonade, screwed the cap back on. "Here's the deal, Kale. If Mo wants ya, that's fine with me, but if you got some other prospect, you'd best be chasing that. This is hard work, long hours, hot days. Your fellow carnies'll be like family, but they're the kind of family that'll stick a knife in your back if you let 'em down. Settin' up those rides is life or death, for the guys doin' it and for the kids ridin' em. If you can't take this job as serious as that, then you don't belong here."

"I think I can," Kale said. A trickle of sweat slid between his shoulder blades, from nerves as much as the relentless sun. "I mean, I can."

Tony nodded. "Then go do it."

Kale followed Mo back toward the tents.

"You're in then," Mo said. "Pay is every week on Friday. I expect you're startin' today?"

"Umm… yeah. I just need to run home and grab a few things."

"Best shake a tail feather." Mo tapped his watch. "Showtime is three o'clock sharp."

19

Kale parked in the driveway and gazed at the giant house he'd called home for most of his life. His hands were slick on the wheel, and he dreaded going inside and telling his parents what he intended to do.

Something whacked his window, and he started.

Thorn grinned. "What are you doing in there, meditating?"

Kale sighed and stepped out. "Where are Mom and Dad?"

"In the house. Mom, Zinnia and Sage are getting ready to go to Ann Arbor, and I probably don't need to tell you that Mom was kind of pissed you took off last night."

"I figured. Where are you going?"

"Out to the barn." Thorn held up a dirt bike fender. "Getting this and the seat fixed on my bike today. I'd love some help if you're not grounded," he called over his shoulder as he headed to the barn.

As Kale walked through the front door, he encountered his mother coming down the stairs, Sage's Beetlejuice duffel bag slung over one shoulder, Grover wriggling in her arms.

She narrowed her eyes at Kale, then thrust Grover toward him. "Put him out, please, Kale. He's terrorizing the girls."

Kale looked at the fluffy gray cat. "Grover, are you being a pest?" he asked. He set Grover on the front stoop and closed the door. As he turned back into the house, he found his mother waiting for him.

"You stayed with Annie last night?"

"Yeah, at the fair."

"Hmm…"

"I wondered if I could talk to you and Dad for a minute?"

She studied his face and then nodded slowly. "You can always talk to us. He's in the kitchen."

Kale followed his mother to the kitchen. His dad sat at the table, a pile of paperwork spread before him.

"I swear they make three duplicates of every single health and insurance form and insist you complete each one by hand. Ludicrous." He shook his hand as if it ached.

"Honey, Kale wants to talk to us about something." Kale heard the tension in his mother's voice as she sat next to his dad.

Frank looked up as if just realizing Kale had walked in. "Oh, hi, Kale. Good morning."

"Morning." Kale rubbed the back of his neck. "Let me just start by asking you guys not to freak out. You've always said to never hold back the thing that needs to be said, so I'm just going to go for it." He was talking fast. "I've decided to join the carnival with Annie—to work there." He forced his eyes up from the table to his parents' faces.

They stared at him, neither attempting to conceal their dismay at his admission. His mother's mouth hung open, her eyes huge.

"Kale…" His dad interlaced his fingers on the table. "You're a very intelligent, very capable young man. I don't think… no, I *know* a traveling carnival is an unwise choice."

"Absolutely not," his mother stated. "No, Kale. The answer is no. How can you even be considering such a thing at a time like this? We just found out Sage is sick again."

"Mom, it will only be for the summer. In the fall, I'll come back and help with the kids. They're doing their own thing right now anyway, and you and Sage will probably be spending a lot of time in Ann Arbor. And…" He considered his next words, knew they'd sting. "I'm twenty. I've helped with the kids and the house my whole life. It's not wrong to do something I want to do. You can't—"

"Oh, yes, I can." She stood and paced away from them, gesturing with her hands. "You still live under this roof, and that means our rules." They were strange words coming from his mother, a woman who prided herself on giving her children freedom and the ability to carve their own path.

"What your mother is trying to say is that… is that we only want the best for you. And sometimes at twenty, we can be very distracted by the glitz and glamour of things like… well, a carnival, for instance. But what we see on the outside is not what happens on the inside."

"Exactly." Lucy turned and slapped a hand on the table. "Drugs, Kale. And felons! I'm not one to judge. Those people need work too, but not you. No, no, no. The world is your oyster and you're not going to throw it away, getting mixed up with a traveling gang of drug addicts and felons."

Again, the words seemed not to be his mother's at all—a woman who'd spent years teaching literacy at the Muskegon Correctional Facility when her children were young, who advocated equality, and who constantly pushed her children to see beyond labels. "Mom, do you hear yourself right now?"

Her eyes filled with tears. She seemed to be skirting the edge of hysteria. "Frank," she said, seeking backup. "Please… tell him he can't go."

Frank stood and hugged his wife. Kale squirmed in his chair, feeling terrible for upsetting his mother, but not willing to back down. He'd made his decision. He was going with the carnival. He was going with Annie.

Lucy started to speak, but Frank took her hand and shushed her. She worried at the scar on her face that cut a pale line through her right eyebrow and caused her right lower eyelid to droop slightly. It had become her go-to tic whenever something bothered her.

"Okay, let's be rational about this, shall we?" Frank asked, guiding Lucy back to her chair. She stared at Kale with red-rimmed eyes. "How soon would this start?"

Kale glanced at the ceiling. "Today. They need me to start today."

Lucy stiffened, but Frank put a hand on her shoulder. "Okay. Let's compromise. You go for the summer, but you check in daily. I mean it, daily, just so we know you're okay. None of this funny business that's been going on lately where you disappear all day without a word."

Lucy shoved Frank's hand off her shoulder, stood, and stormed from the kitchen.

"Jesus," Kale murmured.

"Kale," his dad warned.

"Sorry. Jeez. I just don't understand why she's so mad."

Frank sighed and rubbed the hollows of his eyes. "She's not mad. She's scared. Your mother doesn't do scared well."

"Clearly."

"She has a point, though, Kale. These people you'll be travelling with, they're not Stevie, Ben and Zach. Some of them will be in that line of work because it's the only thing they could get. Some of them may have problems and they may resent you just for being there."

Kale thought of Cliff and nodded. "I can hold my own, Dad."

His dad looked skeptical. "You're a man now. As hard as it is to see our firstborn grow up, we can't stop time. But you need to go into this with eyes wide open. Do not assume anyone in that carnival has your best interest at heart."

"Except Annie," Kale said.

His dad said nothing for a moment. "I agree with your mom that this is poor timing, but I understand what's happening with your siblings can't dictate your life. Still..." Frank leaned forward and touched Kale's hand. "Give this a long think, Kale. If you commit to this, you won't see much of Sage this summer and... none of us know —" He stopped abruptly when Sage appeared in the kitchen doorway.

"Mom forgot to pack Oogie Boogie," she said, holding up her stuffed green Oogie Boogie from *The Nightmare Before Christmas.*

"We can't forget him," Frank said, standing and taking the toy.

"Hi, Kale," Sage said. "I didn't know you were home."

"Just got here. How are you feeling?"

"Pretty good," she said. "Mom found us a hotel that has a pool, so we get to go swimming. You should come."

Kale stood and walked to Sage. He kneeled in front of her and hugged her, eyes brimming. She looked at him, surprised.

"I've decided to work for the carnival for the rest of the summer, so I'm probably not going to be home much."

"That's okay, Kale. Don't be sad. I knew you were going to."

He cocked his head. "Oh, you did, huh? And how did you know that?"

She leaned close to his ear. "One of the drifters told me."

The skin on the back of his neck prickled.

Zinnia bustled into the kitchen and gave Kale a dirty look. "Dad, Mom needs you to load the car."

"I'm on it," Frank said. He patted Kale on the back. "You call every day. Understand?"

"I will, Dad."

Sage followed Zinnia and their dad back down the hall before he could ask more about what she'd said.

~

Kale packed a backpack with a few necessities—toothbrush, change of clothes, deodorant. He eyed his work table, covered in leather scraps, including the bracelet he'd been making for Calla. He'd come back for that stuff. Right now, he didn't have time.

As he walked out the front door, he saw his mother arranging bags in the back of her car. Her eyes locked on his and he cringed at the hurt there. As he passed her in the driveway, he paused and put a hand on her shoulder. "Mom, please don't be mad. It's not for long. I swear."

She swiped at her eyes and hugged him. "Your birthday is in three days. The twenty-first."

"I know. Crazy, right?"

"I'd like you to bring Annie over. Okay? You have the mornings off, right? We'll have breakfast together."

"Okay, Mom. I will."

"Promise?"

"I promise."

"I'd like Annie's phone number too. Here." She held out her cell phone. "Just add her to my contacts."

Kale raised an eyebrow. "Why do you need her number?"

"I'm not going to call her and demand she talk you out of this if that's what you think. I'll feel better about you being in the carnival if I have her phone number as well."

"All right." He took her phone and added the number for the cell he'd recently bought Annie. "Satisfied?"

"Hardly," she murmured. "Be safe, Kale."

He kissed his mother's cheek and climbed into his car.

20

Kale had two hours before he had to return to the carnival. He found Stevie mowing the lawn at the Hampstead place. She'd secured a blue bandana over her hair. As his car coasted to the curb, she looked up and frowned.

Kale stepped out and shoved his hands in his pockets. Stevie didn't shut off the mower, didn't acknowledge him at all.

"Hey," he yelled as he got closer. "Stevie! Hey!" He jumped in front of the mower.

She glared at him and killed the engine. Her face was sweaty, her clothes flecked with sheared blades of grass. "What, Kale? What do you want?"

"I want to talk to you. I left you a message."

"So?"

"So why didn't you call me back?"

"Are you for real right now? You've done nothing but blow me off for two weeks. You didn't even bother to text us yesterday morning to say you weren't showing at the dock. I don't even know who you are right now."

"I was planning to be there, Stevie. I was, but Annie called me in the middle of the night and something crazy had gone down. She thought she got drugged at a bar. I had to go pick her up. She was stranded and freaking out."

Stevie pulled her bandana off her head and wiped her face with it.

"And what? You dropped your phone in the toilet? You were trapped in the only place in a hundred miles that has no cell service?"

Kale's shoulders slumped. "We fell asleep. It was so late and—"

"Whatever, Kale. I don't care."

"Just hear me out. Annie has a stalker and when she called me, I thought it might have been the guy, that she was really in danger."

"She has a stalker?" Stevie's expression was skeptical.

"Yeah. I mean, I found an I.D. that belonged to someone else and she told me, but she seemed really reluctant to talk about it, which I totally get."

"Wait. She had an I.D. that belonged to someone else? To who? The stalker?"

"No. I guess it was a friend of hers who she pretended to be for a while, so he couldn't find her. Norma Fenn, but that's not the point. I'm afraid it was one of the guys from the midway who drugged her."

"That's shocking, considering they all seem like such stand-up guys."

"Which is why I'm going to work for the carnival."

Stevie stared at him. "You're kidding, right?"

Kale shook his head. "No. I'm not kidding. They hired me. I start tonight."

"You're running away to join the circus? That's literally the most pathetic thing I've ever heard." Stevie glared at him.

"Wow, good luck to you too." Kale started away, then stopped and turned back. "Sage's cancer is back."

Stevie recoiled as if he'd slapped her. "What? Are you serious?"

"Yeah. I just thought you should know." It had been a cruel delivery, and he already regretted saying it the way he had.

"And you're still going to work at the carnival?"

"Only for the summer. It's not that long."

"You're making a mistake, Kale. Can you not see that? You're throwing away your whole life for Annie."

He opened his car door, but turned back before climbing in. "I love her, Stevie. Once-in-a-lifetime kind of love. What better reason is there to change? I'm sick of school and riding around with you and Ben and Zach. What I have with Annie is... it's like nothing I've ever experienced."

Stevie's face darkened. She shrugged. "It's your life, Kale. If it sucks that bad, then maybe being a carny is a better option." Her voice wobbled as if she might cry, but she turned away, bent and started the mower.

Kale started his car and slammed on the gas, shot into the street. He didn't look in the rearview mirror as he sped away, but gripped the wheel to still his shaking hands.

How could she be so dismissive of what he'd found? So what if he blew off school for a little while? The lawn business would be just fine without him. Shoot, they could hire Thorn—he'd been begging to work with them for two years. Kale's family would be fine. Everything would be fine.

"Whatever," he muttered, wishing his anger was enough to calm the quaking in his body.

His first official day as a carny was a hard one. The temperature climbed steadily throughout the afternoon, peaking at ninety-two degrees. Kale spent the day running from ride to ride to give other carnies a break. In the times between he picked up trash.

When they climbed into the tent that night, he was sticky and exhausted. He'd intended to lie down for a few minutes and then wake up for a shower, to spend some time with Annie. Instead, he fell into the void of sleep.

"Get up…"

Kale heard the whisper, felt the tickle of breath in his ear. He opened his eyes. Annie leaned over him. She'd lit a candle on her little table, which offered the only light in the space. Her silhouette danced on the interior of the red tent. A soft patter of rain hit the nylon exterior.

"Hmm?" he murmured, reaching for her, trying to pull her onto the sleeping bag.

She laughed. "Uh-uh. I'm not getting in. You're getting out. Come on. Put some shorts on."

"But I'm so comfortable," he complained.

"The point of life is not comfort." Annie picked up the candle and held it over his bare chest, tilting it sideways.

"Don't even," he told her, mesmerized by the flame.

"Then you better get moving quick." She tipped the candle further and a tiny drop of red wax landed on his skin.

"Hey," he gasped, reaching for the candle.

She pulled it away. "There's more where that came from."

"All right, all right. Put that thing down before you burn us alive in here." Kale sat up and searched for his shorts, found them crumpled in the corner. He struggled into them.

He yawned again, longed to lie back down. The day had been long and hard and hot and he felt like his head had only just hit the pillow.

"Is it morning already?" he muttered.

"No. It's three a.m."

He gaped at her. "Then why are we awake?"

She smiled and kissed him. "Because we're alive. Come on."

Annie unzipped the tent and stepped out. He followed her, cringing at the warm rain.

"It's raining," he complained.

"Exactly," she told him. "Come on. Come dance with me."

She pulled him across the field, both of them barefoot. Annie stopped and put a finger to her lips, though he hadn't said anything. He heard it then, barely audible beneath the soft rain. Someone was playing a violin.

"It's Vinnie," she said.

"The guy who works the Ferris wheel?"

"Yep, he plays it every night."

"Huh. Who would have thought?" Kale murmured.

"You gonna dance with me or what?"

Kale looked at Annie, perhaps seeing her for the first time since she'd woken him. Her black hair was damp from the rain, her grey t-shirt dark and plastered against her skin, which glistened. He took one of her hands and twirled her around, then pulled her close, awkwardly swaying to the sound of the music. He'd never been a dancer, but there was something about moving with her, some rhythm that simply existed between them.

The following morning, Kale woke surprisingly refreshed despite his early-morning tryst with Annie. He thought of how he'd left things with Stevie the day before and grabbed his cell phone, shot her a quick text.

Kale: I'm sorry about yesterday, the way I told you about Sage.

He climbed from the tent. Wet grass squished beneath his bare feet.

He yawned and reached his arms over his head. Few moved among the tents and campers. The gray sky cast a dreary morning light. The world smelled of damp earth, a scent that made Kale think of worms.

He turned back to the tent and froze. Someone had scrawled words in black marker on the red nylon.

Die, bitch.

21

Kale stared at the words, breath whistling between his teeth.

Inside the tent, he heard Annie moving. He searched for something to grab, but there was nothing outside the tent he could use to wipe the words away.

Annie stuck her head out. "Morning," she told him, her smile falling away. "What's wrong?"

"Somebody wrote something really nasty on your tent."

"They did?" She climbed out and stood beside him. Her face paled. She turned and scanned the field, crossed her arms tight against her body.

"Do you have any idea who did it?"

When she looked at him, her eyes were tear-filled. "This proves it," she breathed. "He found me."

"The stalker?"

"It has to be," she whispered.

Kale wrapped his arm around her waist. He searched amongst the other tents and campers, half expected to glimpse a man skulking away.

"Got some coffee started over here, y'all," a voice called from behind them.

Kale turned to see Margaret waving at them. "What do you want to do, Annie? Should we tell Mo?"

Annie shook her head hard. "No. They don't want drama. I'm not giving them any reason to get rid of me."

"He wouldn't do that," Kale said, though he didn't know what Mo would do.

"Let's just get our stuff out and pull this down."

"The tent?"

Annie nodded, her lips in a line.

Across the field, Cliff ambled from the bunkhouse. He gazed at Kale and Annie for nearly a minute before turning and walking toward the shower trailer.

"Are you sure it wasn't Cliff?" Kale asked.

"Cliff? Why would he do this?"

"I don't know. I get a bad feeling about him."

"He wouldn't jeopardize his job. If he loses this place, he's got nothing."

Kale thought of Annie's call two nights earlier. She'd believed someone had drugged her. "Could the stalker have been at the bar the other night? Could he have drugged you?"

Annie tugged at her leather bracelet. "I don't know. He could have. I used the bathroom a couple of times. But if he followed me, why didn't he…"

She said nothing more, but Kale knew what she was thinking. Why hadn't he taken his opportunity to attack her outside the bar?

"I'm scared, Kale."

He hugged her closer, wanted to assure her she didn't need to be, but how could he know?

"When could he have done it?" Kale wondered. "It rained last night. It must have been before the rain, but… weren't you awake?"

She shook her head. "I fell asleep just after you and woke up about two. It must have been sometime in there, and we didn't see it when we got out of the tent because it was dark."

"Who stays up late? We should ask around and see if anyone saw who did it."

"Yeah," Annie sighed. "I want to get this down first before anyone sees it."

"Yeah, of course. I'll empty the tent. You go get a couple cups of coffee." He turned her to face him. "It's going to be okay, Annie. I'm here with you now and you're going to be okay."

She smiled, her eyes misty. "Thank you, Kale. I can't tell you how much that means to me."

Kale tilted her face up and kissed her. He watched her make her way to Margaret and then he climbed inside the tent and started gathering their stuff.

Despite the dismal mood in which the day had begun, closing night at the carnival passed in a rush of excitement. Annie and Kale were carefree again, all thoughts of a stalker, of cancer, of disappointed parents fading beneath the reverberating music, the laughter of customers and the dazzling lights.

At ten o'clock, a fireworks show closed the final night. Annie and Kale managed to get her ride covered and when the brilliant-colored sparks rained down they sat at the highest point on the Ferris wheel. She relaxed between his legs, head leaned back on his shoulder, oohing as each firework exploded bigger and brighter than the last. Chin resting on her head, Kale marveled again at his extraordinary luck in finding Annie.

After the carnival ended, there was no sleep for the crew. Kale and Annie dismantled the Pirate Ship with help from Dan the Dragon and two other carnies. As it had the previous week, the night passed in a flurry of laughter and stolen kisses.

Kale managed a quick phone call to his dad and found out Sage would start chemo at the hospital back in Muskegon. They weren't going to waste a minute in treating her. The news took a bit of air from his bubble, but when he climbed into the tent with Annie at two a.m., all the problems of the world melted away.

Brisby Amusements arrived in Fremont early Monday morning and they worked non-stop unloading and assembling the massive rides.

Kale wasn't sure when he'd lost sight of Annie. They'd been working together assembling a kids' teacup ride when Mo had called her to help at the Pirate Ship. Hours had passed. Kale had been so focused he barely remembered the last time he'd seen her.

He made his way to the back yard. They hadn't yet set up their tent. It still sat folded into its bag in the trunk of his car.

Margaret stood at a picnic table by her camper, cutting open packages of hot dogs.

"Hey, Margaret, have you seen Annie?"

"I sure haven't, hon, but if I see her, I'll let her know you're looking."

Kale started back toward the midway. He saw Duke coming toward him, an irritated look on his face.

"Do you know where Annie is?"

"Beats me, but she took my friggin' bike again without askin'. I got half a mind to beat her ass when she gets back."

Kale narrowed his eyes at the man. "I'd think twice about that."

Duke chuckled. "Skinny little thing like you gonna stop me? You just tell her, if she does it again she ain't gonna like what I do to her."

Kale wanted to punch the guy. Instead, he turned and stalked away. Duke was right. He had a hundred pounds on Kale. If they got in a fight, Kale would not come out on the other side unscathed, if he came out at all. Not to mention Duke had a point. Annie had stolen his motorcycle at least twice, but perhaps more often than that.

Kale called Annie's cell phone. It rang without an answer. She'd never set up a voicemail. He called it a second time, feeling a cold sweat break out under his arms.

"Where are you?" he muttered.

If she needed to go somewhere, why hadn't she just asked him for the keys to his car? It didn't make sense.

He walked back to the midway and covered every inch. He asked every carnival worker save Cliff if they'd seen Annie. No one had.

As the hours passed, Kale's panic inched higher. He wanted to call the police. He knew Annie would be livid if he did, but something was wrong. Suddenly the writing on the tent reached a new level of ominousness. Why hadn't he insisted they tell Mo, call the police, something?

He walked to his car and paced the perimeter of the parking lot. His cell phone rang, and he snatched it from his pocket. Annie's number appeared on the screen.

"Where are you? I've been looking everywhere."

She didn't respond, but Kale heard her crying. "Annie? What is it? Are you hurt?"

"I…" She took a gasping breath. "I need you to come right now… to the boathouse. I need help."

"You're at the boathouse? How'd you get—"

"Just come. Now. Hurry."

"Okay. Wait, should I call the police? Do you need an ambulance?"

"No." Her voice cut sharply through the phone. "Just you. Please. Hurry."

The line went dead.

Kale's pulse raced as he sprinted to his car and drove too fast from the lot, spewing dirt and pebbles in his wake.

As he sped down back roads, painfully aware that he was doing ten, sometimes fifteen miles per hour over the speed limit, his mind raced with what might have happened. Had she been hurt? Attacked?

Maybe it was nothing, a bad day that had spiraled. His sisters sometimes had those. More than once, Zinnia had told him it was the curse of being female.

He searched for harmless explanations, clung to those, as he raced toward the isolated property.

~

The property was empty and quiet when he climbed from the car. He started toward the camper, but Annie appeared at the treeline. She took three steps and sank to her knees, burying her face in her hands. He ran to her, knelt and gathered her against him.

A strong metallic odor drifted off of her and Kale pulled back, realizing her hands and shirt were streaked in dark red. The smell was unmistakably blood.

"Annie… oh, Jesus. What's happened?" He examined her, searching for the source of the blood, a cut or wound.

"It's…" She struggled to form words through her cries. "It's not mine."

He frowned, still clutching her sticky hands, trying to understand what she'd said. "Is it from an animal?" But he knew it wasn't. The tortured look on Annie's face told him the blood had come from a person.

"He…" She swallowed hard and wiped at her wet eyes, leaving streaks of red across the tops of her cheeks. "He followed me here."

"Who?" Kale looked beyond her toward the woods, feared for a moment a man would lunge out, blood-soaked, carrying an ax.

"Byron. The guy I told you about."

"The stalker?"

She nodded and went limp against him. "He attacked me," she whispered, "and I fought back."

"Where is he?"

"In the boathouse."

"Okay. I should… I better go and… restrain him."

"He's dead."

22

Kale pushed her back and looked into her face. "Are you sure?"

She nodded.

"Oh, shit. Oh, shit." His mouth had gone dry and the scent of the blood made him queasy. "Okay," he said finally. "Okay. It's okay. He attacked you. It was self-defense. I better just… I better go double-check. Why don't you go to the stream and clean the blood off?" He gestured at her face and hands. "If you're okay being alone for a few minutes. I'll come right back."

She hugged him hard. "Thank you," she murmured.

He helped her stand and watched as she trudged toward the stream. She looked exhausted, as if she'd been in a fight to the death, and apparently she had.

Kale walked to the path in the woods, his feet heavy, his breath short and erratic. His heart thumped against his ribs and he tried to calm down, to convince himself that she might be wrong. The guy might still be alive. Kale had to be alert, ready in case Byron suddenly leapt from behind a tree.

The door to the boathouse stood open, and Kale moved closer to that rectangle of darkness that revealed nothing within. He smelled the stink of blood as soon as he stepped inside. Light trickled in and lit the dust motes. He searched the dark corners and, after a moment, spotted something at the base of the stairs. He inched closer and froze.

It was not a man lying there, but something bloody and human-sized, wrapped in a huge sheath of plastic. Long strips of black electrical tape had been wrapped around the body. The plastic was thick and difficult to see through, but Kale recognized smears of blood and glimpses of colored fabric, as if she'd first cocooned the body in a blanket. He peered closer. It was not just any blanket. It was his blanket—cream-colored and decorated with black paw prints.

Kale squatted, his vision swimming. He tried to see what lay beneath the plastic and the blanket, but it was hidden.

"Oh, God." He stood. His stomach rolled, and he staggered back out of the boathouse, bending over and dry-heaving. Nothing came up. He hadn't eaten since that morning, toast and coffee and a few bites of eggs at the picnic table in Margaret's camp. It seemed like another time. How could that moment and this one have existed in a single day?

When his stomach steadied, he stood again and walked back into the boathouse, keeping his distance. She'd wrapped the body in plastic. How could they possibly tell the police she'd killed the man in self-defense?

"The autopsy will prove it," he murmured, already thinking ahead to hours in the future when they'd be separated and sitting in the over-bright interrogation rooms with detectives demanding to know what had happened. They had to call the police, and then he'd call his parents. Yes, that was the logical next step.

"Kale?" Annie spoke behind him. He whirled, startled, to find her standing in the doorway. She'd cleaned off the blood and changed into a Brisby Amusement shirt, and a pair of jean shorts.

"Annie," he said, his voice revealing the tumult in his head. "Why did you wrap him up?"

She walked into the boathouse, glancing at the body. "I knew they'd never believe me. The police. Byron's family has money, connections. One of his uncles is a judge, another is a detective. They'll send me to prison. They'll stop at nothing. I'm a carny, a foster kid, a nobody. The only way is to get rid of him. I tried to do it alone. I was going to drag him up the stairs and push him off the platform. He was too heavy. I didn't want to involve you in this."

Kale rubbed his temples and closed his eyes, searching for the way out of the nightmare they'd descended into. "Annie... we have to call the police." He pulled his phone out. "We have to. We'll unwrap him and set him up right where he was when he... died. And then I'll call my parents. They'll get a lawyer and meet us at the police station."

Annie plucked the phone from him and tucked it into his shirt pocket. "It's too late, Kale. I'm telling you, it doesn't matter who they hire. They'll never defeat Byron's family. We'll both go to prison. I should never have called you. I'm sorry. I've ruined your life."

"No, stop. Don't say that. Come here." He wrapped his arms around her and stroked her hair.

Annie kissed him and clutched his waist. The kiss grew longer, deeper, and despite the horror of the moment, the thing that lay feet away from them, he felt her body pressing against his.

Her hands slid under his shirt, up his back. She pulled his t-shirt over his head, and he picked her up, carrying her outside, intending to take her all the way back to the camper, but once out of the boathouse, she wriggled from his arms and dragged him down into the tall grass. With his shorts around his ankles, she climbed on top of him.

They didn't speak for several minutes after, but lay panting in the grass. Exhaustion tugged at Kale's limbs, beckoned him into the void.

Gathering his courage, he forced himself to stand.

"Where are you going?" she asked.

He stared down at her, beautiful and vulnerable in her nakedness. He had to protect her.

"I'm going to"—he gestured at the boathouse—"take care of it. Maybe I should I should just push it into the water from the first floor."

Annie shook her head. "It will be right under the boathouse then. It needs to be further out in the lake."

He swallowed thickly. "Okay."

She sat up, eyebrows knitted together. "Are you sure?"

He nodded.

"Let me get dressed so I can help you."

He shook his head. "No. It's better if I do it alone."

"Okay."

He started toward the open door.

"Kale?"

"Yeah?" He turned back.

She was holding her shorts bunched in her hands. "There are bricks upstairs, and duct tape. You should… weight it."

His stomach churned. He felt sick. Sick at what he was about to do, sick that they'd just made love feet away from a corpse. Who did that? What kind of person did that? *Me,* he thought. But they'd been desperate and scared, and that brought out something primal in people. They'd needed to comfort one another.

The boathouse stank when he walked in. The scent of the pungent lake mingled with the stench of blood. His vision grew blurry, and he rubbed his eyes. He was strong. He had to be strong for her now.

Not looking at it, he grabbed the edge of the plastic-wrapped body and lugged it up the stairs, cringing each time it thumped against a step. Annie walked through the door beneath him. Their eyes locked for a moment and then he pulled the body onto the second floor.

It was lighter than he expected and when he reached the second level, he realized he'd been holding his breath. He let go of the plastic and walked outside onto the little platform, gulping air.

Across the lake two great blue herons stood in the weedy lake bed. They turned and stared at him. He blinked at the birds, wishing they'd go away, wanting to scream at them so they couldn't watch what he was about to do. Heavy grey clouds filled the sky and the first droplets of rain fell.

He walked back into the boathouse and grabbed the bricks and duct tape. He worked quickly, unspooling tape and ripping it with his teeth, securing bricks to the bottom and top of the body. He attached three bricks to each end, then stood and dragged the body through the door to the end of the platform. Rain spit down from the darkening sky. He lifted the end of the body and for an instant the magnitude of what he was about to do hit him. There was no going back from this moment, no retreating.

Lightning sheared the clouds across the lake, followed by an ear-splitting crack of thunder.

"Rest in peace," Kale murmured. He leaned forward and shoved the body off the edge. As he watched it fall, his phone slipped from the pocket of his shirt. He snatched at it, but caught only air.

The body hit the lake, releasing a plume of water. His phone disappeared behind it.

23

The rain fell constantly, a deluge. It smacked the leaves and pounded the surface of the lake. It was deafening, and Kale felt trapped. Mosquitoes buzzed in the boathouse, filled his already thrumming ears. Annie slept on the mattress, her breath low and deep.

Kale couldn't imagine how. How she could stand even the darkness behind her eyelids. How she could see anything except bloody plastic.

He'd wanted to go back to the camper, had been willing to run for it, but the rain had fallen with such fury they couldn't see. They might have gotten lost on their way. Instead, they'd holed up in the boathouse.

Kale shivered as he sat on the edge of the bed, shifting his gaze from his feet to the double swinging doors that opened to the deck where he'd pushed the body off. The scene replayed in his head. He tried to think of something else—anything else, but it weaseled back in, a broken record he couldn't stop hearing.

Wind rocked the doors. The entire boathouse groaned and shuddered. Every sound made him jump.

Darkness descended and Kale lit two of the candles on the wooden floor. Their flames twisted and quivered.

A crack of lightning lit the sky and, through the opening above the saloon doors, Kale saw the silhouette of a person standing on the outer deck. His eyes bulged and he stood slowly, unable to see anything once the blue glow of the lightning faded. Now the world beyond the doors was tar-black.

But he felt the eyes watching him just the same.

Kale bent down and blew out the candles. The room went instantly black and he swallowed the rising panic. At least now the thing on the deck couldn't see him.

He shuffled along the floor until his toes struck one of the spare bricks. He grabbed it and backed against the wall by the bed, watching and waiting.

~

The rain finally slowed to a drizzle well after midnight. Kale shook Annie awake.

"Let's go to the camper," he whispered.

She rubbed her eyes. "Huh?"

"The camper. I want to sleep in the camper."

"Okay." She stood up groggily.

Kale took her hand and held a flashlight in the other, guiding her down the stairs and out of the boathouse. Their feet squished in the wet grass and drops of water fell from the trees and plopped on their heads. Each sound made Kale jump, and he dragged Annie faster. She said nothing.

At the camper, he yanked the door open and practically shoved Annie up the cinderblock steps.

"Kale, slow down. Jesus, I almost fell on my face."

"I'm sorry," he murmured, crowding in behind her. He shut and locked the camper door.

They walked to the bedroom and Annie crawled into the bed, curling on her side. Kale climbed in beside her, but lay awake, staring at the plywood ceiling. He shifted constantly from his back to his side to his stomach. Sleep eluded him.

Finally, worried he'd wake Annie, he moved to the threadbare couch in the main section of the camper. He lay on his side, legs curled to his chest, and drifted down.

As he dozed, a disturbing vision rolled behind his eyelids. *Something slithered from the lake. It dragged itself along the weedy trail to the camper's door. It wrapped bony fingers, flesh hanging loose, around the handle and pulled.*

Kale woke up gasping. The door faced him, closed. No rotted corpse stood at the entrance.

Pale morning light trickled through the windows. Kale stood, giving up on sleep, and pushed his feet into his shoes. Mouth tasting acrid, he searched the camper cupboards for anything to eat or drink that might remove the taste. Nothing.

He opened drawers on the little kitchenette and found a junk drawer scattered with pens, a heart-shaped keychain with the name 'ELLEN' stamped on the silver finish, and a few boxes of matches. His fingers brushed a metal tin tucked in the back. Kale pulled it out, read the label, which stated 'Fresh Breath Mints.' He popped one in his mouth. It was stale, but better than the taste lingering on his tongue.

Kale opened the trailer door and stepped out, surprised by the chill in the air after waking in the stuffy little camper. The temperature had dropped in the night and a silver mist clung to the grass.

The dream followed him as he cut through the woods and returned to the lake. He felt both compelled toward and repelled by the little body of water.

When he reached the edge, his stomach churned. It was as calm and flat as a sheet of glass. Morning fog drifted above the water and surrounded the cattails at the banks.

When he looked at the platform where he'd pushed the body off the day before, he froze. A young woman stood there, peering down at the water as if searching. A wave of dark hair hung over one side of her face and she seemed vaguely familiar.

Kale needed to hide, to duck behind a tree, to run and wake Annie and insist they leave. He did nothing, just stood and stared.

The girl straightened and slowly swiveled her head in his direction. He recoiled. Her right eye was gone. A bloody hole occupied the space where it had been. Her single good eye glared at him.

Kale stepped back, tripped over thigh-high weeds and went down. He landed on his butt. The ground was wet and mushy and instantly soaked his pants. He scrambled back to his feet and looked again at the girl, but the platform was empty.

He blinked at it and then stared at the boathouse, listening for her thumping down the stairs. No sounds broke the eerily quiet morning. He waited, his heart ramming against his breastbone.

She wasn't coming. Any idiot would recognize what that hole in her face meant.

She was dead.

Kale hurried back to the camper, biting his fingernails, though he'd never in his life been a nail-biter. He'd seen the one-eyed girl previously. Though she'd been less clear during the former sighting, he was positive she was the woman who'd rushed into the bonfire and vanished the week before.

"She can't be real," he reasoned aloud.

His mind was shattered. Lack of sleep, combined with the horrible events of the previous day, had him hallucinating.

He found Annie standing outside the camper, a ratty flannel blanket wrapped around her shoulders.

"Brr…" she said. "It's cold this morning."

"Yeah. Let's get out of here, okay?"

"Can we go somewhere with heat and coffee? We could get breakfast. There's a pancake house in town."

Kale nodded. The thought of food turned his stomach, but he desperately wanted to put some distance between them and the thing in the lake.

K ale followed Annie to a booth by the window. They ordered coffee and Annie asked for a stack of silver dollar pancakes. Though Kale couldn't imagine eating, he ordered an omelet, already thinking about a future investigation and how everything they did in the oncoming hours could someday be twisted to prove their guilt or innocence. Guilt, he thought. That was the truth. They were guilty.

The server returned their coffees, and they sipped in silence. Annie pushed her hair behind her ears and yawned. "This coffee is terrible, but I think I may need an entire pot to wake up this morning. How did you sleep?"

"Not good."

"No? I woke once and noticed you weren't in the bed. Just feeling restless?"

He stared at her. "I couldn't stop thinking about… you know."

The server returned with their breakfasts.

"That was fast," Annie said, pouring syrup onto her pancakes.

Kale waited until the server left, then leaned forward on the table.

"Okay. What do we do here? We've got to… talk about our plan," he whispered.

"What plan?" She added more syrup to her pancakes. The sticky sweetness made him queasy.

He rubbed his temples and looked away from her breakfast. His own omelet was equally repulsive. He couldn't imagine swallowing even a single bite. "Well… the police. If the police question us, we have to have a story. We're each other's alibis, so we need to nail that down."

She took a huge bite and chewed thoughtfully. "We were working at the fair and then we spent the night away together. Simple."

"But… you weren't there. The guys at the midway know you left."

"They'll vouch for me."

"You can't know that."

"Sure, I can. And if one of them says different, you'll correct him. You're the most trustworthy guy working there. The police will never believe one of those lowlifes over you."

"I thought they were your family," Kale murmured.

She fixed her eyes on his. "You're my family now, Kale. I don't need anyone but you."

Kale rubbed the back of his neck. At the booth behind Annie, a family sat. Two little girls in matching pink and white dresses giggled as they mimed feeding their dolls pancakes. To the world outside of him and Annie, it was just another ordinary day.

"I need to know what happened, Annie. How did you end up at the property? How did he end up there?"

Annie took another bite, then wiped her mouth with her napkin. "He showed up at the fair and came after me. I hid and then circled around to Duke's camper, grabbed the keys and ran to his motorcycle. I took off and… I just couldn't think of where else to go, so I went to the property."

"Why didn't you run and find me at the fair? Or just tell one of the other guys?"

"No one was around. Everybody'd gone to the midway and I just… panicked."

Her story sounded ridiculous, the kind of story that a decent detective would poke a thousand holes in, but she'd begun to silently cry. Tears streamed down her cheeks.

"I'm sorry," Kale said, grabbing her hand and squeezing. "I know this can't be easy."

They didn't talk for some time. Annie ate her pancakes and Kale picked at his omelet.

"I do have one more question," he said.

She looked at him, her expression pinched. "Okay."

"What's his last name?"

She frowned. "Why?"

He stared at her. "Because I'd like to know…" He dropped his voice. "Because I'd like to know his full name."

"I think the less you know, the better, Kale."

"And I think we're way past that point."

"Byron Smith."

"Byron Smith?"

She nodded, but he'd noticed something in her voice, a hesitation on the last name, as if she were creating rather than remembering it.

After breakfast, they climbed into Kale's car.

"Can we just go to your house, please? I think it'd be good for both of us, just to be in a safe place. For you especially," Annie said.

"No. God, no. I can't. I can't face them right now."

"Yes, you can."

He considered a hotel room, but he hadn't been paid yet by the carnival and he'd blown off his lawn job in the previous weeks. He had fifty dollars in his wallet and little more in his bank account. If they did get a room, he'd be down to zero.

Maybe it wouldn't be so bad. He could tell his mom they were both feeling ill and just escape to his room. Lucy inevitably would try to force soup and supplements on them, but then she'd leave them alone.

"Okay," he said, unsure if he was making a terrible decision, but too exhausted to give it more thought.

They drove to the house on Chapel Road.

The day was gloomy and dim, an unnatural day in July—the gunmetal sky more appropriate for the depths of winter when the sun often vanished behind the gray curtain of sky for days at a time. It suited the somberness of the moment.

Kale wanted nothing more than a hot shower. He felt the grime of the blood, the mud from the damp ground, even the remnants of his and Annie's lovemaking. He parked in the big driveway and climbed out, trudged up the stairs and into the house. Annie trailed behind him. He couldn't seem to look at her.

"Surprise!" a cacophony of voices screamed as he and Annie stepped into the front hallway.

24

In the living room to Kale's right, a dozen-plus people stood bunched together. His family occupied the front of the group, Stevie, Zach and Ben off to one side.

He saw the decorations then. A table piled with presents, streamers dangling from the ceilings. Blue and green balloons bunched around a banner that read, 'Happy Birthday, Kale!'

He'd completely forgotten about his birthday.

His mother rushed forward and wrapped her arms around him. "Happy birthday, honey. Oh, I'm so excited you're here. I was worried you might not make it."

Kale opened his mouth, but found no sound. His mother grabbed his and Annie's hands and drew them both into the room as his friends and family patted his back and said 'happy birthday.' He caught sight of Annie's expression and realized she'd known about the party. She'd brought him there knowing the surprise awaited them.

Rage bubbled in his stomach. He wanted to grab her and drag her outside and scream at her. She looked at him and her green eyes were tear-filled and apologetic.

I'm sorry, she mouthed.

His anger softened. He was too exhausted to feel it. He needed every ounce of energy he could muster to make it through the minutes, or, worse, hours, that lay ahead.

"Were you surprised?" Zinnia demanded, glancing at Annie as if to gauge whether she'd let the secret slip.

"Very," he said. "I didn't have a clue." He almost admitted he'd forgotten his birthday altogether, but held that back.

Zach slapped Kale on the back. "Now we don't have to bribe anybody to buy us booze."

Kale's mother stopped her conversation and stared at Zach, eyebrow raised.

Zach turned red and held up his palms. "Only kidding, Mrs. Goodwin—I mean Lucy."

"Yeah, right," Zinnia said. "You've been watering down my dad's whiskey since you guys were like fifteen."

"Lies." Zach laughed and in a lowered voice said, "It was usually the vodka."

Kale noticed Stevie watching him from across the room and quickly returned his eyes to the floor.

After he made the rounds, smiling and saying thank you as his friends and family wished him 'happy birthday,' Kale settled on the couch next to Annie.

"Why didn't you tell me?" he whispered, unable to hide the hurt and shock at what she'd done.

"I couldn't, Kale. Your mom and sister said they'd been planning the party for months. They called me a couple days ago and asked me to make sure you were here. It would have been my fault if you hadn't come."

"But you still should have told me," he said through gritted teeth. Anger, sadness, terror washed through him. He wanted to run from the house screaming.

"What are you two whispering about?" his mother asked, appearing with two glasses of champagne. She kissed the top of Kale's head.

"Nothing," Kale murmured.

His mother's eyebrows pulled together as she looked at him. "What is it, Kale? Are you upset about the party?"

Kale shook his head. "No. Not at all. It's great, Mom. I just… I'm not feeling well today, wondering if I might have caught a flu or something."

"Oh, no." She frowned. "Well, you have your cake and champagne, open up presents, and I'll mix you up a firewater and you can have a nap. Hmmm? How's that?"

The thought of firewater made him want to puke, but he nodded weakly. "Sounds good. Thanks, Mom."

His dad carried a large sheet cake decorated with a photo of Kale as a little boy hugging his dog, Ernie. After Frank set it on the coffee table, Kale's mother and Zinnia arranged twenty-one candles around the edges of the cake.

As Zinnia lit the candles, Lucy handed everyone a plastic flute of champagne.

"Happy birthday to you," the partygoers sang, swaying from side to side. Kale stared at his feet, color flushing his face. He feared if he looked anyone in the eye, they'd know the terrible thing he'd done.

The song ended.

"Cheers to Kale," his mother announced.

"Happy birthday, Kale," the voices echoed around the room.

He tilted back his glass of champagne, drank until the cup was empty. It sizzled in his stomach and he clenched his teeth together to fight the rising bile.

He glanced up and saw Sage sitting cross-legged on the carpet, Grover in her lap. She had a concerned expression, which she replaced with a weak smile when their eyes met. The cat's fur stood on end and he watched Kale with suspicious eyes.

Kale's mother cut the cake and passed out the pieces. He forked a bite into his mouth, somehow managed to swallow it. Beside him Annie chatted with Aster, who was asking about life as a carnival worker.

"Time for gifts," Kale's mother said. She and Zinnia carried presents from the table and one by one Kale opened them. A six-pack of beer, a floating cooler, a sheet of uncut leather, an air freshener in the shape of a skunk.

"That one's from me and Ben," Zach announced, snickering, when Kale reached for a yellow gift bag decorated in pink and white unicorns.

Kale pulled out a black t-shirt that read 'Barely Legal' in white letters, a toilet paper roll stamped with the words 'Holy Crap, You're 21,' and a six-pack of Natty Light beer.

"I had to bribe my dad to buy the beer," Zach said, grinning.

"And I had to confirm they were giving it to Kale," Kale's mom added.

"There's also a gift certificate to Taco Tom's in there," Ben said. "The halfway decent gift."

"What are you talking about? That toilet paper is classic," Zach argued.

"Thanks, guys. It's all great." Kale stood up. "I'm going to get a drink of water," he announced. As he left the room, he heard his mom telling the partygoers he didn't feel well.

He grabbed a glass and the pitcher of water from the refrigerator.

Stevie cornered him in the kitchen. "I need to talk to you," she whispered.

He looked up, surprised. "About what?" Sweat trickled beneath his arms. Stevie and he had been friends forever. Could she somehow sense what they'd done? What he'd done?

"First, here. I bought this for you. Open it when you're alone. Not with Annie. Okay?" She thrust something wrapped in newspaper into his hand. It felt like a book.

"What is it?"

"Just open it later."

"What do you want to talk about?"

"Kale?" Annie stood in the doorway. "Can we go upstairs now? I have a headache."

Stevie took a quick step back, as if worried about Annie's reaction to her proximity to Kale.

"Sure," Kale said. "I'm just filling a water. I'll meet you up there."

"I'll wait," Annie said.

"Can we talk later?" he asked Stevie. "Both Annie and I are feeling a little sick."

Her jaw hardened, but she nodded. "Okay. Happy birthday."

"Thanks, and thanks for coming."

"I wouldn't have missed it, Kale."

He saw a sad expression on her face and wished he could take her to the back garden and tell her everything.

"Bye, Stevie," he said.

He poured a glass of water and followed Annie out of the kitchen. He called a quick goodbye to the group and apologized for bowing out early, insisting he felt like he was coming down with something.

In his room, he closed the door and leaned against it, heaving a sigh of relief to be away from everyone's watchful eyes.

"Hey." Annie cupped his face with her hands. "What's wrong, Kale? You've been so quiet."

His eyes drifted closed. He couldn't imagine why she asked the question. She'd been there. She knew what was wrong. "I'm scared, Annie. I'm sick about what happened. We should have called the police."

The expression on her face shifted, hardened. "How can you say that after everything I told you? Both of our lives will be over, Kale. Prison if we're lucky, but more than likely, his vengeful family won't ever let it get that far. They'll go after your family. That's what they do. Hit you where you're the most vulnerable. Do you want Sage's blood on your hands? Or Calla's?"

"Of course not, but… I don't know if I can hold it together. I feel like I'm losing it."

"That's because you're tired, Kale. That's all. Once you sleep, you'll feel better."

He said nothing.

"Listen to me," Annie said, tears staining her pale cheeks. "We have to forget it ever happened. Okay? The way soldiers do, or kids who are abused. Every time it pops into your mind, you have to say, 'That wasn't real. It was only a dream.' And eventually, your subconscious will believe it. It's the only way we can go on. Otherwise, this is going to ruin us, you and me. It's going to steal the best thing we've ever had."

Kale said nothing, leaned over and braced his hands on his knees. He'd forced down the cake and the champagne and suddenly it was all coming up. He lurched across the room to his trash can, barely made it. He vomited into the trash, his eyes and nose dripping. When it was over and he was empty, he lay down and pulled his knees to his chest. Annie crouched beside him.

"Here," she said. She dabbed at his face with a cool washcloth, then handed him the glass of water. "We're going to survive this, Kale. Me and you. Okay?"

He looked at her, at the sun playing in her eyes, so big and sad. He could not imagine hurting her, losing her.

"Let's just lie down for a little while," he murmured. "I'm so tired."

They climbed up the ladder into his loft bed. It creaked beneath their weight. When his head hit the pillow, a vision of the body dropping from the platform into the lake rose into his mind and he crushed it. "It was only a dream," he murmured. "It didn't happen."

*I*t was night, the sky a menagerie of glittering stars. The marshy lake was eerily quiet. No chirps or ribbits. No call from the night birds or the bugs. Kale stood on the edge of the wooden deck on the second story of the boathouse. His arms reached wide to either side.

How had he gotten there? He didn't know. His body, tensed, teetered on the edge, tilting forward. He was unable to step back, to slow the momentum of his body as he fell.

The murky water rushed up to meet him and he met it with a gasp, but no water flooded his lungs. The black water swallowed him and as he sank down, still unable to compel his limbs to move, pale figures swam from the surrounding darkness.

Corpses. White, pale corpses snatched at his clothes and hair. Their slippery hands rubbed across his face. One of them, a woman with stringy pale hair and no eyes, reached her hand into his mouth. Her putrid flesh caught on his teeth and ripped away, choking him. He couldn't close his mouth, recoil, swim away.

He could do nothing as they ravaged him, ripped his hair from his head, tore at his bare arms and legs with their teeth.

25

Kale jerked awake. He thrashed and nearly toppled out of the loft bed.

Kale flung the blankets off and climbed from the bed, brushing at his arms, the sensation of being clawed and bitten still present on his clammy skin.

Annie slept, her breath whispering through the darkness.

Kale started from the room, then stopped. He grabbed the gift Stevie had given him earlier that day. He crept into the hall and down the stairs. Lights shone in the backyard and he heard voices—some of the partygoers still hanging around, probably having a bonfire, reminiscing.

Part of him ached to go out there, step into the fold of his family and friends, but he couldn't face them, knew his façade was wobbling.

He took the stairs into the basement. His parents had converted four of the rooms in the basement into spaces for the family—the movie theater, the laundry room, the craft room, and an enormous storage room stuffed with holiday décor and old toys. At the far end of the hall, the former embalming room remained untouched. Their father had intended to sell the old embalming equipment, and several caskets left over from the funeral business, but he'd never gotten around to it.

It was the one room that was always empty in the house and though it was a room Kale had avoided most of his life, he stepped in there now. He sat on a hard plastic chair, averted his eyes from the old caskets and embalming equipment. He unwrapped the gift.

It was a book, *How to Know if You're in a Toxic Relationship*. The image on the front showed two silhouettes. One figure appeared to be hunched over crying. The second figure had their back turned on them.

"Gee, thanks, Stevie." He muttered, flipping through the pages.

Ten Signs Your Partner is Toxic

1. They're controlling and jealous.

2. They isolate you from your family and friends.

3. They use your loyalty to convince you to do things you normally wouldn't.

4. You feel unsafe with them.

5. They tell lies.

6. They don't bring out the best in you.

7. You're not optimistic about the future.

8. You walk on eggshells when you're around them...

He sighed and closed the book, leaned forward and rested his head in his hands.

A sound came from the drain in the floor, a gurgling.

Kale squinted at the metal grate. The sound came again, and this time it was less of a liquid sound and more like a voice. He stood and walked closer, leaned down. Were the voices of one of his family members somehow carrying through the plumbing?

"Kale... I know, Kale..."

He knelt near the drain, straining to make sense of the words. Black water that smelled of swamp and decay burbled up through the grate.

"I KNOW WHAT YOU DID, KALE!" the voice suddenly shrieked. The boggy water splattered his face.

Kale fell back and smacked his head on the edge of the plastic chair. The book in his hand skittered across the floor. He scrambled to his feet, out the door and into the hall. He slammed the door shut behind him and leaned against the wall, trying to catch his breath. His face, which he'd expected to be wet with the fetid water from the drain, was dry.

"Kale?" He jumped at the sound of his name. Sage stood at the opposite end of the hall.

"Oh, Sage. It's you. You startled me."

"What are you doing down here?"

"I... umm... couldn't sleep."

"It's because of Annie."

Kale frowned. "What do you mean?"

Sage tilted her head as if listening to someone. "They don't want me to say."

"Who doesn't want you to say?"

"Sage? Are you downstairs, honey?" Lucy called and then her feet appeared as she plodded down the steps. "Oh, Kale. You're down here too? Are you feeling better?"

"A little. I'm heading back upstairs now." He ruffled his sister's hair. "Good night, Sage."

His mother caught his hand and kissed it.

"Night, Mom."

"I love you, birthday boy."

"I love you too."

S omehow Kale slept, but he didn't wake refreshed. A headache lurked behind his eyes as he opened them to sun bathing his room in morning light.

Annie was already up. "I just got out of the shower," she announced, towel-drying her hair. "God, that felt good. I forget what it's like to have an actual hot shower with decent water pressure. You should get in before we head back to the fair grounds."

"We're going back to the fair? Do you think that's a good idea?"

"Yes, I do. Duke is gonna be pissed about his motorcycle, but he'll get over it. We'll have to drive back to the property to get it. Plus, it's like you said, we need to act normally. Going back to the fair is the normal thing for us to do."

"But... what are we going to say?"

"I'm going to eat crow. We're going to make up a really good story about why we missed set-up, and... they'll let us back on."

"Mo doesn't seem like a very sympathetic boss."

"You'd be surprised," she said. "Anyway, don't worry. Let me do the talking."

Kale fiddled with the corner of his pillowcase. "Maybe... maybe we shouldn't go back."

Annie draped her towel over the back of his chair and stared at him. "And do what, Kale? I told you, the midway is my life. I don't have this"—she gestured at the room—"this family and this house and this life waiting for me."

"You could have it with me. We could stay here for a little while and—"

"Why?"

"Why?"

"Yes, why? Two days ago, you were all in. Me and you against the world. And now you just want to throw it all away?"

"No, it's not that at all."

Annie's eyes welled.

He stood and wrapped his arms around her. "I'm…" He wanted to say yet again that he was scared, terrified about what they'd done.

"I know you're worried, Kale, but let me tell you how I feel. Free."

"Free?"

"Yes, free for the first time in years. I've been running for years and now…" She seemed to marvel at the thought. "I'm liberated. He's gone. He'll never hurt me again. I am totally free."

"I didn't think about that," Kale admitted. And he hadn't. What had it been like for her? Years of running from a stalker who had connections to police? Who seemed above the law?

"If you need to quit the carnival, then quit. I'm not going to make you stay with me, Kale. I love you too much for that. But please, for me, don't ever tell anyone. I am finally, for the first time in longer than I can remember, light, as light as a cloud."

"You're right. Of course you're right. I'm sorry. It was you or him, and the world is better off."

"And we're not going to talk about it anymore. Okay? After this moment right now. Can we do that? Can we never speak about it again?"

He wished it were that simple to erase it from his mind, but he nodded. He might never be able to extinguish the memories of that bloody body bag tipping into the water, but he could bite his tongue. Annie was right. If they were going to have any kind of future, they needed to let it go, forgive each other and themselves.

~

"Good morning, you two," Lucy chirped when Kale and Annie walked into the kitchen. "I'm afraid you missed the other kids. They've all gone off to do chores except Sage, who went back to bed. But I made buckwheat pancakes."

"Thanks, Mom," Kale said, grabbing two mugs and filling each with coffee. He handed one to Annie, who sat at the table.

"Annie, can I make you a plate?" Lucy asked.

"Thanks, that'd be great," Annie told her. "I'm starving."

Lucy heaped several pancakes on a plate and set the plate in front of Annie. She pointed at a glass pitcher shaped like a cow. "That's syrup. I also have peanut butter, if you prefer."

"No. Syrup is great."

Kale shook his head when his mother tried to hand him a plate of pancakes.

"Kale." She narrowed her eyes at him. "You need to eat. Even if you're not hungry."

"I'll have a banana," he said, grabbing one from the fruit bowl.

"What are you two up to today?" Lucy asked.

"Back to the fair," Kale said, unable to disguise the reluctance in his voice.

"Do you have to? Why don't you both stay here and rest?"

"No, we have to go back," Annie said. "We'll be fired if we don't."

Lucy frowned, but didn't push the subject.

They drove to the property, but stayed only long enough for Annie to jump on Duke's motorcycle. Kale followed her in his car back to the fair. Her dark hair blew out behind her and she appeared lighter, more free, as she herself had said. Kale had to keep this secret for her sake. She'd had a hard enough life without his conscience sending them both to prison.

They parked at the fairgrounds and started toward the midway. As they approached the work trailers, Duke broke away from a small crowd near the shower trailer. He was red-faced, his fists at his sides.

Annie didn't back down, but as they got closer, Kale grabbed her hand and stepped in front of her.

"Where the fuck is my bike?" Duke spat, trying to push Kale out of the way.

"Whoa, back off." Kale shoved Duke.

Duke sidestepped him and lunged again for Annie. She raked her fingernails across his cheek. He cocked a fist back, but Kale jumped in front of it, taking the punch to his shoulder.

Duke tried again to reach for Annie, but the other carnies had noticed the commotion. Mo raced toward them, grabbed a handful of

Duke's shirt and shoved the man away. Duke jumped to his feet and got in Mo's face.

"That little bitch stole my bike!" he screamed. "What are you gonna do about it, Mo?"

Mo held up an arm, blocking Duke from getting by him.

Annie, who moments earlier had looked ready to claw Duke's eyes out, burst into tears. She dropped to her knees. "I'm sorry, I'm sorry," she sobbed, holding up the keys to Duke's motorcycle.

Kale looked from Annie weeping on the ground to Mo, whose fierce expression grew confused. "What the hell is going on, Kale?"

"She… we… Something happened, something bad. Can we talk in private, Mo?"

Mo snatched the keys from Annie's hand and thrust them at Duke. "Duke, take a walk, cool off. Your bike is right there. It looks just fine."

Duke grabbed the keys and strode to his motorcycle. He climbed on and spit dirt at them as he squealed from the lot.

"Annie, you better have a damn good reason for this shit."

"She does," Kale started, but he had no idea what to say. The only story that rose into his mind was the truth.

"I do," she said quickly, cutting Kale off. "Kale found out his sister has cancer."

Kale stiffened beside her.

"His baby sister. I just… panicked and went to find him, but I forgot my cell phone and I got lost and… and…" Her eyes welled up and spilled over.

Mo's gaze shifted from Annie to Kale. "Is that true?"

Kale nodded, hoping Mo didn't remember Annie had disappeared from the midway hours before Kale left. His eye twitched, and he smoothed it with his fingers, swallowing the bile suddenly rising into his throat. He took a step away, sure he was about to be sick.

"Kale… Are you okay?" Annie put a hand on his back.

"Yeah… I'm just…" Kale took a deep breath and stood up straight.

"Your sister's sick?" Mo asked.

"Yes, Sage. She has a brain tumor."

Mo's expression remained hard, but after a moment he nodded slowly. "My own sister died of cancer. Cancer is a nasty business. I was ready to can you both after this. Understand? It can't ever happen again. And you"—he pointed a finger at Annie—"steer clear of Duke. You still got a job, but you ain't gonna have a head if you cross that guy again, and I'm not puttin' up with this monkey business. You need to go somewhere, take the damn bus."

Mo stalked away. After he was gone, Annie grabbed Kale's arm and pulled him close.

"I'm sorry. I'm so sorry I used Sage being sick. I couldn't think what else to say, and I knew if you told him the truth he'd call the police and things would get so much worse. Can you forgive me?"

Kale nodded. "Let's just go get changed. We don't have much time before the carnival starts."

<h1 style="text-align:center">26</h1>

They didn't speak of it and for Annie, it seemed, forgetting was not hard. And for hours at a time, Kale, too, could forget.

During the carnival he was busy, distracted. In the moments when the midway was buzzing and the lines for whatever ride he worked were growing longer, the memory of what they'd done faded. When laughter and shouts and music filled the air, he could get carried away from that horrible moment at the lake, but at night… at night, it all came rushing back.

He stood beneath the lukewarm spray in the bunkhouse shower, scrubbing furiously at his skin. The day had been long and hot, but it wasn't sweat from the day he wanted to scrape away. It was the memory, the sensation of the plastic beneath his fingers, the stickiness of blood that had clung to him from Annie's bloody hands and clothes.

He climbed into the tent with Annie, but when she tried to make love, he couldn't perform.

"You're just tired," she assured him. "Get some sleep. Tomorrow will be better."

He agreed with her, and after hours of listening to the dwindling voices of the other carnies, he fell asleep.

Kale was back at the boathouse, standing on the deck that overlooked the lake. The water bubbled and thrashed. Slimy heads, flesh dripping, poked from the dark water. They were an army of the dead surrounding the boathouse, shoving through the doors, dragging their withered bodies up the stairs. They scaled the weather-beaten exterior. Their fingernails splintered and chipped off. Their skin slid away, leaving gaping chasms into their ribs and chest cavities.

Kale stood frozen. There was nowhere to run, no way to escape.

The saloon-style doors swung open and the woman with one eye staggered through them. She didn't slow, but charged at Kale, her rotted lips peeling away from filthy teeth.

She hit him and they tumbled off the platform toward the frenzied water below.

Kale woke slick with sweat. He turned his head and saw Annie asleep beside him. Shivering, he stared at the roof of the tent and waited for the dawn.

The following several nights at the carnival passed in a blur. When closing night rolled around, Kale didn't look well. He'd caught sight of himself in the mirror during a bathroom break and barely recognized the person staring back at him. His eyes were bloodshot, his face sallow. He'd barely slept after the previous night's horrific dreams. He'd barely slept in days.

That morning, Annie had plied him with coffee and donuts and insisted he take a nap before the show, but he'd merely lain in the tent, afraid to fall asleep and again meet the one-eyed woman at the lake.

He forced himself along the midway, emptying trash, smiling at customers, offering breaks to his fellow carnies.

Kale saw a woman pushing a cart filled with buckets of long-stemmed red roses. "Can I get one of those?" Kale asked the woman as he dug a few dollars from his wallet. It felt like eons had passed since the easy, love-filled days of his and Annie's earlier courtship.

"Ah, yes, a rose for the one you love. Take your pick."

Kale chose one in full bloom. It wouldn't last long. They didn't exactly have a water-filled vase to put it in. As he started toward the Pirate Ship, he passed Cliff coming the opposite way.

Cliff eyed the rose and sneered. "Man, does she have you fooled."

Kale intended to ignore the comment, but he took only a few steps and turned back. "What's that supposed to mean?" he demanded.

Cliff turned and smiled. "You're a smart college boy, ain't ya? Let me give ya a hint. That girl runs the best con in this whole place and you're the easiest mark I ever seen."

"Screw off," Kale muttered.

"Ever asked yourself what happens to the posters of the missing girls?" Cliff asked cryptically.

"What are you even talking about?" Kale was irritated with himself for playing into the guy's hands, showing even a remote interest in his comment.

"I saw her once—Annie. She tore one of the posters down and ate it. Ripped it into tiny little pieces and stuffed them into her mouth. Swallowed the whole thing."

"Whatever, Cliff. Stay away from Annie and stay away from me."

Kale turned and stormed away. He'd squeezed the rose too hard, and a thorn had pricked the soft flesh between his thumb and forefinger. A drop of blood bloomed on his skin and he slowed, a wave of dizziness sweeping through him. He saw again the blood trapped beneath the plastic, heard the splash as the body hit the lake.

"Whoa there, spinach," Vinnie said, grabbing hold of Kale's shoulder. "You about stepped right in a pile of horse dung."

Kale shook the man off, grumbled a half-hearted "thank you," and stepped around the horse manure. He'd broken the stem of the rose and though he could have easily given Annie the top half, he walked it to a trash can and tossed it inside.

"Hey, Kale!"

He looked up and saw Stevie striding toward him.

"Hey." He patted at his hair, as if that might improve his haggard appearance. "What are you doing here?"

"I found your location on the Brisby website, figured out this is where you'd be tonight."

"Okay, well, thanks. It's good to see you. I like the new shirts." He pointed at her blue and green tie-dye shirt with the name of their lawn company, Lawn Slayers, in funky white letters.

"Thanks. Zach had them made. We've got one for you if you ever come back."

Kale crossed his arms. "I will eventually. I just—"

"It's fine." Stevie waved him off. Her gaze darted around. She turned and glanced behind her.

"What's wrong?" he asked. "Who are you looking for?"

She stepped closer to him, dropped her voice. "Listen, I need to talk to you. It's kind of urgent. Can you meet me tonight? Alone?"

"Why? What's up? Is it Sage?" His stomach dropped.

"No. It's not Sage, but it's important. No Annie, just you."

He frowned, knew Annie'd be upset if he left her behind. "What am I supposed to tell her? She'll be pissed if I just leave."

"Say I'm having guy troubles, needed some insight."

He raised an eyebrow. "Guy troubles?"

"Just say it, Kale. Meet me in town. There's a Denny's. It's open all night."

"Okay. I can be there by ten thirty, maybe a little earlier. It's closing night and we'll be tearing everything down, so I can't stay long."

"Thank you." She threw her arms around him and whispered in his ear, "Be careful."

"What? Why?"

She pulled away. "We'll talk about it tonight."

As Stevie walked toward the parking lot, Kale noticed Annie near the bathrooms watching her go. He expected Annie to approach him, ask what Stevie wanted, but she merely turned back toward the Pirate Ship.

After Stevie left, Kale walked to the Lucky Duck game and gave the carny working it a break. He struggled to focus on the contestants and didn't bother attempting to draw in players. He wanted to know what Stevie had to tell him. Equally he dreaded seeing her, convinced she'd discovered what he and Annie had done. He wracked his brain trying to imagine how she could have found out, but though it seemed impossible, he couldn't shake the fear she was going to confront him about his participation in covering up a murder.

At the close of the carnival, he searched for Annie. He checked their tent and the bunk trailer and asked several of the guys, but no one had seen her.

He finally asked Margaret to tell her he'd gone to see a friend and would return soon. As he drove from the parking lot, he slowed.

A silver Volkswagen Jetta occupied a space at the edge of the lot. It looked similar to the car he'd seen the woman with the gold scarf climb into at the Muskegon fair—the woman who'd been searching for Annie. He stared at it for a moment, wishing he'd paid more attention the previous time he'd seen it, noticed some distinction, but nothing stood out.

He dismissed it and headed for the diner.

K ale arrived at Denny's at ten thirty p.m. He eyed the tables, searching for Stevie. She wasn't there. He stepped outside, looked up and down the street for her car. She'd parked it across the road at one of the meters.

Kale crossed the street and peered into the driver's side. Empty. He walked to the shops behind the car and gazed through the windows, but most of them were closed and dark.

The far-off sound of a police siren echoed. It grew closer. The flashing red and blue lights pierced the dark. Kale's body grew cold as he watched the police cruiser turn onto the street where he stood. It screeched to a stop just a block in front of him. Behind it an ambulance barreled down the road, its lights and sirens joining the police car.

Kale walked slowly toward the emergency vehicles and then he ran, tripped on the curb and flew forward. He landed hard on his palms, felt the impact reverberate into his shoulders. He scrambled back to his feet and into the alleyway.

A group of people stood several yards down. Paramedics carrying a stretcher parted the onlookers. Two policemen ushered the crowd back.

Kale caught a glimpse of something—no, someone—lying on the concrete. He saw the unmistakable tie-dye shirt.

"Stevie," he whispered, plunging forward.

A cop caught him around the waist.

"That's my friend," Kale shouted. "Stevie!"

Her face was bloody. For a moment as the stretcher passed, he saw her up close. Her eyes were swollen shut; blood had turned her blonde hair dark. She looked dead.

Kale sat in the long, too-bright hospital corridor. No one had been out to give him details and, when the swinging doors opened at the opposite end, his body tensed. It wasn't a doctor, but Stevie's parents, Joe and Miriam, hurrying toward him. Stevie's older brother, Jacob, followed on their heels.

Kale stood, and Miriam rushed to him. She burst into tears.

"Kale, what happened? The police called us. They said Stevie was hurt. Where is she?" Joe spoke fast and loud. His face looked pasty, his eyes wild beneath the fluorescent lights.

"Kale..." Miriam tried. "Is she... have they...?" She couldn't get out the words.

"Have they said how she is?" Jacob asked. "They didn't tell us anything on the phone. Dad said they just told him to get down here right away."

Kale looked between their faces, his own tears threatening. "I don't know. They haven't been out. I asked a nurse, and she said she'd tell someone to come out, but that was a half hour ago and there's been nothing."

The doors at the end of the hall opened again. This time, a man in a white coat stepped through. A police officer flanked him.

Joe broke from the group and strode toward the two men. "Where's my daughter? Is she okay?"

"Mr. Duran?"

"Yes, I'm Joe Duran. Please, how's Stevie? Is she okay? Can we see her?"

Miriam clutched Kale's hand as her husband, the doctor, and officer advanced towards them. The seconds stretched. Shoes slapped linoleum as the men got closer.

"Stevie is stable," the doctor explained. "She's suffered a major head injury and we've put her in a medically induced coma as we wait for the swelling in her brain to go down."

Breath rushed from Miriam's lips and she sagged against Kale.

"She's alive," Kale whispered, his own knees weakening at the news.

"Can we see her? I need to see her," Miriam insisted.

"Yes. You can't go in the room just now, but you can see her through the window."

"You're Kale Goodwin?" the officer asked.

Kale looked at him and nodded.

"I'd like you to accompany me back to the station, if you could— answer a few questions."

"Yeah, of course."

"I'll call you as soon as she wakes up," Miriam told him.

"Thank you." Kale followed the officer, then paused. "Umm... Mrs. Duran, I lost my cell phone. Can you call my girlfriend's phone? Annie?"

"Yes, of course. What's the number?"

Kale gave her Annie's phone number, and then left with the police officer.

"Let's just go through your day," the detective advised Kale.

"Starting with... umm... what? Waking up or—?" Kale asked.

"Start with when you and Stevie decided to meet."

Kale rotated his paper cup of water on the chipped table. "Umm... okay, yeah. She came to the carnival earlier tonight, or I guess yesterday evening. I wasn't expecting her. She just showed up and said she had something important she wanted to talk to me about. She asked if I could meet her at the Denny's. I said sure, after the midway closed at ten. I got there about ten thirty and went into the diner, but didn't see her. Her car was parked down the block and I looked for her. That's when I heard the sirens and I saw the police. I had a bad feeling, so I ran into the alley and I saw her."

"Why did she want to meet?"

"She didn't say."

"You have no idea whatsoever?"

Kale picked at the wax rim on his water cup. He saw Stevie's face again and then her bloody hair as the paramedics led her away. That image dissolved into another—the body as it fell from the platform, the sound it had made as it hit the water. Some sick part of him wanted to blurt it all out, unburden himself of that horrible truth, but it had nothing to do with Stevie. The cop wasn't here for that, and admitting it now would only muddy the investigation into Stevie's assault.

"No... I... my sister is sick. She has cancer. She had it and then got better and recently it came back and I thought... I thought it might have something to do with Sage, my sister."

"Stevie and your sister are friends?"

"Not exactly. Sage is only twelve, but Stevie and I have been friends since we were babies. She knows my whole family. She talks to my other sister, Zinnia, pretty regularly, and I thought maybe Zinnia told her something and she was passing it on to me, something to do with Sage."

"Why wouldn't your sister have told you directly?"

Kale shrugged. "I don't know. She would have, maybe... but I lost my cell phone. I've been working for Brisby Amusements. I've been on the road and busy, so not super-available."

"I see. But Stevie knew how to find you. Were you in regular communication with her?"

"She looked up the midway schedule. Before she showed up, I hadn't talked to her since the other day. She came to my surprise birthday party at my parents' house."

"Does Stevie have any enemies? Anyone who'd want to hurt her?"

Kale gaped at him. "Enemies? God, no. You think someone who knew her did this? Not just a random thief or whatever?"

"We have to consider every possibility right now."

"But how would they know she was there? Stevie lives in Muskegon. That's where we're from."

"Someone might have followed her. Did you tell anyone at the carnival you were meeting her? Any other workers?"

"No. No one. I just can't believe anyone who knows Stevie would hurt her. She's a really good person, kind, funny. It doesn't make sense."

"Crimes like this rarely do. It's odd how badly she was beaten. A person trying to grab a wallet can do that without nearly murdering someone."

The color drained from Kale's face. He felt sick. "Murder? You think someone tried to kill her?"

"She was hit in the head with a blunt object two, maybe three times. One time would have incapacitated her. The additional blows were meant to do more than render her unconscious."

"Oh, God…" Kale rubbed his face.

"You said she visited you at the fair?"

"Yes."

"And what time was that?"

"Around eight."

"And then what happened?"

"She left, and I worked the Lucky Duck game until ten and then I went to the diner."

"But you didn't get there until ten thirty?"

"No. I had to close the game and then I looked for my girlfriend to tell her I was leaving."

"She didn't go with you?"

"No. I couldn't find her."

"How would she have felt about you meeting another young woman?"

"Fine, I'm sure. There's no…" Kale shook his head. "We're just friends, and Annie knows that."

"Annie's your girlfriend's name?"

"Yes."

"Annie what?"

"Annie Carson."

"She's not the jealous type?"

"Not at all."

"And do you have any idea what Stevie did after she saw you at the fair? Did she hang around, ride some rides?"

"No. She left right after she talked to me. I watched her walk to the parking lot."

"That leaves two hours unaccounted for. What do you think she did during that time?"

"I have no idea. Maybe went to some shops or… I don't have a clue. You could look at her phone, right? See if she texted or talked to anyone?"

"We didn't find a phone or a wallet."

"Damn."

"Yeah, but you could help by writing down her other close friends. People in your circle. Maybe she spoke with some of them."

"Okay, sure." Kale scrawled the names and phone numbers for Zach and Ben.

"Did you see anyone near the alley? Anyone walking on the street?"

"No one. There were people in the diner, but that was it."

"Is there anything else, Kale? Anything that might be important?"

"Nothing comes to mind."

"All right." The detective handed him his card. "If you think of anything that might be relevant, give me a call."

∼

It was nearly four in the morning when Kale finally returned to the fair. He could barely hold his head up. He walked, limbs heavy, to his and Annie's tent. Kale unzipped it, but she wasn't inside. He eyed the sleeping bag, the two pillows side by side. He wanted so badly to crawl in and fall asleep, but he forced himself up and swiveled his head in search of her.

No sign of her amid the handful of carnival workers still awake. The sound of Vinnie's violin drifted from his camper as Kale trekked toward the midway. The full moon offered enough light for him to see as he walked among the darkened rides.

He found her at the carousel sitting on the dragon. She hadn't heard him approach, and he watched her. She had the side of one of her hands in her mouth and she was gnawing at the flesh, her eyes dull and sightless. She'd broken the skin and a line of blood dripped over her wrist.

He blinked at her, suddenly scared, not of her, but for her. Something was wrong with Annie and, though he thought it might be the horrible thing they'd done, he flashed back to the vision of her ripping the paper into the stream at the property. She'd looked similarly detached, almost insane.

"Annie?" He spoke her name and her hand fell to her side.

159

She squinted at him, her mouth dark with her own blood. "Where were you?" she hissed.

"I went to meet Stevie and… something happened to her. She was attacked and beaten."

Annie's expression didn't change. Her eyes, still oddly blank, remained locked on his. Seconds lapsed and Kale began to sweat.

Finally, she moved, swinging one leg over the dragon. She dropped off and trudged across the platform, wiping one arm across her mouth.

"Let's just go to bed," she said, walking past him toward the tents.

28

In the morning, Annie acted as if nothing unusual had occurred the night before. She didn't comment on the swollen red flesh around her thumb. She didn't ask about Stevie.

They spent the day breaking down the rides at the carnival and transporting them to the next location in Whitehall. By midnight, they were assembled, and unlike the previous tear-downs and set-ups, this one had not been filled with lingering glances and the brush of each other's fingers as they passed on the midway. Kale moved zombie-like and, when the work was done, he showered and climbed into the tent, kissing Annie stiffly before lying on the sleeping bag and pretending to fall asleep.

The following day, Kale emerged from the tent to find a cheerful Annie. She pecked him on the mouth and handed him a cup of coffee.

"We have today off to run errands," she said. "I thought we could do laundry, grab some groceries, and then do something fun. How's that sound?"

Kale blinked at her, the sun piercing his tired eyes. He'd had nightmares again the previous night. They lingered. He felt exhausted. "Umm… actually, I think I'd better run to the hospital and see how

Stevie's doing. Then I'd like to stop home and visit Sage and check in. Is that okay? I could be back by noon and we could do errands and stuff."

Annie's face darkened, but after a moment, she nodded. "I could go with you."

"I should go alone. Quality time with Sage and all."

Annie said nothing, but the set of her jaw told him she was bothered by his decision. "I'm going to take a shower." She grabbed her shower kit and walked away without a backward glance.

He'd upset her, he knew, but he wanted to talk with Zach and Ben, try to figure out what Stevie had intended to tell him. She'd made it clear she didn't want Annie present for the discussion and, as much as he hated to admit it, he wanted some time away from Annie. He needed to think, clear his head.

Kale arrived at the hospital to find Stevie's mom in the waiting room. The space smelled of burnt coffee and a muted television played the morning news.

"Hi, Mrs. Duran. How's Stevie doing?" Kale asked, hovering in the waiting room doorway.

Stevie's mom gave him a tired smile and set aside a copy of *Woman's World*. "She's the same—stable, but not awake. Zach was already up here this morning, but the doctors aren't letting us go back. He got to peek in the window at her and that was it. You can too if you'd like. Just go to the intercom over there and they'll buzz you back."

"Thanks, I'll do that."

Kale went to the intercom next to the gray electronic doors. He hit the call button.

"Yes?"

"I'm here to see Stevie Duran. I know she can't have visitors. I just wanted to look in on her."

"Come through the doors and turn right. She's in Room 319. Don't knock on the glass."

The door beeped and swung open. Kyle walked through and turned, making his way to 319. He leaned toward the window, cringing at the sight of his best friend. She lay in the stiff white bed, most of her head wrapped in thick gauze. The parts of her face exposed were a mottled black and blue. A tube ran into her nose and IVs snaked away from her wrist. Always tan from working in the summer sun, her face appeared bloodless.

He leaned his forehead on the glass. "I'm sorry," he whispered.

Someone walked up and stood beside him. He glanced at their reflection in the window and froze. The one-eyed woman stood on his right. Her single eye was fixed, not on Stevie, but on his face in the window.

He turned slowly, but no one occupied the space, apparition or otherwise.

At the end of the hall, a nurse pushed a man in a wheelchair toward him. She smiled sympathetically, as if she knew how injured the girl in Room 319 really was.

Kale hurried back down the corridor and into the waiting room. He was fighting tears. "Did Zach say where he was going, Mrs. Duran?"

"He said he had a bunch of lawns to mow and then planned to come back this evening, but I told him to hold off until she woke up. No point in all of us sitting in this dreary place. When she's awake, you guys will be the first to know."

"Thanks, I appreciate that. I'll see you later."

"Bye, Kale."

K ale climbed into his car and drove to a nearby cell phone store. He explained that he'd lost his phone and needed a replacement. New phone in hand, he called home.

"Mom?"

"Oh, goodness, I've been worried about you. How's Stevie?"

"I just left the hospital. She's still in the coma, but stable."

"Thank the Lord. You tell Miriam we're praying for Stevie."

"I will. How's Sage?"

"We're taking it day by day. She had her first round of a new chemo yesterday, so last night was tough, but she's up this morning and eating breakfast. She told me and Dad she's riding her bike today." Lucy laughed, but her throat sounded thick, as if her laughter was competing with her tears.

"I'm going to come home soon to see her, and you guys too. The carnival just moved to Whitehall, so hopefully in the next few days."

"That will be nice. I miss you, honey. And Kale… is everything okay?"

"Sure."

"You know you can talk to me. You can tell me anything."

"I know, Mom. Thank you."

She sighed. "All right then. I'll tell everyone you said Hi."

"Give Sage a big hug for me."

"I will. Bye, Kale."

"Bye, Mom." Kale ended the call and dialed Zach's phone number, but he got no response.

Next, he texted Ben.

Kale: You guys mowing lawns today?

Ben: I'm down with the flu. Zach's at the Neff property.

Kale: Thanks. I'm going to stop by and talk to him. Maybe I could come see you after.

Ben: I'll be here at home.

Kale drove to the Neff property in Muskegon and parked in the circular driveway behind Zach's pickup and trailer.

He inhaled deeply. He hadn't realized he'd missed the smell in the previous days, the scent of a freshly mowed lawn that so reminded him of Stevie, Zach and Ben.

"Hey, man. How's it going?" Kale asked.

Zach looked up from the flower bed he'd been dumping mulch onto. "Been better. We've gone from a four-man team down to two. One of my best friends is in a coma. The other one is chasing some nutcase across the state. Oh, and Ben has the flu, so I'm flying solo today, which means a property that used to take two hours is going to take me two days."

Kale blinked at Zach, the laid-back friend who rarely got upset about anything. "I'm sorry. I… I can't believe about Stevie. I feel sick about it."

"You should. She was doing your dirty work, after all."

"What does that mean?"

"It means"—Zach dumped the last of the mulch and walked to his trailer—"that she was looking into the background of your new girl-friend, who apparently doesn't even exist."

"What are you even talking about?"

Zach picked up his sound-canceling headphones in one hand, chainsaw in the other. "I don't know, man. Talk to Ben. She told him more about what she was up to, but what I heard wasn't good." Zach stuffed the headphones over his ears, walked to a tree, and started the chainsaw.

Kale frowned at him, guilt at having abandoned his friends replaced by fear of what he might discover.

～

"Kale!" Ben's mother stood outside Ben and Zach's small rental house, stuffing a bag of trash in the green bin by the driveway.

"Hi, Mrs. Young. How are you?"

She closed the lid on the trash can and wiped her hands on her pleated black pants. She strode to Kale and wrapped her arms around him, patting his back. "I cannot even believe about Stevie. What in the world is going on with people today? And I am so very sorry to hear about Sage, honey. How is your mom holding up?"

"She's okay," Kale said when Mrs. Young pulled away. "Keeping busy. That's her way of coping."

"Oh, the poor dear. Let her know I'm going to make a quiche and bring it by this weekend. And how about Stevie? Any news?"

"I was up there this morning and… no change, really. But she's stable."

"I am so glad to hear she's stable, at least."

"Is Ben in there?"

Mrs. Young brightened up and nodded. "He's in there all right. Nasty stomach bug, but he took a turn for the better this morning. He's tired now and his body aches. I brought over soup. There's plenty if you'd like some. Chicken and rice."

"Thanks, Mrs. Young. I might do that."

Kale said goodbye and walked into the little bungalow. He found Ben in the living room, stretched long on the couch. A superhero movie played on the television.

"Kale, hey." Ben muted the television and sat up a little higher, bunching an extra pillow behind him.

"How are you feeling? You've been sick?" Kale sat in a cracked leather chair.

"Better. I wondered if I got a touch of what you had at your birthday party."

"Yeah, maybe." Kale fidgeted in his chair.

"Any word on Stevie?"

"Still not awake, but stable. She should wake up soon hopefully."

Ben sighed against his pillows. "This flu couldn't have come at a worse time; I haven't even been able to go see her. Zach's been swamped with the business and I've barely stepped twenty feet from the bathroom."

"I'm sorry, man," Kale said. "I feel like this is all my fault."

"It's not your fault, Kale. Some thug saw Stevie and wanted to rob her. If you'd have been with her, you probably both would have gotten bashed in the head."

"Maybe, but... I don't know. It's not only what happened to Stevie. I bailed on you guys, the business, everything."

"We're mowing lawns, not curing cancer." Ben winced. "Shoot, sorry. That was in bad taste. How is Sage?"

Kale rubbed his jaw. "Holding her own. I need to go see her. But I wondered if you know why Stevie wanted to talk to me. She showed up out of the blue at the midway, said she had something urgent to talk about, and Zach mentioned her looking into Annie."

Ben looked away, as if uncomfortable at the question. He grabbed a tissue and blew his nose, then aimed at the little trash can across the room. He tossed the tissue. It missed and landed next to the TV.

"I've got it," Kale said, starting to stand.

"Nah, leave it. You don't want to get this crud. I've got to use the bathroom, anyway." Ben stood, braced his hand against the wall as if light-headed, then made his way to the tissue. He threw it in the trash and then walked down the hall, disappeared into the bathroom.

When he returned a minute later, Kale wondered if he'd forgotten the question, but then he started to talk.

"A few days ago, Stevie and I were working on the Frasier property and she started talking about your girlfriend."

"Annie."

"Yeah, except... she seemed to think her name wasn't Annie. In fact, Stevie came up with another name, Norma. She'd found someone named Norma who kind of looked like Annie who'd gone missing from..." Ben scrunched his face as if trying to remember. "Ummm..." Ben held up his hand as a cough cut off his words. He thumped his chest and then cleared his throat. "Ugh, this is miserable. Anyway, Norma was from some place southeast, Lansing area, I think. At least it started with an L."

Kale remembered the driver's license he'd found in Annie's bag. The city had been Leslie. He couldn't believe he remembered it. "Leslie?" he asked.

"Yep. That's it. Leslie. I've never heard of it. Stevie started talking online to someone who knew Norma."

"She did? What did she find out?"

"Just that a girl named Norma came up missing and—I think this was the part that piqued Stevie's interest—the last place she was seen was at a county fair."

29

Kale frowned. He tried to remember what Annie had told him about the girl in the I.D. She'd said Norma was a friend who'd given her the I.D. so Annie could hide from the stalker.

"Was her name Norma Fenn? The girl who disappeared?"

"Sounds right. Stevie also tried to track down where Annie came from and couldn't find any information about a person with that name, which I think convinced her Annie isn't her real name. And there was more. I guess there have been other girls who went missing from fairs."

"Seriously?"

"Yeah. I don't know much. Stevie had some theory about Annie being involved. I don't know why, but apparently there's a forum online about the Carnival Killer in Michigan. A few people have gotten it in their heads that there's a serial killer preying on women at Michigan fairs and carnivals."

K ale did not go to the Chapel Road house. He'd never wanted anything more, but he sensed if he stepped into the house, he wouldn't leave. The thought of being there with his family and then returning to the fair seemed unbearable. Better to stay away.

Girls had gone missing from county fairs, girls who looked a little like Annie. One had even been the friend who'd given Annie her I.D. to keep her stalker, Byron, from finding her.

"Byron," Kale murmured. Had Byron been abducting and possibly killing girls from fairs? Had he gotten wind that Annie was working at one, so he was going after girls who looked like her or girls who'd helped her? It was far-fetched, but Annie had said he was deranged.

Kale bypassed the library in North Muskegon and drove instead to the library on the south end of town. He had to turn over his I.D. for use of a computer, which he did reluctantly, but still figured he was safer searching on a library computer than using his phone, which could easily be checked if he and Annie ever came under suspicion by police.

The hush in the room was interrupted by the scrape of Kale's chair. He did a quick sweep to make sure no one watched him. The three other patrons all stared intently at their own screens.

He typed in 'Byron missing Michigan.'

If the police ever connected him and Annie to Byron's murder, they'd be looking for searches just like the one he was performing now, but he had to do it. He had to know more about Byron.

A slew of results populated, most of which seemed unrelated to the man he searched for. He didn't know where Byron was from. He didn't know the man's last name, his age. On page two, an article caught his eye.

'Two years since the disappearance of eighteen-year-old Byron Low.'

The disappearance had happened in Gaylord. According to the article, Byron had left on a Friday afternoon in August to drive to Michigan's Upper Peninsula, specifically Marquette, to spend the weekend with friends who lived there. Byron had been accepted to Northern Michigan University, located in Marquette, and would be moving there in the fall for school. His parents had last seen him around three p.m. He hadn't been seen since. Police suspected he might have lost control of his vehicle at some point or accidentally driven into one of the many bodies of water between Gaylord and Marquette. Neither Byron nor his vehicle, a 2000 Black Toyota 4Runner, had been seen since.

Kale enlarged the photograph of Byron Low. Goosebumps rose on his arms, his pulse quickening. Byron shared so many features with Kale they might have been brothers. Same curly dark hair and blue eyes. Byron had a stronger jaw, a more chiseled face, but still the similarities were uncanny. What bothered Kale most of all was that the man in the photograph strongly resembled the corpse-like reflection he'd seen in the Haunted Funhouse.

"What the hell?" he muttered.

This Byron couldn't be Annie's stalker. He'd disappeared two years before.

"Unless..." Kale thought about the so-called Carnival Killer. Multiple girls, according to Ben, had disappeared from county fairs. Had Byron gone off the rails? Staged his own disappearance so he could hunt for Annie?

Kale needed to know if this was the same Byron. How else could he connect this guy to the other disappearances? The man might have been a serial killer for all they knew. If so, they'd be off the hook. Not only would the police have to believe their story of self-defense, Kale highly doubted the police would prosecute him or Annie and, if they did, their defense would be clear. A known serial killer had attacked, and she'd defended herself. Simple as that.

Kale returned to the search bar and typed in 'Carnival Killer Michigan.' A single result came back with the exact term.

It belonged to a website called Armchair Detectives. He clicked it to find a forum. At the top, a user named Michigan Sleuth had outlined his theory, including links to multiple missing persons articles.

Michigan Sleuth: *I have a theory that there's a serial killer targeting women at carnivals in Michigan. The first woman, twenty-eight-year-old Regina Price, disappeared from the Isabelle County Fair in the summer of 2009.* Regina's name was a hyperlink, which opened a missing person's page offering the details of her disappearance. *The second woman, Melanie Grant, vanished at the end of August—same summer—and, though it's not confirmed, it's believed she was going to the Oceana County Fair the evening she vanished. The next woman, thirty-year-old Kathy Poindexter, was working at the Cadillac Northern District fair when she disappeared in July 2010.*

Then there was a lull. Maybe the guy traveled to another state to do his dirty work. Maybe he'd satiated the demon within. But three years passed with no disappearances, until June 2013 when Ellen Barnard vanished after saying she was meeting someone at the Huron County Fair. No missing person's link on this one b/c there's been zero coverage! Police think she's a runaway. I beg to differ.

The next disappearance was only two weeks later. Georgia Hought, a carnival worker, vanished from Clare County. The next summer, last year, two young women disappeared. Norma Fenn from the Ingham County Fair, then later in the summer Annie Spencer from a carnival in Kalamazoo. Our killer is searching for younger victims now. Something he got a taste for during his time away?

Theories... this guy works at carnivals. An obvious possibility. My main issue with this theory is these are different companies running these fairs. It's not all the same amusement company.

Another theory, and one I lean toward, is he's a trucker of some sort. Maybe he drives semis, maybe he helps move equipment, delivers food and other products, or maybe he's just a trucker travelling the routes of these fairs, knowing they're an ideal spot to nab young women.

None of these women have ever been found. Let me repeat: NONE of them have been found. This dude knows the areas where he's grabbing these girls, or he's transporting them to some other place to dispose of their bodies (again supports my trucker theory).

Okay, that's all I've got. Do you think there's a Carnival Killer in Michigan?

Kale's eyes drifted back over the names of all the victims. Norma and Annie most jumped out at him, but one more caught his eye, Ellen. Where had he encountered that name recently?

Kale sighed. If the disappearances were all connected, Byron Low made little sense as the culprit. He'd vanished two years before, and the disappearances had started four years before that, when Byron was only fourteen years old. He wouldn't even have had a driver's license.

Kale returned to the screen and scanned the replies. A few agreed it sounded like a serial killer; a few others said it was probably two separate serial killers.

One person, user name Troy-Leslie, commented: *The police have looked into a sexual predator in Norma's case, but were unable to link him. She was last seen speaking with a woman who was working at the carnival with multi-colored hair. This tip didn't come in until six months after she vanished and police haven't been able to locate the worker.*

Another user, screen name Lawn Slayer, posted: *Does anyone know the carny's name? Does Annie ring a bell?*

"Stevie," Kale murmured. Lawn Slayer was the name of their business. It had to be her, and the comment had been posted just days before.

Troy-Leslie: *No name that we're aware of.*

Armchair Detective: *Annie is the name of one of the missing women.*

Lawn Slayer, are you speculating that the last person to see Norma was the Annie who disappeared?

Lawn Slayer: *No, a different Annie who works for a carnival now.*

Troy-Leslie: *Lawn Slayer, does the person you're talking about have multi-colored hair?*

Lawn Slayer: *No, it's dark, but she could easily have dyed it.*

Armchair Detective: *Why do you think she's connected? If there's a serial killer at work, it's definitely a man.*

Lawn Slayer: *Just a hunch.*

KimLovesCooking: *Annie Spencer was my girlfriend. I've been searching for her relentlessly for a year. I believe a carnival worker had a hand in her disappearance, a female worker. Either she lured Annie away for someone else or she was directly involved in what happened to her. I have a photograph of the carnival worker I believe was involved. I'm trying to track her down and I think I'm closing in. I'll be back with updates.*

Troy-Leslie: *Please post the photograph.*

Lawn Slayer: *Yes, KimLovesCooking, please post. I'll know if it's the same girl.*

Armchair Detective: *KimLovesCooking, are you still checking this forum? We'd love an upload of the photo.*

Troy-Leslie: *Lawn Slayer, where in Michigan are you located? Any chance we could meet?*

Lawn Slayer: *Troy-Leslie, I've private-messaged you.*

Armchair Detective: *I strongly discourage this. Either of you could be the serial killer. Just sayin'.*

Several other users also advised Lawn Slayer not to meet privately with Troy-Leslie, but there were no additional comments from Lawn Slayer, Troy-Leslie, or KimLovesCooking on the forum.

Kale wondered if their conversation could somehow be connected to Stevie's attack. He printed the pages, folded them in half and carried them to his car.

30

———————

When Kale returned to the fairgrounds, he went in search of Mo. "Hey, Mo. Have you seen Annie around?"

"She drove into town with Margaret to do some washing and pick up groceries. She's pretty sour at you—she said you were supposed to be back midday."

"Yeah, I got caught up at my family's."

"How's your sister doin'?"

"She's all right. The chemo makes her pretty sick, but then she bounces back quick."

"That's real good."

"I wondered if I could, umm… ask if you know where Annie came from?"

"Came from?"

"Yeah, like what town?"

"Annie joined last year from another outfit. Not sure how long she'd been with them, though."

"She didn't get started with you?"

"Nope. She was workin' for some other amusement, came to one of our shows at the Eastern Michigan Fair and said she liked our style, asked for a job and that was that."

"Do you have any idea what amusement company she was with?"

"Kid, I can barely remember what I had for breakfast this morning."

"How could I find out?"

"The obvious answer is you could ask your girlfriend."

"Yeah."

"Trouble in paradise?"

Cliff, who'd obviously been eavesdropping, came around the camper with a smug look on his face. "Already sick of her, huh? Don't worry. There's more than a few guys ain't bedded her yet. She'll be in good hands."

Fury ripped through Kale and he lunged at the man, snatched the front of his greasy shirt.

Mo, a foot shorter than Cliff, but surprisingly strong, jerked Cliff back and flung him sideways. Cliff stumbled, but got his legs beneath him before he sprawled in the dirt.

"Shut yer yap," Mo snapped at Cliff. "And you keep yer damn hands to yourself."

Cliff glared at Kale, but did as he was told.

"Don't pay him no mind. He can't sleep at night if he didn't push somebody's buttons. That's all I got for you, Kale. We picked her up on the east side and she already knew her way around a carnival. She's a good ride jockey and a tough little cat. I can tell you that much. Not many ladies would travel with this group, though I bet she'd smack me for calling her a lady."

"Did you ever ask her why she joined? Why she wanted to work for the amusement?"

"Why do you think people join this outfit, Kale? Huh? To leave their white picket fence, their great American life? They're leaving Hell with the Devil on their ass. That's the only reason they join up."

"That's not why I joined."

"No, it ain't. You were chasin' the Devil instead."

Another tremor of fury lit in Kale's belly at Mo's remark.

Mo chuckled. "If you don't want the truth, son, don't go lookin' for it. I've got work to do. You best get your preppin' done, 'cause come showtime you won't have a spare minute to scratch your own ass." Mo ambled off.

~

K ale was hungry, and he had laundry to do. The wise choice would have been to go to town to find Annie. Instead, he drove to another library and searched for Michigan fairs and carnivals from the previous summer. The Genesee County Fair was the closest one he found to the Eastern Michigan Fair. Fun Time Amusements was listed as the outfit for the show. He found the Fun Time Amusements schedule. They were on their summer circuit, currently putting on a carnival in Ludington.

Kale opened a map and typed directions to the Ludington fairground. It was only a forty-minute drive.

As he left the library, a moss-green dually pickup rattled toward him. Kale ducked behind the back of the building as Margaret drove by, Annie in the passenger seat.

T he midway for Fun Time Amusements was nearly identical to Brisby. A Ferris wheel, Tilt-A-Whirl, bumper cars, some thrill rides. A row of games and a cluster of quiet food trucks.

Kale walked past the rides to the line of campers and scattering of tents. It was mostly deserted. Like Brisby, many of the workers were probably using the day to run errands. Most of the shows would start again the following day.

Kale spotted a thin man with a salt and pepper goatee sitting at a picnic table, drinking from a Styrofoam cup of coffee and reading a newspaper.

"Hi," Kale said as he approached.

The man glanced up and then looked back at his paper. "Carnival don't start until tomorrow," the man told him.

"I'm not here about that."

"Looking for work?" The man eyed him.

"Not that either. I'm trying to get information about someone who possibly worked for Fun Time Amusements."

The man combed his goatee. "Any trouble a former employee has gotten into isn't any business of ours."

"Annie Carson. She's not in trouble. I'm just trying to find out where she came from."

"Annie Carson? Never heard of her."

"Have you been here a while?"

"The longest save Mr. Granville. Twenty-six years I've been puttin' on this show."

Kale frowned. He'd never taken a photo of Annie and, even if he had, his phone was gone. "Oh, wait. I know." Kale pulled out his wallet and found the picture Zinnia had sketched of Annie.

Kale handed the black and white drawing to the man, who squinted at the picture, then nodded slowly.

"Norma Cross."

"Norma?"

"That was her name. Norma Cross. She joined up with us in Coldwater, stayed on for a season and then bailed without a word."

"She said her name was Norma? Did you ever see any paperwork that substantiated that?" Kale thought of the I.D. Annie claimed her friend had given her to conceal her identity. The name had been Norma, but Fenn, not Cross.

The man snickered. "No. We don't concern ourselves too much with paperwork, especially not on a skinny little thing like Norma. She didn't exactly pose a threat."

"Do you know where she came from? Her hometown?"

The man flipped the page in the newspaper. "I sure don't. Diesel could tell ya some things. He and Norma were pretty tight."

The way the man said the word 'tight' bothered Kale, but he tried not to show it. "Where can I find him?"

The man gestured at a long trailer. "In the bunkhouse. Probably won't like getting woke up, though. Likes to sleep on his days off. Most of them guys do. Drink all night, sleep all day until the show starts."

"Thanks," Kale said, hurrying toward the trailer.

He didn't want to knock on the door and wake up the whole bunk trailer of sleeping carnies. He eased the door open and stepped onto the creaking metal stairs. Behind him, the gaunt man at the picnic table grinned down at his newspaper.

The bunk trailer stank of alcohol and sweat. The sounds of snores filled the over-warm space.

Inside the trailer, a short, portly man sat in a folding chair, hands interlaced on his lap, staring at Kale with beady, suspicious eyes. "Who are you?" he demanded.

"I'm looking for Diesel."

The man glared at him, but said nothing. A curtain jerked open and a tall man in a rumpled t-shirt and cutoff jeans staggered out. "Man, I gotta piss," he said, pushing past Kale without even looking at him and half-falling out the trailer door.

"There ya go," the man in the chair said.

"That's Diesel?"

The man didn't reply.

Kale stepped back out of the trailer, inhaling a breath of fresh air.

Diesel stood at the corner of the trailer, urinating into the grass. His eyes were closed, his head tilted back as if in ecstasy. He had dark hair buzzed close to his head. He was a big man, well over six feet, wiry and lean.

He finished, zipped his pants, and turned toward Kale, scowling. "You been standin' there watchin'?"

"No, I… that guy over there—" Kale gestured at the now empty picnic table. The man was nowhere in sight. "There was a guy over there and he said to talk to Diesel. Is that you?"

The man rubbed his bleary eyes. "Yeah. What? You lookin' for a job?"

"No. I'm trying to get some information on Ann—Norma, I mean."

"Annorma? What the fuck is that?"

"Norma. A girl who used to work here."

Diesel narrowed his eyes at Kale. "You know Norma?"

"Yeah. I met her recently."

"Little skank stole my money and took off. Where is she?"

"I don't know," Kale lied. "She stole your money?"

"Yep. Waited for payday, got me all sloshed and snatched the cash right out of my wallet. Boy, did she have me fooled, all of us fooled. It's always them pretty ones who get ya. Guess I shoulda known any girl named after a killer is gonna be bad news."

"Named after a killer?"

"Yeah, her ma named her after Norma Bates, you know, the mother of Norman Bates—the *Psycho* guy."

"That's what she told you?"

"Yeah. Isn't it true?"

"I don't know." Kale thought back to his first night with Annie. She'd claimed her mother had named her after Annie Wilkes, the deranged character from one of Stephen King's novels. "Did she tell you where she was from?"

"Nawp, but I figure it was up north. That's when she bailed on us, and I got the feelin' it was 'cause she knew people up that way and didn't want to get spotted."

"Where exactly was the carnival headed when she left?"

"Gaylord."

The same city Byron Low had vanished from.

"Did she tell you anything about her life before the carnival? About her family or friends, former boyfriends?"

Diesel scratched behind the elastic of his underwear, which stuck from the top of his jean shorts. "Both parents killed in a car crash. That's all I remember her sayin'."

Kale stared at the guy, wondering if he could be confusing her with someone else. He pulled out his wallet with the hand-drawn picture and held it out.

Diesel's nostrils flared. "That's her all right."

"She said her parents died in a car crash? Not that she'd been in foster care?"

Diesel gave him a strange look. "I told her *I* grew up in foster care, and I did. But she said she was orphaned at twelve when both her parents hit a tree going about fifty miles an hour."

"You grew up in foster care?"

"Yeah, and as a foster kid, I can tell you Norma never spent a day in foster care her whole life."

"How would you know that?"

"It's just somethin' a foster kid knows. Take you." Diesel gestured at Kale. "You got the look of a guy who ain't never gone to bed hungry 'cause your mom smoked too much crack and didn't buy groceries for a week, who ain't never had to sit in a closet, both feet pressed on the door to keep your foster dad from bustin' in and kickin' you in the head til you passed out. Am I right?"

"Yeah. You're right."

"And I'm right about Norma too. Wherever she had it, she had it a helluva lot better than me or any other foster kid I ever met." Diesel spit in the dirt. "I need some pop. My mouth tastes like I been lickin' the bunkhouse floor."

"Did she ever mention a stalker? Someone who was after her?"

Diesel's eyebrows pulled together. "Nah, but she knew I'd have pounded anybody who messed with her. Maybe there was a girl stalkin' her, if that's what you called it. Somebody came sniffin' around once showin' a picture of a girl who looked a lot like Norma, but we run that girl off, said we didn't have nobody like Norma in our outfit."

"Did she say why she was trying to find Norma?"

"She might have, but I sure don't remember it now."

"Okay, thanks, Diesel." Kale started away.

"Watch out for her, man," Diesel called. "Somethin' ain't right with that one."

31

When Kale arrived back at the midway, he found Annie eating hamburgers with Margaret, Dan, and Vinnie.

"You're back," she said. "I saved you a plate."

"Thanks." He sat down and kissed her cheek, hoped his apprehensions didn't show on his face.

Annie using Norma's name proved nothing. She'd said herself she'd used the alias to hide from her stalker. Still, the other inconsistencies niggled at him, like the lie about her parents dying in an accident—or perhaps that was the truth, and he'd been told the lie.

"How's your sister, Kale?" Margaret asked. "Annie told us she's sick. That's just heartbreaking."

"Yeah." Kale swallowed. "It's hard, but she's a fighter."

"What did you guys do today?" Annie asked.

He glanced at her, saw the set in her jaw and feared she somehow knew he hadn't gone to see Sage—that instead he'd been investigating her. "We, umm… just sat around and watched movies again. I helped do some chores around the house."

"Oh, yeah? What chores?" Annie's eyes bore into him.

Kale took a bite of his burger and chewed slowly. "I helped mend the chicken fence. It's been sagging and… I collected eggs and, ugh… that's about it."

"Well," Margaret said, "Annie and I got all our washing done, bought groceries, and Annie colored my roots so I'm a full redhead again instead of red and gray. We even had some time to stop in the library."

"You went to the library?" Kale asked, his mind running. They couldn't have seen him. He'd watched them drive by.

"Yeah," Annie said, adding more ketchup to her burger.

Kale glanced quickly away, the glob of red causing his appetite to wither. "Did you check anything out?"

"Nope, just went to read the papers and surf the web," Margaret said.

"Read the papers?" Vinnie asked. "Neither of you ladies strikes me as the type who are interested in world news."

"Au contraire," Margaret insisted. "Both Annie and I are very informed. You know Annie buys a paper in every town we visit. Don't ya, hon?"

Annie focused on Kale. "Mo said you came back looking for me and then you left again. Where did you go?"

There was an edge to her voice, and he noticed several deep scratches on her forearm. He could see blood beneath the fingernails of her right hand. "Oh... I just went for a drive. You weren't here, so... I just drove around."

Annie said nothing, but he sensed she didn't believe him.

They had one more evening before the start of the next show, and Annie suggested they visit a brewery in town. Kale hadn't officially purchased a single alcoholic drink since turning twenty-one, and she wanted to be with him when he did.

As he sat across from Annie sipping his beer, he struggled to make eye contact.

"What's going on, Kale? You're not talking, you're barely looking at me."

Kale rubbed his face and pushed his beer away. "I don't know if... I can just forget, Annie. I'm really struggling."

Annie's eyes were flinty, her mouth turned down. "You said you loved me. You'd do anything for me."

"And I have."

"What then? You want to leave? You want us to be over?"

"No, God, no, of course not." He slid from his side of the booth into hers, snaked his arm around her waist. He inhaled the scent of her hair, felt the hard ridge of her shoulder tucked into his chest. How had it all gone so wrong? He'd never in his life wanted so badly to rewind the clock and return to those first days when his feelings for Annie had blotted out the rest of the world.

"Kale... I don't know what to do. I wish I'd never called you that day. I shouldn't have involved you, because it's like I poisoned us. I ruined us. I did it to save myself, but... that's not enough for you."

"That's not true, Annie. I'm so happy you protected yourself. I wish I could have somehow saved you or prevented all this, but I didn't, and now... it feels like this really horrible secret and it's only a matter of time before someone finds out."

"No one is going to find out. Not unless we tell them. And if we do that... we're both going to prison."

Kale dragged his beer across the table and swallowed half of it. He choked a little and coughed. Annie patted his back.

"I'm not trying to scare you, but it's true. Most people get caught because they crack, they tell someone or they confess to the police. If neither of us does that, no one will ever know. We can take this secret to our graves. Your family will never know, they'll never judge you. You'll never have to see that look in your mother's eyes. I get you're scared of that, disappointing her, disappointing them all, and don't they have enough to deal with?"

"You're right." He sighed. He thought back to the forum, to Diesel's comments. "Annie, where were you before you came to Brisby?"

She frowned at him. "All over the place. I travelled a lot."

"But... like, where did you go? Did you work for other carnivals?"

Annie's gaze drifted away as if scanning the brewery for someone. When she returned her eyes to his, her expression was both bored and vaguely irritated. "I don't want to talk about this, Kale. My life has been terrible. You would never understand, and... the past is the past."

Annie stood and sashayed to the bar, draped herself across the gleaming surface. The bartender leaned forward, and she whispered in his ear.

A pang of jealousy flared in Kale's chest as the bartender, a good-looking guy in a too-tight t-shirt, laughed as if Annie had just told him the world's best joke.

"Kale," she called. "Come on up here."

Kale glanced at the other customers, many of whom had turned to look at him, as he walked toward Annie.

"Kale, this is Jace. Jace, this is Kale."

"Hey." Kale did a half-wave that he figured looked as stupid as it felt.

"Nice to meet you, Kale. Listen, your beautiful girl here tells me you just turned twenty-one and we have a neat little tradition at Bro's Brewery. You take twenty-one shots of beer in under three minutes and they're on the house. What do you say?"

Kale shoved a hand through his hair. Annie's eyes gleamed mischievously, and the bartender seemed more focused on her than Kale. Kale wanted to say no. His first beer sat heavy in his stomach, but he didn't want to look weak, not in front of Annie or the bartender.

"Come on, man," a guy called from down the bar. "I could do twenty-one shots of beer in twenty-one seconds with my eyes closed and one hand tied behind my back."

The man's girlfriend laughed.

"Live a little," Annie said, running her hand up Kale's spine.

He shivered and nodded at the bartender. "All right, pour 'em."

When they left the bar to walk back to the midway, Kale was drunk. He wove from side to side, Annie clinging to his arm and giggling.

"Wait… look," she said, dragging him toward a dark house tucked behind a wrought-iron fence.

"Hmm?" he asked, squinting toward the house.

"There's a hot tub on the side patio. Come on. We're getting in."

He imagined the lights coming on, an alarm going off, cop cars swarming the street, but he was drunk and fuzzy and allowed Annie to pull him through the gate and toward the patio. No lights ignited and when Annie stripped naked, his mind stopped its stream of worry and his body responded.

For the first time since that horrible day, he wanted nothing more than to touch her, kiss her. She stepped to him and pulled his shirt over his head. She unbuttoned his shorts, and they fell to the floor. When he sank into the hot tub beside her, his breath left in a rush of pleasure. She slid onto his lap and rubbed her silky body against his.

He moaned, and she pressed a hand over his mouth, guiding him inside of her.

~

That night, they returned to the tent, high on their escapade. They made love a second time, and for those minutes, Kale almost forgot what they'd done and what he'd learned about Annie.

Almost, but not quite.

~

It was the worst nightmare yet, because Kale knew it was a nightmare and yet he couldn't wake up.

Everything about the dream reflected reality. He was lying next to Annie, eyes closed, listening to the hushed sound of her breath. The breeze rustled the nylon on the tent. On a nearby road, a car engine backfired.

Something heavy pressed against Kale's chest. His eyelids were leaden. He fluttered them and, finally, with great effort, peeled them open.

A woman sat on top of him. Her wet hair hung from her mushy-looking scalp. It brushed Kale's forehead and cheeks like tendrils of slimy lake grass. Her right eye was missing and the eye still encased in her putrid face was cloudy and glazed.

He wanted to push her off, scream, wriggle away, but he could do nothing. The crushing weight of her forced his breath from his lungs. She did nothing, said nothing, merely hovered over him, that single eye gazing sightlessly down at him, and yet... it didn't *feel* sightless. Just the opposite. He'd never felt such an intense stare, a gaze so full of hatred he'd have screamed like a child if he could muster a sound.

Kale gasped and his eyes flicked open.

The one-eyed woman was gone, but everything else was exactly as it had been. Annie's hushed breath, the scrape of nylon in the wind. When a car backfired, he bolted upright and clutched his chest.

Annie didn't stir. Kale rubbed his face. Thirsty, he searched for their Thermos of water, but couldn't find it. On the little plastic table, Kale's phone vibrated, giving him another start.

He looked at the screen. It was a message from Zach.

Zach: Stevie's awake. Ben and I are headed to the hospital now.

It wasn't quite five a.m. Kale texted back.

Kale: I'll meet you there.

Kale scrawled a note for Annie, grabbed his shoes and keys, and hurried to his car.

32
___

Kale parked next to Zach's pickup and hurried into the hospital.

He walked into Stevie's hospital room to find her sitting up in bed. Zach reclined in a medicine-pink chair while Ben sat close to the bed.

A bandage covered half of her head and sweat shone on Stevie's face, but she smiled at Kale. "All it took to get the four of us back together was me getting my skull cracked?"

"Not funny," Ben said.

Zach laughed. "What makes you think we're here for you? I came for the breakfast sandwiches they serve in the cafeteria."

"Ha-ha," she said hoarsely.

"You look skinnier every time I see you, Kale," Zach said. "Too in love to eat, or did that girl get you hooked on meth?" He tossed a paper-wrapped breakfast sandwich at Kale that bounced off his forehead.

Kale flipped him off. His stomach turned at the sight of the grease staining the wrapper.

"You are looking gaunt," Stevie agreed. "Though I suspect you look better than me."

Ben patted the chair beside him. He bent down and picked up the sandwich, peeling off the wrapper and offering it to Kale.

"No, I'm good. You eat it."

Ben shrugged and took a bite. "Wow, you're right. These are good."

"Jeez, where's mine? I'm the patient here."

Zach tossed another one to Stevie. It missed and rolled off the side of the bed.

"No wonder you got booted from the baseball team in high school," Stevie grumbled while Kale got up and retrieved her sandwich.

"I didn't get booted. I quit so I could play soccer. Everybody knows that."

"How are you feeling?" Kale asked, pulling a chair closer to the bed.

"Like somebody shot Novocaine into half of my head. It feels big and sore and a little deformed. I'm not looking forward to getting the bandage off."

"Are you in pain?"

"Nah. They're keeping me pretty doped up."

"Do you remember what happened?"

Stevie winced and leaned toward her tray table, hand stretched for her cup, but it was just out of reach. Kale grabbed the drink and handed it to her. She put the plastic straw between her lips, swallowed, and cleared her throat.

"I don't know. I heard something in that alley as I was walking by. It sounded like crying, maybe a little girl. I went down to check it out, and I passed a big green dumpster and then…" She touched the bandage on her head. "Nothing. There's nothing. The police said someone hit me."

Kale rubbed his jaw. "I'm so sorry, Stevie. I feel terrible."

She gave him a weak smile. "It wasn't your fault. I'm the one who picked that diner and decided, like some kind of idiot, to walk into a dark alley. Might as well have been wearing a sign saying 'Jump me, I'm naïve.'"

"No way. Who'd expect something like that to happen?"

"I'm with Kale on this one. No one could have seen that coming, and like you said, they basically lured you down there," Zach said.

"It sounded like a girl crying?" Ben asked. "Does that mean a woman hit you?"

Stevie shrugged. "The police didn't say. They came last night when I first woke up. I was struck with a blunt object, was all they'd say. It wasn't found at the scene. Stole my wallet and phone. What a nightmare."

"Did they try tracking your phone?"

"I don't know. I guess I should suggest that."

"Good morning. I see the rest of the gang has arrived," Mrs. Duran announced, bustling into the room with a brown paper bag.

"Please tell me you have vanilla wafers in there," Stevie said, eyeing the bag.

"Vanilla wafers, your robe and slippers, two of your dirt bike magazines and a six-pack of Vernors. But don't you dare tell your doctor about the cookies or the pop. He was very clear that you should be eating what the nurse brings and that's it."

"Oatmeal and applesauce. A feast for a king," Stevie grumbled, taking a bite from the breakfast sandwich. "Mmm... This is good. How do I get them to add sausage and egg breakfast sandwiches to my menu?"

Mrs. Duran shot a disapproving look at the sandwich and then at Zach, but said nothing.

Ben stood. "We better get going, Zach. We've got five lawns on the schedule today."

"Yep." Zach bounced out of his chair. He took out his wallet and withdrew several bills, held them out to Kale.

Kale stared at the money, eyes screwed up. "What is that?"

"Two hundred bucks. A few Lawn Slayer clients hit us with bonuses. That's your cut."

Kale shook his head. "No, I can't. I've been M.I.A."

"Take it, dude. You've worked there as long as we have. These bonuses aren't for the last two weeks, they're for the last year. Come on." Zach waved the money.

Kale took it. "Thanks, you guys."

Zach gave Stevie a fistbump and clapped Kale on the back. "Take your bonus and eat something, man. You look like the guy from that movie Sage likes. The pumpkin guy."

"Jack Skellington," Ben offered.

"Yeah, him."

"Thanks, Zach. Always a pleasure," Kale quipped as his friends left the hospital room.

"Mom, will you go to the cafeteria and get me a cup of coffee?" Stevie asked.

Mrs. Duran frowned. "I'm not sure if that's a good idea. Maybe I better ask your nurse just in case the caffeine—"

"Mom, please. It's a cup of coffee."

Mrs. Duran glanced at Kale and sighed. "Okay. I'll be back in a few minutes. Kale, would you like a cup of coffee?"

"No, thanks, Mrs. Duran. I have to head out soon." Kale waited until

Mrs. Duran disappeared down the hall. "Stevie, what did you want to talk with me about the other night at the diner?"

Stevie picked at the wrapper of her sandwich. "I feel weird about it now," she admitted. "Like it was this huge deal and… maybe it still is. I don't know. There's something about getting bashed in the head that makes you question your motives. I felt like Annie was ripping you away from us, away from yourself even, but then I woke up in this hospital room last night and I thought, *Why do I want to say anything that might hurt what the two of you have?* You said yourself you've never felt anything like it. You're crazy in love. I don't want to be the person who makes you question that."

"I can handle it, Stevie. If Annie and I are going to make it, then I can't be in the dark when it matters."

Stevie took another sip of her water. "Okay… but… maybe it doesn't matter that much. You said yourself she used a friend's I.D. because she had a stalker. So maybe… I don't know. But the name—Norma Fenn. I couldn't stop circling back to it, like that name was just scratching at my brain. I knew I'd heard it somewhere. I finally sat down and looked it up. Norma Fenn is a twenty-year-old girl from Leslie, Michigan who vanished last summer."

Kale brushed a hand through his hair. "I know. I talked to Ben, and he told me some of what you found online, so I looked her up too."

"Okay, so you know she vanished from a county fair?"

"Yeah."

"That had me thinking Annie must be from that area. They must have been friends, since Norma gave her the I.D. Except I couldn't find anything linked to a person named Annie Carson in Ingham County."

"Which just proves she's from somewhere else. I mean, she told me she moved a lot because she was in foster care." Kale thought of Diesel's comment—*I can tell you Norma never spent a day in foster care her whole life.*

"Here's what's also weird. I tracked down the amusement company running the carnival in Ingham County when Norma went missing."

"Was it Brisby? Or Fun Time?"

"No, a place called Sunny Daze Amusements. They didn't have an Annie, but they told me they had someone who sounded like the person I was describing, except her name wasn't Annie. It was Georgia."

Kale frowned, remembering the list of names Michigan Sleuth had cited in his post about the girls he believed had been targeted by a Michigan serial killer. "Georgia?"

"Yeah, and I can see from the look on your face you recognize that name. Did you look at the Armchair Detective site?"

"Yeah."

"So how weird is it that someone who looked like Annie worked at a place called Sunny Daze and used the name of a girl who vanished from a fair? And we know your Annie had the I.D. for another girl who disappeared from a fair, and let's not forget, her current name is the name of yet another girl who went missing from a fair."

"Meaning what?" Kale threw up his hands. "Annie's abducting women from fairs? She's like one hundred and ten pounds. Come on."

"I don't know, Kale. But you can't deny that the number of connections is downright bizarre, even scary."

33

"First of all, you don't know the girl who worked at Sunny Daze was Annie," Kale said.

"No, and the hair color doesn't match. Georgia was blonde. But get this, she had green eyes the guy described as 'hypnotic.'"

"That could apply to a lot of people."

"Could it really, though? Listen, I understand why you don't want to believe this—girl of your dreams and all—but… there's a reason people say love is blind, Kale. Sometimes we cannot see the person we love clearly because we don't want to."

"Did you end up talking to the other poster on Armchair Detective, the one who knew Norma, Troy-Leslie?"

"On the phone, yeah. We had a plan to meet this upcoming week-end. He's Norma Fenn's boyfriend. He's pretty much the driving force behind her missing person's campaign, and he has a really solid detective working the case."

"Why were you going to meet?"

"He said Norma was last seen talking to a carny, a young woman with pink and yellow hair, with green eyes. Does that sound like anyone to you?"

"Annie's hair is black."

"Is that the hill you're going to die on? Her hair is black? Kale, I've met women who change their hair color every two months. It's not difficult to buy a box of dye from the store. And let's not forget that Annie had Norma's I.D."

"Did you ask Troy if Norma had a friend named Annie Carson?"

"Yeah, and he'd never heard of her. He and Norma had been dating for two years. If she'd been a friend of Norma's he'd have known about it."

"Maybe Annie Carson isn't her real name. I mean, she used Norma's name to hide from the stalker. Annie might be an alias. Maybe she was friends with Norma, but Troy knows her under a different name."

"Okay, answer me this. You and Annie have this once-in-a-lifetime connection, right? Don't you think it's weird she wouldn't tell you the truth about her name? Especially if Annie Carson is a fake name?"

"Yeah, it is, but when you've spent so long hiding…"

"You probably need to confront her, Kale. Ask her outright, 'Is Annie Carson your real name?'"

"Yeah." He agreed, but abhorred the thought of actually questioning her. "Can I get the cell number for Norma's boyfriend?"

"I'd love to give it you, but it disappeared with my phone."

"Oh, damn. That's right."

"You could go back to the online message board, get in touch that way."

"Yeah, maybe I'll do that."

"If you do, see if that other poster responded—KimLovesCooking. She also mentioned a female carny. We asked her to upload a picture. That would answer a lot of questions, don't you think?"

Kale rubbed the back of his neck. "Maybe. But that Michigan Sleuth guy said the person targeting girls at fairs has been operating for six years. Annie would have been like fifteen."

"I don't know if I buy that guy's theory. I'm guessing the Carnival Killer thing is just some hare-brained theory by the Michigan Sleuth. I read a few of his other posts. He also thinks there was a witch killing girls in the Manistee Forest and there's an old asylum in Traverse City that's a hotbed for paranormal activity and murders. He doesn't exactly strike me as someone in his right mind."

"Really?"

"Yeah, but there's one more thing. Ellen Barnard."

"She was one of the missing girls, right?" As he spoke her name, the place where he'd encountered the name popped into his head—the heart-shaped keychain in the camper at the property.

"Yeah. Who also went missing from a county fair. She was the first, and Troy told me he's talked to Ellen's sister, Brenda, three or four times. They've been kind of looking into the cases together. Brenda told Troy she went to the fair with Ellen the night before she vanished and Ellen was talking a lot with a girl running the rollercoaster. A girl with funky, purple hair, a bunch of earrings and a chameleon tattoo. Ellen went back to the fair alone the second night and disappeared."

Kale frowned, imagined the line of little silver earrings that ran up the edge of Annie's ear. "Annie doesn't have a chameleon tattoo."

"And I'm not saying it's her, but… it just all seems odd."

An alarm connected to one of Stevie's monitors began to beep.

"What's that?" Kale asked, standing and studying the monitor as if the squiggle of lines might suddenly reveal the reason for the alarm.

"I'm out of something," Stevie explained. "Saline or meds or whatever."

A nurse in purple scrubs hurried in. "Good morning, Stevie. You are very alert today, aren't you? And who is this?" The nurse took one of the bags from Stevie's I.V. pole and hung another in its place, deftly moving tubes from the empty bag to the full one.

"This is my friend, Kale."

"Hi, Kale."

"Hi."

"Stevie, how's the pain this morning?"

"A four, I'd say, creeping up a little though."

Kale studied his friend's face. It was drawn and he could see now the discomfort she'd been successfully hiding.

"We'll take care of that," the nurse said. "I'm adding the same pain medicine we put in last night."

"Thank you."

"You're welcome. This will probably make you sleepy."

"Good," Stevie murmured, sinking down into her pillows.

"I better go," Kale told her. He grabbed her hand and squeezed. Her return squeeze was feeble.

"Listen, forget what I said about confronting Annie about her name."

"Why?"

"I don't know. I just suddenly have a really bad feeling about it. Don't confront her. Do your own research and if you find out she's not who you think, just walk away, pack your bag and go home. Okay?"

Kale rubbed the back of his neck. The advice was so simple, but nothing about his relationship with Annie was simple. They were bound together by what they'd done. Even if he walked away from her, he'd never escape from that.

"Thanks, Stevie. Get some sleep. I'll visit again soon."

Kale left the hospital and headed for the Chapel Road house. He passed a hardware store with a row of bikes parked out front. He slammed on the brakes and turned the wheel, catching one tire on the curb as he bumped into the parking lot. A woman in a minivan behind him blared her horn.

Kale climbed out and studied the bikes. They were Huffy mountain bikes.

The door to the hardware store opened and a silver-haired man popped his head out. "We're runnin' a special on those. A hundred and fifty dollars."

Kale patted the seat of a blue and yellow one. "I'll take this one."

Kale arrived at the Chapel Road house just after eleven a.m. He unloaded the bike and carried it to the steps and into the house, wheeled it toward the kitchen, where he could hear voices.

When he appeared in the doorway, he discovered his mother, Zinnia, Calla and Sage. His mother and sisters were chopping vegetables. Sage sat on a kitchen chair, feet tucked beneath her, drawing in a notebook.

"Surprise!" Kale said.

They all turned to look at him.

Sage's eyes got big. His mother's hand went to her throat. "Oh, Kale," she murmured, voice thick.

Sage stood slowly, as if a sudden movement might make the bike disappear. "Is that for me?"

"It sure is. Come check it out."

Sage ran across the kitchen and threw her arms around Kale's waist. "Oh, thank you, thank you, thank you!"

Zinnia smiled and nodded. "Good move, big brother."

Calla joined Sage in examining the bike.

"Why don't you girls wheel it out front and Sage can practice in the driveway? But wear your helmet," their mother reminded Sage, who made a face.

"It pinches my chin."

"Honey, we can't afford for anything to happen to that precious head right now. Understand?"

"Yes, Mom."

"You guys got it, or do you want me to wheel it out?" Kale asked.

"I've got it," Sage said, taking hold of the handlebars gleefully.

"Kale." His mother took his hand and pressed it to her cheek. "That was unbelievably wonderful of you. Sage had a hard night, and you just made everything better."

"I've been wanting to do it, and this morning when I went to visit Stevie at the hospital, Zach gave me a bonus from the lawn business and it just worked out perfectly."

"How is Stevie? Her mom sent out a group message that she'd woken up," Zinnia said.

"She's good—no memory of what happened, but feeling a lot better."

"That's such wonderful news. This is turning into a lovely day, just lovely. I made bacon quiche last night. Want some? I could heat you up a plate?"

Kale thought of Zach's comment that he needed to eat. "Yeah, but you guys keep working on your veggies. I can make my own plate."

As he ate, Kale asked questions about Sage's treatment and what the family had been up to, anything to fill the space so they couldn't ask how things were going with Annie.

After he finished eating, he rinsed his plate and slipped up to his room, saying he wanted to catch a quick nap before he returned to the midway.

Kale opened his top desk drawer and pulled out his laptop. It was an old heavy thing passed down from his parents when they'd bought a new one two years before. He rarely used it except for school because it often froze if he opened more than two internet windows.

He turned it on, opened a browser window and typed in 'Ellen Barnard missing Michigan.'

Few articles populated the screen. There appeared to be only one news story that had been shared across multiple news outlets. He clicked it. The headline stated: 'Missing Person Ellen Barnard.'

It was little more than a news brief, a single paragraph with no accompanying photo.

The Huron County police are asking for the public's assistance in locating seventeen-year-old Ellen Barnard, who hasn't been seen for nearly two weeks. She may have visited the Huron County Fair. Ellen is five feet five inches tall with blonde hair and green eyes. If you have any information, please contact the Huron County Police.

Few other results matched his search criteria. He saw the Armchair Detective forum. He clicked it and scrolled past the original post about the missing girls, searching for new comments. There were two.

BrendaB wrote: *Hi, everyone. My name is Brenda and I'm Ellen Barnard's sister. It has now been two years since we last saw her. I'm losing hope that I'll ever see her again. The night before she vanished, we went to the Huron County Fair, where she spoke several times with a carny who had rainbow-streaked hair. The following night, Ellen intended to go back to the fair, but we don't have any confirmed sightings. We've never seen her again. If you have any information about what happened, please call me.*

She'd added a phone number.

User Troy-Leslie had posted beneath her message: *Brenda, I'm happy you made it on here. Fingers crossed we both get answers soon.*

The two posts had been made that morning.

Why would Kale call Brenda? He had no evidence that Annie was involved with any of the girls who'd vanished. None. It was just a stupid keychain. It didn't prove anything. He wished he could peel open his skull and smudge it out. And he might have been able to if not for Norma's Fenn's I.D., the one-eyed woman, the body as it hit the water with a splash. His mind had become an asylum of horrific details, none of which made any sense.

He picked up the scraps of leather discarded on his desk, his wood-burning tool, his stencils. The leather rolled beneath his fingertips. He wanted to disappear into that work for a couple of hours, the smell of the burning tool, watching designs and letters magically appear on a cuff or belt. His father had bought a stencil to add to Kale's collection the year before. Kale picked it up. He'd intended to make a wallet for his dad with the quote stenciled on the front—it was one of Frank Goodwin's favorite sayings: *Peace if possible, truth at all costs.* A quote by the German monk and theologian Martin Luther.

Kale took out his cell phone, glanced at the computer, and typed in Brenda Barnard's phone number. He bit his lip and hoped she didn't answer.

"Hello?" a woman's voice asked.

34

"Hi. Is this Brenda Barnard?"

"Yes."

"Umm, hi. My name is Kale, and I saw your comment on the Armchair Detective forum."

She said nothing.

"I… don't even know why I'm calling, and this will probably sound weird, but did Ellen have a keychain with her when she went missing?"

"A keychain?"

"Yeah."

Brenda sucked in a breath. "Yes. She had a keyring with our house key on it and the key to the hair salon where she worked part-time as a receptionist."

"And there was a keychain?"

"Why are you asking this? Do you know what happened to my sister?"

"I don't think so… no, but… well, I went out with a girl who worked at a carnival and, umm… in her stuff she had a keychain."

"Heart-shaped with the name 'Ellen' on it? Is that the keychain you saw?"

Kale's uneasiness gave way to something akin to despair. The Pablo Neruda book he'd pulled the quote for Annie's bracelet from sat face down on his desk. He looked quickly away from it.

"It sounds the same," Kale admitted. "In your post you mentioned

Ellen spoke to a girl working at the carnival. Can you tell me about her?"

"First, please… just tell me about the keychain. Describe it."

Kale touched the metal stencil with the Martin Luther quote as if he might draw strength from it. "It was silver and shaped like a heart. 'Ellen' was engraved in red letters."

"That's it. That's the one. Where is she? Please. Tell me about the person who has that keychain."

"I'd like to hear about the girl Ellen met at the fair first."

"Okay… fine, but please, please don't hang up and disappear. I've searched for years. You're the first person who's given me even a glimmer of hope."

"I won't," Kale promised.

"The carny we met at the Huron County Fair didn't seem like anything special to me, but Ellen gravitated toward her. She had purple hair and wore a lot of funky jewelry. She had a tattoo of a chameleon on her forearm."

"A tattoo?"

"Yes, does the girl you met have a tattoo?"

Kale's shoulders softened. It couldn't have been Annie whom Ellen had met. "No. She doesn't have any tattoos. Did you ever track her down? The chameleon girl?"

"No. I didn't start thinking about her until months after Ellen disappeared. By the time she popped into my head, the amusement company was done for the season and the carnies had scattered. She never came back the following season."

"Couldn't they give you her name? Her information?"

"They said there'd been a fire at the office trailer where employee paperwork was kept. I didn't believe them. I think they probably never kept any paperwork at all."

"Do the police have any leads?"

"The police have never paid much attention to Ellen's disappearance. From the beginning, they labelled her a runaway."

"Why?"

"Because a few years before she disappeared, our dad died in a car accident. It really… changed her. She started skipping school, got into trouble with local police a couple times. When she went missing, they figured she took off and… I guess some part of me believed that at first, too."

"Did she take her stuff? Clean out her bank account, things like that?"

"No. She had three hundred dollars in a savings account she left behind. She had her purse on her that night, but that's it. No extra clothes. It never sat right with me. She was almost eighteen, she could have just packed a bag, told me and my mom she was leaving and left. There was no reason for her to run away. And after weeks and then months went by with no word, that's when I started to believe something terrible had happened to her."

"I'm sorry."

"If that's true, then you'll tell me where this carny is that has Ellen's keychain."

"I will. I swear, but I need to check one thing out first. Okay? I'll call you back tomorrow or the next day."

"No, please, don't hang up. Nothing hurts worse than the silence, the not knowing."

"Listen, you have my number. This is my cell and I'm going to call you back within forty-eight hours. I swear."

"Okay… wait. What's your name?"

Kale squeezed the phone tighter, imagined offering any name but his own. "Kale," he murmured.

"Kale, thank you for calling me. Please call me back."

"I will."

He'd betrayed Annie. By simply making the call, giving this other person his phone number, opening them to a potential investigation, he'd betrayed her. His hand trembled as he set the phone on his desk.

He moved back to the laptop and searched for Norma Fenn. Once he found her missing poster, he felt sick looking at it. The woman looked so much like the one-eyed woman, his skin crawled as he studied her face. He clicked print. He wanted to confirm it was the same girl Annie had an I.D. for before he gave any more information to Brenda Barnard.

Someone knocked on his door, then pushed it open. His mother stood in the doorway. "I packed you some sandwiches and a baggie of Dad's orange and carrot cookies."

Kale stood, slipped his phone in his pocket, and closed his computer. "Thanks, Mom. I probably better head back."

"Did you print something?" His mom turned toward the printer that sat on a bureau in the hall.

"Ugh, yeah, I've got it." He tried to brush past her, beat her to the printer, but she'd already picked the paper up. She tilted her head, studying the image of Norma Fenn.

"A missing poster? Who is this?" She handed the page to Kale.

"Umm… I'm not sure exactly."

"What does that mean?"

Kale rubbed the back of his neck. "It's a long story and… I really should get back. I'll explain. Just not right now."

His mom wrinkled her brow. "Kale, I know something is wrong. Okay? I know it. You've lost ten pounds. You have circles under your eyes the size of Florida. What is going on?"

Kale folded the flier and slipped it in his back pocket. "I'm just worried about Sage and Stevie, Mom."

She reached a hand up and caressed his face. "Honey, you can always come home. You know that, right? If the carnival is too much with everything, you can just come home."

35

___

It was after noon when Kale made it back to the midway. Annie was in the tent, curled in the fetal position.

"Hey," he said, climbing in.

She didn't turn and look at him. He saw a smear of blood on her hand, but she quickly stuffed it beneath the sleeping bag.

"Annie, I'm sorry I just left. I wanted to let you sleep and Stevie was awake, so…"

She said nothing.

He put a hand on her shoulder and pulled her toward him. "Will you talk to me, please?"

Her face was blotchy, as if she'd been crying. "You're going to leave me," she said. "I know you are. I'm damaged and I'm too much and you're going to leave."

"That's not true. I just went to see Stevie. She's doing better."

Annie's face darkened, and she rolled back over. "What did she say?" Annie asked. "Does she remember what happened?"

"Not really, no. Why don't we go grab some lunch before the show starts? I passed a place on my way back that looked good. Greek food. You said you love gyros, right?"

Annie sat up and swiped at her face. "You were gone for more than six hours. We had such a great night last night and this morning I woke up and you were just… gone."

Kale finger-brushed Annie's tangled hair, then tucked it behind her ears. "The guys were at the hospital, Zach and Ben, and then I went home for a bit. I bought a new bike for Sage and wanted to drop it off."

"Hmm… how is Sage?" Annie asked absently.

"Good. She loved the bike."

"That's nice," she mumbled. She picked up the hand mirror on her table and cringed at her reflection. "I look terrible."

"You look beautiful." He leaned in and kissed her, taking the mirror and setting it down. "Come on. Some food will make you feel better."

Annie followed Kale from the tent and they walked to his car. Kale climbed in and bit his cheek when he realized he'd left the folded flier about Norma Fenn sitting in the passenger seat. He grabbed it and shoved it quickly into the glovebox as Annie slid in.

At the restaurant, Annie ordered a gyro and a cup of coffee. Kale opted for Mediterranean flatbread, but he struggled to eat it. A million thoughts swirled through his head, but he tried to keep his face unemotional as he picked at his food and made small talk.

"I heard Margaret saying it looks like rain tonight," Kale said.

Annie swallowed her bite of food and nodded. "Probably. The show might get rained out. I hope not. I like the nights when the carnival is packed and there's constant energy and sounds and lights. There's nothing more depressing than an empty, dark midway."

"Yeah."

"I'm sorry for… the way I was in the tent, crying and… it's just… when even your parents didn't love you, didn't want you, it's hard to trust that anyone else does."

Kale took Annie's hand. He kissed each of her fingers. "I do love you, okay? And I'm sure your parents didn't abandon you because they didn't love you. Maybe they left because it was the best thing… because staying would have been a harder life, a worse life."

"Maybe," she whispered. Annie pulled her hand from his and stood from her chair.

"Where are you going?"

"I left my chapstick in the car."

"Oh, okay." Kale watched her leave the restaurant and walk to his car. He nibbled the edge of his flatbread. It tasted too salty, and he struggled to choke it down.

Annie returned and sat across from him.

"Find it?" he asked.

"Yep." She stared at him for a moment, her eyes oddly blank, and then returned to her gyro.

After lunch, they walked to Kale's car. "Do you need anything? We could stop at the store."

"No. I'm good."

Kale parked at the fairgrounds. As Annie climbed from her seat, his eyes drifted to the glovebox. He thought of Annie returning to the car for her chapstick.

Kale opened his door and climbed out. Annie was already halfway across the parking lot. She didn't look back at him as she slipped beneath the arch and into the fairgrounds. He reached back into the car, popped open the glovebox and pulled out the flier. He tucked it in his pocket.

They had to talk about it. Sooner or later, he had to ask about Norma Fenn, but first they had to get through the carnival that evening. The following day, he'd ask her about everything.

~

Opening night was a success.

For the first time since joining Brisby Amusements, Kale was in charge of a ride. He ran the carousel, opening the gate as children flooded the platform, shouting gleefully as they chose their horses. Their parents snapped pictures from the metal fence that surrounded the ride.

He barely saw Annie throughout the night, as their breaks didn't overlap. Despite the added busyness of running the carousel, Kale thought constantly of the missing girls, of the desperation in Brenda Barnard's voice, of the heart-shaped 'ELLEN' keychain. All the disturbing mysteries had become a sore spot, a rotted tooth endlessly throbbing. When the rides finally went dark at ten, he was exhausted and the beginnings of a headache were brewing.

Annie stood waiting for him at the tent when he arrived.

"Whiskey?" she asked, holding up a plastic cup. "My feet are killing me. I needed something to take the edge off."

"No, I'm good, thanks."

She knocked back the drink and dropped the cup into a plastic bag they used for garbage. "Here." She reached into her apron. "I grabbed us each a bag of peanuts before the concessions closed."

"Thanks. I'm starving." He hadn't eaten since lunch that day, and even then, he'd barely touched his food.

"I'm going to take a shower," Annie told him. "Want to join me?"

She'd pushed her sunglasses up on her head to keep her hair out of her face. Something about the style made her look younger, more innocent. Annie was a person who'd been abandoned, used, hurt. She needed someone on her side. He hugged her and kissed her temple.

"I've got a headache," he murmured. "I just want to lie down."

"Okay." She pulled away and ruffled his hair. "See you soon." She grabbed her shower tote and left.

Nothing in Annie's demeanor betrayed that she'd seen the flier in his car and yet he suspected she had, and with each passing hour his dread about the looming conversation grew. He sat in the tent and shoved a handful of peanuts into his mouth.

Annie's backpack lay on its side in the corner of the tent. He bit his lip and stared at the bag. He wanted to look at Norma's I.D. He wanted confirmation it was the same woman who'd vanished from the Ingham County Fair. He also wanted to look at Annie's I.D. There had to be an address. He could find out where she was from.

It was a terrible invasion of privacy and Annie would be furious if she caught him. He looked through the flap in the tent. No sign of her. After another moment warring with himself about whether to look, he set his peanuts aside.

He shuffled to the bag and unzipped it, pawing for the loose I.D. that had belonged to Norma. His fingers brushed over Annie's cell phone, a tube of mascara, a loose earring. He felt a wallet and withdrew it.

Kale recoiled as if he'd pulled out a dismembered hand.

To any onlooker, it was just a tattered old wallet, but Kale recognized it instantly. He'd made the wallet, burned initials into the soft dark leather on the cover.

It was Stevie's.

36

—————

Kale flipped the wallet open. Stevie's driver's license lay encased behind clear plastic. He read the name: 'Stevie Pamela Duran.' He peered into the bag and spotted another item he recognized, Stevie's phone. Its case was custom with the name 'Lawn Slayers' in funky black calligraphy. With the tip of his finger, he nudged the phone over and saw the shattered screen.

A shadow moved outside the tent, and Kale thrust the wallet back inside Annie's bag and shoved it away. He stared at the flap, waiting for it to unzip, for Annie to poke her head inside, demand to know why he'd been looking in her backpack.

Breath held, he waited, but she didn't appear.

He counted to ten and then forced himself to his knees. He crawled from the tent and onto the prickly grass.

Margaret and Dan sat at their picnic table. Vinnie stood nearby, eating a hotdog from a paper plate. Three other carnival workers clustered around a plastic table that held a radio. 'Cryin'' by Aerosmith streamed from the speakers.

"Kale, come on over and have some dinner," Margaret called.

Kale stood frozen, the lyrics to the song rolling through his head. Steven Tyler's lyrics, 'the killin' kind' of love, mingled with Kale's terrible discovery. He felt like he might get sick. He took a couple of stumbling steps and then he ran across the field, through the midway, and beneath the arch that announced the fair. His feet pounded across the cement and he didn't slow until he hit his car, throwing out his palms to stop himself.

He climbed behind the wheel, realized he'd begun to cry. Warm tears rolled down his cheeks and dripped onto his t-shirt. He started the car and slammed his foot on the gas, peeled out of the parking lot, sending a plume of dust and pebbles into the air.

~

He drove without direction, sped onto the highway, hands gripping the wheel so tight his fingers ached. When his eyes grew heavy, he maneuvered toward the house on Chapel Road. It was after midnight when he turned down the long driveway. Lights shone upstairs in two bedroom windows. Kale couldn't handle facing his family. He reclined his seat and dozed off.

~

Kale shivered and tried to roll sideways, reaching into the dark for a blanket. His thigh hit the steering wheel, and he came to in his car. The temperature had plummeted. An icy glaze covered the interior of the windshield. When he drew breath, it was so bitterly cold it burned his lungs, and his exhalation was a puff of white that lingered in the thick air.

He became aware of a figure next to him in the car and, as he turned his head, the figure blinked. Fat bluish eyelids scraped over jelly-like eyeballs, white and goopy and dribbling on his putrid cheeks. The skin of the young man was pruned as if he'd been in a bathtub for weeks.

Kale recoiled, hit the driver's side door, and fumbled for the handle. He jerked it and fell out of the car onto the driveway. The cold air of the car rushed into the warm night. Kale, breath ragged, crawled away, stones biting into his palms and knees.

"Hi, Kale."

He whipped his head toward the voice. Sage sat on the front steps of the house. She wore her blue fleece robe decorated with little yellow and white monkeys. Her tangle of dark curls was wild on her head.

"Sage," he breathed. He struggled to his feet and then turned to look at the car, bracing himself for the dead thing.

"He's gone," Sage said.

Kale gaped at her. "You saw him?"

She nodded. "He's very sad."

"What is he? Is he a…?"

"A drifter, yeah. He came with Annie."

"What do you mean, he came with Annie?"

"He was around her when you brought her here that first day. There were a few who sort of came and went. He's tried to tell me his name, but I can't quite get it. It starts with B. Brian maybe."

Byron.

Kale rubbed his hands together, still cold from the car. When he walked to Sage, pins and needles shot through his feet as if they'd fallen asleep. He sat beside her, shivering, flexing and releasing his toes, trying to invite some sensation back into them.

"How did you know he was here? Did you come outside because you knew he was here?"

"He came to me first. I woke up to the cold like you did. They do that sometimes, make the room really cold. He was standing in my doorway and I knew he wanted me to follow him, so I did."

"But… weren't you scared?"

"No. Most of them are… not mean. Sometimes it's like once they realize I can see them, they hang around just to not be invisible."

"Some of them are mean?"

Sage picked at the chipped blue nail polish on her toes. "Yeah, some of them feel really heavy. Like… you know what it's like visiting Mrs. Drabble? The way her house feels and how you just know she doesn't like you and doesn't want you there? Some of them feel like that."

"When you walked out you saw the… drifter get in my car."

"Well, he didn't open the door. He was just in it. And so I waited for you to wake up."

"Did he tell you anything… like how he died?"

"No, but I think he was murdered."

His skin crawled. "Why do you think that?"

"When I followed him from my room, I saw lots of holes in his back."

Kale sagged forward, balanced his elbows on his knees and pushed his hands through his hair. "He's not a hallucination. If you see him and I see him, he's not a hallucination."

"He's real."

"Why am I seeing this stuff? I've never seen it. I don't want to see it."

"Because you love Annie and they've attached themselves to her."

"Does she see them?"

"No, because she doesn't want to."

"What do they want?"

"I don't really know. Sometimes they're just trapped here, I think."

"What do you mean?"

Sage frowned. "It's like they don't know they're dead, or they know, but for some reason, they can't leave. Like they're stuck."

Kale rubbed his temples. The headache he'd felt coming on earlier was back and worse. "How do you handle seeing this stuff, Sage? It's freaking me out."

"They won't hurt you, and... I don't know, sometimes it's kind of nice. I've seen Grandpa Goodwin. It bugs him that Mom and Dad turned the casket room into a movie theatre." She giggled. "I've also seen Ernie."

"Our dog?"

"Yep. When I feel really sick, he gets on my bed and lies with me."

"I'm so glad to hear that some of what you see is good."

"Yeah."

"How have you been feeling?"

"Not too bad. Better than last time when I was getting the chemo. It's a new kind, and it's easier on the system. At least that's what Dr. Mercer says."

"That's a relief."

"Yep." She stood up. "I better go back to bed."

"Good idea." Kale stood and hugged her.

She started into the house, then turned back. "Aren't you coming in?"

"No. I think I'll sit out here for a little while, and then I need to head back to the fair."

"Okay. Love you, Kale."

"Love you too."

～

K ale arrived back at the fairgrounds just after seven a.m. He hadn't slept again after the encounter in his car.

He'd opted instead for breakfast and five cups of coffee. The eggs and bacon had been delicious, but he'd struggled to eat them, constantly turning over the discovery of Stevie's wallet in his mind. He'd analyzed a hundred scenarios, searching for a reasonable explanation for Annie having Stevie's wallet, and every time he returned to a glaring truth. Annie had been there when Stevie was attacked. Annie might even have been the one who'd attacked her.

He had to confront Annie. He had to, but despite rehearsing the conversation again and again, when he parked at the midway, his stomach knotted into a ball.

"Annie, we have to talk," he murmured under his breath as he climbed from the car and walked across the parking lot. "I found something in your bag."

As he came upon the back yard, he saw a group of people standing near his and Annie's tent.

"What is it? What's happening?" He ran across the field.

He saw Mo, Margaret, Dan and others jumbled together, and then he saw the tent and slowed. Huge slash marks marred the fabric. It hung in tatters from the flimsy poles.

"Annie?" Kale asked, moving closer.

No one stopped him as he sank to his knees and crawled forward. His nose perked. The metallic odor of blood emanated from the tent. He could see it, not red like the bright nylon, but darker, a deep maroon, almost brown.

37

"Annie…" He spoke her name again, though it came out as little more than a whisper. He could see enough of the tent's interior to know she wasn't inside. He reached for the opening, but Mo's hand fell on his shoulder.

"Back up, Kale. Don't touch anything. Police have already been called. Just back up now."

Kale swallowed, arm outstretched, fingers frozen, as if he might still reach in and pull Annie out. The sleeping bag they'd first made love on, slept on night after night, lay in a crumpled, bloody ball in the corner of the tent. Her little table was overturned, her plastic tote of toiletries strewn about.

He didn't know how long he knelt there, was shocked when a police officer nudged him up and guided him away from the tent. He wasn't alone, but surrounded by other officers. Voices overlapped as they questioned the carnival crew and spoke amongst themselves, shouted orders.

Their words arrived in fragments, shards of glass impossible to piece back together—each stung as it was uttered.

"Too much blood, couldn't have survived." It was that string of six words spoken by a middle-aged policeman in hushed tones into a radio that snapped Kale back to reality. He moaned and tried to break away from the officer who'd been guarding him.

"Hold on, now," the cop said, grabbing him roughly by the arm. "You need to stay put."

"That's my tent," he said, voice wavering. "My girlfriend's tent, our tent."

"I know that," the officer said. "Your boss over there told me that, which is why a detective will be along to talk to you in just a few minutes. I need you to calm down and stay put."

"But she's hurt," Kale blurted, gesturing wildly at the tent. "We've got to help her, follow the trail of blood or get dogs. Where are your dogs?" Kale looked beyond him, expecting to see a man with a row of canines—German shepherds or bloodhounds—rushing to the scene, but there were none. Instead, the field and the parking lot beyond appeared alarmingly quiet. There was a lack of urgency, the kind that came when police suspected the victim was already dead, that there was nobody to save.

"Murder investigation..." The words floated to them.

The officer shot Kale a warning look, as if he might take off, might suddenly leap a car or pull a gun from the waistband of his pants. *Just the opposite*, Kale thought. His knees were wobbling, his whole body threatening to sink down and down.

Somehow, he stood there. He locked his knees and fixed his eyes on the blades of grass. He counted each blade and when his thoughts tried to slide back to the bloody tent, he focused harder, counted louder in his head, until everything else ceased to exist.

"Walk me through the last twenty-four hours," the detective told Kale.

They sat in a brightly lit room with skidmarked linoleum floors and an overhead fluorescent light speckled with dead bugs. The man, who had introduced himself as Detective Granger, had a narrow, clean-shaven face. His blue eyes were deep-set and intense, and Kale squirmed as the detective watched him.

"Umm..." Kale murmured, rewinding back. "Yesterday morning, I got a text—well, technically, it was on Annie's phone, a phone I bought her because she didn't have a cell phone, and I'd lost my phone. Anyway, we got a text that my friend who was in the hospital had woken up. I left Annie a note because she was still sleeping and I went to see my friend Stevie."

"What's the friend's full name and the name of the hospital?"

"Her name is Stevie Duran, and it's the hospital in Big Rapids. Paramedics took her there after she got attacked."

Granger raised an eyebrow. "Attacked?"

"Yes, someone attacked her in an alley in Fremont. They hit her in the head and robbed her. She was in a medically induced coma, but then she woke up, so I went to see her. We talked for a little while and then, umm…" Kale scratched at his chin. "I left and stopped at a hardware store to buy a bike for my little sister, which I took home."

"Where is home?"

"My parents' house in Muskegon."

"The address on your driver's license?"

"Yes."

"And what'd you do after that?"

"I talked with my family for a bit and then went back to the midway. Annie and I had a late lunch at a Greek place."

"Which Greek place?"

"Aphrodite's Café."

"How were things between you at lunch? Any arguments?"

"No. None."

"And then what did you do?"

"We went back to the midway and worked the carnival until ten. Annie went to take a shower and I"—Kale swallowed, moved his hands to his knees—"looked in her backpack."

"Why?"

Kale massaged his temples, a flurry of images racing through his head—the body as it hit the water; the earnest, smiling face of Norma Fenn, and then the version of her dead, missing one eye; the damn heart-shaped keychain; and Annie, beautiful, wild, green-eyed Annie at the heart of it all. He needed to confess everything, could feel the pressure of it pulsing behind his eyes.

Except every crime show he'd ever seen involved some schmo spilling his guts without an attorney and going to prison for murder. Kale had to wait, talk to a lawyer before he admitted what he and Annie had done. Still, he couldn't conceal everything. For Annie's sake, he had to tell at least some of the truth.

"Well, a while back, Annie dropped her backpack and this driver's license fell out for a girl named Norma Fenn. I asked her who it was, and she said it belonged to a friend of hers. I guess Norma had given Annie her I.D. because Annie had a stalker and… well, she was hiding from him, so she used the I.D. to conceal her identity. Anyway, I mentioned the I.D. to my friend Stevie, and she looked into it and found out a girl named Norma Fenn went missing from the Ingham County Fair last summer. I wanted to look at the I.D. and see if it was the same girl who'd gone missing. But when I opened Annie's bag, I found, umm… I found my friend Stevie's wallet."

"This was your friend who was recently attacked and robbed?"

Kale nodded.

The detective's eyebrows knitted together. "Why would Annie have Stevie's wallet?"

"I don't know. It was stolen when Stevie got attacked?"

"Do you believe Annie attacked your friend?"

"I have no idea."

"What did you do? Confront her about having Stevie's wallet?"

"No. I… I took off. I ran to my car and just drove away."

"Why?"

"I couldn't handle it. I didn't want it to be real."

"Did you take Stevie's wallet with you?"

"No, I put it back in Annie's bag."

"Why?"

"Because I didn't want Annie to know I found it."

"Because she'd be angry with you?"

"Yeah, partially for snooping in her stuff, but also… I… I love Annie and it felt like… how were we going to make it through something like this?"

"Why would you want to make it through something like that? If my girlfriend attacked my friend and stole her wallet, I wouldn't be too keen to hold on to the relationship."

Kale's eyes filled and spilled over. He clenched his jaw and wiped hard at his face, irritated at his inability to keep his emotions in check. "When I met Annie, I felt like she was the best thing that had ever happened to me. I… was struggling to let go of that… that fantasy."

"I see. So, what happened after you left?"

"I just drove for hours. I got on the highway and drove until the sun set and then I went home."

"Home?"

"To my parents' house in Muskegon."

"So, your parents can give you an alibi?"

"No, I didn't see them. I didn't go in because it was late. But I saw my little sister, Sage. She came outside, and we talked at like three in the morning."

Granger leaned back and crossed his arms. "Your little sister came outside at three in the morning?"

"Yes."

"Why?"

Kale thought of the wasted man in his car, the dead man. "She just couldn't sleep, I guess." Kale dreaded the thought of what Sage would tell the police if they interviewed her.

"Okay… and you said you lost your cell phone, right?"

"Yes."

"So, you don't have any issue with us subpoenaing your phone records?"

"Of course not, subpoena away. I'd gladly give you my phone if—"

"You hadn't lost it," the detective interrupted. "Right."

"I would, and I did lose it."

"Where did you lose it, Kale?"

"I…" He searched for a lie as the image of it dropping into the lake surfaced. "I don't know. Someone probably picked it up after I set it down at the fair in Fremont."

"So, when we get your phone records, the last place your phone will have been is at the fairgrounds in Fremont?"

Kale stared at him, stomach sinking. The last place his phone would ping was at the property, and if police searched, they'd find it likely embedded in the muck of the lake.

Right next to the plastic-wrapped body of Annie's stalker.

38

"Yes," Kale lied.

"Okay, let's circle back. You said Annie had the I.D. of this other girl"—Granger glanced at his notes—"Norma because she was hiding from a stalker. Tell me about the stalker."

Kale rubbed the back of his neck. "His name was... is Byron. Byron Smith, she told me, and I guess he comes from a family with like... connections. A judge and a detective, I think."

"Okay. And where is Byron Smith from?"

"I don't actually know."

"So, she mentions a stalker, but doesn't tell you where he's from?"

"No, it was pretty traumatic, and she didn't like to talk about it."

"I get the sense *you* don't like to talk about it, Kale. If my girlfriend went missing and left behind a bloody tent, I'd be shouting this stalker's name from the rooftops, demanding police bring him in ASAP, and you haven't said a peep about him until two minutes ago and even then you mentioned him in passing. Why is that?"

Kale swallowed, felt as if the deception was all over his face. "Shock, I guess. And... I feel like... like you're wasting time on me when you should be out there looking for Annie, finding the guy who did this."

"That's the thing, Kale. The only way we can get closer to who might have hurt Annie is by speaking with the people who knew her best. That happens to be you. And I'm sure you're aware, in most cases like this, the guy who did the hurting had skin in the game, so to speak. He knew the victim, probably knew her really well. Knew which tent out of all those tents in that field she'd be sleeping in, knew what time everyone else would be sound asleep and he could creep in and… do whatever he did."

"I wasn't there."

"I didn't say you were. But someone was there, Kale. Someone who knew that stuff I just mentioned. Who do you think that was?"

"I don't know," Kale whispered.

"You don't know? Wouldn't Annie's stalker be the likely culprit?"

"Yes, but… I don't know who he is."

"You just told me his name is Byron Smith."

"That's the only thing I know, his name."

"Hmm…" Granger took another note. "Interesting that you don't have a lot of confidence in that name. Is that because you don't have much confidence in Annie's name?"

"What do you mean?"

"I mean Annie Carson doesn't exist. There's no birth record for Annie Carson. All of her documentation with the carnival was fake. The social security number she put on her paperwork doesn't even exist."

Kale rubbed the hollows of his eyes and stared at his shoes.

"You don't seem that surprised, Kale. Why is that?"

"I don't know. I think when I found the I.D. for Norma and she told me she'd used an alias, I thought it was possible that the name Annie was also fake."

"Let's shift tack here." The detective slid a photo onto the table. "Do you know her?"

Kale stared at the photograph of a pretty woman with red-brown hair swept over her shoulders, a scattering of freckles on her nose and cheeks. He picked up the picture, holding it closer to his face. "I… yeah. I think I recognize her. She was at the Muskegon fair. I saw her." He almost said "looking for Annie," but held it back, still unsure how much he should reveal.

"This is Kim Hyland."

"Kim," Kale murmured, thoughts shifting to the forum, where user KimLovesCooking had posted she believed she was onto someone, a female carny who might have had a hand in Annie Spencer's disappearance.

"She went missing a week ago. And do you want to know where she'd been headed? To the fairground in Fremont."

"She's missing?" He remembered the Volkswagen Jetta parked in the lot at the Fremont midway. It had appeared untouched, as if it hadn't been driven in days.

"How about her? Recognize her?"

The girl in the photo was unfamiliar. Bleached blonde hair that brushed her shoulders. Blue-green eyes and a heart-shaped birthmark high on her right cheekbone. His eyes drifted to the girl's dangly celestial earrings. He flashed back to an earlier moment, Sage complimenting Annie on her earrings—moons with little stars dangling from them— identical to the earrings the girl wore in the photo. 'Someone told me they're lucky,' Annie had said.

They were only earrings. They didn't prove anything. Probably thousands of them were made and sold every year.

"No. I don't recognize her."

"You sure? I noticed some hesitation there."

"I'm sure. I've never seen her before."

"This is Annie Spencer. She disappeared from the Kalamazoo fair last summer, August. She's the reason Kim was headed to the fair in Fremont. According to her mother, Kim and Annie Spencer were a couple. Kim was convinced a person who worked for Brisby Amusements was involved in Spencer's disappearance."

"Okay, yeah… I read about Annie Spencer online. There's a guy who thinks a serial killer is targeting women at carnivals in Michigan?"

The detective leaned back, interlaced his fingers. "You read a theory about a serial killer targeting women at carnivals?"

"Yes."

"And your girlfriend disappeared this morning from a carnival and this is the first you're mentioning it. Why is that?"

Kale stammered, searched for a reasonable answer. "I don't know… I thought… the stalker, probably." But as he spoke the words, he too wondered why he hadn't offered up the theory of the serial killer.

"Kale, did you go to the Kalamazoo County Fair last summer?"

"No, absolutely not. I… I only ever go to the one in Muskegon. Well… I've been to the Ionia Free Fair a couple times, but no. I've never been to the Kalamazoo fair."

"And where were you on August eighth last year?"

Kale gaped at the detective. "How should I know? It was almost a year ago. I have no idea, but… my mom has a calendar. Maybe there'd be some clue in that or… I don't know, phone records or something."

"We're working on a subpoena for those."

"Already?"

"Let me run a theory by you, Kale. Here's what I think happened. You got into Annie's bag last night and found your friend's I.D. You were pissed, rightfully so. Your friend was attacked. You leave the fairgrounds for a couple of hours. Maybe you're trying to cool down, but you just get angrier. You return to the fair sometime in the early morning hours and you confront your girlfriend. The fight gets physical. You don't mean to hit, to hurt her, but you do and it's bad. She's bleeding everywhere. You carry her out to your car and you find somewhere to dispose of her body, then you hurry back to the midway to ensure all your Brisby co-workers see you arrive and feign horror and grief at the ripped-up tent and your missing girlfriend."

Kale's mouth hung open. "No, absolutely not. That's not what happened."

"No? You sure about that? Now's the time to come clean. After today, I can't help you."

"I don't know what happened to her," Kale said through gritted teeth.

"Okay. That's fine for now, but let me tell you something. I think you know a lot more than you're saying and sooner or later, whatever you know, I'm going to know it too. Things would look a whole lot better for you if you gave me the whole story instead of leaving me to dig it up. Sometimes I uncover all kinds of secrets once I start doing that."

"I'd like to go now. Can I go?"

The detective leaned back in his chair, held up his hands, palms out. "You're free to go. For now, anyway."

It was nearly ten p.m. when Kale found himself side by side with Mo on two plastic chairs in the police station waiting room. He'd ridden to the station with an officer and had no car, so he'd called his dad for a ride.

Mo looked at him sidelong and frowned. "I swear to God, kid, if you brought this nightmare down on us, I'll curse the ground you walk on."

"I didn't," Kale whispered, not bothering to pick his head up off his hands. His elbows were balanced on his knees and he sat perched forward as if he might throw up, which was not an impossibility.

"Then who?" Mo asked.

"I don't know. I wasn't even there. I went home last night."

"So you say."

Kale didn't argue. He suddenly hated Mo and the midway and all the other carnies.

"Did anyone see anything last night?" Kale asked.

"Worried you were spotted?"

"No," Kale said through clenched teeth. He wanted to shout it, but knew better than to look hysterical in front of the cop working the desk, a man pretending to be occupied with paperwork who likely hung on every word they said. "I was not there! My sister will vouch for me. Nobody at that midway will put me there because I was not there. Please." He softened his voice. "Please, if anyone saw anything…"

Mo glanced at him, then shook his head and sighed, annoyed. "At midnight, Annie was just fine. Came over to Margaret's camper and had a beer. And then"—Mo sat up straighter and narrowed his eyes at Kale—"she looked at her phone and said she was going to meet *you* in the parking lot. That's the last I ever saw her."

Kale's mouth fell open. "What—no. That doesn't make sense. I never talked to her last night."

"Sure." Mo leaned back, crossed his legs at the ankles, and closed his eyes.

~

"**K**ale—Kale."

He woke to his father's voice. His dad had a hold of one of his arms and was gently rocking his shoulder. "Hey, buddy. Wake up. Come on. It's time to go."

Kale turned and found Mo's chair empty.

Groggily, he stood and followed his father through the double glass doors into the dark parking lot. His dad said nothing, just kept a hand on his shoulder, guiding him toward his van. Kale climbed heavily into the passenger seat. His dad settled behind the wheel. He started the car and reversed it, then shifted and pulled onto the street.

"Dad, I—"

"You don't have to talk about it right now, Kale. If you need some time, I can drive you home and help you to bed and, in the morning, we can talk about it."

"Something happened to Annie, Dad. Someone hurt her and..." His voice caught. Tears rushed hot over his cheeks. "She might be... she might be dead." The word 'dead' came out hoarse, barely audible, but his dad caught it and his face tightened.

"Don't jump to conclusions. Okay? There's no proof of that yet, so don't you believe it, understand? Don't you believe it."

Kale swallowed and wiped his face. "My car's at the midway. We probably—"

"No, it's not. The police impounded it. They had a search warrant and they're workin' on getting one for the house, too."

"The Chapel Road house?" Kale asked, surprised.

"Yes. Not that they're going to find anything. I told 'em they were barking up the wrong tree. Problem is, you're the only tree in the forest just now, so that's where they're at."

Kale swallowed, saw the bloody plastic-covered corpse as he'd sent it flying into the lake, heard the splash. Annie had washed Byron's blood off after she'd killed him. What if there'd still been blood on her clothes, her shoes? What if she'd left blood in his car? What if they became convinced Kale had hurt her?

"I screwed up, Dad," he murmured after his dad parked at the Chapel Road house and silence filled the car.

"I've already spoken to Miriam and Joe Duran. Jacob will be coming by as soon as he can get away, tomorrow or the next day at the latest."

"Stevie's brother? Why?"

"Because he's a defense attorney. You didn't... confess anything to the police, did you?"

Kale stared at his father, his face mostly in shadow. "What do you mean?"

"I mean, did you give the police any kind of confession? Did you say you did anything to Annie?"

"No. God, no. Of course not."

"Good."

"Dad, I didn't do anything to Annie. I'm not... that's not what I'm talking about."

"Oh, thank God." His dad's shoulders softened. "I didn't believe you could have, but the police implied... Well, it doesn't matter what they implied."

39

Only his mother awaited them when Kale and his dad returned home from the police station. She sat at the table sipping a cup of tea. When they walked in, she stood and hugged him, smoothing down his hair.

"Oh, Kale. I'm so sorry. I've been beside myself since you called. Is there any news on Annie?"

Kale shook his head.

"That's all right. We can't give up hope. For her sake and yours, we all have to have faith right now."

Kale held very still, tears percolating, ready to rush out. "Can we talk tomorrow? I need to go to bed."

"Oh, of course, yes. I'm sure you're exhausted. Can I get you anything first? Zucchini and carrot soup? Leftover quiche?"

He hadn't eaten a thing all day, knew if he tried, he'd be sick. "No. I'm fine. Good night."

He left his parents watching him from the kitchen and trudged upstairs to his room. He heard the sound of Zinnia playing guitar through her closed bedroom door. He slipped into his room and climbed into the bed. The sheets and pillow case still smelled of Annie. He pushed his face into the pillow and cried until he fell asleep.

K ale dreamed he slept in the tent at the midway. Someone stood outside, arm rising and falling. A knife jabbed through the nylon and ripped it open. Slivers of the sky shone through the tattered fabric. Gradually the slits grew wider.

Kale blinked at the knife holder.

Annie stared down at him, a blood-covered hunting knife clutched in her hand, a grin frozen on her face.

K ale jolted awake. Sunlight filled his bedroom. He climbed from bed, his stomach rumbling, a vision of the dream, Annie's maniacal smile, following him from the room.

In the kitchen, he found his mother, Sage and Calla. They sat around the table, an array of photos and colorful paper scattered across the surface.

"Goodness me, you must have been worn right out," his mother said. "It's after noon." She stood and hugged him.

"Morning," he grumbled.

"That bike is so dope, Kale. I get serious air on the third root now," Sage told him.

"Dope?" their mother asked, frowning.

"She means cool, Mom," Calla explained. "Not drugs."

"Well, if you mean cool, why don't you say cool?"

"Because the bike is beyond cool," Sage said.

"That's awesome," Kale told her. He opened the refrigerator.

His mother hovered behind him. "There's overnight oats in there or bacon quiche."

"The oats are good," he murmured, pulling out a mason jar of oatmeal soaked in yogurt. He added a handful of blueberries to the jar and sat at the table.

His mother followed him and leaned close, dropping her voice. "We didn't tell them about… anything yet. Okay?"

He nodded. "That's probably for the best." He turned back to the table. "What are you guys working on?" he asked, eyeing the photos.

"The family scrapbook. Zinnia had the pictures printed, so we're putting it together."

Kale took a bite of his oats and cringed. He'd forgotten to add honey, and the sourness of the yogurt overwhelmed the blueberries. He stood, added two spoonfuls of honey from the bowl on the counter, and poured a mug of coffee.

"How did you sleep?" his mom asked.

"Decent."

"Dad went to drop off a tractor he sold last week, but he'll be back early this afternoon. I thought we could make homemade pizzas tonight?"

"Ooh, yeah," Calla said. "Do we have goat cheese?"

"Lots of it." Sage wrinkled her nose. "No, thank you."

"We also have parmesan and mozzarella. There are plenty of options for everyone to make the pizza they want. How does that sound to you, Kale?"

"Good," he said, though his thoughts had wandered to Annie. What had happened to her? Who was behind it? There was only one place he knew of that might hold the answers to where Annie and her stalker had come from—the property with the camper and boathouse.

"Mom, can I borrow your car?" he asked.

His mom frowned and touched the little scar beneath her eye. "Where do you want to go, honey?"

"I'd like to go visit Stevie at the hospital."

"Well, I could take you. I'd like to visit Stevie. We could pack up some zucchini brownies Dad made."

"No, I'd really like to go alone. I need some time to think and… I can't do it here."

She forced a smile. "Sure, of course you can take my car. The keys are in my purse."

"Thanks, Mom." He finished his oatmeal, rinsed his dish in the sink and loaded it into the dishwasher.

"Kale. Please be careful, okay?"

"I will."

Sun glinted off the hood of his mother's car as Kale drove toward the property. He glanced repeatedly in his rearview, expecting flashing lights, Detective Granger coming to arrest him for murder.

He breathed a sigh of relief when he passed the blackened tree on the side of the road and flicked on his blinker to turn down the two-track. He parked and climbed from the car; his breath caught as he stared at the camper, remembering his first day there with Annie.

The camper door stuck, and he wriggled it open.

"Annie?" He called her name, but only silence returned.

He hadn't expected her to answer, but some part of him had hoped she'd staged the whole thing and run away to escape what he'd discovered in her bag. But she didn't know what he'd discovered.

Had Byron's family abducted her? Was Byron even the person in the lake?

He was going to check. The thought of it terrified him, wading into the water, pulling out the body, but it was the only way to know for sure.

Moving quickly, he opened and closed drawers, finding little of interest. Utensils, kitchen supplies, camping stuff—no paperwork, no revealing information. He opened the junk drawer and pulled out the 'ELLEN' keychain, slipped it into his pocket.

He lifted the kitchen benches to see if they had storage beneath. They did, but he found only musty blankets and a scattering of mouse poop. A row of cupboards stood above the paisley bench that served as the camper's couch. He opened the first one to find a kerosene lantern, a box of latex gloves, and a gallon jug of water.

The next cabinet appeared empty, but when Kale reached into the far back, his fingers brushed a box. He pulled it free. It was a shoebox, and the lid was taped shut. Kale grabbed a paring knife from a kitchen drawer, his hand unsteady as he slit the tape.

He lifted the lid. A small black cassette, the kind used in older video cameras, sat inside. Also in the box were a pair of handcuffs and a prescription bottle with the label rubbed off. Kale unscrewed the cap and studied the pills. The bottle was half-full with little white pills that looked similar to aspirin.

Kale slid the cassette in his pocket. He hadn't seen a video camera in the camper, but figured he could find some way to view the footage once he left.

In the tiny bedroom, Kale got on his knees and peered under the bed. He saw the plastic binder and reached for it. From the dark space beneath the frame, something moved. Kale froze as the one-eyed woman peered at him from the shadows. She reached a skeletal hand out and closed her bony fingers around his wrist. He screamed and flung himself back, cracking the back of his head on the thin camper wall.

He scrambled out of the narrow space and stood, panting, waiting for her to come slithering out. She didn't. Seconds ticked by, then minutes. He couldn't crouch down again, peer under the bed. He grabbed a wire hanger from the alcove that served as a closet, bent the hook and fished it beneath the bed, yanking until the corner of the binder emerged. He snatched it quickly and left the room, closing the door behind him.

Kale walked to the paisley couch and sat down, flipping it open. The first article was the one he'd glimpsed when he'd originally discovered the binder. 'Man Killed in Fiery Crash.'

Kale skimmed the article. Two people had been involved in the crash. The man had died. The woman had survived with non-life-threatening injuries. Their names had not been released to the public.

The following page held a single yellowed photograph of a man with sandy hair wearing sunglasses, holding a young girl on his shoulders. The girl's hair was lighter, silver-blonde. She held a colorful pinwheel in her hand. Behind them was a familiar structure in what might have been its glory days. Kale leaned closer to the image of the now-defunct boathouse. It had been painted white then, and through the open double doors, he could see a small boat inside.

Was this the man who owned the property, the man Annie had described as the brother of one of her foster dads? Had there even been foster dads? Diesel had said Annie—no, Norma— had claimed her parents died in a car crash.

Kale flipped back to the previous page. Could Annie's parents have been the man and woman in the accident? According to the article, only the man had died.

Kale scanned the following page and frowned. It was another newspaper article. This one was dated July 2009, six years before.

Woman Vanished from Isabella County Fair

Twenty-eight-year-old Regina Price, a nurse from Rosebush, Michigan, has not been seen since July sixteenth, nearly two weeks ago at this writing. Her last known whereabouts are the Isabelle County Fair. She met two co-workers that evening who saw her walking toward the parking lot at eight p.m.

Those same co-workers alerted police the following Monday when she did not arrive for her shift at the Mount Pleasant Hospital, where she'd been employed for more than six years. It was highly unusual for her to miss a shift and even more unusual that she didn't call in. When her friends were unable to locate her, they reported her missing.

During their investigation police located Regina's car, still locked, in the parking lot at the Isabella County Fairground.

Regina is five feet three inches tall with shoulder-length brown hair and blue eyes. She was last seen wearing khaki shorts, a lime-green top and white sandals.

If you have any information about the whereabouts of Regina Price, please contact the Isabella County Police.

No photo accompanied the article.

On the opposite page, a similar article highlighted another missing woman. This one included a photo of a pretty woman with dark blonde hair cut in a bob. She wore dangly hoop earrings and her lips were painted a dark red.

Have You Seen Melanie?

Melanie Grant, thirty-two, of Hart, Michigan, hasn't been seen since Saturday, August twenty-seventh. Melanie, a single mother of two young boys, was reportedly last seen at the Oceana County Fair. That evening, when she did not return home, the babysitter of Melanie's boys phoned Melanie's ex-husband, who contacted police.

Melanie's mother told reporters that Melanie's sons are her life. She'd never, under any circumstances, leave them. Melanie's mother is trying to remain hopeful, but she fears the worst.

Though police have not reported any persons of interest or even that they suspect foul play in Melanie's case, sources close to the investigation say they're looking closely at Melanie's ex-husband's whereabouts on the night of August twenty-seventh.

Both articles were related to women Kale had read about on the forum where Michigan Sleuth surmised a serial killer was targeting women at Michigan fairs.

Kale sniffed and wrinkled his nose, smelling something burning. Tendrils of dark smoke began wafting up from the floor of the camper.

40

Kale jumped to his feet, searching for the source of the smoke. Tucking the binder under one arm, he grabbed the handle of the camper door, turned, and pushed. It didn't open.

He tried again, wriggling the knob. Still no movement. It was somehow barricaded from the outside. The smoke grew thicker, black. Flames began to shoot from the bedroom.

"Oh, crap… oh, no…" He hurried to a window, dropped the binder, and forced it open.

He punched the screen out, but didn't dive through. He tried to scan the area outside the camper. Someone must have been out there. They'd set the camper on fire. Unless it had been a fluke, some sort of wiring malfunction.

He couldn't see anyone. Kale tossed the binder out on the grass and then glanced back at the shoebox. He threw out that too, then pushed a leg through and, leaning heavily on the ridge of the window, flopped out, landing on his hands and knees. No one attacked, but behind him, the flames spread through the camper. Smoke billowed from the window he'd climbed out of.

Kale grabbed the binder and shoebox, sprang to his feet, and ran to his mother's car. He slid behind the wheel, slammed the door and depressed the locks.

In the rearview mirror, plumes of black smoke rose from the treeline. He could not see the boathouse through the forest, but suspected this additional stream of dark smoke originated there. Anything the trailer or boathouse held, be it evidence of murder or clues to what had happened to Annie, would soon be obliterated.

Kale set the binder and shoebox on the passenger seat and threw the car in reverse. How long would it take for someone to alert the fire department? He had to get out of there.

"Shit, shit," he muttered, adjusting his mirror as he reversed.

A woman stood on the trail and he screamed and jerked the wheel, stopping inches away. She watched him from her single eye before dissolving into the trees.

He jerked the wheel back to the right and hit the gas. The car's tires spun, but it didn't move. He'd driven into the mud along the embankment of the stream. He tried again, but the car's engine only revved with no movement.

"Calm down, calm down," he repeated, shifting into forward and pressing the gas pedal. The car inched forward. He shifted into reverse and the car inched back. He repeated the process twice, three times, until finally the tires caught and the car shot forward. He pulled back into the opening near the inferno that was the camper. He turned a circle and aimed toward the trail leading back to the road, sickeningly aware that he might be driving toward a head-on confrontation with a fire truck or cop car.

He sped down the trail. The car lurched onto the road. The tires caught the pavement and squealed as he yanked the wheel to the side. As he accelerated away from the property, he spotted a car abandoned on the side of the road only a few hundred yards from the property. It was a silver Jetta. He let off the gas and stared at it, tempted to stop and examine it thoroughly.

Faintly, he heard the sound of sirens.

Kale pressed on the gas pedal.

It was everything Kale could do to remain at the speed limit as he drove home. His entire body trembled and sweat poured from beneath his arms. Someone had burned the camper and the boathouse. Had it been Byron's family seeking vengeance? Or something more twisted?

He thought again of Michigan Sleuth's theory about a serial killer targeting women at carnivals. Could Annie have been a victim of the serial killer? And if so, what was the link between the property that she regularly escaped to and the man who'd likely abducted and murdered multiple women? The binder of articles simply didn't make sense.

He glanced at it on the passenger seat, considered pulling over to read the rest, to see if there was any clue hidden in the remaining pages, but it'd be safer to wait until he got home.

Something bumped his seat from behind. He frowned and glanced over his shoulder, but couldn't get a good view into the backseat. His mother probably had stuff sitting on the seat and it had fallen to the floor.

As he turned onto Chapel Road, a flicker of movement caught his eye. He stared at the shape as it rose up in the seat behind him, assuming for a moment that it was another ghostly apparition.

It wasn't. The shape of a person was solid, their face hidden behind a rubber Halloween mask with black mesh eyes and a stitched red mouth.

The person's arm shot up and something encircled Kale's throat. It pulled tight, yanking his head back against the headrest. It felt like an electrical cord and his fingers scrambled to get beneath it, but whoever controlled had begun to twist and pull it back. He swung his arms behind him, thrashing, trying to hit the masked attacker. They made no sound. His lungs shrieked and he jerked against the restraint, but it only pulled tighter, suffocated him more.

He'd lost his grip on the wheel and as he bucked against the cord, his foot left the gas pedal. The car coasted to a stop in the middle of the road.

The person clamped a rag over his nose and mouth and the pressure on his neck released. He sucked in a desperate breath that stank of chemicals. An acrid taste filled his mouth. He reached for the rag, but his arms, tingly, lost feeling and slowly sank to his sides.

Kale's vision grew fuzzy and shrank to a pinhole. His tongue lay heavy in his mouth. All sound grew muffled and then he faded and was gone.

41

"Kale! Kale!"

Kale felt pressure, a wetness on his mouth, and a burst of air filled his lungs. He gasped and choked. The breath he sucked in burned. Zinnia crouched over him, eyes searching his. Behind her, Thorn and Aster stood huddled together, tears streaming down both of their faces.

His final moments rushed back—the cord around his throat, the chemical-soaked rag, the sensations of dying. He reached up and searched his neck. The cord was gone. He was no longer in his car. He felt the dirt road beneath him, pebbles biting into the back of his head.

"What... where..." he rasped, grimacing at his scorched throat.

"You're on Chapel Road. We just found you lying in the ditch."

He wasn't dead. He hadn't died. "Mom's car...?" He turned his head, saw Zinnia's car still running in the center of the road.

"It's not here, Kale. It was just you."

He pushed himself up with his hands and winced at the burst of pain in his head.

Zinnia braced a palm against his back. "Don't get up. We should call an ambulance."

Kale touched his throat. "Water."

"I've got some." Thorn ran to the car and reached into the passenger side. He returned with a canteen of water.

Kale sipped it and cringed. It felt like swallowing rocks. "I'm okay," he whispered, looking at Aster, whose tears had not stopped.

"Should I run home and get Dad?" Thorn asked, looking from Zinnia to Kale.

Kale shook his head. "I'm all right."

He started to stand. Zinnia and Thorn flanked him, each wrapping an arm around his back.

"Thanks," he murmured as they helped him to the car. He slid into the passenger seat, head throbbing.

Zinnia climbed behind the wheel, hands shaking as she shifted into drive. "What happened, Kale?" she asked.

Kale leaned his head back in the seat and closed his eyes. "Someone strangled me and then put something over my face. They must have been in my backseat."

"You don't know who it was?" Thorn asked.

"Do you think it's the person who hurt Annie?" Aster's voice was small.

Kale rubbed his throat. "I don't know. They were wearing a mask."

"They stole Mom's car," Zinnia said.

"We'll call the police at home," Kale said.

Kale's family swarmed him at home. His mother forced him into a chair. His father delivered painkillers and a glass of ice water before phoning the police. Zinnia ran upstairs for healing balm to put on the tender skin on his neck.

When the police arrived, the entire Goodwin family had gathered at the kitchen table. Though Lucy had tried to make Calla and Sage go upstairs, they'd put up such a fuss she'd finally agreed they could stay.

Two officers took Kale's statement. They offered to alert paramedics who could look at his neck, where a deep burn remained from whoever had strangled him. He told them no.

When they left, the house was eerily quiet.

Sage finally broke the silence. "Maybe we should watch a movie? Just to… get everybody's minds off things."

Lucy smiled and kissed her daughter's halo of curls. "I think that's a fine idea. Movie room?"

"No," both Aster and Thorn said as one.

"It's too dark down there," Aster added.

"Yeah," Thorn agreed.

"The family room it is," Lucy said, standing. "Zinnia, can you bring the zucchini brownies? I'll fill up a pitcher of goat's milk. We can just have a nice family evening like old times."

Kale didn't move as each of his family members, save his dad, stood and headed for the living room.

"I think you should join us, Kale," his dad said. "I know it's probably the last thing you want to do."

"It's not that," Kale murmured, touching his neck. "I'm afraid, Dad. I'm afraid for all of us in this house. Whoever attacked me… they have my wallet. They know where we live. I don't know if they tried to kill me, but… they came pretty damn close."

Frank nodded slowly. "You're right. We can't afford to take this lightly. Let's get some guns out of the safe, hmm?"

"Mom won't like that."

"She'll understand."

"Okay." Kale followed his dad into the basement, where his gun safe was tucked into the storage room.

They maneuvered around old tricycles, dollhouses, and an old sewing machine. His dad opened the safe and handed Kale a shotgun. He took out a revolver for himself. The pistol had been Kale's grandfather's, and he'd never seen his dad shoot it.

"Does that thing even work?"

Frank eyed the gun. "I hope so." He grabbed two boxes of ammunition from the safe and they each loaded their gun. "I'm going to tell your mom we got them out, but I don't want to alarm the other kids, so let's keep them out of sight, shall we?"

"Yeah." Kale wrapped his in a blanket and slipped into the living room. He slid the gun beneath the chair he sat on.

His dad, carrying the much-easier-to-conceal pistol, strapped it into a holster across his chest and put a zip-up sweatshirt on.

Frank leaned down and whispered in Lucy's ear when they returned to the living room. Her face paled, and she glanced at the blanket-wrapped gun beneath Kale's chair. She nodded slowly.

"Kale, wake up."

Kale opened his eyes. The room was dark except for a trickle of light from the hallway. He'd fallen asleep on the couch in the living room. "Dad? What is it?"

"Get up, son. You need to come to the kitchen."

Kale stood. He braced a hand against the back of a chair to steady himself.

He followed his dad into the kitchen, where Zinnia and his mother sat. "What's going on?" he asked.

"Honey…" His mother stood and walked to him, took his hands in hers and kissed his knuckles. "This is going to be upsetting, okay?"

"What? What happened?"

"The police found your mom's car," his dad explained.

"They did? Where? Who was in it?"

"It was abandoned not far from here. On Martin Road."

"Okay? Why are you crying?" Kale stared at Zinnia, whose eyes welled with tears.

"Is it Annie? Did they find Annie?"

"They found something in the car, Kale," his dad continued. "Jacob is on his way here, and the police probably won't be far behind."

"What are you saying? What did they find?"

"A body or… part of a girl's body. She… had a Brisby Amusements shirt on."

"A body? Are you saying… that she's dead?"

"There was a body in the trunk of Mom's car, and yes, she was dead."

Kale's eyes bulged. "In Mom's trunk? Is it Annie? Are they saying it's Annie?"

"We don't know. Jacob called the house, and he filled us in. His girl-friend works in emergency dispatch and she heard the call and told him."

"Do they… they think it's her? It looks like her?"

"Oh, honey." His mother started to cry. She pulled Kale into a hug.

"It might not be her," his dad said. "Okay? That's the thing to remember right now. This girl they found… it's not good."

"Why can't they tell if it's her? I should go to the police station, right? I should go see if it's her."

"Kale…" His dad took his hand.

Zinnia cried harder. Kale's mom moved from Kale to Zinnia and pulled his sister close, her own eyes full of tears.

"There's no head on the body and there are no hands," his dad whispered.

Kale blinked at him, reeled away, and walked into the table. He shot his arms out and pressed his palms against the smooth surface. "Oh, God… oh, my God. No." He shook his head, tried to erase the words, unhear them. He stood and staggered to the back door.

42

___

Kale sat on the ground in the garden. He'd been picking up rocks for a half-hour, one after another, picking them up, rubbing them between his fingers, dropping them, picking up another.

All the while, his mind plodded through the previous days with a hundred images of Annie. Annie that first night working at the Pirate Ship, the sparkle in her green eyes, the sweep of her dark hair. Annie kissing him, snuggling into him, sleeping curled against him. Annie furiously chewing at her raw thumb. Annie gone, a bloody tent in her place.

The back door opened and his dad stepped out. "Jacob's here, Kale."

What had Kale done so wrong to bring them to this point? Why hadn't he insisted the very first night at the midway that she call the police, alert them to the presence of her stalker, a man she'd gotten a restraining order against? Kale had wanted so badly to keep her, to not displease her, that he'd tossed away all his common sense. He should have protected her. He hadn't.

"Kale," his dad repeated.

"I'm coming." Kale climbed to his feet and followed his dad into the house.

Jacob stood in the kitchen talking to Lucy and Zinnia.

"Hey," Jacob said, clamping a comforting hand on Kale's shoulder. "Why don't we have a seat?"

Kale nodded.

"We're going to get out of your hair," Lucy said, gesturing at Zinnia and Kale's dad to follow her. "We'll be in the living room. I put two glasses of water on the table, but if you prefer, I could make some tea?"

"No, I'm good. Thanks, Lucy."

Kale sagged into a chair. Jacob sat opposite him.

"Hey. How ya doin', Kale?"

"I'm not good."

"That's to be expected in circumstances like these."

"How's Stevie?"

"Better. Fewer pain meds last night than the night before, steady improvement."

"At least there's one good piece of news today."

"It's been a rough day for you. Why don't we talk about the last couple of days? Can we do that? Because the police are going to be coming here and you're going to have to be very careful about what you say from this point forward."

Kale opened his mouth, then realized he wasn't even sure where to begin. He slumped back in his chair. It was time. He had to tell someone. "This is confidential, right? Anything I tell you stays between us."

"Yes, and if my being Stevie's brother makes you uncomfortable, I understand. I can give you the name of someone else at my firm if you prefer. Sometimes it's easier to be totally open with someone you don't know."

Kale shook his head. "I'd rather it be you."

"Okay, go ahead." Jacob flipped open a notebook.

Kale rubbed his face and pushed his hands back through his hair. "A week ago, Annie called me at the midway. She was at this property she goes to up in Newaygo. I couldn't find her at the midway that day. Something had happened and she said to come right away." Kale paused and took a sip of water. "I drove there and Annie came running out of the woods covered in blood."

Jacob blinked at him, but said nothing.

"I thought she'd been hurt, but then she said it wasn't her blood."

Jacob frowned and picked up his pen, but didn't write anything.

"She said her stalker had followed her to the property and attacked her."

"Stalker?"

"Yes, she said his name was Byron Smith. She'd told me about him before this happened. She said he was an old boyfriend who became obsessed with her and tried to kill her."

"And she was covered in his blood?"

"Yes. She said she needed help because he was too heavy. She had… she killed him."

Jacob set the pen down again. He steepled his fingers on the table. "Okay. You saw his body then?"

"Yes… well… not technically. He was in the boathouse, but he was wrapped in this really heavy-duty plastic and all taped up."

"She'd wrapped him in plastic?"

"Yes."

"And you didn't call the police?"

"No. I wanted to, but she said he came from a family of people in the criminal justice system, cops and judges. She insisted we'd both go to prison."

"Why would *you* go to prison?"

"Because I helped dispose of the body."

"Okay. Tell me about that."

"Like I said, he was in the boathouse and he was too heavy for her. I dragged him up to the second floor, where there's a platform that juts out over the lake. I secured bricks to the body and pushed it into the lake."

Jacob's eyes briefly closed. When he opened them, he looked concerned. "This is not ideal, you participating in that, but… maybe this all makes sense. The stalker followed Annie, attacked her, she defended herself and killed him. Out of fear, she covered it up. His family suspected she was behind it and took revenge."

"Yeah, exactly. She was so scared of his family. She said they have all kinds of police connections and that they're not afraid to play dirty."

"Tell me more about this property. Do you have an address? It shouldn't be hard to pull tax records and see who owns it. That's a quick way to home in on Annie's identity."

"She said it belonged to the brother of one of her foster dads. I don't have an address for it. I doubt there is one, but it's in Newaygo County on Boneset Road."

Jacob frowned. "Boneset Road? Where have I heard that name before?" He clicked his pen and scrawled the name. "It'll come to me. Let's talk about your alibi for the timeframe when Annie went missing."

"I was here, but I didn't come inside."

"Why not?"

Kale remembered opening Annie's bag, discovering Stevie's wallet. He cringed at the memory. Why hadn't he just confronted her then and there? They could have fought about it or figured it out or whatever. It would have changed everything. "The evening before I came here, I found Stevie's wallet and phone in Annie's backpack."

Jacob looked taken aback. "Why did she have Stevie's wallet and phone?"

"I don't know."

"Did you ask her?"

"I freaked out and left the midway. That's how I ended up here at home. When I went back, she'd been taken and there was… blood in the tent."

Jacob rubbed his eyes and blew out a breath. He stood. "I think I'll make a pot of coffee. I need to be sharp for this."

"I'll help," Kale offered. He grabbed a French press and bag of ground coffee while Jacob filled the kettle with water and turned on the stovetop.

Jacob leaned against the counter. "The police believe whoever attacked Stevie has her wallet and phone. Basic deduction implies that since Annie had those items, she attacked Stevie."

"Maybe… maybe Byron's family, whoever hurt Annie… maybe they attacked Stevie, and they planted that stuff in Annie's bag."

"Is that plausible? Was she often without her bag?"

"Well… not often, but when we worked the carnival, it stayed in the tent."

"Okay. That's an angle to consider. We should also consider that Annie herself attacked Stevie. Why would she do that?"

"God… I don't know. She wouldn't. Right? I mean, she had no reason to hurt Stevie."

"Why was Stevie there that night? Why did she ask you to meet her at the diner?"

Kale frowned. "Because she'd been looking into Annie. She thought something was up with Annie."

"Explain."

"I guess it started when I found a driver's license that didn't belong to Annie. The name on the I.D. was Norma Fenn. I mentioned the I.D. to Stevie because Annie said the girl on the license, Norma, had given her the I.D. to help hide from her stalker. Stevie apparently recognized the name Norma Fenn and started doing some digging. She found out Norma Fenn was a girl from downstate who'd disappeared from the Ingham County Fair last summer."

"Hmm… and Annie had the girl's driver's license?"

"Yeah, but like I said, the girl and Annie were friends. Norma had given her the I.D. so Annie could use her name as an alias to hide from Byron."

"But when you met Annie, she went by Annie, right? Not Norma?"

"Right, but she said it had been a couple years since she'd had trouble with Byron, so she stopped using the alias."

"I see. And that's what Stevie wanted to tell you."

"Pretty much. She also mentioned trying to track Annie down, find out where she was from, but she couldn't find anyone by that name."

"Which makes sense considering the issues the police are having right now figuring out who Annie was."

"Yeah." Kale sighed.

"Which brings us back to why Annie might hurt Stevie. If she had any reason to suspect Stevie had discovered she wasn't who she said she was, that might be a motive."

"Maybe, yeah."

The kettle whistled and Jacob poured steaming water into the French press. Kale opened a cupboard and grabbed a coffee mug. He hesitated and then pulled out a second mug for himself. He needed sleep, but feared what nightmares would come when he did.

"Did you tell Annie why you were meeting Stevie?" Jacob asked, returning to the table.

"No, no way. In fact"—Kale weighed his next words, realized the implication before he'd even spoken them—"I couldn't find Annie when I left to meet Stevie."

"Is that odd? Did you guys normally meet after the carnival ended in the evening?"

"Always."

"And after Stevie was attacked, and you returned to the midway, did you ask Annie where she'd been?"

Kale shook his head. "After everything that happened that night, I pretty much forgot about it. I was so fried when I finally made it back to the fair. It was the last thing on my mind."

"How did Annie seem when you got back?"

Kale remembered finding Annie on the carousel, blood dripping down her wrist, coating her teeth where she'd chewed her own thumb.

"She seemed… upset that I'd left the night before and not told her."

"But you said yourself you couldn't find her."

Kale nodded.

"Kale, this is all pretty concerning, and it doesn't look good. This girl is missing, and right now, you're person of interest number one. I think the best move will be to tell the police everything, and I mean everything, including the murder of Byron and disposing of him in the lake."

"There's more," Kale murmured.

Jacob poured each of them a cup of coffee.

"Today, I drove to the property where we got rid of the body. I went in the camper and searched. I found a binder under the bed. There was an article about a car accident and there were a bunch of articles about girls who'd vanished from county fairs."

Jacob sipped his coffee, his expression unreadable. Despite being eight years Stevie's senior, Jacob had always been the goofy older brother. He loved to play practical jokes on Stevie and their parents. Now he looked like another person altogether, a gravely serious person. "Do you have the binder?"

"No." Kale hung his head. "It was in my mom's car." Kale remembered the tape he'd tucked into his pocket. He fished it out and held it up. "I do have this, though."

Jacob took it, turning it over in his hand. "A video tape?"

"Yeah. I found it in the camper in a shoebox that was all taped up and kind of hidden. There was other stuff in the box too—handcuffs and a bottle of pills."

Jacob raised an eyebrow. "Handcuffs?"

Kale nodded.

"That's disturbing. We need to find a way to watch this. Hold on." Jacob took out his phone and typed a message.

"Who did you text?"

"A friend of mine from college. He's a tech guy, specifically likes the old-school stuff. He might know how to transfer the footage from this tape so we can watch it. How about the binder? Did you find anything else important in that?"

"I didn't get a chance to read the whole thing because smoke started coming up through the camper. It was on fire."

"Someone lit it on fire while you were in it?"

Kale nodded.

"Why didn't you call the police?"

"I freaked out because Byron's body was in the lake… I don't know. I just keep making the same stupid mistakes over and over again. I ran. The door had been… locked somehow from the outside. I couldn't get it open, so I climbed out a window, jumped in my mom's car and fled. I saw smoke in the sky, I think from the boathouse. I'd almost made it home when all of a sudden someone in a Halloween mask sat up in the backseat. They put a cord around my neck and started strangling me. They must have climbed into my car at the property. I couldn't breathe and then they shoved something over my face, a rag or something. I think it had chloroform on it. I passed out and woke up to Zinnia giving me CPR on the side of Chapel Road."

43

"That's pretty scary. And it means you're probably in serious danger. Whoever attacked you also put a woman's dismembered body in the trunk of your mother's car."

Hearing the words spoken aloud brought a new wave of despair rushing through Kale. "It has to be Annie's, right? Someone killed Annie?"

"I don't know that, Kale. We can't know until they identify her, and… based on the condition of the body, it may take a while."

"And in the meantime, we just… wait? How can that be okay?" Kale stared at Jacob, unable to imagine what the hours, days, maybe even months ahead would feel like.

Jacob looked at him seriously. "I've known you your whole life and I believe you, Kale, but let me tell how the police are going to view your story. You went to an isolated property Annie had originally taken you to, a place where the two of you disposed of a body. Conveniently the place got set on fire, all evidence destroyed. Your mom's car was abandoned less than a mile away from your house, walking distance back here. The police are going to surmise that you went to the property, dismembered Annie, put her torso in the trunk of your mother's car, faked an attack and theft of the vehicle and lay on the side of the road until your siblings found you."

Kale gaped at him. "But I didn't. That's not true. Why would I put her body in my mom's car? Why wouldn't I just leave her at the property?"

"I understand why you ask that, but murderers sometimes set up elaborate ruses to shift the focus away from them. Sometimes those ruses make them look even guiltier. I believe you're telling the truth, but the police won't. They think you're orchestrating this whole thing, so it's up to us to prove that someone else is behind it. We have to find out who the stalker was. Otherwise, we can't track down the family and see if they're involved."

"That was partially why I went to the property," Kale murmured.

"You thought there might be information about him there?"

"Yeah, and if I didn't find anything, I was going to…" He glanced at the hallway, wondered if his parents and sister had been listening the entire time. He half-hoped they had. It would save him from telling it all again and seeing the look in their eyes when he did it. "Pull the body out of the water."

Jacob studied him, his expression doubtful. "You thought he'd have I.D. on him."

Kale rubbed the back of his neck. "I wanted to see his face."

"You realize a level of decomposition would have taken place. Whatever is in that lake isn't going to look like a picture of this guy."

"Yeah."

"It's obvious to me that someone is either trying to frame you or kill you, Kale. Which do you think it is?"

Kale took a drink of his coffee. It tasted bitter. "They could have killed me in my car, strangled me all the way. Whoever lit the camper on fire… they let me escape."

"It seems that way, yes. And for all their attempts, you look pretty unharmed."

Kale touched his throat. "Yeah."

"So, they want to frame you. We're going to have to prove you're innocent."

"Isn't it the other way around? The police have to prove I'm guilty."

"If that was how the justice system really worked, I'd be out of a job."

～

Before Jacob left, he gave Kale specific instructions to not be alone, stay armed, and be around people at all times. Only his mother was still awake when Jacob headed out at nearly two in the morning. Lucy insisted on packing a Tupperware of zucchini brownies for him to take.

Alone, Kale and his mom sat in the living room. The clock above the couch steadily ticked the minutes away.

"Why don't you stretch out on the couch, honey? Try to get a little sleep."

Kale rubbed his grainy eyes. "I really don't want to." He did want to, he desperately wanted to sleep, but hated what awaited him there.

"I have melatonin. That gummy kind that Sage likes. Want one of those?"

Kale shook his head. "It's okay, Mom. Why don't you go to bed? I'll be fine."

She stood and grabbed the remote from under the TV. "How about we watch something? It's so quiet in here I can hear the grass rustling outside."

"Sure," Kale said.

He barely paid attention as his mom flipped on the television and started a Spider-Man movie. He'd gone through a phase in childhood when Spider-Man had been his idol. He'd dressed as Spider-Man for Halloween, insisted on having a Spider-Man backpack, Spider-Man lunch pail and coat with a hood that looked like Spider-Man's head.

The opening scene of Peter Parker getting bit by a radioactive spider drifted at the periphery of Kale's gaze. He rested his chin on his chest and blinked, his eyelids growing heavy.

Someone knocked on the door, and Kale jerked awake. He sat alone in the living room. It was dark and quiet, but the sound of the knock echoed in his head.

He sat up and waited for it to come again. No sound but the ticking clock. Had he dreamed it? His eyelids, so heavy, drifted closed.

Three more knocks reverberated down the hall from the front door. Kale's eyes shot open.

He stood and groggily made his way to the front door. He peered through the frosted glass that flanked the entrance. A person stood there, a dark shape barely illuminated by the sliver of moonlight that splashed the yard beyond.

He thought back to Jacob's warning the night before. 'Don't be alone, and stay armed, just in case.'

Another sound emanated from the opposite side of the door—scratching, as if the person on the front step were dragging their fingernails down the wood door.

Kale stepped back, cringing at the sound.

"Don't answer it." Sage's voice came from behind him.

Kale reeled around, clutching his chest. "Crap, Sage. You scared me."

She stood at the top of the stairs wearing a Beetlejuice t-shirt that fell to her knees. She lifted a finger to her lips.

Kale frowned and looked from Sage back to the door.

The door handle turned and then rattled, shaking the door in its frame.

Kale looked back at Sage, whose eyes were fixed on the door. She swayed slightly. Her face had gone pale and sweat made her face shiny.

"Sage?" He took a step toward her. "Are you okay?"

She said nothing, but suddenly she was falling forward, eyes slipping closed.

Kale took the steps three at a time and caught her as she plummeted head-first down the stairs. He wrapped his arms around her waist and sagged back against the wall. She'd lost weight, felt feather-light in his arms.

A strip of light appeared beneath the door to his parents' bedroom. The door swung open and his mother stepped out, eyes big. Kale's father was close behind.

"Kale?" his mother said, frowning, and then she spotted Sage. She rushed forward and helped ease Sage up. "Frank, hurry, come get her."

Frank lifted Sage from Kale's and his mother's arms. He held her against him, head on his shoulder, legs dangling.

"What happened, Kale?" his mother asked, putting a hand to Sage's forehead. "She's burning up."

"She was standing on the top of the stairs and she started to fall. I ran up and caught her."

"Oh, thank God."

"I'm going to carry her to her bedroom, Lucy. You better call the night nurse," Frank said.

"Let me take her temperature first. Kale, can you get the thermometer out of the medicine cabinet?"

"I'm on it." Kale hurried up the last of the stairs and down the hall. He flipped on the light in the bathroom, illuminating the tile floor and old-fashioned claw-footed tub. The medicine cabinet had once been a metal locker in the basement embalming room. The door screeched when he opened it. He found the thermometer and turned back to the door.

Another reflection met his in the mirror. A man, his face burned beyond recognition, stared out from charred, leathery-looking skin. His eyes were two green slits in his blackened face.

44

—————

Kale gasped and dropped the thermometer.

He didn't bend to pick it up, but continued watching the man, noticing too that he could smell him. The bathroom reeked of scorched flesh.

"Kale?" his mom called.

Kale blinked. The man's reflection no longer occupied the glass. Kale snatched the thermometer from the floor and hurried out of the bathroom, leaving the light on behind him.

Kale's mother took the thermometer. "Sage, honey, open your mouth. Let's take your temperature."

Sage parted her lips. Her eyes, feverish, shifted from Lucy to Kale. "He got in, didn't he?" she whispered.

"Let's get this under your tongue." Lucy slipped the thermometer in place, then turned to look at Kale. "Who got in?"

Kale shook his head, staring at Sage, whose eyes had slipped closed. "No one."

Frank appeared in the doorway, cell phone pressed against his ear. "The nurse says we better take her to the ER, just in case. Kale—"

"I've got it. The other kids will be fine. I'll let them know what's happening when they wake up."

The thermometer beeped.

"It's one-oh-five," Lucy said, her voice strained.

"I've got her," Frank said. "Go get the van started." He reached one arm behind Sage's back and another beneath her legs.

"What can I do?" Kale asked.

"Um… you start the van. I'll get my purse and Sage's hospital bag."

Kale stood and left the room. He hurried down the stairs and paused at the door. With a deep breath, he flipped the lock and jerked the door open. No one stood on the front stoop.

Because he's already inside.

Kale shuddered and hurried to the van. He opened the driver's door and leaned in, pushed the key into the ignition and started the engine. He went to the side and opened the back door so his dad could easily slide Sage into the backseat.

His parents appeared at the front of the house.

"Are you okay, Kale?" his mother asked as Frank loaded Sage.

"I'm fine. Just go. Call as soon as you know what's happening."

"We will." She kissed his cheek and climbed into the back, lifting Sage's head and settling it into her lap.

"Keep the doors locked and keep"—Frank dropped his voice—"a weapon handy, just in case."

"Okay. Thanks, Dad."

"Wait!" Zinnia flew down the front steps, holding Sage's stuffed Oogie Boogie. She came around the van and handed the toy to Lucy.

"Oh, Zin, thank you." Lucy's eyes welled up as she snuggled the plush toy close to Sage.

"Go," Zinnia said. "And call us soon."

Zinnia and Kale stood in the driveway and watched the tail lights grow small and then disappear.

"Did we wake you up?" Kale asked.

Zinnia shook her head. She wore a matching pajama set she'd likely sewn herself, decorated in smiling bananas and lemons. "I've been online all night. I've found some stuff out. Come look."

"What stuff?"

"Stuff about Byron Low, the guy who disappeared from Gaylord."

"Were you listening when I was talking to Jacob?"

"Yeah, sorry. I know I shouldn't have, but that antique air vent above the refrigerator leads right into the living room. Me, Mom and Dad heard everything."

"Ugh…" He rubbed his temples. "How did they seem when they heard it?"

"Scared, sad, but not the way you think. I know you're afraid you've let them down. You're wrong, Kale, okay? Mom and I talked a lot about you and Annie and you joining the fair. She knew you were… in love, just totally neck deep in your feelings and not quite seeing clearly. What happened isn't your fault."

"But the things I did…"

"Don't worry about that right now."

Kale followed Zinnia into the house. He locked the door and secured the deadbolt.

In her room, she turned her desktop so he could see a private message screen.

"Are you talking to someone on here?"

"Yep. His name is Carter, and he produces a podcast called *Mysterious Michigan*. It's all about disappearances, unsolved murders and weird Michigan urban legends. He covered the case of Byron Low last year."

"I don't think Byron's the stalker, Zinnia. She must have given me a false name."

"Or maybe his name was real, but the story was a lie. Maybe she was the stalker."

"Come again?"

"Carter talked to Byron's friends and more than a few of them said they believed Byron's crazy ex-girlfriend killed him."

"Crazy ex-girlfriend?"

"Yep. Georgia. Apparently, she was stalking him after the break-up, showing up at the places he would be, allegedly even breaking into his house—his parents' house, mind you. Sometimes stuff would be missing. Innocuous stuff like a teddy bear his grandmother had made him. One time he got home to find all of his fish dead in the aquarium and when he opened it, the water reeked of bleach."

"Someone poured bleach into his fish tank?"

"That's what he believed. He also came home once to find a dead bird lying in the center of his bed."

"Really?"

"Yeah. He had two close friends, and they gave Carter the dirt on all this weirdness."

"But what makes you think he was connected to Annie?"

"She worked at a carnival."

"Who did?"

"His girlfriend. He'd met her that summer at a fair in northern Michigan. They dated for two months and then he ended it because he was leaving for school and apparently wanted out. She didn't take it well."

Kale brushed both hands through his hair. He sat down on the edge of Zinnia's bed.

Across the room, the door creaked and swung closed. A shadow passed beneath the door.

Zinnia stared at it, mouth turned down. She stood and peered into the hallway.

"One of the other kids awake?" Kale asked.

She shook her head and sat back down at her desk. "Stuff like that happens sometimes, but usually only when Sage is home," Zinnia murmured.

Kale thought of Sage's mumbled words as she lay feverish on her bed. *He got in, didn't he?*

"Did the police ever look into the ex-girlfriend?" Kale asked.

"Yeah. She had an alibi they couldn't poke holes in."

"What was it?"

"She was with another guy that night. He was a carny. He vouched for her."

"Even if all this is true, I don't see how it changes anything."

"If Annie has lied to you since you met, if other people who have vanished are linked to her, she may not be missing. She may be the one setting all this up."

"There was a dead body in Mom's car, Zin."

"According to this site, there are a bunch of girls who have vanished in the last two years alone."

"Meaning what? Annie murdered those women and put one of them in Mom's trunk to frame me?"

"Is that theory any more unbelievable than what we're currently working with? A stalker attacked Annie, she murdered him and now his family is taking vengeance on both of you by murdering her and framing you for her death?"

The lights flickered and went out.

"Shoot," Kale murmured.

They came back on. Zinnia's computer had turned off and now it started the process of rebooting. She seemed unperturbed. "There's been a lot of activity in the house lately."

"What do you mean?"

"Lights flickering, faucets turning on, cold rooms. Sage and I have talked a lot about it. And you know what she says? Annie brought them."

Kale frowned. "She mentioned something like that to me too."

"But you don't believe Sage? You think it's all in her head?"

Kale thought of the one-eyed woman, the man with the wasted face, and now the last apparition, burned beyond recognition. "I believe her," he murmured. "Have… you ever seen them?"

Zinnia pushed her cursor around, clicking to open the internet. "The drifters?"

"Yeah."

"No, but I've seen what they can do." She gestured at the computer. "Listen, there's something else about Annie."

"What?" Kale asked softly, wishing she wouldn't tell him, but of course she would.

"I *had* seen Annie before you brought her to dinner here. She looked so familiar, and the other day it came back to me when I went into town to check out some books from the library. Last winter when I still worked the front desk at the library, Annie came in. She looked different. Her hair was all tucked up under a ballcap and she had a hooded sweatshirt on, also pulled up.

"That's why I paid attention to her. She looked… suspicious, but I kept thinking, *Who steals books from a library? That's just crazy.* And then I got a really good look at her, at her eyes, which are, as you know, unique and very pretty—like jade gemstones. She was watching me from between the bookcases."

45

"You're sure it was her?" Kale asked, puzzled.

"Positive."

"Huh. I don't even know what to make of that."

"Neither do I, but I think we can both agree it's strange and that… things may not be what they seem with Annie."

A yawn overcame Kale and he rubbed his eyes. "I don't think I can do any more of this tonight." He gestured at the computer.

"Yeah, you need to sleep."

Kale stood and started for the door.

"Hey," Zinnia said.

Kale turned back.

"I'm sorry this is happening to you."

"Thanks. And listen, if I actually manage to fall asleep and you wake up before me, will you make sure the kids are good and keep the doors locked and—"

"I've got it, Kale. Go sleep."

K ale slept a deep dreamless sleep, and when he woke to Grover meowing at his bedroom door, he felt the best he had in days. The fuzziness had largely dissipated from his head.

He picked up the hefty gray cat and walked him downstairs, deposited him in the living room. He found his siblings in the kitchen.

"I made French toast," Zinnia announced. "Grab a plate."

"Thanks. It smells good." He sat at the table where Aster, Thorn and Calla had finished their breakfast and were playing a game of Scrabble. "Who's winning?" he asked.

"Aster, as usual," Thorn grumbled.

"Mom called," Zinnia said. "Sage is doing better. They're not really sure what spiked the fever, but they're discharging her in a few hours."

"Oh, good." Kale ate his breakfast, then slipped back upstairs to his room.

Kale sat at his computer, opened the internet and started searching for articles about the man killed in the crash he'd read about in the binder from the camper. Kale didn't know if it would get him closer to discovering Annie's real identity, but he could think of no other options.

Zinnia poked her head in his room. "Hey, the kids want to go to the store and buy some 'get well' stuff for Sage. Do you want to go?"

Kale's phone rang and Jacob's name appeared on the screen.

"Hold on," Kale told her. Kale picked up his phone. "Just one second, Jacob." He turned back to Zinnia. "No... I better stay here."

"If you want us to pick something up for you, send me a text," she said.

"Thanks." He put the phone back to his ear. "Hey, Jacob. What's up?"

"I wanted to give you a couple of updates. First, police found a few things in the search of your car that aren't good."

Kale heard the trail of voices as his siblings headed out of the house. "My mom's car or my car?"

"Your car."

Kale frowned. "What did they find?"

"A bloody scarf. It was under the mat in the trunk, stuck in the spare tire well."

"What? No. I didn't put that there. What color was the scarf?"

"Apparently the parts not covered in blood were gold."

Kale closed his eyes, saw the red-haired girl with her gold scarf searching for Annie at the Muskegon fair. "I know whose it is."

"Yeah, so do the police. It belongs to Kim Hyland. Her mother has already identified it."

"I swear I didn't put it there. I have no idea—"

"Don't worry about that yet. Let me get all this out first, okay?"

"Okay."

"They found a bloody hunting knife beneath the passenger seat wrapped in a towel."

Stunned, Kale sagged back in his chair. "I don't understand."

"It's simple, Kale. Someone wants the police to believe you committed not one, but two murders."

"What am I going to do?"

"Nothing yet. Police are still gathering evidence. They're days, if not weeks, from charging you. They don't have definite proof that Annie or Kim are dead. Our best way to get in front of this is to come clean about everything, but we'll do that together, okay? I'm working on setting up a time with Detective Granger tomorrow. I'm coming back to the Chapel Road house this evening and we're going to go over every detail and lock your story down. Don't panic."

Kale's hand had grown sweaty on the phone and his stomach had shrunken to a stone. "Umm… Zinnia and I found some stuff last night, stuff about Annie that might relate to all this."

"Good, keep digging. But save it for later, okay? I'm on my way to a meeting and only have about four more minutes. I took your tape to my friend this morning and we reviewed it."

"You did? What was on it?"

"Some pretty troubling home video of unconscious women being raped."

"What?"

"Yeah, I know. Is it related to what's happening to you? I tend to think so, but the guy in the video was pretty careful to keep his face out of the camera. The women, on other hand, are fully exposed."

"And they're unconscious?"

"Yeah, it's sickening. And we'll be taking it to our meeting with Granger, but first I want to find out who owns that property."

"Okay, well, I can send you the coordinates if I pull up a map on my phone. Do you think that should work?"

"Yeah, I've got a guy—I'll forward it to him. Email me those after we end the call."

"Okay. I will."

"One last thing. Are you sitting down?"

"Yeah."

"The medical examiner completed the autopsy on the body found in the trunk of your mother's car."

Kale waited, chest tightening.

"It's highly unlikely that it's Annie's. Approximate date of death is more than a week ago. Cause of death was blunt-force trauma and stabbing, and she was also submerged in water for an extended period of time, likely since the day she was killed."

"Holy crap."

"Yeah."

"So it wasn't Annie in the trunk?"

"It doesn't appear that way. Okay, I'm walking into my meeting. I'll plan to be at your place by five tonight. Good?"

"Yeah. Thanks."

Kale sat in silence for several minutes, dumbfounded by the news. It was good news, and yet… a chill crept up his spine.

He still held his phone. He punched in Annie's number and waited. He didn't know what he expected—for her to answer, for someone else to answer.

It rang five times and then someone picked up.

"Annie?" he said.

No response. No sound of breath. Nothing.

The seconds ticked by, minutes. He swallowed, slowly ended the call and set the phone down, suddenly wishing he'd gone with Zinnia and the other kids.

Despite sunlight streaming through the window, the bright smiling face of his pup on the wall, the absolute ordinariness of his surroundings, Kale felt the shadow of fear fold around him.

"Stop freaking yourself out," he murmured, a command he'd often given to himself as a boy when he woke from a nightmare to a dark room where he imagined some monster with razor-sharp teeth and a taste for the blood of children hid beneath his bed.

He forced his eyes to the computer and scrolled the articles for a fatal car crash in Newaygo County in 2010. He found one and clicked it.

'Man Killed in Newaygo County Car Crash Identified as Rick Barnard.'

At the top of the article, a full-color picture of Rick Barnard was on display.

Kale studied the photo, pulse quickening. The man was handsome, with sandy-colored hair and familiar green eyes—Annie's eyes.

The man killed last week in an automobile crash on Boneset Road in Newaygo County has been confirmed as forty-two-year-old Rick Barnard of Bad Axe, Michigan. The crash occurred at approximately ten p.m. The name of the second individual in the car has not been released to the public, as she was reportedly a victim of Barnard's who had been abducted earlier that evening. The investigation into the alleged abduction is ongoing.

Kale stared at the picture, eyes flicking back to the last name, Barnard, and then to Boneset Road.

Music suddenly broke the silence. Kale tilted his head, listening. Had one of the kids come back?

He stepped from his room. *Crazy*, the Aerosmith song he'd heard the first night he'd met Annie, floated down the hall.

The song swept him back as if the melody had sliced a hole in the air beneath his feet and he'd fallen into another dimension—that perfect night not so very long ago and yet an eternity before. For an instant it was all there—the strobe lights on the Himalaya, the rush as they whipped around the track, the stomach drops, the smells of French fries and fried dough, but most of all those fleeting glimpses of Annie, her head tilted back as she laughed.

The lyric 'crazy for you, baby,' skipped and repeated again and then a third time. Kale shook his head, breaking the reverie. He hurried down the hall, following the sound of music to Thorn's room. The refurbished laptop that Thorn shared with Aster sat open on his desk, the song playing on a music program.

Kale grabbed the mouse, hand trembling, and maneuvered the cursor to exit out of the program. The song ended.

He turned around and studied the room, searched for a sign someone else had been in it. Other than the closet or under the bed, there was nowhere to hide.

Kale grabbed a tomahawk Thorn had made from the windowsill. He stepped to the closet and quickly pulled open the door. Clothes hung from hangers. Stacks of jeans sat on a high shelf. The floor was scattered with Thorn's shoes. No one lurked inside.

He closed the door and crept to the bed, tightening his grip on the weapon as he sank to his knees and peered beneath it. Little more than dust bunnies and a few balled-up clothes occupied the dark crevice.

The tinkling sound of bells floated up from downstairs. Kale stood and stepped to the doorway, listening. The bells hung on the handle of a door that led into a utility room.

He opened his mouth to call out, assuming Zinnia had forgotten something, but suddenly a figure filled the doorway across the hall to Sage's room. It was the one-eyed woman.

She'd never been as clear as she was in that moment, and as he gazed at her, he realized without question he was looking at the ghost of Norma Fenn. Slowly, she lifted a finger to her lips. He blinked at her, through her. She faded and was gone.

Kale frowned, and when he heard someone start up the stairs, their footfalls muffled as if they were trying to be quiet, he slipped behind Thorn's door and pressed his back against the wall.

46

Someone moved slowly down the hall, pausing as if peering in every room, but saying nothing.

If it had been Zinnia or another of his siblings, they'd have called out, made their presence known. His pulse quickened, and he tried to slow and quiet his breath.

The floorboard outside Thorn's room creaked. Kale pushed harder against the wall, palms flat on the smooth plaster.

The intruder paused. Kale imagined their eyes sweeping the room. A moment later, they moved on down the hall.

Kale slipped out and softly crept down the stairs. The deadbolt and door lock were secured. Biting his lip, he reached for the deadbolt. Above him, the floors creaked as the person moved back toward the staircase. Within seconds, they'd be in full sight of him standing at the front door.

Kale pivoted and fled down the hall and turned into the stairway that led into the basement. He cringed at the groan of each step beneath his feet.

If he'd have been anywhere else in the house, a dozen exits through windows and doors would have been available. In the basement, there was one path in and one path out. The stairs at the end of the long hall. Why had he run to the basement, of all places?

He hastened to the embalming room and slipped through the door, his clammy feet leaving impressions across the tiled floor. A bead of cold sweat slid down his spine.

Three coffins sat crowded on one side of the room. The embalming table stood front and center beneath a hanging halogen lamp. Shelves on one wall still contained the old embalming equipment. There was nowhere to hide except inside a coffin.

He crept toward the one closest to him and tried to lift the lid. It wouldn't budge. On the floor behind the casket, he noticed a crumpled-up blanket and pillow. He stepped closer and crouched down. How long had it been there? Had one of his siblings slept in the embalming room? He doubted it. A single black hair clung to the white pillowcase.

Kale lifted the blanket and froze. Annie's backpack sat on the tiled floor. Next to it lay her cell phone.

Hands shaking, one ear perked for any sound in the hall, he unzipped the bag. The binder and the shoebox that had been in his mother's car were crammed inside.

Whoever lurked upstairs hadn't just broken in. They'd already been in the house.

From the hall, he heard the gentle screech of a door swinging in.

Kale eased the bag back onto the floor. He picked up the cell phone, but when he tried to turn it on, the screen remained blank. He frowned and flipped it over. The battery had been removed.

"Kale!" a voice called out, a familiar voice, Annie's voice. "Kale. Where are you? I know you're here alone. I've been watching."

Kale stared at the closed door, paralyzed. He'd been mourning her possible murder and yet… some part of him had suspected, had feared it was her all along.

"Kale, why are you hiding from me?" she called. "You said together forever. Nothing could tear us apart. Nothing." Her voice carried from the hall and he tried to imagine what doorway she stood in. The theatre room, the laundry room?

Gritting his teeth, he tried again with the lid. It released an audible groan and Kale froze.

Had she heard it?

"Uh-oh, Kale," she called. "Somebody just walked through the front door. Let's see who's joining us. We're down here," she yelled.

Kale stared at the door. Had someone come home or was Annie bluffing, trying to lure him out of his hiding spot? He heard a muffled voice, his mother's.

Kale strode to the door and pulled it open.

Annie stood halfway down the hall, a handgun pointed at his mother and Sage, who stood on the stairs.

"Come on, you two, keep coming." Annie glanced back at Kale. "Isn't this perfect? One big happy family. Three for the price of one."

"Annie," Kale said. "They're not a part of this, okay? Just… let them walk back upstairs. They'll leave. Won't you, Mom?"

Sage's bottom lip quivered as she looked from Annie to Kale.

"They're not a part of this?" Annie asked. "Are you sure about that, Kale? I think they *are* part of this. Come on, let's all go have a little chat down there in the embalming room. Yeah?"

"No," Lucy said. "Annie, whatever is going on, this is not the solution."

Annie swung the gun toward Kale and pulled the trigger. Kale ducked and covered his head. She'd intentionally aimed high, and the round lodged itself in the wall.

"Annie! No," Lucy screamed.

Sage clutched her mother, face buried in her side.

Annie grinned, turning from Kale to Lucy and Sage. "He's right, Lucy. Go ahead and leave. I'll finish him and maybe myself, too. Don't worry, I'll do it in the embalming room and you can just sweep our blood and brains into the drain."

"We'll do what you say," Lucy said, voice wavering. "Please don't hurt my son."

"Mom, no."

Lucy patted Sage's head. "Please, Annie. Can Sage go? She won't call anyone. She'll just go upstairs and sit in the back garden."

Annie laughed. "God, you must think I'm dumb. Don't worry, I'm used to it. Carny life and all that. One of the perks of that job is how totally people underestimate you. No, Sage can't go upstairs. Both of you into the embalming room. Come on." She trained her gun on Kale. "Any sudden moves and your son's forehead is going to explode."

Lucy grabbed Sage's hand and hurried toward Kale. They slipped past him, his mom's face lined with fear, into the embalming room.

"Go ahead, you too," Annie told him.

Kale walked in behind his mother and sister. His mother hugged him, Sage sandwiched between them. When she released him, Lucy pushed Sage behind them.

Sage clutched both Kale's and their mother's hands.

"Annie," Lucy said. "Don't do this, honey. We can help you. Whatever is wrong, we can make it better."

Annie stared at Lucy, her lips pulled back from her teeth. "Make it better? Is that what you just said?"

"Annie—"

"Don't call me that," Annie snapped. "My name is not Annie."

Lucy glanced at Kale, confused.

"My name," Annie said, hands tightening on the gun, "is Ellen. Ellen Barnard. Does that ring any bells for you, Lucy Goodwin?"

The color drained from his mother's face.

"What is she talking about?" Kale asked.

"Maybe that's not the name you'd remember," Annie said. "Maybe the name you'd be familiar with is Rick Barnard. That one sound familiar?"

Lucy trembled beside Kale. He moved closer to her.

"Annie," Kale pleaded. "Please don't do this. My mom is right. We can help you. Let us help you."

A thin sheen of sweat coated Annie's upper lip and her eyes glittered with some combination of rage and madness. "Help me?" she mocked. "Your slut mother ruined my life. She ruined my mom's life and my sister's life and most of all, she ruined my dad's life. She took him away. And she's going to pay for that."

Kale's mother's breath had grown short and fast.

"Mom, are you okay?" he asked.

Lucy lifted a shaky hand to the scar above her eye.

"Not only did you ruin our lives, you never even told your family. They don't have a clue." Annie shook her head, as if impressed. "Now that is some next-level deception right there. I thought I was a good liar, but you've been carrying this secret for five years. It's literally written on your face."

47

Kale wanted to ask what Annie meant, but he could feel his mother struggling. He held her hand tighter.

"Annie, whatever it is, it's over now. It's in the past. We can still have a future, you and me. Let's just..." He swallowed the lump in his throat. "Let's just walk out of here, get in the van and go. Remember what we talked about? Driving to Canada or Mexico, living in some little cabin. Just me and you."

Annie cocked her head and studied him. "I almost wanted that. You almost tricked me into believing we could have that, that you loved me, but you never did. Did you? Because when I called on you to prove it, you turned on me. You stopped loving me and you started investigating me. And you know what? I thank you for that, for directing me back to my purpose."

"I did love you, Annie. I do love you."

Annie's mouth turned down. "That love you're talking about? I created that. I picked you for a very simple reason. You're Kale Good-win. You're the firstborn child of your whore mother. There was never gonna be a cabin, a happily ever after. Every single thing we did, I orchestrated to dismantle your life. Every single thing.

"The only end was going to be you dead. That's what this has been about, making you dead, Kale, so your mother can understand, so she can wake up and sink into despair, so she can walk through this house and see a million things that remind her of you and know you're never ever coming back.

"Everything I did served that single purpose. Getting you to walk away from your family, to stop listening to your overbearing mother, to turn on your morality, to pick me over your own soul. It was so easy. A few tall tales about being followed and you were mine. With enough time you would have killed for me. You would have followed me to hell and smiled the whole way."

Kale stared at her, unable to see in this ugly, hateful person the girl he'd fallen in love with.

Because she never existed.

"Lucy, did your beloved son tell you what he did? How he wrapped that poor girl's body in duct tape and bricks and dumped her into a nasty little lake?"

"Girl?" he breathed.

Annie grinned and nodded. "Yes, a girl. Kim was her name. I'm sure you remember her, Kale. Gold scarf and that face full of disgusting freckles. My mistake taking on the names of the ones before. Annie Spencer was Kim's girlfriend. No wonder Annie was so excited to come to the property with me. She was tired to death of that self-important bitch." Spittle flew from her lips as she talked.

She took one hand off the gun and bit viciously at the side of her thumb. Then, as if she realized she had less control of the gun, she quickly reasserted her grip.

"Kim was only too willing to jump on Duke's bike with me when I promised to take her to Annie." She laughed. "I actually had her convinced Annie and I were lovers and Annie had been hiding out at the property for a year. I swear people are so gullible it's sickening. They'll believe anything if it's what they want to hear. But you know all about that, Kale. Don't you?"

"Your dad was sick, Annie," Lucy said. "He—"

"Shut up!" Annie screamed, finger tightening on the trigger.

"No, please don't." Kale stepped in front of his mother.

"We just..." Lucy said. "We went for a drive that night. Sage had been so sick and your dad Rick was at the hospital a lot. He sat with people who were dying. It was the most extraordinary thing and... I was so very sad and lost. He said, 'Let's take a drive and talk.' He gave me a bottle of water and... I lost consciousness. He drugged me, Annie."

"More lies. Lies, lies, lies. You lured him away from the hospital that night. You wanted to steal him from my mother, from our family, and when he didn't want you, you killed him."

"That's not true."

"Then why doesn't your son know, Lucy? Hmm? If the big bad man wanted to hurt you and you saved your own life and killed him, why doesn't Kale know?"

"He does know. He doesn't know your father's name, but my children know I'd been driving with a person from the hospital and we were in a terrible accident and that person died."

"Was murdered," Annie snarled.

"It was your dad?" Kale asked, eyes widening.

"Your mother was trying to take him away from us. Another whore trying to ruin our lives, and she did it. She was the one who finally did it."

"Annie, he was going to hurt me, and… he hurt other people, other women."

"They deserved it," Annie muttered. "Every one of them got exactly what they deserved."

"The video," Kale murmured. "It was your dad."

"Shut your stupid mouth," she snapped, again pulling one hand from the gun to tear at her thumb with her teeth.

He thought of rushing her, but he couldn't be sure she wouldn't squeeze off a round first, maybe two, and who would they hit? His mom? Sage?

Kale glanced down at Sage. Her lips were moving and her eyes were fixed on the door. The door creaked and swung open wider.

Annie glanced toward it, shuffling to the side. "Whoever's out there, show yourself or I'll kill all three of them."

The lights flickered.

Sage shuddered and her voice changed. "Ellen…" Sage spoke in a shrill tone. "Ellen, why are you doing this to me? Don't do this." Sage made a howling sound and slapped a hand over her eye. "I can't see. I'm dying." Her voice faded and a long shuddering breath passed from Sage's lips.

Annie's hands faltered. She dropped the gun slightly so Sage was square in front of the barrel.

"No." Lucy blocked Sage and Kale stepped toward Annie.

"Don't move," Annie hissed.

Sage pushed her mother aside and moved back into the front.

The door creaked and then suddenly slammed hard. Annie jumped and whirled to point the gun at the closed door. She swung it back and trained it on Kale. "Who's out there?" she yelled. "Who?" She glared at Lucy. "Is it your husband? Is he out there?"

Lucy blinked and glanced at Kale. A surge of hope swelled in his chest. If his dad was in the house, he'd have called the police. He'd be armed and figuring out a way to defuse the situation.

Lucy shook her head. "After they discharged Sage, I dropped him off at the equipment auction. His friend offered to give him a ride when it's over."

"I hope you know better than to lie to me," Annie told her.

"It's true. I swear it." Lucy looked at Kale and he could see in her face that it was true. His dad had not come home with them.

Sage stared at Annie. When she next spoke, her voice was rapid, fear-filled. "Norma... why? You were my friend. I thought—" Her words were broken off by a terrible guttural scream.

Lucy gasped and Kale crouched near Sage. Her face was white, her eyes rolled back. "Sage..." He shook her shoulders. "Mom, what's happening to her?"

48

"Stand up!" Annie shouted. "Don't touch her. Get away from her. Both of you. Stand back."

Sweat poured down Sage's face, her eyes glazed. She held tight to their mother. "Georgia," she whispered, her voice low, masculine. "Georgia... what did you give me? Call someone... call 911."

"Stop it!" Annie screamed, again training the gun on Sage. "Stop it or I'll kill you. I'll kill all three of you."

The door swung open and missed Annie by only an inch. It slammed into the wall and a chunk of plaster broke loose and splattered on the tile floor. The hallway lights flickered. Annie stared at the darkened doorway.

Kale stepped forward, but his mother grabbed his arm. Her other hand was clamped firmly on Sage.

Kale turned. Annie looked terrified, insane. She was pointing the gun at Sage, her finger tightening on the trigger. The door swung and hit Annie's elbow. She lost her grip, but didn't drop the gun. Lucy sprang at Annie and Sage began to crumple to the floor. Kale caught her and eased her down.

Lucy grabbed hold of the gun and tried to jerk it away. Annie shrieked and ripped the gun back. She brought it forward and slammed it into Lucy's face. Lucy gasped and clutched her mouth. Kale lunged towards Annie and shoved her hard. She used her free hand to grab him, sinking her fingernails into the flesh of his forearm.

They both sprawled through the open doorway into the hall. Somehow, Annie still had control of the gun. She pulled the trigger. The bullet ripped past Kale's head and lodged in the wall behind him. Kale froze.

Annie climbed slowly to her feet and focused the gun on Kale. She released another shot, missing him intentionally. "The next one is for Sage and then your mom if you don't do exactly what I say."

Still in the embalming room, Lucy started toward the door, but it slammed shut between them. Kale heard her wiggling the knob.

"Go," Annie snarled. She gestured down the hall. "We're going outside."

"Kale!" Lucy yelled. "Don't go with her. Don't go." The doorknob shook harder, but didn't open.

"Now," Annie hissed.

Kale wanted to get Annie out of the house, away from his mother and sister. He followed Annie's orders and walked down the hall and up the stairs. He opened the front door.

Annie bumped the back of his head with the barrel of the gun. "Don't you dare run. If you run. I'll kill them both, Kale."

He nodded.

"Go to the van. Get in, both hands on the wheel. Don't move them." Annie kept the gun trained on him as she circled in front of the van and climbed into the passenger seat. "Start it," she demanded.

"There are no keys," he said.

"Where are they?" she snapped. "You stall for one more second and I'm going to blow your brains all over that window and then I'm going to go do the same thing to your baby sister."

Kale gritted his teeth and reached for the driver's side visor. He pulled it down, and the keys fell in his lap.

"Start it. Drive."

He turned the key and maneuvered the van down the long driveway. "Which direction?"

"Left," she commanded.

As he turned from the driveway, he reached for his seatbelt.

"No seatbelt," she snapped.

Kale released the strap and let it fall back into place. He drove down the dirt road, passing the trails he and his siblings had ridden their bikes on. His mother's 'SLOW DOWN' sign still marked what was left of the squirrel carcass.

Kale wondered how long it would take for his mother to escape the embalming room to call the police.

"Where are we going?"

"Don't talk," she hissed.

Kale glanced at her. Her hand wove up and down with the gun. She was getting tired. The gun was getting heavy.

"The property," she said.

"Why? It's a crime scene. There are probably cops crawling all over that place."

She said nothing. He glanced at her, noticed cuts along her forearms, sharp and thin, as if she'd been dragging a razorblade in little criss-crosses over her skin. "Annie… it was a car accident. Your dad and my mom."

"She murdered him on purpose. It was in the police report, so why don't you shut your ignorant mouth?"

Annie ground her teeth. The sound made his skin crawl. Annie reached up and plucked a piece of hair from her head and then another. Each little ping gave him a start. He watched the hairs drift from her fingers and coil on the gray carpet.

"What do you mean, it was in the police report?" He wanted to keep her talking, but he also wanted the truth, the whole story.

"Your *mother* jerked the wheel. Her seatbelt was buckled and my dad's wasn't, so she grabbed the wheel and drove them into a tree."

"You heard what she said. He drugged her. She's telling the truth. I know what was on that video in the camper."

"Shut up!" Annie whispered, and something in her tone made him glance her way.

Her skin was shiny and waxen. A weird little smile clung to her lips that were so chapped they looked bloody. Her eyes were as vacant as a porcelain doll's.

He could feel her losing it. The gun wavered and her whole body swayed with the movement of the van. What if he drove them into a ditch? Just slammed on the brakes and jumped out? He glanced at her.

"Do it, Kale. Whatever you're thinking about. Do it." She cackled. "You won't, because you are a fucking coward."

He gripped the wheel harder, searched for an opening to present itself.

The silence stretched. Annie watched him and he stared at the road, sweat pouring from beneath his arms, his eyes flickering again and again to the rearview mirror, praying for flashing lights. There were none.

"I talked to your sister this morning," he said.

He felt her shift, grow rigid.

"Brenda knows you're alive, Ellen. She's desperate to see you. She said you met a carny at a fair right before you disappeared. A girl with a chameleon tattoo. Did you kill her too?"

Annie shook her head slowly. "I became her."

"What does that mean?"

Annie didn't answer. Almost imperceptibly she rocked from side to side.

"For someone so fixated on other people ruining families," he said, "you've done a pretty good job of destroying your own."

"Your mother destroyed my family."

"Really? You sure it wasn't your rapist dad who did that?"

She said nothing for nearly a minute. "I know you, Kale, and you're not going to bait me. Save your breath."

A calm had fallen over her, a steadiness that unnerved him.

They were going to the property. Jacob knew about the property. He'd send the police there. Better still, maybe police and firefighters still lingered from the previous day's fire. But why would they? They likely hadn't linked the property to any crime yet. Still, any number of things could shift in Kale's favor. He just had to stay alive long enough for help to arrive.

Kale turned onto Boneset Road.

"Faster," Annie told him.

He frowned. "We'll miss the turn."

"I said faster!" She waved the gun.

Kale stared through the windshield, depressing the gas pedal. He glanced over. Annie's eyes flicked from Kale to the side of the road. Kale realized she was looking ahead at the huge black tree with the plastic flowers. The place where her father had died.

He finally understood what she intended to do.

"Faster," she shrieked.

49

Kale vice-gripped the steering wheel, his knuckles turning white. For an instant the burned man was there, standing in the center of the road, with his charred misshapen face and glittering hateful eyes. The van barreled through him and he scattered like dust.

Annie grabbed the wheel and tried to yank it sideways. It didn't budge. Kale held it tight. She shrieked and tried to bash him in the head with the gun. He ducked, and the barrel grazed the side of his head.

"No!" She screamed as they passed the tree.

She fired the gun, the crack deafening. Fire roared through Kale's forearm. The bullet shattered the driver's side window. He slammed on the brakes.

Annie, caught off guard, was flung forward. Her hand smacked the dash and the gun clattered to the passenger side floor. Kale had braced both feet on the floor and his chest slammed against the wheel. He flung open his door and fell out while the car was still rolling. He stood and ran into the woods.

A shot rang out behind him, but he didn't look back.

Kale tore through the forest, aware that at any moment a bullet might explode the back of his head.

He leapt over fallen logs, nearly twisted an ankle in some loamy soil, but he didn't stop until a stitch in his side became unbearable. His forearm wept blood into his shirt, where he clutched it against his stomach.

He'd sprinted for at least fifteen minutes when he finally ducked behind a tree, pressed his good hand into the sore spot above his hip, and doubled over wheezing for breath. Black spots swarmed behind his eyes, blood loss and fatigue threatening to overwhelm him.

Kale tried to listen, to hear if she'd followed him, somehow kept pace, but his own breath and heartbeat drowned out all other sound.

After he caught his breath, he peered around the tree, scanning the forest. She could easily have been concealed behind any of a dozen trees in his view, but he heard nothing.

Hurrying, the cramp still knotted in his side, he limped to the next tree and the next. No branches snapped around him. A crow called from the tree above. Kale glanced up, but continued walking.

He had no clue what direction he was headed, how deep the woods went, how long he'd have to walk to find civilization. The bleeding would continue and there'd come a point when he wouldn't be able to go on, when the fuzziness at the corners of his eyes would go full-blown and he'd lose consciousness.

Kale gazed through the wash of trees, endless, indistinguishable. If he went the wrong way, he'd bleed to death in the forest.

Sweat dripped into his eyes and he rubbed it away. As he scanned the woods, he caught movement from the corner of his eye. He pressed himself against a tree, sure Annie had followed him, but as he stared at the shape, he saw it was not a person at all, but a gold scarf that had caught on a branch. It undulated as if moved by a breeze, though the forest was still. It fluttered, broke away from the branch and vanished.

He turned in the direction of the scarf and started walking.

A half-hour later, Kale stepped from the treeline into the weedy ditch beside a paved road.

A car barreled toward him. It wasn't a van, he knew that much, but still, as he walked closer and lifted his arm to wave for help, a part of him feared Annie's face, frozen in a diabolical grin, would be staring at him through the windshield.

The car slowed and stopped. Kale limped toward it. Two men sat in the front seats. The driver was Detective Granger. He rolled down his window.

"Just the man we're looking for," Granger said.

Kale let out a whoosh of breath and nearly sank to his knees.

Granger stepped out and opened the back door. He eyed Kale's blood-soaked shirt. "Let me see."

Kale winced as Granger peeled his limp arm from his stomach and examined the wound. He turned his arm over gently. "Through and through shot, so that's good. No bullet lodged in there. Guess we better get you to a hospital."

Kale slid into the backseat and closed his eyes.

50

The bullet hadn't done irreparable damage. It had passed cleanly through Kale's forearm without hitting bones or damaging nerves.

As he sat in the hospital bed, his family arrived. They crowded into the room and surrounded him, hugging and crying and bumping his arm, and despite the pain, he'd never been so happy to see them.

Sage looked exhausted and pale. He used his good arm to pull her onto the bed beside him. After a while, his nurse came in and sternly told the Goodwin group, "Two visitors at a time." Kale's dad offered to take the other kids to the cafeteria and left Sage and Lucy behind.

Lucy pulled a chair close to the bed. Sage had fallen asleep. "My matching bookends," she murmured, pushing a curl off Sage's forehead.

"Do you think she's okay?" Kale asked, considering Sage.

"Okay for now. But this morning took a lot out of her. Out of all three of us." Lucy touched his bandaged arm. "How's your pain?"

"Not bad now. They gave me some painkillers when I first got here."

"I was so scared," she whispered. "When Annie got you out of the house, I was absolutely terrified."

"It was better that way. If we'd have stayed, who knows what might have happened."

His mother nodded. "Thank God you escaped."

"Mom, can we talk about it? About what happened the night you were in the accident?"

Her hand drifted to her scar. "I thought you might want to. I'm sorry I didn't tell you earlier. I never could have imagined..."

"It's not your fault. Don't think that even for a minute."

"Yes... I know, and yet... I still feel responsible somehow. And as angry as I am at what Annie did, I feel very sorry for her."

"Yeah," Kale sighed. "It might take me a while to get there."

"I met Rick Barnard at the hospital in Muskegon. To tell you the truth, it didn't even cross my mind to question his intentions. I was forty-one years old, had six children, was holding vigil at the hospital during those terrible weeks after Sage's radiation. I was long past the age of thinking anyone would target me in that way.

"I didn't meet him for the first time the night of the accident. I'd talked with him three or four times by then. He visited the dying and offered grief counseling to families, sometimes for free. He said he travelled all over the state doing it. He was so easy to talk to and he listened. He'd sit there for two hours and listen to me bemoaning all my fears. Dad was working so much then just trying to keep us afloat."

"I remember," Kale murmured. "Those were hard days."

"They were. And that night, I just felt so hopeless. Sage had been sick and throwing up for two days, terrible headaches. I remember sitting there and crying until I was bone dry. Rick listened, and after a while, he said, 'You know what you need? A little break from this place.' He suggested we go for a drive. I could talk if I wanted or I could just stare out the window or take a nap. Whatever I needed. I said yes. Had it been almost any other night, I probably wouldn't have, but that night was a terrible low point and so... without a moment's hesitation, I said yes."

Sage grumbled in her sleep and shifted. Kale moved so more of her head was propped in the crook of his shoulder.

"As soon as we climbed in his car, he reached in the backseat and handed me a bottle of water. He always kept a case, he said, because crying dehydrates you. 'Drink up,' he told me, and I did. And then..." Lucy touched her scar again. "I don't know. I don't even remember passing out. The next memory I have is waking up, my head against the glass of the passenger side window. Everything was heavy and I could barely lift my head. I knew he'd drugged me. I could feel it in my body, slowing everything down, and he was beside me at the wheel."

"Did he say anything to you?"

"No. I couldn't even talk, that's how out of it I was. And yet some part of me, my instincts perhaps, knew that I was in big trouble and that if I was gonna have any chance of surviving the night, I had to do something quick. Somehow, I grabbed the wheel and yanked it. I had buckled my seatbelt, and he hadn't. I'm sure he didn't think I had enough awareness or motor control to do anything. The car swerved, and we hit a tree at full speed."

Kale thought of the big black oak on the side of Boneset Road, the faded plastic flowers. He wondered who had put them there—Ellen, most likely.

"I didn't mean to kill him. I truly didn't, but I'm sure that's exactly what he intended to do to me after whatever else." She shuddered. "Rick went through the windshield and hit the tree. My head struck the dash, split my face open. I shattered my right wrist."

"You must have been terrified."

"I was. I remember staring at him through the destroyed windshield, all crumpled on the hood of the car. I sat there for so long, thinking he was going to wake up. And then I started to smell gas." She closed her eyes. "Do you... Do you want to hear this? Because if you'd rather not—"

"I want to know. Tell me, please."

Lucy sighed. "I smelled gas and I couldn't get my door open. I pushed myself into the backseat and climbed out through one of those doors. I made it twenty or so feet when the car exploded into flames. And..." She pushed her hands through her dark hair. "He started screaming. He wasn't dead. And I... there was nothing I could do. I just sat on the side of the road and waited for the police."

Kale leaned his head back against the pillows. "That was really brave, Mom. You stopped a terrible person from ever hurting anyone else."

"He'd mentioned he had daughters, but I knew nothing about them. After the accident, a lawyer contacted me, said I should file a civil suit against his family for damages." She shook her head in disgust. "As if they hadn't gone through enough. The death of a husband, of a dad, and the realization of why it had occurred? It must have been an absolute nightmare for them."

"Did his wife ever try to contact you?"

"No. I was afraid of that. For probably the first year, every time the phone rang, I felt sick, but she never called and with time... I tried to forget what had happened, but... we can never really forget, can we?"

EPILOGUE

Two weeks after Kale was discharged from the hospital, he drove to Alma to meet Brenda Barnard at a bookshop that was halfway between his house in Muskegon and her house in Bad Axe.

Kale parked at Poe's Books and Café and stepped from Zinnia's car. As he reached the sidewalk, a white Escort pulled up to a meter. Brenda Barnard had told him she drove a white Escort.

She climbed from the car, looking tense, and searched through her purse, plucked out quarters and fed the meter.

To Kale's surprise, Brenda looked almost nothing like Ellen. Brenda had brown, frizzy hair tied back in a ponytail. Her gray eyes blinked behind thick-lensed glasses. She wore a loose-fitting t-shirt that stated 'Read, Return, Repeat' and a pair of knee-length jean shorts.

"Brenda?" he asked.

She gave a little jump and nearly dropped her purse. "Kale?"

"Yeah." He stepped forward, offering the hand not in a sling. "Nice to meet you."

She forced a smile. "Thank you for meeting me. I'm sure this feels unusual. At least it does for me."

"My barometer for 'unusual' has been pretty skewed this last month."

Her eyes flicked to the blue sling. "How's your arm?"

"It's okay. I'm just grateful it wasn't my right. Have you been here before?" He walked toward the café door.

"Yeah. It's a drive, but I try to get here a couple times a year. It's very warm, not the temperature, but the feel of the place, you know?"

"Yeah. I like it already." Kale held the door open for Brenda.

He followed her between shelves to a back corner café with couches and upholstered armchairs. A man stood behind the counter, stocking bags of coffee.

"If it isn't my favorite bookworm," the man, nametag Charlie, said, beaming at Brenda.

"Thanks, Charlie. No books today though. I've come for the coffee and comfy seats."

"Those are never in short supply. What can I get ya?"

"I'll have the cinnamon latte."

"And for you?" Charlie asked Kale.

"Hmm… umm… why not, I'll try the cinnamon latte too."

"Coming right up."

Brenda chose two chairs nestled in the corner. Sun from a skylight lit the amber floor. "Have you heard from Ellen?" she asked.

"I was about to ask you the same thing. No, I haven't."

"That's probably a good thing, huh? I keep looking out the window, sort of perking up anytime I hear a car on our street. Not so unlike those first weeks and months after she went missing. Always waiting for her to come home."

"I'm sorry. I can't imagine how that must feel."

"Like a fantasy now. She's not coming home. When they find her, if she's alive… she'll go to prison." Brenda took off her glasses and cleaned them on her t-shirt. Her eyes were red-rimmed.

"Yeah, I'd imagine you're right. Can I ask if… if it was shocking to you, all of this stuff, or if—?"

"If there'd always been something wrong with her?"

Kale nodded.

"Some part of me always suspected that something wasn't right with Ellen. It's terrible to say that, but after my dad died, she spiraled. She'd always had black moods and other stuff, self-harm stuff. She was hospitalized after my dad died for burning herself with cigarettes and cutting herself. Even before he died, she had this ability to mimic people. She could… look different and talk different, pick up accents easily. She liked to dress up, but it wasn't just clothes. She'd try on a whole person.

"It bothered me, but I figured I was just jealous. Ellen was always so beautiful, with those sparkling green eyes and pale blonde hair. She was always blonde, but I know after she left, she started dyeing it. She was fair-skinned, the type of girl who got cast in the lead of every play. She looked like a Disney princess. When we were young people would stop my parents to comment on their stunning daughter. And even though she looked delicate, she wasn't weak and demure. She could be loud and forceful. She knew how to get her way.

"I was the opposite—the steadfast one, the school nerd. I had no boyfriends and lived most of my life with my nose buried in a book. After Ellen left, our house became so quiet. My dad and Ellen were the loud ones, the animated ones. My mom and I were all but invisible."

Kale imagined the Chapel Road house always buzzing with noise and activity. "That must have been hard."

"It was. And I'm not sure what's worse, living in their shadows or living in the silence now that they're both gone."

Charlie appeared with two large mismatched mugs. He slid them onto the table. "Enjoy," he said.

"Thank you." Brenda smiled at him.

"Did you and Ellen know after your dad died what had really happened?" Kale asked.

Brenda sipped her latte. Her hand shook as she put the cup back on the table. "Not at first. My mom said it was a car accident, but eventually we learned the truth. Police had questioned her about my dad. She was obviously shocked that another woman… that your mother… had been in the car, and your mom told the police that she'd turned the wheel on purpose because he'd drugged her. Ellen and I eavesdropped when the detective came. We heard everything. Your mom claimed she'd met my dad at the hospital."

"While my sister was sick."

"Yeah. He was a grief counselor and he often went to hospitals and sat with people who were alone or just counseled people for free in the waiting room. He was that kind of guy… but he had another side too. Moods like Ellen. He'd disappear sometimes for three or four days at a time. My mom never questioned him because he was a master of the silent treatment and it would just spur him to leave again.

"After he died, two more women came forward with stories about rapes. They didn't know what had happened. They'd been unconscious, woken up with him in his car, but they could feel... that he'd done something to them. Obviously, no charges were pressed because he was dead, but... we had no idea about the other women, the ones he'd met at fairs who... never made it back home. The ones they found at the property."

Kale cringed as he thought of the boathouse and the lake and all the bodies it had concealed. Detective Granger told him they'd pulled five women out, one man. The first three were attributed to Rick Barnard—those had been in the water for five or more years. The others were suspected to be Georgia Hought, Byron Low, Norma Fenn and Annie Spencer. Ellen's final victim, Kim Hyland, had been in the water and then removed, dismembered and put in the trunk of Kale's mom's car. Also in the lake they'd discovered the submerged Toyota 4Runner that had disappeared with Byron Low.

Though Ellen had set fire to the camper and the boathouse, the lower floor of the boathouse, the boards rotted and wet, had not burned and police had discovered a cardboard box concealed beneath a canvas tarp filled with the wallets and personal effects of her victims. They'd also found more than a hundred photographs of Kale and the Goodwin family. She'd apparently stalked them for over a year before she homed in on Kale.

"I'm trying to understand why Ellen blamed my mom," Kale said. "I mean... other women came forward about what your dad had done. They tested my mom's blood after the accident and it was positive for rohypnol-the date rape drug."

"For Ellen, my dad could do no wrong. They were... inseparable. Sometimes I think she even hated me and my mom for taking his attention away." Brenda sighed. "It feels wrong talking about her like this, like I'm betraying her, but then I think about the last two years, how we searched for her and cried for her, and all the time she was living her life... acting out these sick fantasies or whatever it was."

"What do you think it was?"

"Vengeance with you. The others? I don't know. She used their names, stole their identities. Maybe she was trying to be someone else. Is there ever really a reason that makes sense?"

"What about Byron Low? She obviously didn't steal his identity."

"Yeah, I've thought about him. Ellen had a lot of boyfriends growing up and she had a pretty familiar pattern. Fall head over heels in love, get the guy wrapped around her finger, and then possess them."

"Possess them?"

"That's what it seemed like. Like she owned them, they'd do anything for her, and when they stopped, she was vicious. She'd do sick little things to get revenge. She got arrested her freshman year in high school for slashing her boyfriend's tires. Another ex-boyfriend accused her of intentionally hitting and killing his dog."

"Really? Did he know for sure it was her?"

Brenda shook her head. "He couldn't prove it, but..." She sighed. "A part of me always believed it."

"What does your mom think about all of this?"

Brenda looked at the floor. "We haven't really talked about it." Her eyes darted up to his and then away. "That sounds strange, doesn't it? My mom has always struggled with... alcohol and... other things. It got worse after my dad died and we found everything out, but even before that, it was a problem. Then when Ellen disappeared, our mom just gave up—stopped leaving the house. I already worked full-time, but I took on a second job to cover our expenses. That's part of what makes me so furious at Ellen now, that she could have done this to our mom, who she knew was fragile.

"That's part of the reason I wanted to talk to you." Brenda smiled, but there was no joy in it. "I just wanted so badly to talk to someone about all this, someone who knows what happened."

Kale took a sip of his latte, unsure how to respond. His family had talked of little else in the preceding weeks. They'd hashed over Annie's motives, the murders, all the tricky things she'd done to deceive Kale. She'd created the fictitious stalker, set herself up as the victim, so that Kale could play the hero. And that's exactly what he'd done.

"About a year after my dad died, my mom confided to me one night. She was deep in the whiskey, slurring. She told me that while she and my dad were in undergrad—that's where my parents met, at Western Michigan University—he was accused of date rape. A girl in my mom's sorority said my dad put something in her drink and raped her. He was kind of a big man on campus and people believed him over the victim. She dropped the charges, but she showed up at my mom's dorm one night and warned her that he'd choked her too. The girl was sure he'd intended to kill her, but one of his roommates had knocked on the door."

"And your mom still married him?"

"He was very charismatic and handsome and my mom was crazy

about him. She didn't want to believe it, so she didn't. She grew to regret that, and I guess alcohol is her escape of choice." Brenda gestured at the shelves. "Books are mine."

"What was Ellen's?"

"Pretending to be someone else."

"Do you think she's doing that now?"

Brenda sighed. "She has to be, right? How else has she managed to not get caught? They found your family's van, so obviously she doesn't have a vehicle. The property is crawling with cops, so she can't hide out there."

"Did you ever look for her at the Boneset property after she disappeared from the fair?"

"Once, but..." Brenda shrugged. "We didn't even consider it a possibility. There's no running water, no electricity. It belongs to my uncle, who lives in Costa Rica, and he hasn't been back to the States in like twenty years. I've never even met him. My dad used to take us there as kids, but he took Ellen more than me. I preferred to stay home with my books."

"Do you think Ellen knew what was in the lake? The women your dad had killed?"

Brenda took off her glasses and rubbed her eyes. "I want to say no, but... what are the chances that both she and my dad independently of each other used the lake as... a dumping ground? I feel sick just saying that. I don't know. Maybe... maybe she found one of the women. Maybe he confided to her what he'd done. But the coincidences—the fact that she targeted people at fairs just like he did..."

"Why do you think she did that?"

"It was something they loved, Ellen and my dad. They'd travel to county fairs all over the state, go on the rides, bring home cheap stuffed animals and plastic bags of goldfish that Ellen would leave sitting on her windowsill until they died." Brenda shuddered.

"The day I met Annie, someone had put tickets to the Muskegon County Fair under my windshield wiper blades."

"She was very good at knowing how to get people to do what she wanted."

The bell above the café door dinged. Kale turned quickly, not comfortable having his back to whoever walked in. It was an elderly man wearing muck boots and a straw hat. He barely glanced at Kale and Brenda before heading for the gardening section.

Kale fiddled with the handle on his mug. "The day I last saw Ellen, she tried to yank the wheel while I was driving to the property. She tried to repeat what happened between your dad and my mom. I think she meant for us both to die. I wonder if—"

"She walked into the woods and killed herself and the police haven't found her body?"

Kale nodded.

"Maybe," Brenda said.

"But you don't think so?"

"That'd probably be the best thing, right? It means no more victims. It means your family is safe, but… if I've learned one thing about Ellen, it's that nothing is ever as it seems."

"**O**h, my heart, it's the whole gang," Lucy said, walking into the kitchen at the Chapel Road house with a stack of pizzas.

"Woot, woot!" Zach pumped his fist. He stood and grabbed the pizzas. "Let me take those off your hands, Mrs.—"

She raised an eyebrow.

"Lucy," he quickly corrected.

Kale and Stevie sat side by side at the table. The bandage on her head was gone, but they'd shaved half of her head and a track of ugly black stitches marred her scalp.

"You guys leave tomorrow?" Stevie asked.

"Yep, the whole Goodwin posse is Texas-bound. MD Anderson, here we come," Kale said.

"That's the big cancer hospital?" Zach asked taking a bite of pizza.

"Yeah. They've approved Sage for a clinical trial."

"When did you get the van back?" Stevie asked.

"Three days ago. The window is fixed and the car place detailed it, so hopefully it doesn't smell like that milkshake Thorn spilled three years ago anymore."

"Hey," Thorn argued. "I didn't spill that milkshake. Aster hit it with her elbow."

"I did not," Aster snapped.

"And neither of you," Lucy added, eyes narrowed on the twins, "mentioned it until it had curdled and the entire van smelled like rotten milk."

"How long will you be gone?" Ben asked.

"The brain cancer trial lasts for three months," Zinnia offered. "But most of us will only stay for four weeks, then we have to trek back because I'm starting at U of M and the other kids have to be back in school. Plus, Kale will be starting his leather-working internship. My mom and Sage will stay on their own for the last two months, with my dad flying down every other weekend."

"Can you say 'house parties?'" Zach asked, leaning forward and unsuccessfully trying to wink at Stevie and Kale.

"Yeah, I'm down with that," Thorn agreed.

"Don't count on it," Lucy said. "Unless by 'house party' you mean 'coming over to help the kids with their homework?'"

"Absolutely, that's what I meant." Zach grinned. "And Ben is totally a history buff. He bores me to tears with biographies of Civil War generals and such things. He'll have these kids getting straight As."

"Leather-working internship?" Stevie asked.

Kale nodded. "My dad talked with a guy at an auction last week who's a leathersmith. He owns a couple of stores and has agreed to take me on as an apprentice."

"That's awesome, Kale. Congratulations," she said.

"Thanks."

Sage appeared in the kitchen, Grover balanced in her skinny arms.

"You're getting pretty strong, Sage," Stevie said. "I picked up that cat earlier, and he feels like he weighs fifty pounds."

Sage wrinkled her forehead. "I know. He's getting so fat. I wish he could go with us to Texas."

"Don't worry, I'll keep an eye on him for you. I'll text pictures and everything."

"Good. I don't want him to get lonely." Sage turned to their mother. "Could we have a bonfire and eat outside?"

"I was just thinking that," Frank said, grabbing a bag of marshmallows from the cupboard. "And afterwards we'll roast marshmallows."

~

They sat on stumps eating pizza around the fire. The smoke drifted toward a sky brimming with stars.

Kale excused himself to use the bathroom. A light wind shook the trees. As Kale made his way toward the house, something blew across the stone path. It was a crumpled piece of paper. He bent and picked it up, unfolded it to find a missing person's flier for Ellen Barnard. He'd never seen one before, hadn't even realized Brenda had made fliers of her missing sister.

Gooseflesh prickled his neck, and he turned quickly, scanning the back garden, the trees at the edge of the yard. He saw no sign of Ellen, but beyond the light cast by the bonfire, everything was in shadow. She could be anywhere.

He walked into the house, pulled his phone from his pocket, and punched in the number for Detective Granger.

The man answered on the first ring.

"I think she's here—Annie, I mean Ellen."

"She's not, Kale. I was just about to call you. We picked her up today."

"You did?" Kale sagged against the counter. "Alive?"

"Yeah. She was driving a stolen car, got pulled over, and fortunately the officer didn't buy her story. It took about five hours of interrogation before she finally admitted to who she was."

"Where did she get arrested?"

"About five miles from your place in Muskegon."

"You're kidding."

"No. She might have been headed there, it's hard to say. But the important thing is we've got her."

Kale blew out a breath. "What happens now?"

"She's been booked and she won't be getting out of jail anytime soon. There'll be a trial, but that's a few months off at least. It all depends on how quickly the prosecutor can go through the evidence."

"I'll be called as a witness?"

"Yes, I'd imagine you will, but I'm not going to speak for the prosecutor."

"And… the body, my pushing it in the lake—"

"Again, I'm not the prosecutor, but there's a good chance you'll be offered immunity for that in exchange for your testimony. You'll have to discuss it when the time comes."

"Okay. Thanks, Detective. Does Ellen's family know? Her sister, Brenda?"

"Yep. We notified Brenda and her mother."

"Has Ellen confessed to anything?"

"Nothing but her name. She's asked for an attorney, so our hands are tied."

"Okay… ummm… she didn't ask about me or anything, did she?"

"No, she didn't. I've got to hang up now, but Kale, the worst is over. Go enjoy your life."

～

After Kale and his dad finished securing suitcases to the roof of the van, Kale climbed into the far back next to Sage. Her stuffed Oogie Boogie sat between them.

"Ready for this?" he asked.

"As long as Dad doesn't let Thorn pick the music."

"Hey." Thorn twisted around in the passenger seat. "I heard that."

"I meant for you to," Sage called.

"I'm in charge of music," Zinnia said. "I've already made a huge playlist. I put everyone's songs on it, so it's fair."

"I vote for Simon and Garfunkel," their dad said, starting the van.

"I second that," their mom said. She sat on the bench seat behind their dad and next to Zinnia.

"Don't worry, Simon and Garfunkel are on the playlist," Zinnia said.

Aster and Thorn groaned.

"And so are Bruno Mars and Maroon 5," Zinnia told the twins.

"What about my songs?" Sage asked.

"I added the entire soundtrack to *The Nightmare Before Christmas*."

Aster, Thorn, and Calla groaned.

"You three hush up," Zinnia said. "I'm hitting play."

Their dad pointed the van down the driveway. As the wheels started rolling, a familiar song poured from the speakers—the Shins' 'Phantom Limb.' Goosebumps rose along the back of Kale's neck.

"Skip this one, please," Kale said.

Zinnia turned around. "What? You love the Shins."

"Not anymore."

"Wish you would have told me that when I made the playlist," she grumbled.

The next song started, 'This Is Halloween' from the *Nightmare Before Christmas* movie. Another trio of groans filled the van.

Sage swiveled in her seat, looked out the back window and waved.

Kale craned around. "Who are you waving at?"

Sage faced forward and buckled her seatbelt. "Norma. She's leaving too, for good this time."

Don't Miss the next Troubled Spirits novel:
After She Fled

THE TRUE STORY THAT INSPIRED GRAVE DEVOTION

In 2018, a young woman who worked at a Florida hair salon ended her shift and vanished without a trace.

In the coming days, investigators were mystified. They checked into the woman's ex-husband and boyfriend, but could find no evidence of their involvement. Police questioned other salon staff members who worked with the woman. They discovered that a newer female employee had abruptly quit after the stylist disappeared. The new employee claimed she had a stalker and couldn't be involved in police matters. The co-worker had worked at the salon for only a month.

Days after the stylist disappeared, police discovered the stylist's vehicle abandoned in the parking lot of a store. When they reviewed footage from the store, they observed the co-worker, who had evaded police, parking the missing stylist's vehicle.

Investigators found the co-worker and arrested her. What followed was a series of discoveries leading to the true identity of the co-worker who'd been using a false name during her employment at the salon-a name which belonged to a young woman who'd died in a car crash. As detectives dug into the woman's background, they uncovered a tangled web of lies. The woman had used over eighteen aliases in the previous twenty years.

When crime scene technicians examined the salon where the stylist was last seen, luminol revealed a gruesome crime scene with blood smears on the walls, chairs, sinks, and floor. Surveillance video of the salon parking lot revealed the stylist's co-worker carrying large trash bags to the dumpster the night the stylist disappeared. Additional video from a nearby store showed the co-worker purchasing gloves, cleaning supplies and an electric knife. It was disturbingly clear the co-worker had brutally murdered the stylist.

After a difficult trial, during which the accused co-worker had frequent outbursts in court, a jury convicted her of the brutal slaying of the stylist.

The stylist's body has never been found.

Police suspect the woman with many aliases, who some called a chameleon, had likely murdered before.

ALSO BY J.R. ERICKSON

The Troubled Spirits Series

Dark River Inn

Helme House

Darkness Stirring

Ashwood's Girls

Still Falling

Flowers in Her Bones

Black Hollow Hideaway

Grave Devotion

Or dive into the completed eight-book stand-alone paranormal series:

The Northern Michigan Asylum Series.

Do you believe in ghosts?

ACKNOWLEDGMENTS

Many thanks to the people who made this book possible. Thank you to Team Miblart for the beautiful cover. Thank you to RJ Locksley for copy editing Grave Devotion. Many thanks to Will St. John for beta reading the original manuscript, and to Emily H., Saundra W., Travis P., and Sandra S., and Robin W. for finding those final pesky typos that slip in. Thank you to Ellen Barnard for offering up her name as a character in this novel. Thank you to my amazing Advanced Reader Team. Lastly, and most of all, thank you to my family and friends for always supporting and encouraging me on this journey.

ABOUT THE AUTHOR

J.R. Erickson, also known as Jacki Riegle, is an indie author who writes ghost stories. She is the author of the Troubled Spirits Series, which blends true crime with paranormal murder mysteries. Her Northern Michigan Asylum Series are stand-alone paranormal novels inspired by a real former asylum in Traverse City.

These days, Jacki passes the time in the Traverse City area with her excavator husband, her wild little boy, and her three kitties.

To find out more about J.R. Erickson, visit her website at www.jrericksonauthor.com.